THE LOST BROTHER

The Days of Joseph

Book 2

JOHN NOBLE

For my Dad, who taught me the secret to accomplishing anything.

Table of Contents

Chapter 1
Starlight

The air around Joseph glowed.

Amid the darkness, he stared across a world bathed in silver starlight. In the distance, the western hills loomed like dark sentinels, backlit by the shining band of stars that arced across the sky. Meanwhile the fields of barley stubble stretched across the valley like a sea of thin spikes, their copper tint washed out in ethereal midnight.

At his feet, a luminous puddle of white starlight splashed down around him. Before he could puzzle out what it all meant, he found his eyes drawn out past the fields of cut barley.

To those who came.

They blazed like stars. For a moment they reminded him of the Messengers, the ones he'd seen as a child, men in burnished armor with long swords that glowed like embers. Yet the stars coming towards him weren't the Messengers Joseph remembered.

They were his brothers.

His eyes roved across the gleaming lights that swept through the fields and somehow Joseph just… understood. Eleven orbs, one for each of them. Ten were large, pulsing off powerful tongues of white fire, yet each slightly different. Simeon's star flared with a ferocious strength, Reuben's swirled chaotically, and Levi's pulsed with a focused, dangerous calm. Joseph could recognize them all in a heartbeat. And apart from those ten stood the eleventh, smaller but burning all the more fiercely for it.

Benjamin.

Normally his brothers rushing towards him would have twisted Joseph's gut with worry, but in the hazy moment he felt only a surreal clarity. Somehow, they were *supposed* to be here. Where else would they be if not here — together.

The orbs swept closer until—

Joseph blinked as a vast radiance abruptly washed across the valley. He turned east, watching, transfixed as a pair of orbs, the sun and the moon, both soared above the low hills. And now he recognized them too. The moonlight flashed sharp and somehow harsh, while the yellow orb that rose beside it flickered with wispy tendrils of subdued gold, like a fire burned low. The sun grown old.

Dad and Leah.

The sun and moon crested above the wide valley then fell towards the ground in graceful arcs. They touched the fields with a shudder that trembled the very earth itself… except for him.

The entire valley shook at the gravity of their coming, but the puddle of light around Joseph's feet never wavered. Instead, it grew strong, bright… powerful, even as his brothers' stars dimmed and arrayed themselves before him.

For the briefest instant the lights twisted and morphed, streamers of starlight tracing ghostly figures amid the surreal scene. His eyes danced across them all— his step-mother and father, with his brothers fanned out behind them.

His family.

And as one, the sun, and moon, and stars all bowed.

***

Joseph awoke with a jolt, sucking in a sharp breath. The wondrous world of starlight was gone, replaced by the pitch black of his tent. Yet the images of the dream remained etched in his mind.

He stared into the darkness above, his breaths slowing. What had that been? He'd experienced his share of dreams before, but mostly bizarre nightmares or incoherent strings of images. They were always a slurry of nonsense scenes that only made sense in the strange realm of sleep and slipped away the instant he awoke.

But this had felt different, more crisp… almost real. And the images weren't fading either, instead they remained seared into his head. The distinctive patterns of his brothers' stars felt remarkably sharp in his memory. If he'd had a whitewashed wall to paint on, he knew he could have recreated each of the blazing figures in intricate detail.

Relaxing his tense limbs, Joseph lay there, puzzling over the dream. He ought to get back to sleep, he realized, it'd be a long day ahead. Yet the images kept nipping at his mind, a mental dog that wouldn't leave him be.

Eventually, Joseph rolled off his mat and sighed. He groped a moment in the darkness, his hands searching for a tunic. Finding one, he slipped it on and stood, taking special care not to bump little Benji on his own bed mat nearby. Feeling his way to the entrance of the tent, he brushed aside the flap, and headed outside.

Instantly the cool morning air breezed over him. After so many days working beneath the tyranny of the burning sun, the chill left him refreshed. The breeze picked up, rustling the leaves of distant terebinths and wafting the sharp, earthy, smell of fresh cut wheat. For a few seconds he stood perfectly still, lost in the familiar scents, until finally he glanced east, to where the first purple haze of dawn crept over the hills. And with the light, the questions crept right back.

What had he just seen?

In the predawn gloom, Joseph paced the well-trodden dirt in front of his tent, mulling on the problem. It had been a dream, but… people also said dreams could hold hints of the future. And Father had witnessed his share of dreams. Joseph knew about those, visions of Messengers guarding Dad on a journey, voices from a God that bridged between the world he could see and… somewhere else entirely. Dad had even told him about a dream, from years ago, when Joseph had been almost too young to remember, where his father had been warned to leave Harran. And that dream had come true. In their own way all of those dreams, visions, whatever they were — they had all come to pass.

And this wasn't the first strange dream he'd had.

A few weeks earlier, there had been another. He'd seen all of them working in the fields, helping the farmers of Mamre bring in the harvest. Suddenly their sheaves of grain had all stood up, moving as if by magic. His brothers' sheaves had gathered around his in a similar array to the one he'd just witnessed... and as one, their sheaves had bowed down low before his.

So what did that mean?

Were his brothers all going to come bow down before him? A part of Joseph scoffed at the idea. With the frostiness between them right now, his siblings would need spearpoints prodding at their backs before they bent a knee to him.

Yet in the dream they had.

He entertained the bizarre possibility for a moment, cautiously rolling it through his mind. Eventually, his brothers might be forced to come to him. They could hate him all they wanted, Joseph mused with a spark of cold satisfaction. Didn't matter though, because one day Father would be old like Grandpa Isaac, too old to restrain the organized madness of their camp. And when that day arrived, Joseph knew full well that the responsibility to manage father's affairs would fall to him.

Then his brothers wouldn't have a choice.

To the east more brushstrokes of dawn rose above the hills, dyeing the sky in a haze of lush purples that gently faded to red. Joseph watched, his eyes picking out the faintest streak of green that marked the transition between the colors. His focus lingered on the horizon, but his mind cradled the memories of his dream.

They would come to him, he realized with a spark of vindication. His brothers would come to him. The possibility lit in him a renewed fire for the day ahead. Sometimes he hated them. They were cruel and petty and jealous. And yet, he realized with a flush of triumph, they couldn't stop what was happening, could they. Father had chosen him, and one day he would lead the family.

Issachar might scream, Simeon might kick and fight in frustration. But it wouldn't matter.

One day Reuben, Simeon, Levi and all the rest *would* bow before him. They wouldn't have a choice.

It was a heady feeling, the image of his family finally showing him the respect he deserved. He could see it in his mind's eye, and held tight to the image as it filled him with a moment of wondrous calm. One day. One day all of them would bow down and honor him.

One day.

A few moments later Joseph's thoughts of sleep were long forgotten as he strolled through the sluggish camp. They'd pitched their tents on a slight rise in the land so as not to flood in the wet season. From here he could see down the wide valley toward the town of Mamre that capped a broad hill to the south. He vaguely considered grabbing some breakfast for himself and Benjamin, but paused when he saw a girl duck out of a tent two dozen paces ahead. She was carrying a clay jug nestled in one arm, and from the way she moved, clearly hadn't noticed him in the predawn gloom.

In an instant Joseph's plans shifted. He broke into a stealthy walk to follow, making sure to keep his distance. He allowed her to go a good hundred paces from her tent, before abruptly stealing up behind her at a jog and lightly tapping her shoulder, "Hey, Myrrha."

Myrrha shrieked.

She jumped a solid half-cubit into the air and spun, nearly fumbling her jug, absolute panic on her face.

Then she saw him.

Joseph couldn't stop laughing, even as her eyes narrowed to razors, her voice furious. "WHAT IS WRONG WITH YOU?"

She angrily swatted at his shoulder, but Joseph barely noticed past his chuckles, "Oh, you should have seen…"

"That was *not funny,* Joseph," Myrrha snapped.

"It was a little funny."

Her face twisted in an indignant scowl, "I thought I was about to die."

"I could tell." Joseph let out a deep, belly laugh.

She fixed him with a glower that said she was trying *really* hard to be angry with him. Finally, she swatted at his shoulder one last time and clutched the jug to her chest with a sullen, "I could have dropped this, you know."

True. But she hadn't. Besides she'd pulled a few fast ones on him over the years. Jokes went both ways. "Here, I'll make it up to you," he offered, still grinning from ear to ear. "I'll carry the jug."

It was a sizable jug, and she'd definitely struggle to lug it back completely filled with water. For a moment Myrrha glanced at the jug, then him, frowning like she wasn't quite done being upset.

Finally she puffed up one cheek, thinking, before letting out a long hiss that ended with a grumpy, "Fine." She shoved the jug into his arms, "Come on."

She took off at a sharp pace, and Joseph let out one last chuckle as he followed.

They walked in silence through the gradually brightening camp. The sun had yet to peek above the horizon, but the predawn rays cast sufficient light to see where they stepped. Myrrha was headed for the pool at the base of the hill, where most of the camp would go for their drinking water, and Joseph knew the path by rote.

After another moment of silent treatment, she glanced back, her voice sulking. "What were you even doing? You just wake up early to terrorize people?"

"No, I…" he hesitated, trying to find the right words, "…couldn't sleep."

He pulled alongside Myrrha, and her eyes met his, a flash of concern worming past her frown. "Is Benjamin not…?"

"No, he's fine." Joseph shook his head. He'd been sleeping in the same tent as his baby brother since well before spring. "He's actually slept a lot better the last few weeks," Joseph added as they walked. "Probably because he's been helping with the harvest. He's usually pretty wiped by the end of the day."

Myrrha finally managed a trace of a smile. "Well, that's some progress at least."

"Yeah," Joseph nodded absently, even as he considered the other topic on his mind, the thing he was almost afraid to say aloud. Finally, through all the uncertainty slipped out a simple, "I uhhh… I had another dream." He drew his lips tight and added, "Last night."

Myrrha didn't immediately answer. Instead they walked several paces, the words hanging between them. Joseph hesitated, then turned his head to find her regarding him with curious eyes. "You mean a dream, like—"

"Yeah," Joseph nodded. "Like the last one. I was here, but not *exactly* here." He vaguely gestured around with his free hand, hoping that made some sense. "Everything was different, quieter maybe. This time I saw these fiery orbs that came and bowed down."

As he spoke the two finally reached the pool, a sort of shallow well, excavated deep at the base of the hill. The surface was unremarkable, a roughhewn slab of rock covered over most of the opening, keeping out the worst of the leaves, dust, and general nastiness. To one side, a set of stone steps led down six cubits to a vault beneath. In the faint light, Joseph could only barely pick out the spot where the steps vanished into the dark pool.

Moving more by memory than sight, Joseph carefully dipped his feet into the cool waters, sending dark ripples bouncing across the surface. Stooping down, he dunked the jug, filling the vessel nearly to the brim. He'd carried enough water pots to easily judge by weight when it was full.

He'd also slipped on the steps enough times to tread cautiously until he was back at the top, where he presented it to Myrrha, "One water jug. Full, as requested."

Myrrha giggled as his mock formality, "Thank you kind sir. I'm sure I can manage from here."

"Myrrha, I wouldn't…"

But she'd already taken the large jug, visibly straining and letting out a surprised, "Oh," at the weight.

Yeah, it was full for *him,* which was not the same as full for *her.*

"Here, I've got it." Before she could protest, Joseph had scooped the heavy water pot back into his arms.

For an instant she looked like she might protest, but Joseph headed her off. "Seriously, Myrrha, I don't mind."

He really didn't. If anything, he enjoyed helping. He could tell it bothered her sometimes, as though a part of her resented her need for help in the first place. Yet, it was always a bright spot in his day. Finally, she relented with a sigh. "Alright," followed by a belabored, "Thanks."

"Not a problem." The two started their trek back up the hill. They walked a moment before Myrrha spoke, "You're not going to tell anyone? Right?"

"Huh?"

"About the dream?"

"Oh that…" Joseph adjusted his grip on the jug. "Definitely not."

He'd made that mistake with his first dream. Joseph wasn't entirely sure what response he'd been expecting, maybe a bit more respect and consideration. But all he'd gotten for mentioning the dream was scorn. He could still hear Judah's sneering, "Oh look, it's the little dreamer who wants to be king."

That had happened right as the harvest began, and since then his bothers had stopped talking to him entirely. Yet another wedge hammered in between them.

It seemed there were more and more of those lately. Things had never been fantastic between him and Leah's side of the family, but since Mom had… passed, the relationship between him and his brothers had devolved from bad to straight up dysfunctional. Wedge, after wedge, after wedge, after wedge— everything just kept prying them apart.

Deep down he craved that moment when his brothers would bow down before him. A moment that would finally eat up their overweening arrogance. But unless that moment was scheduled for sometime this afternoon, he didn't particularly want to bring it up today, or tomorrow… or anytime soon really, at least not within earshot of his brothers.

"I'll keep this one to myself," Joseph added, as they walked. "It's already going to be a busy day."

"It is?" Myrrha asked, suddenly confused. "I thought we were finished with the harvest?"

"We are finished," Joseph explained, "but Father and I are going into town today to collect our share of the crop. And I'm sure there'll be plenty of cooking for tonight."

He saw Myrrha relax, nodding, "Oh, well that'll be nice."

Yeah, Joseph nodded. The end of harvest meant they'd have a celebration. Dhra and his helpers would whip up all the food anyone could eat, and for the first time in two weeks, they could relax for the evening.

The two were nearing camp. By now, the gathering dawn cast a warm glow across the sprawling city of goat-hide tents. More people had appeared outside now, sluggishly wandering through various morning chores — feeding geese, rekindling coals from ashy fire pits, and of course, a trickle of people heading down to draw water. Soon there'd be a line down at the well.

Myrrha's tent came into view and the girl suddenly hesitated, "Joseph, I uhh… I need to carry the water."

He shot her a confused glance. "It's really not a problem."

"I know, but my mom. If she sees, she'll…"

Myrrha's voice trailed off, embarrassed and Joseph cocked an eyebrow, lost. "She'll... what? Is everything alright?"

"It's fine. Mom just doesn't want me to..." Myrrha struggled a moment, her hands grasping for the right words, like she might pull them out of the air. Finally, she seemed to deflate with a frustrated insistence. "It's dumb, okay. But I need to carry the water."

Joseph felt like he was missing something, but, "Alright," he shifted the jug into her arms, watching her stagger a half-step under the weight as she firmed up her grip.

"Thanks." Myrrha gave an appreciative nod, even as she took a deep breath at the obvious strain.

"You sure you don't need a hand?"

"I'm fine." Myrrha smiled, a bright, buoyant grin that left Joseph smiling too. "I'll see you later?"

Joseph hesitated at the cheerful goodbye. A part of him almost said more. Something important. Something he'd meant to speak with her about for weeks. He'd kept waiting for the right moment, except it seemed like that moment never came, always spoiled by the details. He almost just blurted it out, but before he could summon up the words, Myrrha had already spun to go, and just like that, the moment faded.

"Yeah," Joseph murmured, as Myrrha hurried off the last two dozen steps to her tent. "Later."

Chapter 2
The Chosen One

After leaving Myrrha, Joseph hurried back to his own tent. He poked his head inside to see young Benjamin awake and fiddling with a few of his stones. For the boy's age, he had amassed an impressive collection. Specifically, all the roundest, most vibrantly colored pebbles that Joseph and his brothers had picked from the streams near Harran and Shechem over the last twenty years.

Benjamin looked up at the swish of the tent flap, bright-eyed, as usual. "Joseph. Game?"

The last few months Joseph had been slowly introducing his little brother to "Pebbles" a game Reuben had invented.

When Joseph had been younger, they'd played for hours to pass the time. The core concept was to knock the other player's pebbles out of a circle, with a few quality-of-life rules tacked on for fairness.

The rest of Joseph's brothers had outgrown the game, but most had kept their pebbles. It hadn't been a simple task, but even despite their animosity, Joseph had persuaded several to donate their collections to Benjamin. Most notably, he'd convinced Dan to give up his trove, which had been an absolute coup. That meant his brother now had *the* premier pebble collection in camp, a rainbow of colors in every different size.

Benjamin had yet to master the game… at all. But Joseph knew he'd get there. Then the other boys in camp had better watch out.

At the sight of Benji's grin, Joseph was sorely tempted to stay. In other circumstances they could have played a few shots and eaten later. But not today.

"I have to meet with Father," Joseph explained.

Benji's bright joy morphed into glum disappointment, with a frown like the boy had been robbed. "But—"

"I'm sorry, Benji. It's important," Joseph explained hastily. "Maybe this afternoon?"

Before his little brother could protest, Joseph set about the daily challenge of making himself presentable. A basin of water sat in one corner, still cold from last night. He gave his face a quick wash, and wet down his hair, then beelined over to the wickerwork basket where he kept his clothes. Sliding off the top, he pulled out a delicately folded tunic and held it up, allowing the folds to neatly drop out.

For a moment he regarded the garment, a vibrant Egyptian blue robe with elaborate silver embroidery. Myrrha's work. A smile tugged at Joseph's cheeks. The cotton fabric was light and airy, perfect for being outside in the heat. That said, he hadn't touched it since the beginning of harvest. It would have been a travesty to ruin such beautiful craftsmanship out in the dusty fields, snagging threads on bits of stubble.

Today though… the tunic might be just perfect.

Slipping the long-sleeved garment over his head, Joseph grabbed his best waist strap from the basket. He had several, ranging from simple leather strips to a thick, elaborate belt with a silvery buckle emblazoned on the front. Again, excessive for working out in the fields, but perfect for today.

When he was finished, Joseph stepped back, giving himself a quick once over. The tunic hung down a little past his knees, neatly cinched around the waist, and the sleeves rippled with bands of intricately patterned silver. He patted his hair to ensure it had been tamed from its usual early morning birds' nest, then took a deep breath.

Excellent.

At a minimum, he wouldn't show up looking like a vagrant and embarrass Father. Dad had entrusted him with a lot of responsibility today and—

Right, the tablets. He'd almost forgotten. Hurrying over to another basket, Joseph pulled off the top to find a stack of wooden slates, each with raised outer edges and a thick layer of dark wax coating the middle. Four of the tablets were hooked on a brass ring, and Joseph briefly flipped through them. That helped assuage the swirl of nightmare imaginations from yesterday night where he walked into their meeting carrying a pile of blank tablets… but no, these were definitely the right ones.

Tucking them and a bronze-tipped stylus under his arm, Joseph glanced back to see his brother engrossed in his colorful rocks. "Benjamin, can you go with Abby to get food today?"

"Huh?" his brother glanced up.

"Abby and Nathanial," Joseph said, seriously, "go with them to get food."

"Okay," Benjamin nodded absently and returned to his game. Joseph watched, hoping his little brother didn't completely forget breakfast and spend the whole morning flicking pebbles.

Abby knew to check on him though. Joseph sighed; he'd be fine… probably. Before he could dwell on the issue enough to second guess himself, Joseph took a deep breath, ducked and pushed aside the tent flap.

Time to meet the new day.

Outside he blinked at the brightness flooding the sky. The sun had just crested the tree-capped eastern hills, drowning the purple streaks of dawn in a brilliant light.

Joseph headed for his father's tent.

He wasn't the first to arrive, but not the last either.

Father was already there, of course, as was Grandpa Isaac, a genuinely ancient man who'd been blind longer than Joseph had been alive. Grandfather had maintained a surprising sharpness of hearing though, and as Joseph swept aside the tent flap to step inside, he saw Isaac glance toward him, even before Father did.

"Good day," Joseph nodded. Several of his brothers had already arrived, specifically Judah, Levi, Reuben, Asher and Gad, not that any of them looked particularly pleased to see him. Joseph even caught Levi's expression momentarily twist in a sneer at his choice of clothing.

Father smiled though, gesturing to the familiar cushion at his right. "Joseph, come sit."

Joseph did, pausing before Isaac with a respectful, "Grandfather."

Even without his eyesight, Grandpa Isaac extended Joseph a frail hand. "Good morning, my boy."

Grandpa called all of them *my boy,* even Father. He also had this unnerving *thousand league stare* where he'd seem to look straight through you when he spoke. Obviously, being blind, he wasn't looking at anything at all, but the body language was still there, and it took a conscious effort on Joseph's part to push away the oddness of the interaction. Benjamin in particular had shied away the first time he'd been old enough to meet Grandfather. Well… that was until he'd realized that *Saba* would let him eat whatever he wanted, and possessed a trove of fascinating stories about far-off lands. Then they'd gotten along famously.

Assuming his usual seat, Joseph busied himself arranging his tablets in a neat stack. Father leaned over, "Is everything prepared?"

"Yes," Joseph nodded. "I've totaled everything up and—"

His Dad held up a hand for him to stop. "Good. We'll discuss it later."

Back at the entrance, the flap swished again, and Simeon stepped inside, offering a perfunctory nod to Dad, but pausing at Isaac with a surprisingly respectful, "Hello, Grandfather."

He made for a spot next to Levi, strolling past Joseph with a sneering, "Morning, Princess."

Joseph's hands balled into fists, his eyes tracking Simeon like arrows, but he managed an aloof reply, "You spend all night thinking that one up?"

The words took an amusingly long second to lance home. But when they did, Simeon froze, slowly turning with venom in his glare.

A few years ago, Simeon might have made a crazed attempt to strangle him right there, but Joseph had grown up since then. He *might* still lose a fair fight with Simeon, but it was no longer a certainty. Besides, even if Simeon had been of a mind to fight, Father still ran everything around here, and Father had chosen *him*.

Simeon's faced burned with impotent fury, but Joseph matched his glower, and Simeon slowly lowered himself down to sit.

The tension nearly crackled in the air, refusing to dissipate until finally Dan and Naphtali poked their heads in with twin greetings, *Morning, Father,* and provided some distraction.

Soon everyone had arrived, and Dhra brought in an unusually scrumptious breakfast. Heavy bowls of honeyed oatmeal, and thin strips of pan-fried lamb. After so many days of rising at dawn and heading straight to work, Joseph found himself struggling not to gorge himself straight away. Finally, after a quick blessing, he dug into his oatmeal and…

It was delicious. Dhra had nailed the flavoring, a dousing of honey with just a pinch of cinnamon. The oats had been boiled to a perfect consistency so that they dissolved into a lumpy mush. The sweetness lit up his mouth, and for a while, even Simeon's nastiness was forgotten as Joseph's focus narrowed down to his oatmeal and strips of crispy lamb bacon.

When Joseph looked up, his father had already put aside what was left of his own meal, his gaze wandering across the tentful of them. "So, Joseph," Dad's eyes jumped to him, "Did you sleep well?"

It should have been an easy question, but it caught Joseph by surprise. For an instant his mind flashed back to last night, to his dream, the stars gathering around him and…

"I… umm… yes," Joseph stammered.

He must have given something away, because Father regarded him with a curious stare, before adding, "And Benjamin is doing well?"

"Never better," Joseph said, his composure trickling back. "He helped winnow the barley yesterday and slept all night."

Saying Benjamin *helped* was perhaps a generous description. Winnowing involved tossing the husked grain in the air so the wind blew away the light chaff and left the heavier grain. Benjamin had… sort of grasped the concept… emphasis on the *sort of.* Mainly he'd tagged along with Nathanial, both boys basking in the excitement of a place where he could wildly throw things in the air and no one minded. But Joseph figured it was their enthusiasm that counted.

Dad chuckled at the mention. "I saw. I don't suppose you counted him on the worker rolls?"

"I, uhh…" the short answer was, no. He hadn't felt entirely right, counting his little brother alongside full grown men. Admittedly, Benjamin had outshone them all in enthusiasm, but he'd occasionally proved more of a hinderance than a help. Joseph recovered with a quick, "I didn't, but I can if you'd like me to."

Father smiled and shook his head, "That's quite alright. I wouldn't want us to mis-represent ourselves."

Before Joseph could say more, Father stood, wincing slightly at the motion. He raised a hand to silence the small conversations that had been gradually breaking out.

"Good morning, boys," Father said. "I want to congratulate all of you on your hard work these last few weeks. I know it's been a monumental task bringing is the harvest, but now it's time to reap some of the rewards of our diligence."

That bit about rewards garnered a tentative clap from Issachar in the back, and Dad continued, "I'll be heading into town today to take delivery of our share of the harvest. There'll be a feast tonight, and in a few days, we'll begin moving the animals to greener pastures for the summer. For today though, I'd encourage everyone to take a well-deserved rest. You've all earned it, and you all have my thanks."

There were more claps at that news. Everyone definitely needed a day off at this point. Dad settled back down beside Joseph, working a bit longer on his oatmeal, while the rest of the tent dissolved into a haze of discussions.

The rest of his brothers had effectively been dismissed, and soon Gad and Asher both stood to leave. But Joseph waited as Dad finished up, flipping through his tablets twice more, then moving on to fidgeting with the sleeves of his tunic.

He found his eyes constantly drawn to the three patterned silver bands that looped around the sleeves. Each sleeve was traced with repeating geometric swirls that smoothly flowed from one pattern to another as though elements in some master plan. When Father had gifted him the robe, Joseph had assumed he'd had it commissioned from a tailor in the city. That was, until later that evening, when Myrrha had slyly found him beside the fire.

"You like it?" she'd asked.

"It's beautiful," Joseph said, admiring the shifting amber glow of firelight on the silver stitching. "It matches the moon."

"I was thinking it would match the stars, actually."

Joseph caught an odd sort of satisfied pride in her tone. He glanced over, surprised to see Myrrha grinning, an impish light in her eyes, even as she bashfully glanced away.

And suddenly he realized.

"You made this?"

If anything her beaming smile widened, "Just the embroidery."

Joseph touched the intricate silver patterns, seeing them in a new light. "I love it. Where'd you get the idea?"

Myrrha glanced up, that impish light still in her eyes as she teased, "It was your idea."

"Mine?"

"You probably don't remember. It was months ago, you were drawing a bunch of swirls in the dirt with your staff and I thought, well…" Her voice trailed off in a shrug, her cheeks shading. "I just stitched a design I thought you'd like."

Joseph allowed himself a smile at the memory. Strange how she'd just… known. He doubted anyone else in camp would have even noticed, probably would have scuffed out the marks he'd drawn with their foot. Yet Myrrha just paid attention, and so she'd made something spectacular. Remarkable, really.

"Are you ready?" his father's voice interrupted

"Huh…" Joseph jolted back to the present where his father watched him with expectant eyes. "Oh, yes." Joseph mumbled, hastily gathering his tablets as his dad stood.

Jacob helped Grandfather Isaac stand, the old man leaning on Father's arm as though he might be blown over by the breeze. "Where would you like to be while we're gone, Father?" Jacob asked.

"Depends, my boy," Isaac mused in a raspy voice. "Will it be sunny outside?"

"It should be blazing."

"Excellent," Grandfather said with a smile. "I'll take a spot where I can feel the heat then. Best way to stay warm you know. Much better than being wrapped in blankets."

Dad chuckled but nodded, helping Grandfather totter toward the entrance.

"Talita?" Jacob called to a mousy young girl seated a few tents down, who stood up at her name and hurried over.

"Talita, would you help Master Isaac find a spot at the front of the tent, and fetch him anything he may need."

"Yes, sir." Talita gave a respectful curtsey.

The girl was certainly an unusual one. She'd been part of grandfather's entourage when they'd come south after the Shechem debacle. Maybe she was just shy, but she got along remarkably well with Grandfather. Some people became impatient with the way he often sat and chatted all day, but she seemed to appreciate it. Very odd, at least in Joseph's reckoning.

The girl guided Isaac away, and at last Joseph found himself alone with Father.

"Alright then," Father declared with perhaps a hint of nervous excitement to his own tone. "I believe we have somewhere important to be."

Chapter 3
Golden Problems

The walk to Mamre led them a mile up the valley, toward the low hill upon which squatted the sprawling metropolis. Even from afar the city loomed like a giant. It dwarfed Shechem, Jebus, and Shiloh. And although Joseph couldn't remember to compare, Father claimed it was nearly as large as Harran. Just like Shechem, Mamre, the city, was named after the Amorite *'King' Mamre the Great,* as distinguished from *Mamre* his father, and of course *Mamre* his grandfather, who had also incidentally gone under the moniker *Mamre the Great.*

Technically the town was called Kiriath Arba, *The Four Quarters,* but it was often just referred to as Mamre, since some Mamre or another had ruled there as long as anyone could remember.

Their camp had been pitched to the north of the city, on a low rise shaded by an ancient oak grove. Joseph followed his father as he limped down the slope towards the freshly harvested fields that blanketed the valley floor. Father still kept a good pace, but Joseph could swear his limp had gotten worse of the last few years… ever since… since Mom had…

Joseph pushed away the unwelcome memory and focused on the present, searching for a distraction. "Are you doing okay, Father?"

His Dad glanced over, before keenly grasping the unspoken meaning behind the question. "I'm not that old, Joseph," he said with a wry expression. "Not yet."

Father took a few more steps before continuing, unprompted. "I've been meaning to ask if you've given any thought to our discussion a few weeks ago? About finding a wife?"

Joseph's breath stuck in his throat, and an anxious twinge staked at his gut. He uhh… he *had* thought about it. He'd thought about it a great deal, actually. Probably more than Dad. He'd talked it over a hundred times in his head, imagined a hundred permutations of this conversation, trying to hammer down exactly what he wanted to say. But now that the moment had arrived, he wasn't sure he wanted to have this talk.

"I…" Joseph struggled to find the right words.

"I sent a messenger to your Uncle Esau before the harvest began," Father continued as they walked. "Your uncle has a daughter who he thinks might make an excellent match."

Joseph gulped back a stubborn lump in his throat. None of his imaginary conversations had started with that unwelcome bit of new. "What if… what if that's not what I wanted?"

"Well, you ought to at least meet her before declining," Dad said. He chuckled to himself, "You might be surprised. There's something quite entrancing about a young lady."

"And," his father added, energetically, "if, you two don't feel like things would work out, there are a number of eligible young women in your Grandfather Laban's family in Harran. I'm not sure if you remember Kaela, but she would be coming of age herself now. I could send a message to inquire…"

Dad's voice faded to the background behind the cacophony of Joseph's own worries. That wasn't what he wanted at all. Marry some girl from Harran he'd never met.

"Dad?" Joseph interrupted, and his father paused with an expectant look. "What if I found someone around here?"

Instantly he could tell his father didn't like that idea. "You mean someone from Mamre?" Dad scowled. "You would really do better to marry…"

Father's voice trailed off and he paused, controlling his expression and seeming to collect himself before coming at it from a new angle. "That's certainly a possibility," he agreed in a strained tone. "But I'd caution you that it might not be the wisest course. I'm not sure you and a girl from the city would make good partners."

That also wasn't quite Joseph's point, but before he could explain, Father kept right on talking, "Our world is so different from anything that a woman from Mamre would understand." Father nodded towards the city. "The furthest most of them have ever been from this place is a day's walk. And yet, just in your own lifetime, we've come from Harran and traveled the length and breadth of Canaan. Your great grandfather Abraham traveled even further, from Ur to Harran all the way to Egypt and everywhere in between. He pitched his own tent here, yet when he passed though, the people of Mamre were in the same place as they are now, living behind their walls in the city, static."

Joseph paused to dwell on that possibility. In truth that didn't sound so terrible, to be bound to one place and not always be moving. He might enjoy having a permanent home beyond just whatever hilltop they camped on.

It might be nice to finally just belong… somewhere.

Dad seemed to take his silence as proof that he needed more persuading and continued, "One day, Joseph, everything we have — the camp, the herds all of it — will become yours. Everyone will look to you to manage the business of our camp, to make wise decisions and safeguard them. And when that day comes, you'll want a wife who understands the world we live in and the decisions we have to make."

Dad hesitated a moment before adding, "Before we left Harran, I asked Leah and your mother both what they thought we should do. If we should go. There was danger for us in Harran but also danger returning to Canaan. Do you know what they said?"

Joseph shook his head.

A smile danced across his father's face as he halted to answer, "They were both willing to walk beside me and leave. Despite having lived in Harran all their lives, they weren't afraid to leave when the time came."

As they'd talked, they had come down into the valley where a small dirt path wove its way through the fields of golden barley stubble. From here they could see Mamre ahead, its low walls running a long circuit around the hilltops.

Father cast a pointed look toward the city on the rise above. "A girl from Mamre won't see the world like that. How can she? She'll have lived here, in her house with her friends and neighbors and family. What would she think of living in a tent when a storm pounds it in the night? Or about moving the animals to find water and grass? And what if you have to leave forever one day? You don't want to wake up ten years too late, only to discover that, down in your hearts, the two of you want different things."

"Your mother… she understood what our life means, and both of us were stronger for it. But a girl from Mamre?" Father gestured at the looming city. "How could she? A girl from a place like this can never truly understand our world and the sacrifices we have to make."

Jacob ended on a definitive note, as though that thoroughly settled the question. He kept his steady pace toward Mamre, but, watching him go, Joseph's gut still churned like an anxious flock of starlings. That hadn't really answered his question at all. Because what if he *wasn't* talking about a girl from Mamre? What then?

Joseph had so much more to say, yet this conversation wasn't going at all like he'd hoped. Silently following his father, the two took the footpath through the valley and past the sprawling fields of barley stubble. The unsettled silence slowly soured until they reached the base of the hill and found themselves looking up at the city above.

"When we get inside and start the negotiations," Dad finally broke the quiet with a serious look in his direction, "I want you to stay quiet until I ask you to speak. You understand?"

Joseph had been planning to do that anyway, but he nodded his agreement. Then, piping up anyway. "Father, if you don't mind my asking, yesterday I got the numbers you wanted, but Eshakol already had one of his own scribes there to tally everything. Was there some reason I needed to be there as well?"

Joseph didn't mean to complain. Instead of wearing out his arms at the threshing floor, he'd enjoyed a leisurely day of tally keeping at the granaries. He'd been captivated by the bustle of frenetic activity as a steady stream of men toting heavy baskets stockpiled the harvest.

It hadn't made sense why they needed multiple people to do it though. He'd certainly elicited a number of confused looks from the local scribe, Arvad. The man had seemed almost offended by his presence.

Dad silently traipsed up the hill a few more steps before answering. "Perhaps I simply wanted to ensure that their tallies were accurate."

The words took a moment to sink in, but when they registered, Joseph sucked in a shocked breath. "You think they're cheating us?"

"Now I never said that," his father answered, deadpan. "And you would be wise not to either."

"But..." Joseph struggled for the right word, "you suspect."

"Let's just say that your grandfather is very old. Perhaps he hasn't been able to keep a watchful eye on everything that he should," Father remarked evenly. "Last year, when the harvest was tallied, we ended up with substantially less grain than I expected. Hence why I had you collect your own numbers."

Joseph nodded eagerly, "So if he tries to lie to us, we can call him out on it."

His father ground to a halt fifty paces from the gate, shooting Joseph a glare to make him wilt, "Absolutely not."

"Wait, then why did you have me—"

"Joseph, this is why I haven't mentioned this *to anyone* until now. One must be very cautious with accusations, they are dangerous tools in the hands of the reckless. *If* Mamre is being honest with us, then calling him a liar is an insult, and *if* he's cheating us, then the same accusation is a grievous embarrassment. Either way it's the sort of stain he can't easily remove. We are *not* trying to make an enemy of him. That would not be wise."

Dad turned back towards the city and resumed his limping walk. "Many men have sabotaged themselves by negotiating a winning trade, but losing the trust of the man across the table, myself included. That mistake was part of why we had to leave Harran. And while we certainly need the extra barley, we need Mamre's good will far more if we are to remain here." He paused an instant before adding, "If we want both, then we will have to be clever."

Close ahead the towering city gate loomed large, a thick edifice of mortared limestone, fitted with fat towers to either side. Down at the foot of the gate, a watchman stood his boring sentry duty.

Despite their only having lived near Kiriath Arba for the last couple years, the guard recognized his father even from ten paces away and gave a deferential nod as they approached, "A fine day, sirs."

"Indeed, and to you as well." Father returned the nod. Then they passed beneath the long shade of the gateway and stepped into the great city that was Kiriath Arba.

Chapter 4
Mamre

This time of morning, the plaster walled homes cast long shadows across the road, with only the occasional slash of dazzling sunlight slipping through the gaps between. Already the city hummed with activity: the gentle honks of geese mingled with the background chatter of conversation and the percussive *bang-bang* of the forge across town.

Most of the houses towered two stories tall, their rooftops rustling with the sheets, robes and tunics that fluttered like banners in the wind. The gateway marked a major avenue, and alcoves on lower floors of many houses had been converted into storefronts. Already several owners were energetically hawking their goods.

"Fresh fired pots! All sizes! Never been used! A quarter shekel copper for—"

"Eggs, fresh laid yesterday and—"

"Skewers, get your hot skewers! Lamb, goat, and goose! Only a gerah each!"

The skewer woman stepped out half in their way as the two passed, "You here to sell more rams today, my lord?"

"Not today, Isilnah," Jacob said with a polite nod. "Next market day though."

The woman seemed only slightly deterred, "Of course, sir. A skewer for you and your son? Complimentary, of course."

That sounded great actually, Joseph thought, a bit of lamb would—

"Unfortunately, we just ate," Joseph's father said in a voice as though it really was a tragedy. "Perhaps later."

"I'll be expecting it, sir."

Jacob dodged past the pushy woman before she could make any more conversation, and Joseph hurried to follow. He glanced back longingly to where Isilnah was busy seducing the next set of passersby. She'd never offered *him* free food.

"I could go for one of her skewers," he tentatively suggested.

"As could I," his father agreed, deadpan. "But we'll get them later, and we'll pay for them. Otherwise, she'll expect ten times the price off the next animal she buys."

They passed a bakery where a dozen different types of bread and a pastry were laid out for display and oozing an aromatic symphony. Finally, they made it to the wide open square. Today was a market day, which meant the broad, paved area was covered over with various booths and stalls. The earliest shoppers were already busily perusing the wares, although Joseph didn't spot quite as many as usual. The day after a harvest always tended to be a bit slow, and this morning the market lacked its typical wild excitement.

His father's camp might be relatively new to the city, but Grandfather had made his home here for years. In that time, Isaac's people had become a staple of the weekly markets, and secured a permanent spot in one corner of the square. Joseph could even see their familiar red awning poking over the heads of the crowd, although amid the business of harvest, they hadn't brought in any animals to sell today.

Animals weren't all they sold though, maybe not even the majority. They also sold rawhides and wool, plus just about anything they made in camp. There was cheese, of which they had a truly endless supply, along with fats and tallow which they'd process into soap or candles. Additionally, several people in Grandfather's camp were expert tanners who could craft leather into anything from boiled armors, to sandals or aprons. Meanwhile, many of the women pooled together to sell fabrics and clothes.

Today they didn't pause to browse at the square though. Instead, Father led him down another wide avenue. Unlike most of the packed earth streets around town, here a layer of well-worn cobblestones pressed at his feet through thin sandals. The houses lining this lane were larger too, several with wooden balconies jutting out over the street. Their plaster washes were painted over with a dazzling riot of reds and yellows. Up on one balcony, Joseph caught a group of young girls garbed in a blaze of blues, yellows and oranges. They were gesturing toward people in the road below, but abruptly pulled back out of view the moment they realized he was watching them.

At the far terminus of the street loomed a house, grander still, almost a small fortress jutting up like a mighty pine among terebinths. Tall walls sectioned it off from the rest of town, and a miniature gateway with yet another guard marked the entrance.

This time the guard at least paid attention to who they were. His posture remained relaxed but reasonably alert, a short spear in hand. Dad spoke with him a moment, explaining their business before they were finally nodded through into the courtyard beyond.

Joseph had never been in the inner sanctum of Mamre's personal fortress but it was… big. Big and more than a little intimidating. They strolled through a short tunnel of stone into the broad courtyard at the center, ringed by an extravagant colonnade. Joseph craned his neck back to see the top floor where the colonnade supported a raised balcony that ran all around the courtyard.

A blur of servants and slaves in tan work tunics bustled past them. As Joseph pulled his gaze back to the ground floor, he noticed a man robed in embroidered blue strolling towards them. Finally, a face he recognized, at least briefly, from the harvest.

Eshakol, Mamre's steward, raised a hand in greeting, "Jacob." The man then gave a respectful bow as he came close. "Excellent, I was hoping you'd make it before noon."

"A pleasure, as always, Eshakol." His father nodded, then gestured to Joseph. "I'm not sure if you've met my son, Joseph."

The steward regarded him a moment with a flicker of recognition before, "I don't believe we've been formally introduced."

Eshakol nodded them toward the house, "If you would, follow me."

He led them inside the palatial abode, passing more servants and a sprawling kitchen. Joseph's nose caught the delectable scent of roasting lamb, and passing a doorway, he glimpsed a whole haunch, slow simmering on a spit.

Heading up the stairs, the steward escorted them through a hallway with a red dado covering the bottom half of the wall. The upper half was lavishly painted, each frame a scene from local myths. Joseph knew enough to at least recognize several: Ba'al poised in a battle against Yam, huntress Astarte stalking the desert lions, and a gloomy Anat descending into the underworld.

At last they turned into a sitting room, where the morning light spilled in from an open window. There they found a middle-aged man seated at a low table, dressed in a fine black tunic, and finishing up his breakfast.

"Jacob," Mamre's gaze rose to meet them. Unlike Mamre's father, who according to local rumor, had earned the uncharitable moniker, *Mamre the Fat*, this Mamre was a lean, athletic man still clutching to the prime of life.

Mamre stood and strode across the room, grasping Jacob's arm in greeting. His gaze flicked to Joseph, who had only ever seen Mamre from afar and found the king surprisingly imposing up close. Mamre's sharp eyes regarded Joseph's embroidered tunic, clearly piecing together the meaning of such a princely garment, but with an obvious flash of confusion.

"Is this your first son, Jacob? I could swear last time I met one he looked older. Thicker beard maybe?"

At the mention of facial hair, Joseph's hand self-consciously felt at his chin. He'd been trying to grow out a beard for the last several years, and only recently improved from a trimmed stubble to the beginnings of a real man's beard that might rival his older brothers'.

Fortunately Dad explained, "Technically he's not my oldest. This is Joseph. He's the firstborn from one of my wives."

Mamre regarded him a moment longer before simply nodding with a disinterested, "Hmm."

He looked to his steward in the doorway, "Eshakol, go fetch the scribe with yesterday's tallies."

The steward vanished with a bow, and Mamre gestured them to the table, "Please sit."

They did, and as Joseph laid his tablet aside, a young slave girl who had been standing unnoticed in the corner hurried forward. She quickly gathered the remnants of Mamre's meal and swept outside. Joseph's eyes briefly followed her, although neither of the older men seemed to notice.

When he looked back, Mamre had deftly produced an Aasha board from a cloth padded case. It was packaged with a sack of pyramidal dice and a lavish set of carved game pieces, half in amber and half in turquoise. "Would you enjoy a round while we wait?"

Dad accepted instantly.

Mamre must have known, Joseph figured. Dad would *never* turn down a game of Aasha. Joseph had never quite matched his father's enthusiasm, but he understood the appeal. The game possessed that savory combination of thrill, chance and risk, with a little bit of strategy thrown in. Levi, Judah, Naphtali, Gad and Issachar all enjoyed it, and Joseph dimly recalled participating in family tournaments when he'd been younger. Grandfather Isaac had the real Aasha treasure though, an incredibly ancient board that *his* grandfather Terah, had brought all the way from Ur. The simple set was carved from cypress wood with the markings almost worn to invisibility with age. Not that anyone really needed them though.

The basic premise was for both sides to race down a central lane, with each player rolling their dice to move their soldier token a certain number of squares ahead. Landing on an enemy soldier would bump it back to the start, and certain squares gave a chance to roll again. The first player to move his entire squad to the end won. That meant incredible comebacks were always a distinct possibility, and the betrayals could become rather personal.

The two went at their game with a gusto. Mamre quickly snuck through two soldiers before a spate of poor rolls allowed Dad to get one across and three more stacked on the board.

As they played, Joseph busied himself shuffling through his tablets, mentally reassuring himself that he had everything he needed. When he looked up from his triple checking, he saw Eshakol had returned, along with a man who he recognized as the scribe from yesterday, Arvad.

The scribe did a surprised double take at seeing him as well. Behind him, dice clattered on the table and Father let out a disappointed sigh. Meanwhile the steward stepped into the room with a deferential bow, "My, lord."

Mamre waved them forward. "Ahh, yes, come in, Eshakol. We won't be long."

In a moment the steward and the scribe were seated cross legged next to Mamre, the scribe with his own stack of tablets to match Joseph's. All of them watching as Mamre and Father quickly played out their last few rounds.

Joseph winced as Mamre scored several lucky rolls to bump two of Father's pieces in quick succession, before hitting a four and hopping his final soldier off the board in a decisive win. Ouch.

Father sighed and shook his head, but otherwise took the loss well enough. "Well played." He reached across, shook

Mamre's hand, and the two settled back across the table for the more serious discussion.

"It's been a busy few weeks, so you'll have to remind me, Jacob," Mamre declared, "what were the terms of our deal?"

"I believe, it was a quarter of the total, plus an ephah per day, per worker." As he spoke, Jacob produced a smudged and battered scroll from his robes and handed it across. "This was our tally of days worked," he said. "I expect yours is similarly close. I counted about five hundred."

Mamre passed it off to the scribe who spent a quiet moment comparing the tic marks they had used to record the days each man had worked against a tablet of his own. Finally, the scribe looked up with a nod. "We show four hundred and ninety-two."

"I find that number acceptable," Jacob agreed.

"Excellent," Mamre said in obvious high spirits. "Now for the share of the harvest. Arvad, what was the total—"

"Actually," Jacob interrupted him mid-sentence, "if you don't mind, I had my son here also do the tally on the harvest total. We had a teacher come through last year and give him some instruction as a scribe. I thought this could be an opportunity for him to practice his skills." Before Mamre could object, his father turned to him, "What were your totals, Joseph?"

Despite Joseph's nervous anticipation, the question still caught him by surprise. He gulped, a flock of swallows taking flight in his stomach. "I, uhh..."

He'd memorized the total barley tally last night, but now that he needed it, the number flitted away like a hunted hare. He rapid fire shuffled through his tablets before his hands finally found the one he wanted. "My total for the harvest was... eleven thousand six hundred and sixty-seven ephahs."

Joseph looked up to see the other half of the table staring at him in dismayed shock. A frown had slipped onto Mamre's face, but the man quickly shoved it back down beneath his pleasant veneer. The steward and the scribe were noticeably less apt at hiding their thoughts though, and after a flash of hesitancy the scribe gestured to him, "May I see?"

"Of course." Joseph eagerly handed over the wax tablets he'd scribbled out his work on. He was pretty sure he'd done the operations correctly.

Arvad's expression creased in a frown when he saw the work, his voice allowing just a hint of disdain, "You did it in the Egyptian style?"

"Yes," Joseph nodded, "I thought it was simpler, and I included the tables…"

His voice died in his throat as he saw that Arvad barely seemed to be listening. This probably wasn't the venue to discuss how he felt Sumerian arithmetic was a lot less intuitive.

Across the table, Arvad shuffled through Joseph's work before abruptly frowning, "Your last doubling, did you use the tables?"

Uhhh… no. Joseph's face flushed with a hot panic. The man whom Father had hired to teach him, an Egyptian scribe named Tefibi, hadn't struck Joseph as having the best grasp on Sumerian math. He'd also come across as a bit… eccentric. As in, there were potentially very good reasons why he *wasn't* plying his trade in Egypt anymore.

Anyway, they'd spent an inordinate amount of time on the nuances of fractions and learning various doubling operations, most of which were intended to be done from prewritten tables.

For example, to multiply 7 x 15 ½ he would break down 15 ½ into all its various powers of two, and represent it as ½ + 1 + 2 + 4 + 8 = 15 ½ . Then he could reference the 7's table to look up the results of each of those component operations. So 2x7 was 14, 4x7 was 28 ect. All that remained was to add those numbers from the table together to get a total.

In this case, 3½ + 7 + 14 + 28 + 56 = 108 + ½

Unfortunately, Tefibi had been an absolute fanatic about *not* being reliant on the solution tables. In retrospect, that should have been a warning sign. He had this bizarre habit of pointing to himself and proudly proclaiming, *the tables are in here.* That meant, instead of learning the really fascinating and complex operations that he'd been excited about, Joseph had wasted his first weeks drilling on the tedious memorization of fraction decompositions and basic multiplication pairs.

Across the table, Arvad nodded half to himself, "This should be 512, not 520."

Joseph's breath caught in a panicked rasp at the back of his throat. *Ezû...* His mind flashed back to yesterday, recalling his bleary-eyed calculations as twilight had crept across the sky. The hieratic for 2 and 20 looked painfully similar. Had he been tired and put down the wrong numeral? He swallowed, frantically hoping he hadn't ruined all of Father's carefully laid plans with such a fool-headed mistake.

Joseph only dimly heard Father next to him, "Does that change the total very much?"

"Well, your tally will be short by eight cartloads," Arvad answered absently. "So you can bump the total up by a hundred and sixty ephahs..."

His voice abruptly trailed off into a horrified, breathless silence. Joseph looked up to see Mamre still smiling, but with a strained tension twitching at his cheeks. The steward at his left looked downright unsettled and Arvad stumbled over his words, "I'm mean... ummm... uhhh..."

"Well, that's not too bad," Father declared, still jovial as ever. "So, a quarter is what, a hair under three thousand?"

"Ummm..." Arvad scrambled, suddenly thumbing through Joseph's tablets. Mamre shot the scribe a concerned glance, his veneer cracking a hair. The scribe found the tablet with the division math and regarded it a moment, before saying, "Well accounting for the error that'll be... two thousand nine-hundred and fifty-six plus a half, plus a quarter." The scribe gulped.

"And of course," Jacob added, glancing back at Mamre. "There are the four hundred and ninety-two ephahs for the workmen themselves."

"Of course," Mamre agreed reluctantly, but added, "and where are you going to be storing all of this, Jacob?"

"We have two granaries that'll hold about six hundred each."

Six hundred and thirty-two… specifically, Joseph mused. Dad had asked him to work out the numbers a couple months ago, although Joseph wasn't entirely sure why. He'd spent half a day measuring and calculating the precise volume, only for Father to nod with a nonchalant *that sounds about right,* when he'd delivered his answer.

There were a few moments of haggling as Father negotiated to rent one of Mamre's giant granaries to hold the remainder of the harvest. Still chagrined over his lackluster calculations, Joseph was only dimly aware of Dad and Mamre's discussion. He accepted his tablets back from Arvad and spent a long moment staring at the one frustrating line where, sure enough, he'd copied a doubling incorrectly.

Dad's voice abruptly rose with a sort of jovial finality to it, enough to start Joseph out of his distracted daze. He looked up as Dad said, "How about this, we'll take the twelve hundred ephahs, keep the two thousand in the granary and leave the remaining balance. That should be fair compensation, plus some extra for being a good partner. Does that sound reasonable?"

Almost *too* eagerly, Mamre nodded in agreement. His hand snaked across the table to shake Father's and cement the deal like he was afraid it might dry up and blow away in the east wind.

Joseph blinked in surprise. If he was doing his sums right, Father was letting Mamre have about 250 ephahs just to rent a granary. That was the sort of one-sided bargain Dad typically wouldn't have poked with a spearpoint, let alone accepted.

Except for today.

Today, Father accepted Mamre's hand with a broad grin. He didn't even seem to question it.

Watching left Joseph with the lingering feeling that something had gone horribly wrong, especially after all Dad's talk about Mamre cheating them. A sudden nervousness gripped at him. This wasn't his fault, was it? Had he made a mess of the negotiations and upset Dad's plans?

There were a few moments of the usual pleasantries. Mamre seemed obviously pleased with the deal he had struck, and finally Father stood, "We should be going. We'll be having a celebration tonight and still have many preparations to make. I'm sure you understand."

"Of course," Mamre rose with a polite nod and gestured them toward the door. "Until next time, Jacob."

The steward led them back out through the painted hallways and downstairs to the atrium. Joseph clutched his stack of wax tablets close, hurrying to keep up until the two found themselves back in the smooth paved street in front of Mamre's palace and headed for the city square. The whole time Father didn't say a word, and Joseph could swear he felt the tension swirling tight.

It seemed things had gone well, at least from reading Mamre's expression, yet his mind was still stuck on his carelessness nearly bungling the whole negotiation. If anything, it seemed Father's quick thinking had salvaged the situation. And now Dad wasn't saying anything. Was he upset and hiding it because they were in town? Dad had trusted him with one thing, keeping the tally and…

Finally, he spoke up, more than a little embarrassed. "I'm sorry, if I ruined things Father," Joseph mumbled.

Jacob glanced up absently, a far-off distraction in his eyes. "What was that, son?"

"The tally," Joseph said, "I'm sorry I messed it up."

Father blinked, not understanding, "What do you mean?"

"Well… my calculations were wrong."

"That?" Joseph could swear his dad had an expression like he was only just now remembering. "You were close enough?"

Joseph hesitated, even more confused, "But… I didn't ruin…"

Jacob paused in the middle of the street, regarding him with a flicker of understanding. "Son," he said softly, "last year the harvest was better than this one. Do you know what our *share* was?"

Joseph shook his head *No*, and Dad continued. "A little over fifteen hundred ephahs."

Joseph's eyes went wide. Fifteen-hundred? But that was less than half what they'd…

Father nodded grimly, "You can see why I was so concerned. My goal was to get a deal that didn't leave us buying grain from Mamre before the end of winter. Given that we just walked away with thirty-two hundred ephahs, a hundred more or less doesn't matter."

Father smiled, "We did *very* well today, son."

"Come on." Jacob turned, setting off for the square, which even from a distance, Joseph could see was now substantially busier than it had been earlier. "We can celebrate with a few of Isilnah's skewers," Dad said. He took a few steps before adding, "and don't let her give them away for free. Like I said, we'll pay for them one way or another, best to do it up front."

Chapter 5
A Night to Remember

Eight hours later, the sun painted long shadows across their camp amid a haze of frenetic activity. Ducking into his tent, Joseph scanned the shadowed space for his brother. "Benji? You there?"

A childish giggle escaped from behind a pile of baskets in the corner. Stepping close, Joseph peered behind the pile with a quiet, "Boo."

Benji shrieked in mock terror and tried to run, but Joseph easily scooped up the small boy. "Come on," he said. "It's time to eat."

"But I don't want to get eat-ed," Benjamin squealed, writhing madly in his arms.

Joseph sighed with an exasperated, "We're not going to eat you until tomorrow. Tonight it's lamb. Now put your sandals on."

"No!" The young boy went limp in Joseph's arms, trying to slide free, but Joseph held him firm and his gaze cast across the room, finally alighting on a tiny pair of battered leather slippers.

Getting them on was a challenge though, the sort of job that really required two pairs of hands. Typically, Myrrha would have been around to supply the extra pair, but after she'd scurried off this morning, Joseph hadn't seen her at all. Instead, he finally resorted to laying his ornery little brother on the ground to force the shoes on, mumbling past the little boy's kicking, "Benji… we're going… to be… late."

Finally his brother was ready, and before he could fiendishly unlace his sandals, Joseph grabbed him up again, "Come on."

"But it's your turn to hide," Benjamin insisted.

Joseph blinked. Had they been playing hide and seek? No one had told him. Regardless, they could do that later, right now he was starving.

Stepping out into the red streaked evening, Joseph caught a deliciously spicy fragrance wafting from their stewpots, mingled with the wondrous scent of honeyed bread. Above it all rose the aroma of crisped meat from where Dhra had three full sheep and as many goats spitted and slow roasting over a string of simmering fires.

Already the collective excitement was strained taut as a bowstring, and half the camp hungrily milled near the feast. Nearby, a smaller crowd marked where Abby and Tannah were passing out a mountain of honey tarts to sate the ravenous masses.

"Joseph, can we get one?" Benji squirmed to point at the tarts.

"We might be too late now," Joseph remarked dryly.

It took a moment battling through the throng to get anywhere near the front where Abby was more holding back a mob than handing out food.

"I said *one* each, that's two," she snapped at Asher.

"One's for Gad."

"Oh, just like he got an extra for you? Get!" She flicked him away, and Joseph pushed his way into the gap. Benji proudly held up his fingers as he asked, "Two?"

Instantly Abby's face transformed into a smile. Joseph was certain he saw one of the herdsmen swiping a pastry out of the corner of his eye, but Abby barely appeared to notice. She piled two tarts into Joseph's free hand, with a warning look at Benji, "Don't eat that too fast."

Joseph nodded and set to extricating himself and his little brother from the tangled mass of people.

They had just slid out, finding a spot where a ravenous Benjamin could start munching on his snack, when Father's booming voice rose above the camp. "EVERYONE, IF I MAY!"

It took a moment and several more shouts to tamp down the general roar, but finally the noise died off, and Dad continued. "I know you're ready to eat, so I'll be short. I want to congratulate all of you for your hard work these last few weeks. That includes not just those of you in the fields, but everyone who prepared the food, carted the grain, and even those who tended the herds so others could work. You've all played an important part in our bounty this year, so tonight we shall all share in that. I want everyone to eat well, enjoy yourselves and sleep in tomorrow." Father raised his hands with a final shout, "Let's feast!"

A cheer rocked the camp, and Joseph sat back, watching as a line instantly coalesced near the food. Dhra was busy ladling out giant scoops of meaty stew, while grandfather Isaac's cook, Muza, carved off slabs of roast lamb and goat for the hungry masses.

Joseph was content to wait a few moments, savoring Abby's delicious tart. Benjamin hungrily demolished his snack, but Joseph tried to eat slowly, enjoying each bite. The circular outside was puffed up, and the center had been pressed flat and spread with a thick honey butter. They made them in a dome-shaped oven, sticking the pastries on the inside wall and cooking hundreds of them en masse. And if you ate it just right, Joseph had found you could nibble a little of the gooey middle with each bite.

As he ate, he watched the milling crowd, glimpsing Levi, Judah, and Issachar all caught up in the mad rush for food. But even with hundreds of people in the camp, Joseph didn't feel much urgency. They had prepared enough food to feed everyone, and he knew from experience that they'd be sitting on a mountain of leftovers tomorrow.

Besides, he didn't see Dad in there, muscling people aside for a bowl of stew. Might as well try to act similarly dignified.

Benjamin was… less patient. "Can we eat now? Can we eat now? Can we eat now…" Joseph shot his little brother a warning glare, but the moment he looked away, "Can we eat *now*?"

He lasted about two minutes before, "Fine. Come on."

The wait was still long, but at least all the people who might have punched someone for the first bowl of soup had gone. And when Dhra ladled a steaming helping into Joseph's bowl, he shivered at the delicious scent.

Usually Benjamin, Myrrha and himself might have sat at the entrance to his tent. Myrrha would be grinning as they helped Benjamin through his meal. Today though, he couldn't see her anywhere. Pausing to look around, he finally caught Myrrha's distinctive yellow and blue patterned shawl, seated near her mom and several older women. She didn't look terribly happy either. She sat a pace back from the others, her shoulders hunched as she mostly stared at her food. He watched, wondering what she'd done to get in trouble, before a hungry Benjamin grabbed his attention with a shrill, "Joseph, come on!"

Heading towards his father's tent, Joseph noted with no small satisfaction that Dad had also chosen patience and wasn't yet back. Grandpa Isaac was there though, and Benjamin nearly spilled his stew hurrying over to shout, "SABA!"

The old man grinned at hearing him. "Benjamin, come on over, my boy."

In a moment the two were getting along famously, Benjamin sitting next to Isaac and digging into his meal with a gusto, while Joseph tried to pace himself. That proved difficult. The mutton had been roasted to perfection, and Dhra had been simmering the stew so long that the broth had taken on a fantastic flavor.

Father returned a moment later with dinner for himself and Isaac, smiling when he saw them. "Enjoying everything?"

Joseph nodded, swallowing a mouthful of stew. Now that he'd started eating, it was difficult to stop.

He eventually did have to pause, although only to tear up Benji's slice of meat into small, manageable chunks. Fortunately though, his little brother could handle the stewed vegetables just fine. Frankly, Joseph wasn't entirely sure how the boy still had room after scoffing a whole tart, but Benji put down most of his stew, plus the mutton. Impressive.

While they ate, the sun sank lower in the west, streaking the clouds in scarlet. And as the light faded, torches slowly sprang to life across the camp, bringing with them the trill of music.

While a steady stream of people hustled back for second and third helpings, he saw two of the more rhythmically inclined members, Hana and her husband Aram, find a spot in the center of camp. Hana struck up a slow beat with a timbrel, while Aram matched it on an assortment of leather drums. The two musicians came from grandfather's side of the camp, and they seemed able to play just about anything. Sometimes they'd perform for an entire hour, elegantly sliding from one tune to the next, or even transitioning to something they'd made up on the spot. Certainly they constituted a dramatic improvement over the somewhat haphazard performances he'd grown up with back in Shechem.

The musicians started out with a steady beat, then without breaking pace, they slipped into *Dawn over the Tower,* an old favorite. Soon the entire camp was tapping along and as they hit the last note, they ramped up the pace and launched straight into *The Wayward Goat.* By the time they'd finished, the sun had set, leaving a fading light, and more players had joined them, with a flute, another timbrel, and a pair of lyres all adding to the performance. Meanwhile several younger women gathered with the players, adding in their sonorous voices, while others in the camp chimed in with a few… less talented contributions. He even caught his father humming along.

As they sang, Benjamin poked at his arm, frowning and one hand on his stomach. "I don't feel good," the boy mumbled.

Wow, what a surprise.

"Just lay down, okay? And stop eating everything in sight."

In answer, his little bother's frown deepened, like that was a profoundly unreasonable request.

Before Benji could say more, Joseph's attention was stolen as the impromptu band took up the fast-paced notes of another song, *The Wind from the North.*

As they did Aram shouted, "Everybody come on in! Men on the outside, women inside!"

There were shouts of excitement from across the sprawling camp, and Joseph glanced at his father, "Can you watch—"

"Go," Dad waved him on. "You only get to be young once."

Joseph nodded, and a moment later he joined the excited circle. He'd been aiming to dance with Myrrha, but had ended up four spots down from her. Meanwhile, the band had played the first verse without words a few times to let everyone get organized. The moment the chaos coalesced into a semblance of order though, they kicked into the first verse, this time for real.

Joseph found himself across from Fannah in her tan work skirt. She grinned as they launched into the dance. Four steps in place, walk past, turn, four more steps, move in, then arms up, palms together as they circled each other.

The dance was something grandfather's camp had picked up years ago, apparently a variation on a Philistine original. The first time Joseph had tried it, he'd made an absolute fool of himself. That he'd learned at all was only thanks to Samas and Abby, who knew it by another name, and had spent several hours the next day teaching him the steps.

Now though, the moves came almost without thinking. He and Fannah stepped in perfect time, and when the chorus came, everyone belted it out:

And the north winds roar
And the thunderheads rumble
And the lightning strikes around
While the old man he does grumble

And the winds tear at the trees
While the earth it creaks and shakes
But the old man stares the storm right dooooown
With a glare that makes the north wind quake

The verse ended and as one the women rotated to a new partner. According to Abby, there was a version with just a single partner, but that would have been absolutely scandalous. He knew Leah already didn't appreciate the dance, and he'd heard enough of the older women complain about it to know she wasn't alone.

Fannah spun away, and Joseph found himself across from a woman he only dimly recognized. She was older than him, but wearing an encouraging smile. They launched into the second verse and Joseph soon lost himself in keeping time to the music, right until Myrrha twirled into the spot in front of him.

Then he nearly missed a step. Somehow it had slipped his mind in the last two minutes that she was moving down the chain. She froze also, only for an instant, but long enough to be a quarter beat behind. When she did catch up, their eyes met and even in the dark, he could see her demure smile.

The music didn't pause and Joseph found himself still stepping through the dance, with Myrrha keeping pace. This was the fourth and final verse, and as they came to the end both lines stepped apart. Joseph bowed, Myrrha curtsied, and the band hit the final notes with a cheer.

Across from him Myrrha grinned, her colorful yellow and blue shawl draped over her shoulders, and an abashed glow on her cheeks. Joseph broke the silence, "You're an excellent dancer."

That wasn't anything particularly new, but she nodded and glanced away, blushing, "You too."

There followed an awkward pause, until Joseph asked, "You want to go sit down?"

Myrrha seemed to glance at something behind him, her voice uncertain, "I ummm…"

"Oh, come on," Joseph insisted, adding a teasing. "You're not trying to avoid me, are you?"

Myrrha still hesitated, before abruptly seeming to make up her mind. "Okay," she agreed with a furtive whisper.

The music began to swell once more as they left, and Joseph led for his tent. They found their usual spot near the entrance. Even as they sat though, Joseph saw the girl cast a cautious glance around for the third time.

"Everything okay, Myrrha?"

She didn't answer immediately, instead letting out a frustrated sigh as she plopped down next to him. "It's my Mom. She's…" Myrrha shook her head. "We've had some disagreements."

Joseph didn't know how to respond. In the moment, the only thing that came to mind, was his own conversation with Dad earlier, the disastrous one about choosing a wife. The memory of their talk had plagued him all day, harassing his thoughts whenever he slowed down enough to dwell on it.

He wished he could go back and have another chance at explaining what he wanted. He knew what he *needed* to tell Dad. That he absolutely didn't want to marry his long-lost cousin from Harran. And certainly not one of Uncle Esau's daughters that he'd never even seen, let alone met. Just the possibility left him nauseous.

Except what would Dad think? When they'd spoken this morning, he'd seemed so certain that he knew the best way.

Glancing at Myrrha, the words slipped out, "I know what you mean."

The girl looked over with a sudden sharpness in her gaze, and Joseph clarified, "About… disagreements."

Myrrha relaxed, some of the tension visibly draining from her shoulders, but she still didn't look at him. Instead, she stared straight ahead, gazing at nothing in particular as the music picked up yet again until, "Does it ever feel like everything just becomes more complicated the older you get?

"Only all the time," he agreed dourly.

Myrrha nodded half to herself, then added a contemplative, "Sometimes I wish we could just go back to the way things were before." She paused, "You remember the time we stole all of Bilhah's honey cakes and hid in those bushes up the mountain to have our own little feast?"

Joseph chuckled at the absurd memory. They'd been twelve and in their infinite genius, they'd stacked all the little cakes away in a wicker basket. Bilhah had almost caught them too. They'd bumped into her on the way out of camp, before she'd realized anything was amiss and she'd given them a probing glare, demanding to know what they were doing. He'd been sure she was about to look inside, except that Myrrha had spun a marvelous lie and claimed it was only a bunch of wool that they were off to pick clean.

"Yeah," Joseph grinned. "Do you remember her face when she went after the herdsmen trying to figure out who'd taken them?"

Myrrha nodded, a smile sneaking onto her face and a giggle slipping out.

A breeze whisked across the camp, blurring the music as it passed and leaving a slight chill on Joseph's arms. Next to him Myrrha tugged her shawl close around her chest. "You know," she said after a moment, "it's dumb, but I think that may have been my favorite day… ever. Nobody caught us, the cakes were delicious, and we got to just sit there for the entire day, no chores, no one to tell us what to do." She breathed a fond sigh, and turned to look at him, their eyes meeting, Myrrha's strangely serious. "Do you think it's wrong, to want to go back and live in that day forever?"

The sudden intensity in her gaze caught Joseph off balance, and the only thing he could think was to make a joke. "I don't know, would I still have to get sick afterwards?"

Her eyes narrowed in mock admonition, "You know what I mean."

Joseph laughed before, "I'm not sure, I suppose…" his voice trailed off as his gaze swept across the camp, the question tumbling in his mind. He remembered that day in a mix of images and feelings, little moments all strung together amid a happy, excited haze. And beneath it all he'd felt a wonderful calm like he was… home. As though for that one day, he had been exactly where he belonged.

Glancing across the camp now, it tore his heart that he felt almost exactly the opposite. Many of the faces were the same, and except for becoming larger, their camp hadn't really changed. They still herded the same animals; everyone did the same chores and yet…

Joseph blinked as a surge of loneliness swept over him. He couldn't pinpoint where it had come from, but in that instant, he felt so horribly isolated, as though no one really understood him at all. It was like he didn't quite belong anymore, and in a flash, he also understood exactly what Myrrha meant.

"No," he mumbled, glancing over to see Myrrha staring at him with a look as though he'd sunken into a momentary trance. "I don't think it's wrong at all, wanting to go back and live in that day." He swallowed, "I wish we both could."

Sitting next to Joseph, Myrrha nodded, silent, and for a time neither spoke. Joseph's own thoughts inexorably slid back to *the thing,* the thing he'd meant to talk with Myrrha about this morning, the one that had been haunting him for weeks now. He'd kept putting it off, always waiting for the right moment. But perhaps this *was* the right moment, he realized, or as close as he would ever get.

The thought prodded him that last step forward and before Joseph could stop himself words began to slip out, "Myrrha I've been wanting to—"

"Myrrha!"

Joseph jolted, and Myrrha nearly jumped in shock. Her eyes locked on the furious figure of her mom stalking towards them. "What are you doing?"

"I…" the girl glanced from her mother, to Joseph, then back, like a trapped gazelle.

Joseph frowned, dismissive, Myrrha might be scared of her mom, but he, quite frankly, wasn't. And this was kind of important. "We're not *doing* anything."

Althea scowled, her eyes boring in on Myrrha, "Come with me," she snapped.

"Althea," Joseph made to stand, "she didn't—"

"Joseph," Myrrha's hand appeared on his shoulder and he turned to see her with a desperate plea in her eyes, "Please, just…"

She left the sentence hanging, yet somehow perfectly clear.

"I'll be fine." Myrrha mumbled.

Even so Joseph almost stopped her, almost told her mom that she wasn't leaving. Althea didn't get to disagree, not with him. Except he hesitated at Myrrha's expression, a nervous, almost scared frown. Joseph was gripped by the abrupt sense that he was interfering in business that he didn't understand, and if he wasn't careful, his meddling might just shatter something in the dynamic between then. Something he couldn't quite define, except to say it was important.

He hesitated, staring right into her eyes "You sure?"

Myrrha nodded, relief sweeping her features, like whatever ledge he'd been walking close too, they both knew he'd stepped back. She held his gaze one last instant before turning to her mother who curtly nodded for them to go.

Joseph stared after them a moment. Althea's steps sharp and tense, while Myrrha trailed her, seeming very small in comparison. An unsated curiosity nipped at him. What was going on? It was rare to see Althea upset. He could recall it happening *maybe* once or twice, but typically with good reason.

Had Myrrha done something? Joseph watched as the two women headed back in the direction of their tent, the question poking his mind like a sharp rock beneath his bedroll. Finally, on the spur of the moment, he rose to tail them.

Chapter 6
Horizon of Stars

In the firelit night, following Myrrha wasn't difficult. At the center of camp, the music blazed away in a flurry of beats, shouts, and dancing, that was growing wilder as the evening wore on.

Joseph clung to the shadows near the tents, avoiding the central bonfire. He kept far enough back that, even if Althea turned, he would just be one more dark-shrouded figure amid the chaos of the feast. A wash of people coursed around him, some carrying steaming bowls of stew, while others laughed over honeyed pastries. A group of partiers stumbled past and Joseph caught the lingering scent of wine in their wake. He nearly stumbled over a man and woman, two shadowed figures illicitly kissing behind a nearby tent. They both jolted at seeing him, but in the dark it was nearly impossible to make out faces. Joseph turned and hurriedly navigated a new path.

Myrrha and her mother finally paused near their tent. Althea glowered at Myrrha, and Joseph fought back the urge to step in and help. Amid the cacophony of the party, he might as well have been watching pantomime. Althea pointed an accusing finger, while Myrrha threw up her hands, frustrated. The two gestured, obviously at loggerheads, while Joseph snuck in close enough to catch snippets.

"…just hide away in the tent?"

"Myrrha, you know exactly what I expect you…"

"NO! I DON'T!"

As though they were afraid of making a scene, both their voices lowered another moment until, "I AM YOUR MOTHER AND YOU—!"

"NO!" Myrrha screamed, before abruptly catching herself. Joseph gulped, watching as her head swiveled left and right, like she was afraid she'd been heard. Then, with Althea still talking, she wheeled and stalked off.

"Myrrha, you get back here!"

But Myrrha wasn't listening. Joseph watched as she hurried through the maze of tents, out into the blackness beyond the camp. For an instant he hesitated, his eyes jumping back to Althea. The woman stared after Myrrha, took a half step like she was about to follow, then paused. One hand rubbed at her forehead before she finally turned away with a wounded frown.

Joseph's eyes leapt back toward Myrrha. She was gone now, lost to the shadows beyond their camp, and with barely a pause he plunged straight into the darkness after her.

Fortunately, tonight the moon waxed above, a half circle of pale light that bathed the world in a quilt of murky shadows. Still, Joseph had nearly sprained his ankle enough times in the dark to stride carefully as his eyes slowly adjusted.

Passing through the outer ring of tents, the mingle of shouts and tunes in camp gradually faded into an indistinct jumble behind him. He paused, his eyes roaming the grassy hillside until... there. He caught a silhouetted figure amid the faint glow that shrouded the world, and picked his way towards her, until at last he caught a new sound close ahead— long, miserable sobs.

"Myrrha?"

The girl drew a sharp breath in surprise, "Joseph?"

He stepped closer to find her sitting, a dark sentinel amid the short grass. He settled down beside her, and for a time Myrrha didn't move, just stared off into the star-strewn horizon, her shawl pulled tight.

"Are you okay?"

Myrrha gulped audibly, then said, "You shouldn't be here."

She probably couldn't see in the dark, but Joseph still cocked an eye with a skeptical, "Shouldn't I?"

No answer. Instead she sniffled, her hands firmly in her lap. For a time, the dull noise of the night washed over them: the soft chirps of crickets and the swish of grass in the breeze.

"Myrrha, what's going on?"

She exhaled a long breath, "It's nothing."

Right, *obviously* nothing.

She wet her lips though, and Joseph knew enough to hold his questions in until, "It's my mom, she… she…" Myrrha's voice wavered like she couldn't quite force out the words until…

"…she doesn't want me to spend too much time with…" her voice cracked, "…with you."

Joseph blinked, his mind racing in bewildered confusion. "With me? Why?"

He might have guessed several possibilities — Leah making some insidious power play to cut off the few friends he and Benjamin still had, his brothers threatening Althea because… why not? The one thing he didn't expect was the forlorn whisper of an answer that Myrrha gave.

"She…" the girl sniffled again, "She says she doesn't want me to get hurt."

The words tumbled out and Joseph's mind froze. Myrrha could have meant a few different things, but the way she said them, the way her eyes darted to meet his… there was only one possible meaning. In that instant, Joseph could swear every wall came down, all the chinks in her armor perfectly aligned, and he could see right down to where Myrrha had just bared her soul.

His chest constricted and he struggled to breathe. She stared at him, her wide eyes reflecting moonlight, even as he grappled for the right words. This was *the thing*, the thing he should have spoken to her about weeks ago. He was never sure how to start the conversation, yet he'd imagined it a hundred times in his mind. "Myrrha, you know I wouldn't hurt you. I... I..."

Joseph almost couldn't force out the words, yet he couldn't *not* say them either. The unspoken truth that had been hanging between them for months was suddenly cracking open before his eyes, and the only choice was to fumble the moment or to grab hold.

"I love you."

The girl gave a small, solemn nod... and then burst into tears.

Joseph put his arms around the sobbing figure, "It's okay." He pulled her close, not sure how to react, even as she buried her head in his shoulder. A cyclone of feelings rushed through him — confusion, concern, panic, but also a reassuring warmth and a strange relief at the simple act of holding her close.

For a time, she sniffled in his arms, but despite her tears, serenity radiated out from where their bodies met. Joseph's mind flooded with a wondrous calm, and for the first time in years, everything felt exactly right. They'd spent so much time together the last few years. Sometimes he'd catch himself watching her play with Benji, his gaze anchored on her like a tent peg in the ground. Once she'd turned and caught him staring, their eyes locking and her cheeks blushing a beautiful scarlet right before he could look away. Then he hadn't known what to think, just that everything felt better when she was there.

Slowly Myrrha's breaths grew more steady, the sobs fading to a cold quiet and Joseph brushed a hand through her dark locks. None of Myrrha's tension drained away though. If anything she seemed to coil herself ever tighter, until finally whispering, "I can't be *her*."

Joseph frowned, "Can't be who?"

"The girl," Myrrha mumbled with a forlorn despair. "The one you're supposed to marry." She swallowed hard and shuddered, "That was what Mom told me... and she's right."

"Myrrha you know that's not true. I—"

"Isn't it though?" she demanded, finally pulling away and fixing him with uncertain eyes. "Joseph, you're… *you* and I'm just…" she paused, seeming to search through several aborted words before offering a dejected, "I'm just *me*."

He looked at her, dumbfounded. "You think I care?"

"Everyone else does. One day you're going to be in charge of everything here. Your father will have you marry some… some… I don't know. Some wealthy girl from far away with rose perfume and beautiful skirts and…"

She tried to pull away but Joseph held her tight against him. "Myrrha, I don't care about any of that," he insisted. "You know I don't. I don't want that girl. I want you. And if Dad insists then… I don't know…" He swallowed, honestly not sure what he'd do in that situation, then sighed, "Maybe I do have to marry some other girl, but… that doesn't mean we can't still be together. If Dad has four wives, I can have two."

Myrrha didn't pull away, but she looked up, fixing him with a wounded stare. "And then what?" she asked dejectedly. "I spend the rest of my life with the other girl, the one you don't want, hating me? Just like Leah and your mother? We do the same dance, but with different faces?"

For once Joseph was taken aback, his arm slipping from around her shoulder. She wasn't wrong. They'd both grown up seeing that resentment fester like a boil. He'd seen his Mom angry and hurt and frustrated. He'd seen his brothers split into dueling camps. So much anger and resentment, all because someone was loved more than someone else. Was this what Dad had thought all those years ago, when he'd married Mom and Leah? That he could just make things work? And were they about to repeat the same cycle once again?

In a flash his voice firmed up, "Then I won't marry her," he said. "I won't marry the girl from far away with the perfume and the dresses." He met Myrrha's gaze with a force in his voice, "It'll just be the two of us. And this time things will be different."

He wasn't entirely sure how he would accomplish all that. He certainly didn't know how he would convince his father, but in the moment, he took Myrrha's chilly fingers with a reassuring grip.

"Do you really mean that?"

He gulped, willing the answer to be *yes* as he whispered the words that came easier the second time. "I love you, Myrrha."

"I love you too."

Their eyes locked for a fleeting instant. Then a force like a whirlwind pulled them together, and a liquid lightning strobed through Joseph's veins as their lips met in a kiss.

For an instant that drug into forever, Joseph's whole consciousness narrowed down to that kiss. She loved him. She loved him and…

The two broke apart, awkwardly gasping for breath. And Joseph couldn't stop staring at her, even as the lightning inside him dimmed to a refreshing tingle.

Myrrha glanced away, and even in the pale glow of the moon, Joseph could tell she was blushing. "I…" she seemed almost surprised at herself.

The breeze picked up, the cool night air whipping at them. Myrrha shivered and huddled close, her figure heavy as she leaned on his shoulder. A wondrous warmth flooded Joseph in spite of the cold. For a while neither spoke, like something as simple as words might shatter the one perfect moment they did have.

Another gust swept across the grass, stronger now, and Myrrha curled close beside him. "I'll talk to Dad. He'll understand." Joseph said. He paused before adding, "He has too," not sure if he was speaking to himself or to Myrrha.

Next to him Myrrha didn't answer. When he turned to her, she was gazing at him, and suddenly the magnetic whirlwind returned pulling them together into another lingering kiss.

As they did a third breeze whipped up, and Joseph wasn't sure if it was a sign the world wanted to drive them apart or just a token of the storm of emotions raging inside. The wind sliced at them both, and breaking apart, Joseph stood, offering her a hand up.

She accepted, and pulled her shawl close, even as he nodded back towards camp. "Come on," he insisted, "we can go talk to Dad."

Myrrha blinked in surprise, a sudden flash of worry on her face. "You mean… right now?"

He shrugged, "Is there a better time?"

Myrrha hesitated, and even in the night, Joseph could swear he caught a twist of panic on her face, "But what if he—"

"He won't," Joseph said, somehow finding a steady reassurance to put into the words. "After the harvest negotiations this morning… he won't."

Across from him, Myrrha shuddered, and he gripped her hand with a optimistic strength. Their eyes locked, and after a long interval she finally nodded with a quiet, frightened, but determined, "Okay."

***

The feast was devolving into chaos as they returned to camp. The wine and beer had begun to flow, and at the center of camp, the dancing hammered on, now backed by the rapid *thumps* of drums. When he'd been younger, this was well past the time when Mom would have hustled him into their tent and to bed. And that had been back when things hadn't gotten nearly so rowdy.

As their camp had swelled and merged with Uncle Isaac's, the chaotic task of managing so many people blowing off steam at once had gradually slipped beyond them. As they returned, Joseph saw Nashu and his apprentice Lerin armed with quarter-staves and stalking like lions at the edge of the chaotic dancing. Usually if the drunken revelry got too far

56

out of hand, the solution was a few sharp knocks to keep everyone in line.

Out in the maze of tents though, with no one to hold it back, the madness was building to a crescendo. People surged around them, some faces familiar, others shadowed. A pair of woozy herdsmen stumbled by, mumbling slurred greetings, and a little further on a clump of women emitted drunken giggles as they passed. He kept tight hold of Myrrha's hand as they navigated around another tent only to find a man woozily leaned over a pool of dark puke.

Joseph wrinkled his nose as the two gingerly stepped around him. He couldn't escape a twinge of hesitation, maybe this wasn't the best time to talk to Dad. His gaze flashed towards Father's tent, hoping to see him, but Joseph couldn't make out more than shadows near the entrance. He was about to retract his suggestion and just walk Myrrha back to her tent, when a sharp scream pierced the muddle of shouts and music…

Benjamin.

Both heard, and both instantly knew that voice. In a flash, Joseph shot her a panicked look, to which Myrrha just nodded. Her hand slipped from his, but he knew she'd be close behind as he broke into a run, weaving through tents until he heard another sharp wail, much closer now. "Let go!"

He rounded the next tent at a pell-mell run and found… his brothers.

Issachar held Benjamin upside down by his ankles, cruelly swinging the little boy back and forth like a doll. Benji screamed, even as Reuben, Simeon, Judah, Gad and Zebulun watched, laughing and sipping at their cups. Simeon called out, "Looks like the little brat doesn't know how to have fun either."

"ISSACHAR!" Joseph's furious roar split the night, and all of them abruptly started at seeing him. "PUT HIM DOWN!"

"Look," Issachar regarded him with a drunken grin, "it's dreamer boy."

Joseph stared at his flailing little brother. "Put him down, Issachar."

He tried to keep the panic out of his voice, but Issachar must have caught it regardless. "Why don't you make me?" His expression twisted in a sneer, "You're the one who's going to be king of us all. Right?"

Joseph hesitated, a hot fury gathering in his chest, as he realized Issachar wasn't about to back down. Then he abruptly lunged ahead, trying to grab his little brother.

Even drunk though, Issachar stumbled a step backwards and out of reach, waving a crying Benji around like a toy and playing keep-away.

"Oh right," Issachar taunted, "I guess you're not king yet, are you?"

Joseph heard Judah and Simeon chuckle nearby, and Benjamin wailed again.

"Issachar, put him down!"

"You mean like this?" A smirking Issachar let one hand slip, so Benji was dangling by only a single leg.

Joseph froze, fury boiling inside as he summoned up every ounce of command he could throw in his voice. "Don't...you...dare!"

Issachar seemed to dully consider that for a moment before, shrugging with an ambivalent, "Okay."

He let go of Benjamin's other ankle.

The boy plunged.

Joseph could swear the fall stretched out into forever. His breath caught like a salamander in his throat as his little brother tumbled a half cubit and smashed face first into the dirt.

Joseph saw red, his eyes honed like knives on Issachar, and he rushed him. Growing up, Issachar had always towered half a head above him. But the last couple years, Issachar had finally stopped growing and Joseph had caught up. Now they were nearly the same size, and right now,

Joseph wouldn't have cared if his half-brother had been a giant.

Issachar sneered, belatedly putting up his arms to fight, and laughing the whole time. Laughing while the helpless kid at his feet cried in pain. Joseph charged close right as Issachar swung a woozy fist straight at his head.

And Joseph blocked.

The motion came more by instinct than intention, but suddenly he'd stepped past the older boy's guard. His half-brother's sneering face hung a tantalizing cubit away and Issachar's eyes widened in surprise. Surging with adrenaline, Joseph threw all his fury, and hatred and frustration into a single devastating uppercut.

Crack.

Issachar's head popped back, the whites of his eyes rolled up, and he tumbled backward, crashing in an unconscious heap.

For a second Joseph stared, a part of him surprised at how quick it had been. He was dimly aware of a stinging fire in his knuckles, and Myrrha near his feet, bundling the sobbing Benjamin into her arms with a reassuring, "It's alright, Benji."

Then a furious dark shape crashed into him. "*Sumaktar!*" Zebulun swore as the two crashed to the ground, Zebulun on top, "*Lā Kēnu Karkittu!*"

Zebulun pulled back a fist and swung. Joseph threw up his arms, but couldn't fully deflected it. Pain flared in his lip and he tasted sharp, metallic blood.

His older brother reared back for another punch, murder in his eyes. Pinned beneath him, Joseph threw a wild backhanded fist, clocking him right across the nose and stunning him for a precious half second.

Zebulun clutched his nose, and writhing frantically, Joseph managed to shove him off. Zebulun crashed to the dirt, and Joseph was on him in a flash. He jammed an elbow into Zebulun's ribs, heard his brother gasp in pain, and pulled back to smash him again when…

"Get off!" Joseph felt strong hands on his shoulder, wrenching him away from Zebulun. Levi's steely grip half-lifted, half-dragged him across the dirt.

Furious, Joseph scrambled upright and threw a wild swing at Levi, but his brother shoved him away. Unbalanced, Joseph stumbled in the dark, tripped and crashed face down on the packed earth, his lip stinging as he gasped for breath.

Nearby he heard Benjamin still wailing, Zebulun's groans, and above it all Simeon's cold declaration, "That little *zû* is going to pay for—"

"Simeon, NO!" Joseph rolled over to see a drunken Simeon struggling toward him with murder in his eyes, while Reuben stubbornly dragged him back.

"You know the brat deserves it, Reuben! Someone has to put him back in his place."

Joseph scrambled to hit feet, spit blood, met Simeon's glare, and stepped forward anyway. "Screw you, Simeon!"

"You just wait, Joseph! You and your precious little *zû* of a brother. I'll—"

"Both of you, STOP!" Reuben frantically interposed between them.

Fighting Simeon was generally considered to be suicide, but right now Joseph didn't care. He hated them. He hated all of them. He rushed towards Simeon only to be dragged to a halt as Levi's arms clamped around him, holding him back. "Joseph, stop!"

"LET ME GO!" Joseph vainly struggled to break free. "You'll pay for this!" he screamed. "One day, when I'm in charge you're all going to pay for this! You hear me?"

"Joseph, just shut up!" Reuben snapped, still holding back Simeon, but now fixing him with a dark glower. "Nobody died and made you king. You had a weird dream, let—it—go."

Joseph tried to writhe free of Levi's grip. "It wasn't just a dream!" He shouted, furious. Right now he just wanted to hurt them. He didn't even care how, so long as it stung. "Look," he ranted, "I had another dream, and this time the sun, moon and eleven stars were bowing down to me! That's you! You hear me? That's all of—"

"WHAT IS THIS?" Father's familiar voice rose above the racket.

Instantly, the night turned more chaotic as Father strode onto the scene, carrying a bright torch to illuminate the madness— Issachar out cold, Myrrha cradling a sobbing Benjamin, Zebulun clutching his ribs, while an enraged Simeon tried to push past Reuben.

Several voices spoke at once.

"Joseph swung first!"

"Issachar hurt Benji!"

"It's nothing. Everything's fine."

Father's bewildered gaze flashed across the lot of them. Simeon had finally given up his wild attempts to fight past Reuben, but when Father stalked close, he wrinkled his nose at the alcohol on Simeon's breath. "Simeon, you're drunk," he snapped. "Reuben, get him to his tent."

There came a collective pause as Father stooped down, wincing at the motion, and felt at Issachar's neck for a pulse. His lips creased in a dark scowl and he rose. The torch flickered as he turned to face the rest of them with a glower, "Levi, Judah, take care of your brother. The rest of you, back to your tents," he snapped furiously. "I don't want to see any of you again tonight. Understood?"

There came a chorus of mumbled acknowledgements, and slowly his brothers turned to leave. Zebulun clutched a nose gushing dark scarlet in the torchlight, while Judah and Levi moved to lift Issachar's limp figure. Joseph wiped his lip, still tasting blood. This was hardly the first time Dad had stumbled onto them to find someone bleeding, unconscious or both. But it still qualified as one of the worst, and Joseph had the ominous feeling that Father's intrusion hadn't solved anything… just postponed the reckoning.

Meanwhile, Father's focus swung towards Myrrha, cradling a sobbing Benjamin in her arms, "Is he alright?"

"Yes, sir… I think."

"Get him to bed then. Then I want you back to your tent as well."

Myrrha gave a respectful nod and rose, "Yes, sir."

Her arms were full with the crying boy, but even so she dipped once in a curtsey, before turning and hurrying off with a *swish* of her skirt.

Joseph turned to follow but…

"Joseph?" Father's voice interrupted. "What happened?"

Joseph hesitated. Over the years he'd learned to just *say nothing* in these situations. Move on, get over it. He didn't need Father to fight his battles for him. That typically just made things worse. Right now though, the rage burned in his chest, hot enough to make Joseph break his own rule, "They were tormenting Benji… for fun."

He left it at that. And before Dad could say anything, he'd spun after Myrrha and hurried off to make sure his little brother would be alright.

He found Myrrha and Benji already back at his tent, and the next hour passed in a blur. He tried to comfort his little brother, while also doing his best to ignore the spike of fury that hammered at him every time he touched the tender knot on the boy's head. And when Benjamin finally calmed down, there came the long chore of coaxing the young boy to sleep.

It seemed to take forever. He recovered from his knock quickly enough, but that just left Benji brimming with a frenetic, frightened energy, and channeling it all into avoiding bed. He wanted to play pebbles, then he wanted to dart around the tent, and eventually he settled on pleading for a story. Joseph obliged, for a while. He spent long minutes recounting a pair of scary tales he remembered from Didi. Finally, Myrrha swooped in, insisting that the yawning boy needed to sleep, and humming a soft lullaby as she scooped him up and settled him on his mat. She didn't hum a single song so much as a medley of gentle tunes and Joseph noticed the singing calmed even his strained nerves.

He was almost disappointed when Benjamin finally dozed off and Myrrha's song faded with him. He'd been staring at her, her hair a rumpled mess after everything that had happened, yet she seemed absolutely beautiful. She turned to him, her cheeks flushing, "I uhh… I should go…" she mumbled. "It's late."

It was only then he noticed the sounds of revelry outside had faded substantially, the music and shouts of partying bleeding away like water from a cracked pot.

He nodded, adding, "Thank you, Myrrha, for… everything."

She smiled, a warm happy grin, "Of course."

She made for the exit, but paused, their eyes locking in a hypnotic gaze that he couldn't seem to break… Then they kissed, quick, simple, both of them suddenly close, holding each other for a passionate moment. And when they split apart, Joseph felt like he could have lost himself in her deep brown eyes.

Myrrha looked away embarrassed, yet beaming. She mumbled a soft, 'good night', then turned away blushing furiously as she pushed past the hanging tent flap and out into the breezy night.

That left Joseph alone with his thoughts. He'd come to hate these sorts of moments lately. Anymore he felt like being alone with himself was just a quick way to become angry. He crawled onto his own bed and blew out the last flickering candle, plunging the tent into utter darkness. But despite his exhaustion, sleep was slow in coming.

His worries about Benji gradually crept back, prodding at the dark corners of his mind. With it came a simmering hatred that kept him even more awake, a cold fury that his brothers would stoop so low. He wouldn't have been surprise if they'd picked a fight with him. But Benji… Benji was a kid. He wasn't part of any of this. He didn't even understand and yet they…

It wasn't right, the thought circled like a vulture a dozen times in his mind, latching on and not letting go. It wasn't right, nothing about this was right. He didn't understand what was wrong with his brothers to make them so horribly evil. But he felt like he had to respond somehow, if not for himself, then at least for Benjamin.

The dream the prior night still sat sharp and crisp in his mind, an image that he could focus on as his hot anger eventually sizzled and died beneath a tide of drowsiness. He was meant to rule over his brothers, deep down he knew it, sure as the sun rose in the east. And as far as he was concerned, that day couldn't come soon enough. The last thing he remembered before he dozed off was a single persistent thought. When the day did come, his brothers were going to pay for tonight… for everything. They were going to pay. They were… they were going to… pay…

Chapter 7
Dreams of Strife

The next morning, Joseph woke exhausted. He must have jolted awake a half dozen times during the night and the dreams he could remember were a shifting cascade of nonsense scenes melded with bizarre nightmares. He felt surprisingly clear-headed though. The sleep had melted away his confusion from the night before, leaving just an icy clarity.

Outside he heard the familiar *mmmahahah* bleat of a goat, and opening his eyes, Joseph was surprised to see a strand of sunlight outlining the bottom of the tent flap. He blinked and rubbed his eyes. Usually he was up with the sunrise, and if not, someone would be sure to swing by and ruin his slumber. Not after feast nights though. This was one of the few mornings when everyone, slave or free, was allowed to sleep in.

Looking towards his little brother's mat, he saw Benji's blankets wadded in an empty bunch, his brother vanished. Probably busy harassing Samas, Abby and Nathanial, Benji's usual escape route from boredom. That was for the best, Joseph mused. He didn't know precisely what the fallout from last night's fiasco would be, but he'd have to go deal with it one way or another, and Benji *didn't* need to tag along for that.

Touching his lip, he felt the rough scab where it had been split the night before, and gave a resigned sigh. Whatever happened, he doubted it would be positive. If he'd only been dealing with Dad, he perhaps could have gotten off free and clear. He had a good case, and Dad understood how tense everyone's nerves were wound. But given how many of her brood had been involved, Leah would undoubtedly find a way to intervene. Then Joseph *would* end up in trouble…

Dwelling on Leah's possible interference also brought the memory of Myrrha and their kiss rushing back as well. He'd been supposed to tell Dad about that too, he recalled despondently. Joseph gave a groggy groan, palms on his forehead as he realized any chance of Father receiving that news positively had been thoroughly shredded. He'd hoped to catch his father in a charitable mood, willing to approve of him and Myrrha being together, even if it wasn't the most conventional marriage.

But now?

Joseph shook his head.

Exhaling another frustrated sigh, he rose and went about the mundane business of dressing. He gave last night's tunic an exploratory sniff and wrinkled his nose at the smell. Might be time to dig out another. He probably needed a bath also, but that would have to wait.

As an alternative, Joseph emptied a pottery jug into a small wash basin and cupped the water in his hands, splashing his face several times. Another few moments had him presentable… sort of. He'd donned a linen tunic, laced up his sandals, washed his hands and smoothed his hair enough to keep the sparrows from mistaking it for a nest. And after a final once over, he swept aside the tent flap and headed out.

This morning the camp radiated none of its usual buzz and bustle. Instead, the eerie stillness felt more like the aftermath of a stampede. Few people were out about their chores for how high the sun stood. Navigating towards his father's tent, Joseph stepped past several shattered clay cups, as well as a puddle of nasty, congealed vomit that he gave a wide berth. As he reached the open middle of the camp, his eyes widened at the sight of a tent across from him, with the entire side smashed in.

Had somebody let a few bulls loose to fight in camp? Joseph shook his head. Apparently, things had gotten more than a little out of hand last night… and not just between him and his brothers.

Joseph found the front to his father's meeting tent pulled shut, probably not the best sign. As he approached, the tent flap abruptly swept aside, and Reuben, of all people, stalked out with an irate frown. Reuben's glower only deepened when their gazes met. Joseph's oldest brother gave a small shake of his head. "You should probably go in." He thumbed toward the tent. "I think Father wanted to talk to *you*."

Reuben nearly spat the word *you* with a simmering disgust in his tone, but Joseph ignored the subtext and headed inside. He was used to the resentment by now.

Father and Grandfather Isaac both sat cross-legged inside. Grandfather lay a bit further back, comfortably propped on several cushions, with Father near the front, far less relaxed. Father looked up at the sound of the tent flap, and Joseph caught a dark scowl on his features that evaporated the moment Dad saw him.

"Ahh, Joseph, excellent." Jacob gestured for him to sit. "I assume Benjamin is okay?"

Joseph swallowed at the reminder, but nodded, "Yes Father, he has a nasty lump, but he seems fine otherwise."

"Good," Dad let out a relieved breath, tapping his fingers as he spoke. "I've already talked with Reuben about keeping everyone in line in the future. And I've also informed the rest of your brothers that they'll be gathering what they need and taking the animals out to pasture first thing tomorrow, instead of next week. I think some space will do you all good."

Joseph pursed his lips at that last part. On the surface that sounded fantastic, but truthfully, he wasn't certain if sending his brothers away would make the situation better or worse. They'd have a few weeks with little to do besides stew on the situation, blame him — and maybe Benji — then return fuming and angrier than ever. Still, he mused, he certainly didn't feel like he could handle them for all of next week either, not if he was going to remain civil.

Regardless, Father spoke with a finality that indicated the decision had already been made. Joseph acceded with another nod. "Of course."

He expected Father to slide along to another subject or perhaps call for breakfast. Instead, Dad regarded him with an uncomfortable, penetrating look before finally asking, "Joseph, is there something you want to tell me?"

Joseph's mind blanked and he gulped back a sudden trepidation. Dad didn't already know about him and Myrrha… right? Joseph had wanted to speak with Father himself. He'd assumed Father would take it better in that context. But he also acutely realized that the morning after an enormous fight wasn't the best time to broach the topic. All of his courage from the night before fled, and instead his head filled with uncertainty. Had someone already told Dad? Maybe seen them kissing last night?

"Uhhh…" he mumbled, hesitant, "I…"

Across from him Father didn't wait for an answer. Instead his fingers peaked as he spoke. "Last night, you were shouting at Simeon, something about the stars?"

Oh… that. Joseph's breath caught, not certain if he should be relieved or perhaps just filled with a different sort of dread. Apparently, there were *two* topics he'd been avoiding. By now he regretted the decision to even bring up his dream. It wasn't something he'd planned to discuss with Dad at all, not until he understood how everything he'd seen in the dream was supposed to happen.

Dad continued right on though, "I asked Reuben about what you meant and he suggested I speak to you, then said something about you wanting to be king? Can you tell me what's going on?"

From the tone of Dad's voice, it was one of those questions that Joseph knew he couldn't readily decline to answer. He considered the situation for an eye-blink. Dad had experienced his own dreams. Right? Or at least visions?

Encounters with God in his own way? And dreams were supposed to be from God.

Joseph rocked back where he sat, then forward, nerving himself. "I've been having dreams," the words spilled out. He caught the confusion on his father's face and quickly clarified, "the unusual sort. They're about…" he stumbled an instant before, "they're about us."

He'd first mentioned his earlier dream to Levi and Judah over a quick meal as they harvested the fields a few weeks before. Then the two had regarded him with a mounting skepticism before Judah finally dropped a mocking, "Okaaaaay?"

Dad didn't let out an ounce of disbelief, instead he simply leaned forward, elbows on his knees and fingers peaking in interest. "Go on."

Joseph did. He explained how his dream had felt astonishingly vivid. How he'd seen his brothers as pools of living light, how he'd seen Leah and Father rise together as the sun and moon and assemble before him… and bow.

He struggled to precisely put the scene into words, but when he finished, Joseph felt he'd done an acceptable job.

Father regarded him with a methodical stare. "That is… certainly an *unusual* dream." He spoke delicately, like he was picking his words from a field full of spikes. "And I wouldn't doubt that you're destined for something very special, Joseph. I've always thought that, and before your mother passed, she told me she felt much the same, like God had purposed you for something wonderful."

Joseph's heart fluttered at that news. Mom had? She'd never said anything like that to him, but then Mom and Dad had always kept their little secrets. For an instant he nearly could have flown, that was until he noticed Father's expression crease in a frown.

"But I'm not confident that you've understood the dream correctly."

"What do you mean?"

"Son, dreams are very complex omens," Father explained. "They can have layers of meaning, and sometimes what you would assume as the obvious interpretation is simply wrong. That's part of why they are so tricky to interpret properly. What you saw might mean any number of things."

Joseph bristled at Father's sudden dismissiveness. Maybe *his* dreams were difficult to interpret, but this one wasn't. If anything, the explanation felt self-evident. "Father it's obvious that—"

"Is it?" Jacob questioned, his arms folding. "Can you be certain? And how do you even know you are remembering it correctly? It's not uncommon for dreams to be muddled when you—"

"Of course I'm remembering it correctly," Joseph interrupted. "How could I forget something like—"

"Then ask yourself, son," Father cut him off with mounting exasperation, "what kind of a dream is that? Will your mother and I and your brothers actually come and bow to the ground before you?"

"Well..." Joseph's voice trailed off, stinging from the way Father had framed things and suddenly feeling very foolish and small, "I..."

"Joseph," his father insisted, "what you saw could mean a dozen different things. Perhaps one day you'll provide some special boon or service for us all. Perhaps when I am old, you're meant to negotiate a treaty and find us a new home somewhere else here in Canaan. Grandfather Abraham always said that God had promised him this land, so maybe you have some purpose to play in bringing that about. But it sounds to me like you've let this go to your head. Frankly I can understand why Reuben would be upset. You can't just try to exalt yourself over everyone."

Joseph swallowed, the words stinging like daggers. "Dad, I'm not just—"

Seated across the tent, Grandfather abruptly interrupted. "Now, Jacob, you shouldn't be so hasty to dismiss these dreams."

Dad turned to Grandfather with a frown. "I'm not being hasty, but I think…"

Joseph didn't hear the rest. He folded his arms, staring at the shadowed linen mats that carpeted the tent floor feeling like he'd just been gut punched. Did Dad really think that? That his brothers were *right* to be upset? That he was trying to lord over them? It wasn't as though he'd asked for the dream. He hadn't asked for any of this. He hadn't even meant to tell them really.

He finally looked up to see Father and Grandfather still debating the point. "… shouldn't ignore your son's interpretation," Grandfather insisted. "The Lord sends dreams to those He wishes to have them. Perhaps He chose your boy for a reason."

Father sighed, clearly frustrated, but keeping his tone respectful, "I understand, but I don't want to start making assumptions about what the dream means."

Father turned back toward him and Joseph caught himself wishing he'd never had the dream at all. Yesterday morning he'd felt such a conviction. He'd known in his heart that he'd understood it. In that moment it had meant he'd been chosen to lead them all, and that there might finally be some justice for how his brothers treated him. But now, facing down Father's scowl, he wished it had just passed him by. Maybe it would have been better that way. Certainly, up until now his dreams had mainly just brought him trouble.

Father's lips drew taut, one hand rapping on his knee, but finally he spoke, "This is certainly all something to keep in mind. But perhaps also something to keep to yourself." He took a long breath, "And at least for now, it might be wise to leave the interpretation to the future."

Joseph gave a subdued nod and swallowed back the bile welling in his throat, "Of course, Father."

"Good," Jacob declared with a decisive finality, "it's for the best."

Maybe it was, but right now Joseph felt like he might be sick. He pushed himself up to standing, "I should probably—"

"Don't leave yet, Joseph" Father abruptly motioned for him to sit back down. "Dreams and the future weren't all I wanted to discuss this morning. I actually have a task for you, a very important one."

He did? After everything Father had just said, Joseph would have preferred to sneak off and spend the day alone with Benji, but he sat still, swallowing back his emotion with a deferential, "Of course. What is it?"

"You recall our negotiations with Mamre yesterday? We promised we would take 1200 ephahs immediately and store them ourselves?" Joseph nodded and Father continued, "I want you to oversee the transfer of the grain. You'll need to deal with Mamre's scribe regarding the final arrangements and ensure everything is properly deposited in our own stores. Do you think you can manage that?"

The task caught Joseph by surprise. Dad wanted *him* to be in charge? He felt like he'd spent most of his life *not* being in charge, doing what Reuben, or Simeon, or Levi, or… any of his brothers ordered. At most he could disagree with Issachar or Zebulun, but then they'd just go grab one of their older siblings and the final result would be exactly the same.

But if Dad actually wanted him to lead things…

"Of course," Joseph agreed, his disappointment from earlier ebbing, replaced by a budding eagerness. "I think I could take care of that."

"Excellent," Father nodded, the scowl from before a distant memory. "In that case, I'd like you to fetch Samas. There are several details we'll need to discuss, and I'd like him privy as well."

Chapter 8
Sheep Among Wolves

Two hours later, Joseph and Samas walked up to the hulking, white stone gate that marked the north entrance to Kiraith Arba. Today two sentries stood guard, both leaning on their spears but watching them with wary eyes. Joseph's skin crawled from the razor gazes they honed on him and Samas, even from afar. Apparently though, by the time they drew close, both guards had concluded they weren't a threat and nodded them through with only a quick check.

Passing into the city, Joseph saw they must have enjoyed their own late night of riotous festivities, at least judging from the mess in the streets. The main road to the square was littered with refuse, but largely deserted. Only a few bleary-eyed women stood outside their houses, sweeping up detritus from the night before. Something intangible felt... off though. The few men they passed cast wary glances at Joseph and Samas, only to quickly look away, flashes of fear in their eyes. Even the meat-skewers woman was nowhere to be found.

Initially, the damage from last night's revelry seemed largely cosmetic, but reaching the central market, Joseph's eyes widened at the sight of several fire-blackened buildings across the square. Charred stumps of roof beams stuck out of cracked plaster walls that were streaked with dark soot. In the center of the square, a number of stockades had been set up, guarded by a pair of stiff-backed guards with gleaming spears. A dozen men sat there, slumped and bruised, their feet locked in the wooden restraints while the sun mercilessly beat down on their heads.

Instantly Joseph's curiosity was piqued, "What do you think—"

"Best leave their business to them, young master," Samas declared, firmly grabbing Joseph's arm as he tried to angle towards the men.

"But—"

"Trust me," Samas insisted, forcefully guiding them both across the square and toward the paved avenue that led to Mamre's lavish home. "It never pays to get involved in that sort of business. I've made that mistake myself."

They turned out of the square and Joseph cast a reluctant glance back, adding. "I was just going to look."

"I know," Samas agreed seriously. "That's how it always starts. But we have enough problems without poking our noses into Mamre's."

Samas's firm insistence was enough to spark another ember of curiosity in Joseph as they strode down the long avenue of opulent abodes. What did he mean he'd *made that mistake himself*? Now that Joseph thought about it, he'd never gotten a solid story on why exactly Samas had left Lagash and ended up out in the back end of Canaan with them. Odd really. Samas was an excellent doctor, so why leave?

Joseph was still working up the nerve to pry into the physician's private life when they reached the entrance to Mamre's small castle. Just like at the main gate, *two* razor-eyed sentinels guarded the door, as opposed to the single man who'd been there yesterday. And this morning both men were kitted out in full battle gear — pointed bronze helms, leather breastplates studded with beaten metal discs, and even arm, shin and thigh guards buckled on to cover every extremity. Their tense posture suggested they were looking for a fight, and Joseph unconsciously gulped beneath their cold glares.

Before they even reached the portico, one of the guards barked a loud, "State your business!"

Joseph already had a cheerful, in-depth explanation worked out to deliver, explaining how they needed to see Arvad about the harvest. But faced with the open hostility of the imposing men, his thoughts fled and his mind went blank. Suddenly his, *Good morning, how are you?* felt woefully inappropriate. Joseph ground to a stop, stumbling over how to articulate everything, "We uhh… we're here for…"

"We're expecting a meeting regarding the harvest," Samas thankfully stepped in. "We are from Lord Isaac's camp. Routine business."

That earned them slightly less hostile glares. The armed men eyed them another tense moment before, "Eshbaal, send a slave to find Arvad," one guard snapped curtly.

The other guard briefly vanished inside then returned to stand stiff-backed at his post, leaving Joseph and Samas to just… wait. The soldiers didn't even make an attempt at conversation, and both Joseph and Samas took the hint to slide back at least a spear's length from the edgy men.

Meanwhile, the sun soared towards its midday heights, and since the avenue ran east-west there wasn't even the consolation of shade from the surrounding houses. Joseph had, once again, donned his extravagant robe, and now that he was wearing a robe, over a tunic, over his undergarments, he quickly found himself breaking into an anxious sweat.

At last Joseph caught a familiar voice from the gate and let out a sigh of relief. "Who was it that—"

"Us, sir." Joseph raised a hand in greeting as Arvad strolled out.

At least the scribe's eyes lit up in friendly recognition, and with a *stand-down* gesture to the guards, he waved for them to follow.

Inside Mamre's manor things seemed even more tense than out in the city proper. Servant girls scurried past, their eyes fixed on the floor, and two other men they passed in the courtyard wore short-swords buckled around their waists. Unlike yesterday when they'd headed to the upper floors, now Arvad led them into a small side chamber laid out like a waiting room. A waterfall of maroon curtains draped across the entrance, and a spread of simple seating cushions were neatly arranged around a low table. Tasteful, but not extravagant. Arvad gestured them to sit, disappeared for a moment, then re-appeared with a pair of thick clay tablets in hand.

"These are the contracts for the final disposition of the harvest," he explained, taking a seat, on a cushion opposite them. "They outline your share and detail that you're expected to take possession of twelve hundred ephahs by the next new moon. Additionally, they state that you intend to rent the use of one of our granaries for the remainder of the year and outline the payment for said service."

Arvad laid both tablets face-up on the table where Joseph could see a mess of words chiseled into them. The scribe impatiently slid them across. "If you're satisfied, I have two men of standing in the city that are available to act as witnesses. I can call them, we'll both make our marks and be finished."

Joseph stared at both tablets a moment, his mind completely overwhelmed and frantically trying to process all that. He knew he was supposed to read everything thoroughly, that was what Dad had said. Yet with Arvad expectantly staring at him, the pressure to just sign felt oppressively real. He hadn't so much as read anything in the last couple months, and even making out the first few words suddenly seemed a challenge. "Umm…"

Once again Samas jumped to the rescue. "We'll need a little while to review everything."

Arvad regarded the man with curious eyes, probably wondering who exactly Samas was to even be here. But finally he nodded and stood. "Of course. I have other business, but I can be back in half an hour?"

"That should be ample time," Samas agreed.

Arvad turned, whisked though the curtains and vanished back into the hallway.

Samas waited a second for Arvad's footsteps to vanish then nodded to Joseph. "Don't let him pressure you. For a contract this important, we can take all the time we need."

Joseph let out an internal sigh of relief, feeling the anxiety vanish now that Arvad's eyes weren't boring into his skull. "Yeah," he mumbled.

He took one of the tablets, his fingers finding the slight yield of unfired clay. "So this one is…?"

"They're both identical," Samas explained. "Or at least they should be. That's something important to check. It's an old trick to offer two tablets that read slightly different, have the recipient check one that reads properly, but then give them one that says something else afterwards."

The doctor took the other tablet, leaning back to begin perusing the text. That was why Samas was here. He could read, both Summerian and Akkadian, as well as more than a little Hieratic. Yet another piece in the mysterious puzzle of how he'd ended up out here.

Joseph, on the other hand, could read Akkadian… sort of. He stared down at his word soup of a clay tablet, his eyes dancing across several phrases he only partially recognized. Father had insisted he learn, and Joseph had spent numerous hours being tutored by the doctor. Samas had taught him quite a lot, but Arvad apparently enjoyed using a number of technical terms that twisted his brain. He made it about two lines, guessing a couple words from context before mumbling an embarrassed, "Uhh, what does this mean?"

"*In recompense for,*" Samas barely had to glance over. "It's just a fancy way of saying paid for."

Joseph nodded, struggling his way through the next line. He really should have practiced this a bit more. *'In recompense for the good—' (toil, fatigue…service?) 'of his men in harvesting and…'*

Joseph paused at *zarû inninnu,* which had to mean… something to do with barley? *Scattering* wasn't right.

Sowing was also clearly wrong maybe... *winnowing* he realized. That had to be it.

So, "*In recompense for the good service of his men in harvesting and winnowing barley, Jacob, son of Isaac is hereby entitled to...*"

Joseph spent a moment double checking the amounts being offered. It seemed right. After what felt like forever, he glanced over to see Samas, patiently waiting.

The doctor nodded to the tablet, "Did everything seem acceptable?"

Joseph wasn't sure if that was a trick question and Samas was just waiting to point out some fine detail he'd missed.

"I... think it's fine."

Surprisingly the doctor nodded in agreement. "I didn't see anything either. Let's switch, then if you're happy we can stamp them and be done."

The second tablet went much faster now that Joseph had worked out most of the words. In a few moments he wrapped up and lounged back on his cushion. "I don't see anything wrong."

"Nor do I," Samas agreed, setting his tablet back on the table.

With that pronouncement, the doctor appeared perfectly content to sit and patiently await Arvad's return. Joseph though, found himself fidgeting at the prospect of doing nothing. His eyes absently skimmed back over the tablet, while his right hand rapped an anxious tune on one knee. They were close enough to the kitchen to catch savory whiffs of something like stew, and soon his stomach set to angrily growling.

Mamre must be entertaining someone, Joseph realized. While they waited, a steady trickle of young serving maids and boys streamed past, trailing enticing smells in their wake. Joseph's stomach gave another insistent gurgle, reminding him that he'd missed breakfast, and finally he asked, if only for the distraction. "So what happens once we stamp the tablet?" As he spoke his hands went to the leather cord around his neck, pulling out the engraved lead stamp dangling from one end that his father had given him that morning. Their family's mark.

"You'll stamp *both*, actually," Samas explained, with his usual precision. "After which they'll add the list of witnesses, then fire both tablets in the nearest kiln. One copy goes to us, and the other stays with them in case there's any dispute. Then it's just a matter of seeing the grain delivered back to our own stockpiles."

Joseph nodded and a moment later Arvad re-appeared, sweeping the scarlet curtain aside, this time with a heavy looking pouch at his side. "Are you two ready?"

Joseph nodded, and Arvad turned back into the hallway just as a young slave boy, not more than ten or eleven, tried to slip past with a hurried bow and an empty platter. "You, boy." the scribe's sharp tone brought the serving boy to a screeching halt. "Go fetch Malsheth and Abdholm on the second floor and bring them here."

"But sir, the cook told me—"

"You think I care what she says?" He swatted the boy on the back of the head. "This is important, go."

The boy cast a worried glance back toward the kitchen, but only a glance. With another quick bow, he scurried off in the opposite direction.

Arvad heaved a deep sigh, stepping into the room, and seating himself on a cushion near one wall.

"Everything alright?" Samas asked politely.

"As much as it can be, given the circumstances," the scribe declared dourly. He looked over to them, "There were some minor agitations last night."

To Joseph that sounded like the perfect excuse to ask about the men in the square. He almost did except that Samas spoke first. "We saw. I take it you have everything under control?"

"We..." Arvad opened his mouth, then seemed to reconsider whatever he'd been about to say. He finally settled on a painfully *un*-convincing, "It's well in hand."

The scribe glanced towards the door with an impatient scowl. "Where did that lazy wretch get off to?" He stood and strode towards the curtain, mumbling, "If he's hiding somewhere, I swear I'll have him…"

Joseph missed the rest as the scribe swept aside the curtain and stepped out into the hallway. Meanwhile, Samas shot him a *wait here* look and stood to follow.

Joseph could just hear the two discussing something outside in hushed tones. Then the sound of clomping, sandaled feet came from the hallway. A moment later Arvad, Samas and two middle-aged men tromped in, both in partial armor and with short-swords buckled around their waists.

At seeing them so heavily armed, Joseph's confusion only increased. How had the relaxed mansion from yesterday transformed into a bristling fortress overnight? With his witnesses here though, Arvad was all business and no explanation. The two other men must not have been literate, since Arvad briefly read the tablet aloud for both to hear. He made certain to get acknowledgements that they both understood, before finally removing a stone emblem from a pouch at his side and continuing in a formal tone.

"Very well, if we are all agreed, then I will stamp for Mamre, King of Kiraith Arba." The scribe quickly marked both tablets before sliding them across to Joseph.

Joseph gulped and nervously gripped his father's own stamp, but he tried to sound equally formal. "And I stamp for… uhh, my father, Jacob son of Isaac."

One of the witnesses gave an amused chuckle at his flubbed formality, and Joseph's face reddened. Arvad barely seemed to notice though. "Excellent." He quickly gathered both tablets, gesturing for the armed men to go. "I'll include everyone here in the list of witnesses and add that beneath the stamps."

"Now" he set the bulky pouch he'd been toting on the table, "in order to retrieve the grain you'll need these."

Arvad opened it to reveal a number of rectangular clay tokens neatly stacked inside. Each token was stamped with a distinctive seal, and Joseph picked one out as the scribe continued. "Each of these entitles you a single wagonload, twenty ephahs of grain from the granary. You'll turn a token in to the guards on each load. You'll *only* use standard ephah sized baskets and the guards will verify that on the way out. If the baskets aren't fully loaded or you forget one, that's your problem. There should be sixty tokens total for twelve hundred ephahs of barley."

Arvad hesitated, then added an expectant, "You should count them, so that we both agree."

"Oh… right." Joseph scrambled to tally the tokens, quickly stacking them in six groups of ten before nodding. "I also have sixty."

"Good." Arvad smiled and stood with a polite dip of his head. "Then our business here is concluded. I'll have both tablets fired tonight and you can collect your copy tomorrow. You can begin collecting your grain whenever you find convenient, but bear in mind that the tokens expire at the next new moon. If you need to make additional arrangements, you know where to find me." He gestured them both toward the hall, "I can show you both out."

Joseph cast a glance at Samas, wanting to ensure he hadn't missed something important, but the doctor simply nodded to him that it was fine and stood to leave.

A few moments later they were back out front, passing between the two alert guards at the gateway and following the paved road toward the square. At the wide square, Joseph's eyes instantly jumped back to the cluster of men still languishing in the stocks. Samas nudged at his arm, "Don't stare too long," he warned, "they might start wondering if you're involved too."

Joseph frowned, "What do you mean."

There was no one around, but even so, Samas's voice dropped to a hushed murmur. "When I spoke to Mamre's scribe earlier, he let drop that it was more than just some mischief last night. Apparently someone decided to go after Mamre himself."

Joseph's eyes widened, and he shot another sharp look toward the men, "You mean like a coup?"

"Don't stare," Samas said curtly. "And yes, attempted coup at least. Hence why it's not a bright idea to be seen watching those men too closely."

Joseph nodded, forcing himself to keep his head facing forward and away from the captives. "So those men are…"

"Probably captured arms-men," Samas said. "Arvad claimed they'd executed one of the ringleaders, but the others escaped. So keep an eye out."

Joseph nodded, gulping as he asked, "So are they going to execute those men too or…"

"Probably just sell them as slaves." Samas kept making for the edge of the square and the road that would take them back towards camp. "Still bad, but I suppose it's one of the small perks to being an underling. They're worth more alive than dead. But like I said, be careful what you poke your nose into. Did you see how everyone else was giving them a wide berth? Anybody that walks over there right now is automatically under suspicion."

Joseph cast one last glance back towards the captives. Now that he knew to look for it, he saw precisely what Samas meant. An invisible bubble surrounded the men, with people and carts detouring well out of their way to avoid being anywhere nearby.

"But it's not a crime just to…"

"Try explaining that to the guards. If they bring in more *traitors* it's a pat on the back for them and money in Mamre's purse the next time a slaver visits."

They'd finally moved beyond view of the sordid scene, back into the long rows of houses and shops with the gate looming some distance ahead. Joseph saw Samas's face turn sour as the doctor added, "Trust me, I've seen it happen. Whole families carted off because somebody stopped to gawk, and nobody who could stop it." He shot Joseph a serious look, "I'll let your father know what happened. We'll probably want to keep to ourselves for the next week or so, let Mamre cool off. And watch yourself. If you're going to be doing grain runs, try to stay out of all…" Samas shook his head in disgust, "…all that."

Chapter 9
A Time Apart

By the time they returned to camp and spoke with Father, Joseph's stomach was aggressively grumbling for food. There were several large tandoor ovens set near Dhra's tent for making bread, basically squat four foot wide, half spheres of baked clay, mud and plaster with coals set inside. A vent hole in the top allowed the cooks to reach in and literally stick dough to the inner walls, while the coals below slowly baked the bread to a crisp outer crust. The design meant they could simultaneously bake more than a dozen rounds of bread in the same oven. Fortunately, Joseph happened to return just as Dhra was reaching into the hole in the top and pulling out one fragrant date loaf after another.

Sliding behind Dhra, he stealthily snagged one, retreating to a safe distance before sinking his teeth into the warm loaf. His first taste yielded a lump of sweet, caramelized date fruit, and even if the bread almost burned his tongue, he quickly tore off a second bite. Joseph scarfed down a good quarter of the loaf before coming up for breath and continuing at a more measured pace. He walked as he ate, wandering over to their still empty granaries and trying to puzzle out how he was supposed to move twelve-hundred ephahs… even with help. Dad seemed to think it was reasonable, but the immensity of the task was daunting. He was still dwelling on the problem when a familiar voice interrupted his vigil.

"So you stole bread, and you weren't even going to share?"

He spun to see Myrrha, ten steps behinds him, hands on her hips as she regarded him with a frown.

He shrugged, "What, you couldn't go steal your own?"

As he spoke though, Joseph tore off a chunk from the half he hadn't been eating on, and offered her some. Myrrha's frown faded to the faintest trace of a smile, and strolling over, she accepted his offering. As she did, Joseph saw a strip of flaxen cloth cinched around her palm.

"Everything okay?" he nodded to her bandage.

"Oh," she glanced at it with a sudden grimace, like she was only now remembering. "Just an angry mama goose. I was out hunting for eggs this morning."

Joseph chuckled, "Sounds like somebody needs to be eaten."

"You'll have to fight her first." Myrrha nibbled at the date bread.

She went quiet a moment as she ate, and Joseph glanced behind them both suddenly anxious. "Your mom isn't going to see us—"

"She's helping Talia with stomach issues." Myrrha said in a tone like she'd already appraised that concern before even saying hello. "The way Talia talks, Mom will be there at least another hour. I begged off to go see if I could find a few clutches of goose eggs which… uhhh…" she glanced at her bandaged hand, "obviously the geese weren't very obliging."

She paused a moment, her voice turning serious, "Is Benji still okay?"

"I've barely seen him all morning, which I suppose means yes." Joseph took a deep breath, trying to arrange the jumble of ideas in his head into a sentence before, "I… Myrrha, about last night. I know we were going to talk to my dad, but… I don't think right now is the best time to tell him about… us."

He glanced over to see her suddenly standing stiff as a statue, her expression quivering with an uncertainty to break his heart.

"It's just this morning," Joseph hurriedly tried to explain, his mind flickering back to Father's obvious displeasure with his dream, "I made a mistake talking to Father this morning, and I don't want to ruin things because… well…just because he's in a bad mood."

Next to him Myrrha was deathly quiet, until finally she swallowed, whispering an unconvinced, "I understand."

She stared at her hands in front of her, not looking up and Joseph added, more forcefully, "I will tell him."

She looked up in surprise and he reiterated, "I'll tell him. I swear. This morning Dad gave me a job. An important one."

"What do you mean?"

Joseph nodded to the pair of large grain silos before them, "He wants me to fill up both of these, with grain from Kiriath Arba."

Her eyes widened, flashing from him, to the vast silos, then back, "*Both* of them?"

"Yeah," Joseph gulped at the enormity of the task, but explaining it all to her now, he felt a small ember of confidence.

"I'm going to do it," Joseph said. He wasn't quite sure if he was trying to convince her or himself, but regardless, he felt that ember of confidence suddenly flicker into a flame. "I'm going to do it, and when I'm done, I'm going to speak to him about us, and he'll listen, and I'll tell him that—" his eyes darted to Myrrha, "that I love you."

Joseph felt like there was something almost magic about speaking the words. Myrrha had been tensed taut as a bow, but now she visibly relaxed, her shoulders loosening. If they'd been alone, he would have tried to kiss her, but standing out where everyone could see, the best he could do was find her hand with his and clutch it tightly. A warmth like liquid sunlight pulsed in his veins where their palms touched, and her fingers squeezed around his with a nod and a whispered, "Okay."

For a moment they stood there.

If he could have, he would have drawn those seconds out into eternity, just the two of them — no complications, no barriers, no worries — just them and a plan, and a future. Everything was right.

Finally though, Myrrha's hand loosened on his with a reluctant, "I should go." As much as he didn't want to, Joseph let her hand slip away, the lingering warmth of her grip slowly dimming.

When he looked over, she smiled, a buoyant, happy grin. "I'll see you around…" she whispered the last word like it was the most special sort of secret between them, "Joseph."

He didn't stare after her as she left. From a distance, he doubted anyone would have noticed their clasped hands, but they might pay some attention if he awkwardly gawked after her. Instead, he forced his eyes back to the two granaries and the enormous task before him.

He could do this.

He could do this for her…

Except he didn't precisely know how.

He might need to ask Dad about that part.

***

Turned out his father did have a plan, specifically in the form of a grain cart and a pair of donkey's to pull it. Father also assigned him two of the camp laborers. Those two being Irran, a heavyset herdsman a couple years older than Joseph, and Myron, a tall middle-aged man with tan skin and a scrawny frame. Both were Uncle Isaac's people. And now that the cows had finished calving and were grazing near the camp, the two were enjoying a few lazy weeks off.

They were also perfectly happy with that arrangement. At least, judging from their frowns when Jacob summoned them and explained what they'd be working on for the foreseeable future. Then there had come deeper frowns at *who* they'd be working for.

Joseph tried to be optimistic, despite the scowls. Maybe his helpers weren't the most enthusiastic, but this could still work. He just needed to stay positive.

Then they'd headed out to hook up the donkey to their cart… and the grousing had started… and kept going… and going… *and going*, as they slowly trundled their way into town.

"This'll take forever," Irran declared to no one in particular as the wagon creaked along. Joseph rode up in the driver's seat beside him, jolting at every bump in the terrain and already wondering when this ordeal would end.

Myron was bouncing along in the back and spoke up, "Maybe we can swap days, Irran? I'll drive the cart and you stay back at camp one day, then I stay at camp and you can drive the next?"

"*Or*," Irran spoke slyly, "maybe one of us can stay in the city instead." He paused before adding, "There are some mighty fine ladies in the city."

Joseph glanced over to see the rough herdsman nodding to himself, hair a disheveled mess, wafting an odor of cow dung, clearly a few weeks from his last bath, and occasionally scratching his beard from the lice. Yeah, he was certain to be a hit with all the 'fine women' of Kiriath Arba.

"I say, that's the best idea you've had in weeks," Myron agreed heartily. "I could go for a day in the city — walk the streets, take in the smells, get me some of that… what do they call it? The special thing that real high and mighty folks have that makes them use those fancy words?"

Joseph frowned. As in, *an education*?

Irran chimed in, "You mean *culture*?"

"Exactly, *culture*," Myron said, almost savoring the word. "I can finally get some for myself. And some wine," he added as an afterthought. "The city always has the best wine."

Joseph sighed. Flicking the reins, Irran turned to him. "What do you say, Master Joseph? One of us will help you one day, and the other one the next. This'll be a rare opportunity."

Joseph blinked. Did they think he was stupid? If he let these two wander off in town, he was fairly certain he wouldn't see them until they stumbled back into camp dead broke and walking off a colossal hangover.

He didn't want to explicitly spell that out that though. Then he'd just earn a flurry of nasty scowls and a reputation as a killjoy. Instead he settled on a vague, noncommittal, "I don't know. We'll have to see."

Maybe they'd just forget about it.

As the cart approached the gates, both guardsmen moved to block their path, spears in hand, and Irran pulled the donkeys to a slow halt. "There now, no need for those. We're just trying to enter the city."

"On what business?" one guard barked, while gesturing his fellow to circle around the back.

Before his two helpers could say anything else, Joseph spoke up, "I'm Joseph, son of Jacob, and we're here to collect grain from the granaries." He lifted the purse of tokens Arvad had given him. "We have the king's permission."

From the rear of the cart, the second guard shouted, "Nothing here!"

The first guard regarded them a moment, and Joseph hoped the man recognized him from earlier that morning. Regardless, the guard finally gestured them through with a curt, "Be quick about your business."

Joseph nodded, and a moment later they passed beneath the squared stone gate, the cart raising them so high that he could have stood and reached up to brushed the upper masonry.

Once they'd were inside the city, Myron and Irran grew a bit more subdued, although he caught the occasional obnoxious whistle from Myron at passing city women. Joseph tensed, hoping the herdsman didn't make a pass at the wrong one.

Finally, they reached the granaries, a walled complex with another imposing gate and another pair of guards. This time though, the guards expressions turned far friendlier when they saw the tokens in Joseph's pouch. "Third building on the right, is the one you want, young master," one of the guards explained, laying aside the stamped clay token in a collection box. "Have your men pull twenty ephahs from there. We're obliged to count them on your way out. You understand?"

"Of course."

The man smiled, stepping aside and gesturing their cart on through. "Then welcome to the King's granary."

Irran gave another flick of the reins and with a lurch the two donkeys tugged them forwards.

When Joseph had been here tallying the grain from the harvest, the place had exuded a wild chaos, men traipsing everywhere, shouting and toting barley baskets. Carts had trundled through, with bare chested workmen swarming to unload the grain, before waving the carts ahead to turn around and squeeze their way out through the pandemonium.

Now, an aura of eerie stillness clung to the granary. A few echoed sounds emanated from the streets outside, but otherwise they faced an empty dirt avenue with rows of double-storied adobe buildings rising to either side.

Pulling forward, Irran reined the donkeys to a halt at their destination, and Joseph hopped down. A tall partition wall with a door separated the granary from the road. Inside lay a small courtyard with stairs leading to the top and several blocked off spouts in the wall through which the barley could be drained in bulk.

He glanced back to see his two helpers still stuck to their seats in the cart, watching him. "Well, come on," he insisted gesturing them with an exasperated sigh. "The faster we load up, the faster we're done."

Neither seemed to share that sentiment, but with a pair of grumbles, the two men hopped down and grabbed some baskets. Positioning the baskets on the ground, Myron pulling down the spout to start the flow of barley.

Joseph watched, his foot tapping the packed earth. He mentally counted the seconds to load each basket and fought off a depressing realization… this was going to take ages.

Chapter 10
Shattered Plans

Judging by the sun, it took from midday to midafternoon to make a circuit from camp, to Kiraith Arba, then back. As they began their second run, Joseph was already reviewing the math in his head and growing steadily more despondent with each sharp jostle of the cart.

Three hours… roughly, was what it took to make a single trip, and they were already in late spring, which meant the twelve daylight hours were about as long as they would ever be. Even if they left close to sunrise, they could maybe do four runs… maybe.

Joseph's math made the depressing reality of their situation simple enough to work out. Sixty runs to move the grain, at four runs a day, was fifteen total. Working six days a week, it would take them a grand total of two and half weeks to get the grain moved.

Two and a half weeks.

Two and a half weeks of sharp jolts every time Irran managed to find yet *another* bump to slam the cart into. Two and a half weeks of gnawing tedium, listening to Irran and Myron babble on about women and drinks and food… and even more about drinks. And worst of all, two and a half weeks of barely seeing little Benji and probably *never* seeing Myrrha… at least not alone.

Halfway back up the hill to Kiraith Arba, his foot anxiously hammered out a drumbeat on the wagon floor. He could have *walked* faster than this.

"Shouldn't we speed up?" Joseph finally suggested, trying to be polite about it, but hardly in the mood to pointlessly waste even more time.

"Don't want to hurt the cart, Master Joseph," Irran calmly responded as though that non answer settled things.

And so they didn't. They hauled themselves back to the granaries with a maddening slowness, then lethargically began filling baskets. Irran wouldn't even bother to hop down from the driver's seat, so Myron worked alone, leisurely filling baskets one… by… one.

Finally the cart was loaded, at which juncture, Joseph received the pleasure of an *even slower* ride through the city, out the gates, down the hill, across the valley, and into camp. There, the two proceeded to discover the *least* efficient way to dump twenty baskets of grain into their stockpile.

By the time they'd finished, the sun had already sunk below the horizon, leaving a fading orange blush of twilight smeared across the sky. Irran and Myron hurried to unhitch and feed the donkeys, but Joseph lingered, his eyes staring at the pitifully small pile of grain they'd amassed thus far.

He'd expected forty ephahs to look bigger. But instead it seemed tauntingly small, little more than an anthill compared to the granary. And they still had an entire second granary just like this one to fill. With a frustrated sigh, he latched the door closed and trudged away.

Between washing off all the dirt of the long day and actually getting food, Joseph didn't return to his tent until well past dark. Benji was already asleep and a single candle flickered near the center-post of the tent, welcoming him back. Myrrha, trying to be considerate after coaxing Benji to bed. That, at least, brought a brief smile.

He'd done vanishingly little physical labor, but apparently all his supervising had strained him more than he'd realized. Joseph found himself fighting back exhausted yawns. With little else to do, he collapsed onto his bed, puffed out the candle, and let the pitch blackness of the tent take him.

The following morning blurred into a repeat of the prior day. They endured another pointless search at the gates, followed by a trip through a city brimming with hushed whispers. Then his helpers settled into the same agonizingly sluggish routine. Irran and Myron worked slower than the seasons, and by the second morning, Joseph found a single constant refrain, "Hurry up."

Every trip drug out into eternity, and the two seemed utterly untroubled by it. That day they managed to cart four loads, but on the next they barely completed their first two trips in time to catch the tail end of lunch. That was the one time he saw the duo actually hustle. They returned, realized everyone else was already eating, and with a shocking eagerness, dumped all their grain in the silos before bolting straight towards the savory scent of stew.

Joseph got his own meal, and made it a point to find Benji, who appeared to have, semi-permanently attached himself to Samas, Abby and Nathanial. Everyone had already finished their food, but he at least got to watch Benji and Nathanial dart around like energetic starlings as he scarfed down his lunch… then headed back to the wagon. Where he waited… and waited… *aaaaaaand* waited.

Where in Sheol had Myron and Irran gone?

Joseph thought he knew most of the best hiding places around camp, but he still had to check three different spots before finally stumbling over his helpers. They'd joined a rowdy crowd of men, huddled behind a row of tents and tossing dice amid eager spectators.

"One more white!" several chanted as a man shook the dice in a cup, "One more white! One more—"

"Hey?" Joseph interrupted with a scowl, "What is *this*?"

Instantly the crowd froze in a stunned tableau.

Irran was near the center of the group, but if he was shocked, he astutely covered it. "Master Joseph," he smiled and offered, "would you like to play a round?"

Joseph's eyes narrowed, unamused. "We still have work to do." His eyes flashed to Myron, "Both of you."

Their expressions fell, but Joseph couldn't have cared less. "Come on," he snapped, furious. He ignored a few mocking chuckles as his two helpers reluctantly slid out of the crowd to follow him.

Stepping away, Joseph glared the two down with a frustrated hiss, "Why didn't you come back to the cart."

"Well, we did, Master Joseph," Irran said innocently. "You weren't there, so we assumed you'd find us when you were ready."

Myron added an apologetic, "Didn't mean no harm by the dice, sir."

Right, Joseph fumed, of course they'd checked. They'd probably glanced over two minutes after he'd gotten his lunch, decided they must be finished for the day and *conveniently* made themselves scarce.

He didn't say much more, but despite the sweltering sun above, it was a chilly crew that headed into town that afternoon. It showed in their pace as well, Myron and Irran seemed to work as slowly as humanly possible to deposit the third load in the camp granaries.

By then it was well past midafternoon. One more trip would have them returning substantially past dark. It burned at Joseph to just let the two sluggards stroll off, but he didn't see an alternative. Tomorrow was a sacrifice day, so they wouldn't be working at all. Finally, seething with frustration, he threw up his hands, "Alright," he scowled, "we're done for the day. Unhitch the donkeys. We'll start again on Rishon." He added a hasty, "Right at dawn. I want both of you here."

From their barely concealed grins, he might as well have announced another feast tonight. Suddenly all of the sullenness was gone amid a pair of polite, *Thank you, sirs*.

Joseph waited there a moment, staring at the slowly growing grain pile, dejected. Nine loads in three days. Abysmal performance. They should have been able to move that in two. When he'd started, Joseph had blissfully assumed they'd get five loads a day at minimum… but apparently not.

He sighed, feeling the bitter sting of disappointment. What was he going to tell Father? That he couldn't even manage a simple task, but that he was definitely ready to start a family of his own? And, oh, by the way, he wasn't about to marry some cousin he'd never met, he was going to marry Myrrha, no matter what anyone said and…

Joseph pursed his lips and rubbed his forehead. That didn't even sound convincing to *his* ears. Certainly he wouldn't help his case if this task collapsed into a disaster. If he took a week longer than he should have. If he proved he *wasn't* capable.

That night Joseph slept in short fits, his dreams punctuated by bottomless baskets that never seemed to fill despite the grain that kept pouring in. He saw strangely empty granaries, and felt a gathering sense of panic as he searched everywhere for Irran and Myron… but they were gone. Piles of baskets crowded in, towering over him before…

Joseph jerked awake, the nightmares fading like mist in the morning. When he groggily rolled out of bed, he blinked, rubbed his eyes, stifled a yawn, and spent several moments wishing he could fall back asleep. Unfortunately, that wasn't an option. He had responsibilities today also.

With the rest of his brothers gone, it fell to Joseph to help Father with the sacrifices, a gruesome affair. They spent all morning slaughtering two rams, draining out the blood and disemboweling the carcasses. That mainly involved slicing out all the organs along with a number of fatty cuts, and tastefully arranging the display on their family altar.

By the time they'd finished he was, quite literally, up to his elbows in blood. He spent the next quarter hour turning a washbasin scarlet as he scrubbed his arms clean. At last though, with the gore washed away, he donned his decorated tunic, and strode out of the tent to join Father, Grandfather and the rest of the camp as they prepared to light the pyre.

Ever since they'd left Shechem, Father had become very particular about offering regular sacrifices. Not that Joseph faulted him. Something about running into the literal manifestation of God had left everyone feeling more religious.

Usually, Joseph noticed a twinge of tension in his chest at their sacrifice. Anticipation, mingled with the memory of what he'd witnessed at Bethel. Would today be the day when it happened again? The day when the sky tore asunder, an invincible light descended, the ground trembled, and they met God once more?

The prospect typically knotted his stomach in nervous fear. And yet, as Joseph's eyes roved across the bundled sheaves of tinder, a part of him desperately wanted exactly that. It seemed strange, but the last time The Lord had appeared, so many of his worries had just resolved themselves. His life had felt like a tangled knot of yarn, but in that instant, a single string had been pulled and suddenly the knot unraveled into a dozen straight threads, at least for a while.

He wondered too if there was something that he could do to… bring God back… if that was even the right way to say it. Dad had insisted that it didn't matter how they arranged the entrails, it was more about the *doing* than the *how* exactly. But maybe Father was wrong, and it did matter. Every one of his brothers arranged the various cuts differently, and of them all, God had sent *him* the dreams, those glimpses of a better future.

So was it because of this?

For a moment Joseph dwelt on the question, only dimly aware of Father speaking the invocation. He only looked up as the pyre flared to life, the sudden heat pricking his skin. Wisps of orange flames reached skyward, while the offering sizzled and crackled within. At his side, Benji's little hand gripped Joseph's tightly, the boy staring at the flames in wide-eyed excitement. Meanwhile Father solemnly stood a pace away, supporting Grandfather, both quietly observing as the sacrifice was consumed by the blossoming inferno.

For a while Joseph remained unmoving, doing his best not to fidget, his eyes on the sacrifice, while his mind went everywhere else and—

"How have things been?"

"Huh?" Joseph started at Dad's voice. For a moment, he assumed Father was asking how work had been going with Irran and Myron, at least until Father clarified.

"How have things been in the city? Everyone's been on edge since the assassination attempt."

Assassins? That's what they were calling them now?

Joseph gave a shrug, "They still check the wagon every time we go through the gates."

Father nodded, and Joseph hesitated before asking, "Do they know how many of them are still out there?"

"I've heard rumors, maybe a dozen," Jacob said. "But the herdsmen know to keep a lookout. Besides, I doubt they'll attack us. After all, they want Mamre."

Joseph nodded, and Father added, "Be careful though. He may try to hide it, but Mamre was worried enough to preemptively cancel the market day next week."

That was a sobering thought, and Joseph scuffed one sandal in the dirt until Father continued in a lighter tone, "What about the grain? I see you making trips all day, is that going well?"

"We've… umm…" Joseph tried to riddle out how to put a positive spin on, *NO*. He might have complained about his two worthless helpers, except that would probably just convince Father that he had *absolutely* no clue what he was doing. Eventually Joseph settled on, "It's going slower than I thought it would."

"Ahhh," Dad gave a knowing nod. "And Irran and Myron?"

"They're uhh…" Joseph struggled to find anything flattering to say at all.

"Difficult?" Father asked, in a knowing voice.

Joseph blinked in surprise, but Father kept his eagle stare straight ahead. "Some people require a firm hand to guide them," Father continued cryptically. "That can be a challenge."

Joseph nearly held his breath, waiting to hear what came next, but Father said nothing. Instead, Dad's gaze lingered on the hissing fire as the sacrificial meat within rapidly crisped to a char. Joseph turned to watch too, his mind still anywhere but on the sacrifice.

So if Father knew Irran and Myron were difficult to work with… was this some sort of test? Had Father engineered all this just to see if he was up to the challenge? The concerning possibility gripped him like a bramble on his tunic. If this was a test… was he already failing?

Suddenly Joseph felt a gathering urgency to make progress. The concerns about coups against Mamre dimmed to the background, behind a more overriding fear— he had to succeed. But how could he with two useless helpers who wouldn't even try?

He was still wondering when Father turned to leave, clasping him on the shoulder with an encouraging, "I'm sure you'll figure it out."

The parting phrase left Joseph almost sick with worry. Would he?

The whole rest of the day he puzzled over Father's cryptic words, hoping to discover a secret ember of advice buried within. Even as they feasted on the remaining cuts of the slaughtered rams, and he spent the afternoon playing with Benji, the words still echoed in his mind. A firm hand?

He rolled the words over and over. A firm hand. He wasn't certain what exactly that meant, but by evening he was beginning to gather some ideas. Maybe Father was telling him to be strong, take charge. He'd seen Father do that before, bend others to his own will, guide them to the place that he wanted. Maybe that *was* the answer. Maybe that was what Father wanted, he just needed to be strong.

As he lay on his mat that evening, Joseph latched onto the idea. Be strong. That might just do it. As he drifted to sleep the words roiled one final time in his consciousness.

A firm hand.

The next morning Joseph woke with the dawn, feeling marvelously refreshed. It was Yom Rishon, the first day of the new week, and he was finally going to get something done. Rolling out of bed, he headed straight outside to find the morning air crisp and chilly, with a stiff breeze that nipped at his arms. In just three steps, his sandaled feet were drenched with the cold dew that lay thick on the grass. The first tendrils of light were only just crawling above the horizon, and with time to spare, Joseph made straight for the cook tent.

Dhra and the cooks were usually up well before dawn to start the breakfast preparations, and this morning Joseph found the usual fare laid out: yesterday's bread, cheese, goat's milk and any meat leftover from the sacrifice. However, Dhra often concocted a special treat for anyone who rose early enough to get it. Today it was *tiganites* or *'teganites'* as he'd heard Althea insistently called them. They were thin little pan cakes fried to a light brown hue. Dhra's recipe was from the far east, although Joseph had tasted so many variations, he had no clue where they'd originally come from. Today's were excellent though, light and fluffy, bursting with honey sweetness, and with a jug of night-chilled cream to drizzle on top. He took one, tasted it, then immediately grabbed two more.

Finding a spot at the edge of the wide circle that formed the center of camp, he spent a moment savoring his breakfast. He watched as a growing stream of people began emerging from their tents, piling up as they crowded around for the breakfast special. Before long, he caught sight of both Myron and Irran. He made certain to keep his eyes on the two as they hurried to the breakfast line, then promptly disappeared back into the ranks of tents that ringed camp

Joseph marked the spot, grinning to himself as he calmly finished off his food. The cakes were excellent, and when he swallowed his last bite, he waited a moment, appreciating the sweet aftertaste, and slow counting to a hundred.

The count would give the two time to finish their own food so they couldn't tell him they'd come around in a few moments, then disappear again.

At last he stood, heading toward the tents where his two helpers had vanished. He found them sitting on a pair of stones and polishing off hunks of cheese. "We need to get an early start this morning," he declared, without announcing himself.

Myron nearly jumped with a jolt of surprise, his neck twisting to stare. Joseph beamed inwardly but hid it beneath a serious expression. Hadn't expected him, had they?

"We need to get the cart hooked up," Joseph said.

Irran recovered from the shock with a deferential nod, "Of course. We'll finish eating and be there soon."

Joseph suppressed a fiendish grin; he wasn't about to fall for that. Walk off so they could find a new hiding place?

Instead he nodded towards the granaries across camp where they'd left the cart, "Let's just head over there now. We've got a lot to do this morning."

Joseph crouched it as a suggestion, but from the looks the two men shot each other, they clearly understood it wasn't. Reluctantly, Irran sighed and nodded, standing to go with a frown. "Of course, young master."

Joseph made sure they were *both* following then led off toward the granaries. Once he turned away, his grin finally spilled out. Step one, get an early start.

Done.

Easy.

Like Dad had said, it just took a firm hand.

Chapter 11
Chasing the Sun

Sitting in the front of the cart, Joseph flicked his long whip at the donkey's hindquarters. The creature lurched ahead for a few steps and the cart shivered as it jolted over a tuft of grass. But then the animal settled back into its usual plodding gait.

He glanced at the sun for the dozenth time. They'd just finished their first run and it was only midmorning. They were on schedule, but only barely.

"Irran, speed the donkeys up."

"Sir, if we go too fast we might damage the cart," Irran cautioned.

"It's not even loaded," Joseph dismissed. "It'll be fine."

Irran sighed with an obvious frustration that Joseph flatly ignored. The cart would be fine.

Irran seemed to dwell on that a moment but finally said, "Of course, young master." He flicked the reins several times with a sharp call, and gradually the cart picked up speed as they headed up the hill toward the city.

Lunch consisted of their usual hide and seek games, but even if the two grown men were acting like a pair of petulant children, they still made progress. It took some cajoling, but the wagon completed two more trips in the afternoon. Each time they entered town, the guards made an elaborate show of inspecting the empty cart that had Joseph rolling his eyes. *Obviously* he was playing the incredibly long game to deliver hundreds of ephah's of grain, *then* smuggle a bunch of rebels into the city. Still, Joseph marked off four loads for the day, and they rolled back into camp just as the sun touched the western horizon.

After a tense day being continuously jolted in the wagon, and haranguing Irran and Myron to move at a reasonable pace, Joseph felt beat-up, both physically and mentally. It seemed odd, yet the exhaustion still seeped into his bones.

Standing at the granary entrance, he stared a moment, his eyes roving across their suddenly *not* so diminutive barley pile. He tried to find that ember of encouraging optimism he'd felt this morning. They *were* making progress. He counted in his head, thirteen loads down, so forty-seven left, which meant… he frowned… twelve more days of… this.

The spark of optimism abruptly faded, and Joseph sighed, sliding the granary door shut as he turned to find his tent.

Joseph had hoped that once they fell into a regular rhythm, the job would cruise along more smoothly… except they didn't. Or perhaps they weren't all working to the same tune. Regardless, the next several days Joseph found himself playing a bizarre game of cat and mouse. Myron and Irran kept discovering ever more ingenious hiding places where Joseph would laboriously track them down. They'd then grouse, and he'd have the absolute joy of being cooped up with the chilly duo for the next few hours as they clattered back and forth to the city.

Just getting them to move was an endless, exhausting battle. And sitting up in the cart seat, Joseph had to stuff back growls of frustration every time he suffered through the saga that was the two trying to load the baskets from the granary.

They had the most absurd tempo to their work. Irran would pull down the grain spigot to fill the basket, trickling in grain from the silo. A simple task, except for his needless precision, inching the spigot open— then closed— then open— and closed *again* as he tried to perfectly top off each basket. That meant loading each ephah of barley took three times as long as it ought to.

Then, once Irran *finally* declared the basket ready, Myron would lift it with a grunt, stagger it over to the cart, hoist it into the back, and adjust it around a bit. Then he'd stare at the basket a second, and emit the exact same exaggerated sigh — every— single— time.

The process was doubly frustrating as Irran couldn't begin loading the next basket until Myron brought it back from the cart. So Irran would stand there, watching Myron work like it was some sort of show. Joseph kept waiting for one of them to realize that, they could unload all of the baskets before they started, or maybe Irran could fetch a fresh one instead of loitering around. Anything would be an improvement really. He tendered the suggestion several times, but no one seemed to hear, or perhaps they just didn't care.

Finally, Joseph hopped down from the cart, and started shuffling empty baskets over to Irran himself. That earned him a pair of odd looks, but he didn't care. If he had to watch this mess unfold *one more time…*

For a change, that actually did speed things up. The next day they finished their fourth run well before dusk, and walking back to his tent that evening, with a bit of daylight left for a change, Joseph suddenly had an idea.

He spent the whole evening with the possibility simmering in his mind. The next day was Yom Shishi, the sixth day of the week, and for the first time since they'd begun, they hit a major milestone. Despite their pace, the pile of barley in Granary One had been mounting up incrementally higher and higher with each load. Finally, late that morning, they dumped in the final cart load, and Joseph opened his satchel to see only 30 tokens left. They were halfway done.

Myron and Irran lugged the final two baskets up the stairs of the adobe building to pour them in through a hole in the roof and Joseph followed. The two unceremoniously dumped their baskets and Joseph peered in through the top at the hill of grain below, "I think this one's full."

Myron blinked, as though that were some great surprise. "It is?"

"Indeed," Joseph nodded. Typically he had *nothing* encouraging to say to the two, but now he managed to find a *Good job* and meant it.

The news that they were half finished, seemed to lift everyone's spirits, and Myron and Irran even traded their sullen grumbles for a few tentative smiles. They made two more runs after lunch, the last finishing maybe an hour past midafternoon. And as they dumped off the barley from the final run, this time in Granary Two, Joseph kicked his plan into motion.

"Let's do one more," he said, hopping back into the cart.

"Sir?" Irran frowned, glancing at the position of the sun.

"Another run," Joseph insisted waving them on up, "it won't take long."

Both men hesitated, obviously unhappy. A part of Joseph worried they might just walk off. Technically he was in charge, but if they did leave he couldn't *physically* force them back. Well… not without help. Joseph gulped back the unsavory prospect of having to plead with Dad to haul them back and get them going again. That wouldn't look particularly stellar for his *I'm a responsible adult, who should make my own decisions about who I wed* case.

He kept up his bluff though. They had time, they could do five loads.

Finally, Irran gave a discouraged sigh, "Of course, young master."

"But sir, we already got four loads?" Myron insisted, uncomprehending. "The barley isn't about to up and walk off?"

"We need to get this job finished," Joseph insisted, quickly tiring of the argument. "One more load won't kill anybody."

He said that, but halfway to the city he began to wonder if he'd made a mistake. Irran was back to his plodding pace, the donkeys panted from the long day, and as they rolled into the city, he looked west to see the sun dipping dangerously low.

The guards eyed them with stern glares at entering the city so late. With the light beginning to fade, a part of Joseph almost wished they'd turn him away, at least then he could go back without looking like he'd given up. But the guards eventually waved them through, and by the time they reached the granary and finished loading, Joseph's foot anxiously rapped on the floorboard, as he eyed the lengthening shadows. For once, Irran forced the tired animals to move at a sharp pace, flicking the reins with several loud cries. They all knew the gates shut at sunset, and no one wanted to spend the night stuck inside.

Pushing their way through the emptying streets, they squeezed out just as the guards were moving to bar the doors, earning a chorus of scowls from the armed men. As the gloom of night spread across the grass, they trundled down the long slope, straining to see in the darkness. The cart bounced at each hillock, the fragile suspension shuddering as the wheels jolted against rocks and struck on tufts of grass that—

CRACK!

The whole cart lurched wildly beneath them, and Joseph's stomach leapt to his mouth at the sickening crunch. His seat, along with the entire front of the cart sagged lower, both donkeys brayed loudly, and in a flash, the loaded cart sagged to an ignominious halt in the dirt.

Irran swore, and Joseph climbed down, almost afraid to look. Peering through the shadows beneath the cart, his heart sank as he saw the entire front axle had snapped clean in half. Hopping down on the opposite side, Irran peered underneath and added a wholly unnecessary, "Looks bad, young master."

Oh really? Joseph slammed his sandal at the broken cart wheel, now dug into the dirt at a wild angle, mumbling a curse of his own. One more load. That was all he wanted and now...

He stared at the damage, bile in his throat as he mentally willed himself to summon up a solution. Anything, so long as it would quickly patch things up. None came. Finally, Irran suggested, "Sir, we should get the donkeys back to camp, before it's too dark.

Joseph barely heard, "Yeah," he agreed numbly, then swore and kicked the broken wheel again. Why? Why? WHY?

***

The next morning, when Father lit the pyre of their sacrifice and spoke the invocation, Joseph stared into the orange flames, wishing more than ever that God might show up today. He wasn't quite sure what he wanted God to do. Maybe fix things... somehow. He glanced at the sky, still clear, with the midday sun beating down... and no sign of the Lord.

As the sacrificial meat hissed and sizzled in the inferno, he whispered a desperate plea, not sure what to say, but acutely aware that things weren't going well. "God..." he said softly, "I don't know what to do."

For a moment he waited, hoping. But as the flames licked hungrily at the meat, and nothing happened, Joseph couldn't escape a sinking disappointment in his chest.

After their pyre had burnt itself low and the camp had eaten, Joseph got down to the more practical issues of the day. Step one was to seek out the camp carpenter, a tall, burly Hittite named Kuwadar. The two hiked down into the valley to examine the wreck. The broken cart still sat out amid the fields of barley stubble, a beacon to his failure. Fortunately, Dad either hadn't noticed, or hadn't asked... probably hadn't asked.

As he walked, the sharp golden stubble stabbed at his ankles if he stepped wrong, and the dry heat pounded his head. When they did arrive, Kuwadar took one look at the shattered axle and shook his head with a frown.

107

That bad?

It took the remainder of the day just to haul the cart back to camp. With his helpers nowhere to be found, Joseph had to hook up a second cart all on his own, bring it out, manually shift over the baskets of grain, then haul them back. By the time he finished dumping the last painfully heavy sack, he was panting from exertion, his arms ached and the sweat kept trickling into his eyes.

Meanwhile, Kuwadar rigged up some ropes to allow another donkey to half tow, half drag the broken wagon back to camp. There the carpenter delivered his stinging prognosis— the cart would need a whole new axle, which meant a trip into town and at least a week of work. Until then, they'd just have to use another cart.

That was a gut punch of an assessment. As they wrapped up that evening, Joseph walked away with a sickening queasiness in his throat. Dad had given him this test and here he was, failing…

He ducked into his tent and froze, as the flickering candle illuminated, "Myrrha?"

"Joseph?" She glanced up from where she knelt next to Benji's bed, tucking in the snoozing little boy. In the fading light, a flickering candle flame illuminated her smiling face in a puddle of orange. But her smile faded to concern when she saw his expression, "Are you okay?"

Joseph didn't answer. Instead he wordlessly slumped down on a cushion, his feet aching from the endless day. In a moment she was next to him, the bright candle set on the mat in front of them. "Things aren't good?" she asked, pensive.

Joseph shook his head, but avoided looking at her. Instead his gaze lingered on the candle as though the answers might be lurking in the amber flame.

"Is it about the wagon?"

"You saw?"

"I think everyone saw." She spoke with a tentative humor in her tone, but Joseph couldn't find it in himself to chuckle.

He felt Myrrha's hand on his arm. "It'll be alright," she insisted, encouraging.

"I don't know," Joseph mumbled. "It feels like things just keep getting worse."

Myrrha went oddly quiet for a second, before, "I mean, I heard the granary's full. That's something, isn't it?"

Joseph sighed. If she was trying to cheer him up, she wasn't doing a great job.

Normally he might not have said anything, but… it was Myrrha so…

"It's more complicated than that," he kept his voice a quiet whisper as he explained, so as not to wake Benji. Yeah, they'd made some progress, but at the price of constantly haranguing his two helpers, and frankly, moving the grain ought to have gone much faster. At this point he was flat-out exhausted. Exhausted from today, exhausted from worrying, exhausted from constantly fighting Myron and Irran. Just the prospect of waking up tomorrow and having to do it all again filled him with an ominous dread.

"Well, then don't," she finally said, oddly insistent.

"Huh?" Joseph frowned and glanced at the brown-haired girl. She'd leaned up beside him as he spoke, one hand sympathetically rubbing his shoulder, and for a moment he swallowed at just how beautiful her face was in the candlelight.

"Joseph," Myrrha said, "you're tired and frustrated and… I know today was probably awful too. So what if you just took a day and stopped pushing so hard. What's the worst that happens, you get two loads instead of four? At least you give everyone a day to cool off."

"Myrrha," Joseph wasn't sure how to make her understand. It felt an awful lot like giving up. "I can't just throw up my arms and stop trying. That's not what Dad…" his voice trailed off amid a tired yawn. He tried to continue the sentence, but an exhausted haze had been slowly thickening in his mind now that he'd finally stopped moving. All he could manage was a weary, "I have to do this."

He wasn't sure if Myrrha understood. For an instant she leaned in as though she wanted to argue the point, but finally she let out a heavy sigh. "I know."

She gave his arm a sympathetic squeeze, then stood to go, a cloud of disappointment on her face. "I… I'm sorry it's been like this," she said quietly. "I hope it gets better."

Yeah, Joseph thought as she turned and ducked through the tent flap to go. Him too.

She'd left the candle at his feet, and after another anxious moment trapped in his own thoughts, he took it. Heading straight over to his bed-mat, he lay down, blew it out with a sharp puff… and that was the last he remembered.

Joseph fell into the deep, still sleep of exhaustion. Yet, the next morning when he woke, he barely felt rested at all. The fatigue lingered, and his arms were sore from yesterday's exertion. Failing to summon up the motivation to *get to it* as Father might have said, he allowed himself a long breakfast. He even returned for a second helping, a way to put off the foreboding dread of what came next.

Apparently, last week's extended game of hide and seek had convinced Myron and Irran that he *also* knew all the good hiding places, because the duo were eating breakfast out in the open this morning.

Finally, Joseph's internal responsibility meter wouldn't let him piddle around any longer, and he strolled over. "Morning," he said, trying to disguise his despondency.

Usually he'd stand, trying to be imposing there until they rose to follow, but today he sat down across from them with a heavy sigh. "Whenever you guys are ready, we can get started."

Irran eyed him cautiously and asked, "They fixed the cart then?"

Joseph shook his head, eyes in the dirt. "No, it's busted up pretty badly. We have a replacement. Guess that fifth load was a mistake after all," he tried to inject a touch of humor into the statement, but it didn't catch.

Selecting a pair of donkeys, the two men followed Joseph over, harnessing them to the cart. Hopping up beside Joseph, Irran flicked the reins to get them moving toward town and glanced over, "So, what's the plan today, young master?"

Joseph stared off south, vaguely towards the city. What was the plan for today, *Don't shatter another axle?* Last night, he'd told himself he'd find the strength to keep pushing the two men, but staring down the exhausting task this morning he... he didn't have the energy. Myrrha's suggestion from the prior night nipped at his mind, *stop pushing so hard.* He still didn't like the idea, but maybe there was an element of truth there.

"Honestly," Joseph said, "if we could just manage four loads today, I'd be happy with that."

He looked up to see Irran watching him beneath bushy eyebrows, with a calculating gleam. "You said just four loads, Master Joseph, then we're finished for the day?"

"Yeah, I think so." Joseph nodded. Something about Irran's demeanor radiated to Joseph that he was being played, but Joseph couldn't imagine how, so he sat back in the cart to watch the barley stubble slide on past.

And then something genuinely bizarre happened. Everything went just fine. They got two loads before lunch, ate, then finished a third, and took a short break before easily completing their fourth trip.

For once Irran and Myron seemed in good spirits. They chatted amiably during the trip and Joseph almost didn't notice how early it was when they finished dumping out the last baskets.

"Well, that's the last for today," Irran announced cheerfully, "Right, Master Joseph?"

Was it? Joseph's gaze caught the position of the sun and did a double take, it was only midafternoon. He looked to the cart, then his two helpers in a sudden disbelief. How had they...?

The thought flashed in his head, that today they actually *did* have time for another load, but glancing at the two expectant men… he had said only four loads.

"Yeah," Joseph nodded, still half numb in surprise, "I guess so." For a while after they'd left Joseph stood there puzzling over the situation. How had they managed that? Same work, same route, but three hours faster. How?

Finally, when he couldn't work out a good answer, he turned to go. Maybe he'd find Benji, or see if Myrrha was hiding in the thick oak forest up the hill from camp. She went there sometimes to card wool, and since he had the rest of the day off, he might as well enjoy it.

Chapter 12
New Seasons

The next few days went *shockingly* well. Joseph would wake with the sun, enjoy a long breakfast with Benji, then find Irran and Myron and get to work. After that miraculous Yom Rishom, he debated setting the goal at five loads for the next day, but a part of him was almost terrified of what might happen if he tried. He felt like changing anything might shatter the spell that finally had everyone working at a decent pace. And so, the next day he stayed at four loads, and again they finished by midafternoon… just minus all the frustration and shouting from the prior week.

Irran and Myron even opened up a little and started talking *to him* instead of *past him* for a change. He got to hear about Makani, one of the maidservants, a girl with long dark hair, forest green eyes, and a smile that made Myron melt… or at least that was how he told it. By the third day, Irran even got around to slyly asking, "I suppose you're getting old enough to be considering a wife, Master Joseph?"

"Yeah," Joseph gave a non-answer, "I suppose," and left it at that. No way he was *ever* going to mention Myrrha to these two. The way they talked, that news would run a circuit around camp and back before he woke up tomorrow.

Even if he didn't want to spill his secrets to Irran though, that afternoon Joseph found himself with his back to an oak trunk, sitting across from Myrrha as she busily stitched a pillow cover. The camp was dotted with sprawling oaks that shaded the tents, but further up the hillside, the grove thickened, transforming into a dense forest of wide trunked behemoths that capped the summit. Unless the livestock got scattered in the forest, the only reasons people came up here were either to avoid everyone else or gather deadwood. Fortunately, gathering wood was a task for the cool of the morning, and with the midafternoon sun still blazing above, Joseph doubted anyone would stumble onto them.

For a time, he watched Myrrha's quick, precise needlework as she rapidly layered yellow threads into a pattern. "So," she finally asked, eyes still on her stitching, "things are going better?"

"Yeah," he paused, then added, "I uhh… I took your advice."

Myrrha did glance up at that, a confusion in her eyes like she'd forgotten what her *advice* actually was.

"When you said to stop pushing so hard," Joseph clarified. "I tried to take a break and… I don't know, suddenly Irran and Myron seemed really eager to get things done. It's strange, you know."

Myrrha's expression glowed, her voice amused, "Well, I'm glad you listened for once."

"I try," Joseph said, then slyly added, "at least when I hear a good idea."

Across from him, Myrrha cocked an eyebrow, suddenly seeming less amused at the insinuation. "*Ooooh*, well you're lucky to be so good at picking the good ideas out then."

Joseph grinned smugly, "It's a gift." Then added, "You know, at this rate, we'll be finished early next week."

He meant it to be good news, but Myrrha didn't respond. Instead she went dead quiet, and Joseph noticed she'd stopped her stitching. Her hand hovered, frozen over the pattern, the needle trembling. "What does that mean," she finally asked apprehensively, "for us?"

Joseph moved close, firmly taking her hand in his, "Hey," he encouraged, "it'll be okay. I'll speak with Dad and…"

Myrrha's gaze was still fixed down on her stitching, and Joseph reached over, guiding her chin up until their eyes met and reiterating, "It'll be okay, Myrrha."

For a second their eyes locked, Joseph leaned in… and the two kissed. In that moment time stood still, just him and Myrrha, her arms wrapping around him while he pulled her close. He almost forgot to breathe, and when they did break apart, all her hesitance had vanished. She stared into his eyes, then leaned in to kiss him once again.

When they finished, she was breathing hard and blushing furiously. As Joseph watched, an abrupt change swept across her face. Myrrha turned away, her cheeks a ruby crimson, while her voice scrambled for a more dignified tone. "I should uhhh…" she groped for the needle that she'd dropped into the short grass, suddenly seeming both flustered and yet very focused on her embroidery, "I need to…"

Joseph didn't want the moment to end. How many opportunities did they have to be alone like this? "Myrrha…"

"No," she mumbled, hastily. "I… I need to finish this."

"Oh please," Joseph rolled his eyes, but sat back across from her. "You're picking a pillow cover over me?"

"No…" Myrrha's face colored an even more embarrassed shade of scarlet, "It's a commission, I need to finish it."

Joseph leaned back on one fist and cocked an eyebrow, skeptical, "Reaaaally?"

"I'm serious," her voice firmed up, "It's for…" she paused, pursing her lips to remember, "Mistress Tellai." She held up the cover, on which Joseph could see half of what resembled a yellow flower, "I think it's their family crest, two yellow roses. I guess she liked one of my other designs." Myrrha's expression lit up with a tentative excitement. "Anyway, Namluh pointed her to me, and now she's expecting it at the market day tomorrow."

"Well, you're cutting it a little close," Joseph snickered.

"Oh, shut it. You're the distraction here."

"Am I?" Joseph grinned fiendishly, "Exactly *how* distracting would you say I am?"

In response, Myrrha narrowed her glare, grabbed a twig and pelted him with it, even as Joseph raised an arm to shield himself, chuckling.

"It's a big deal, okay," Myrrha said. "I think she has a bunch of other stuff she wants embroidered too. If she likes this, it could mean a lot more work."

Joseph sighed, still grinning, "Well, in that case. How about one more kiss, and I'll stop being distracting."

Myrrha glared at him, scowling like she *really* wanted to be upset with him, but couldn't quite manage it.

Joseph added a mockingly serious, "I promise." And, abruptly, her stony expression shattered into giggles.

She blushed, embarrassed, despite that there was no one to see them. "As long as you *promise*," her expression split in a smile, and Joseph leaned in close, his hands feeling her hair as their lips met.

***

The next morning their wagon was joined on its trip into town by dozens of others. Many were smaller carts, most with only two wheels, a single donkey harnessed to the front, and the back piled high with freshly harvested produce, hides, firewood… everything imaginable. Sprinkled among the various farmers from outlying villages, Joseph saw several traders leading strings of pack donkeys. He even noticed one man driving a double-axle merchant's cart, the sides and tarp painted in vibrant blues and yellows.

Joseph and his crew had risen early and made one trip already that morning. Irran and Myron had been working hard for a promise though, and as they pulled through the gathering press at the gate, they guided the cart along a new route. Instead of turning towards the granary, Irran pulled them along one side of the square, where already a thick bustle of people clogged the road.

Technically the market square opened to everyone at dawn. But with so many people coming from outside Kiraith

Arba to trade, many stalls didn't truly open until midmorning.

Moving slowly in the crowd, the trio inched past a pair of intimidatingly well-armed guards near the square. Finally they pulled the cart to a halt in a spot where it only *mostly* blocked the road. In a flash, Irran hopped down and tied the animals' halters around a nearby post.

"Alright," Joseph stepped down after him, waving Myron over as well, "let's meet back at the camp stall at noon. We can grab the second load and head back to get lunch."

Irran nodded eagerly, and Myron glanced past the bustling crowd to the maze of vendors already set up on the square. Joseph had noticed that today both Irran and Myron had small pouches tied on their belts that clinked with bits of silver and copper ore to trade with.

"Alright," Joseph raised his eyebrows, trying to offer final caution, "*Don't* get too lost."

"Of course, young master." Irran nodded, as though that shouldn't possibly be a concern. Both he and Myron turned, swiftly vanishing into the crowd.

Joseph found himself slightly peeved that neither had had the presence of mind to offer to stay and watch the wagon. But in fairness, he wouldn't have trusted them to, which was why he'd already planned on doing that himself. Not far away, he could see the distinctive white and blue raised tarp that marked his family's customary space at the square. They'd stopped close enough that he ought to be able to keep an eye on the wagon from there, and with time to kill, Joseph headed over.

Back in Shechem, everyone from their camp had always been treated as outsiders. They might find buyers for their animals at the market, but afterwards those same people would scurry off with scowls like his family left a nasty stench in the air. Here in Kiraith Arba though, the reception was almost the exact opposite. Grandfather Isaac had pitched his tent near the city longer than many people in town had been alive, and the familiarity seemed to have bred a modest acceptance. Joseph had been genuinely shocked the first time he'd seen someone buy a pair of rams then actually linger to chat afterwards.

Weaving through the press of people, Joseph brushed past a cluster of goats all tied to a post and stepped into the cool shade of their awning. Everywhere a bustle of familiar faces did a brisk business, even as the collective hum of the crowd washed out the individual voices.

Ten steps away, Father was deep in discussion with a middle-aged man that Joseph dimly recognized as one of the local butchers. Next to him, Garash, one of Grandfather's deputies, gestured a well-dressed buyer toward a post with five rams tied to it. Joachim stood off to the left, near a pair of two wheeled carts. One cart was stacked high with tanned hides, while the other displayed a menagerie of finished leather goods: replacement strips for broken sandal thongs, slippers, belts, and larger hides sewn into waterproof tarps. On the opposite side of the family's awning, several eager women clustered around Namluh, picking over her wares, and sure enough, that was where Joseph spotted Myrrha.

Namluh acted as a general intermediary for most of the women in camp. She would take any excess handcrafts they had to sell, then retail everything at a unified storefront. Already Namluh had laid out several different mats in the awning's shade with dozens of items. At a glance, Joseph saw delicate gloves, spools of thread, bolts of wool cloth, various bits of jewelry and goose-feather cushions. Namluh, short and severe, with her hair twisted into a tight braid, already had her scales out to weigh one woman's silver. The next mat over, Myrrha dutifully held up a bolt of wool for a haughty lady, flanked by a pair of maidservants.

Joseph had to wait while Myrrha spent an inordinate amount of time displaying the cloth. She unrolled a length and held the fabric up, allowing the woman to rub the material between her thumb and forefinger. By Joseph's reckoning that was all the information a normal person needed. But the lady engaged in a bizarre sort of dance, poking at the fabric, rubbing it… again, and holding it at a half dozen angles. She then gestured for Myrrha to position the cloth out in the sunlight… he was half surprised the woman didn't attempt to sniff it.

Finally the woman nodded.

Myrrha passed the cloth to Namluh, who glanced at the bolt, then began the typical back and forth trading of disgusted scowls and feigned offense that constituted haggling.

Before another customer could get Myrrha's attention, Joseph tapped her on the shoulder, "Hey."

She turned, regarding him in surprise. Today she'd foregone the modest shawl that she'd typically drape over her head. Instead, she taken to copying Namluh's more relaxed style, her brown hair swept back and tied with a scarf, just minus Namluh's painfully tight braid.

Myrrha mouthed something, the words lost amid the dim.

"What?" He leaned close, cupping one ear to hear over the din of the market.

"I thought you were hauling grain all day," Myrrha spoke up.

"We're taking a break," Joseph grinned, nearly shouting to be heard. "What are you—"

Namlu glanced towards the both of them and stepped closer, her eyes sharp as knives on Myrrha, "Customers," Namluh thumbed towards the crowd. "You can be lazy and make puppy-dog-eyes tomorrow."

Namluh gestured another waiting woman of the city toward Myrrha, whose face had gone scarlet in embarrassment.

Instantly, Joseph found himself low-key looking away, trying his best to pretend that he definitely *hadn't* come over to their tent just to chat with Myrrha…

Nope… not at all… not even on his mind.

One of the herdsmen strolled by, Ashan, an imposing mountain of a cow-herder who they brought along to scare off thieves. He was clearly relishing the job, and Joseph could swear he saw the man flash a roguish smile at a young woman in the crowd who blushed and turn away giggling.

Leaving Myrrha, Joseph found his father just wrapping up with the butcher and handing over the leads to a trio of bleating rams. Dad turned back into their tent his figure sagging with a visible sigh and his limp slightly more pronounced than usual, as he made for where several stumps had been laid out to sit on. His dour expression faded at seeing Joseph though. "Joseph, what are you doing here?"

"Myron and Irran wanted to scout out the market," Joseph explained. "Since there wasn't one last week. I figured we could spare an hour."

It wasn't until he explained things that it occurred to Joseph that Father might not approve. Jacob regarded him a moment with a bemused expression, until, "Well, I suppose as long as the grain gets moved." He paused, "You didn't leave the cart filled with grain, did you?"

Joseph shook his head. "It's just empty baskets." He gestured toward where the hulking cart stood, the seats and harnessed donkey's heads poking over the stream of people coursing by. He sat next to his Dad, staring out at the milling crowd. "Busy day?"

"Exceptionally," Father said, "We're going to run out of animals soon. I sent Kasku back to camp to bring more into town."

Joseph saw his father's eyes alight on a man slowly strolling around the goats like he was choosing his favorite. Father sighed, standing with a grunt, "I'd better—"

His voice cut off as a shout tore the midmorning air. "FIRE! FIRE ON THE ROOF!"

Joseph's head snapped up, suddenly alert. The call had risen from the opposite side of the square, but his gaze instinctively swept back toward his cart… still there. More people took up the cry and the crowd surged around them, a few moving towards the fire, but most flooding away. Next to him Father was already barking orders, "Namluh, pack your things. Ashan, get the animals, we—"

A woman's piercing scream sliced through the chaos, and behind it came men's angry shouts. "Down with Mamre!" "For Lord Issir!" "Death to the king!"

The square erupted into pandemonium. Screams tore the air as people fled in every direction. Nearby, Joseph saw the pair of heavily armed guards he'd passed earlier charging into the square, wading through the river of fleeing civilians and calling, "Protect the king!"

A window briefly opened in the crowd, and he glimpsed a dozen men furiously swarming around a knot of king's guards. Mamre's men bristled like a hedgehog with bronze spearpoints leveled outwards, "To the king! All warriors to the king! Protect the—"

"Joseph!" Father's razor voice sliced through the madness unfolding on the square. "Get your cart! We're leaving!"

Joseph turned just as someone in the wild crowd barreled into one of the tentpoles, and the entire awning crashed forward in a mess in front of them. More people scrambled by, pressing close as they fought to get out of the square. He headed for the cart, and ran straight into Irran's heavyset figure. "Master Joseph," the man said breathing hard, "I think we should—"

"Get to the cart!" Joseph waved him to follow and shoved through the mass, "Wait for our people from the market, then go!"

Irran nodded "Right away s—"

His voice died in this throat, the man staring past Joseph, transfixed. Joseph followed Irran's gaze to see a man with a heavy warbow, standing on the rooftop above their cart. The man drew back the powerful bow and sent an arrow zipping across the square with a sharp hiss that Joseph barely caught over the uproar. Immediately the archer scowled, his lips muttering as though he'd missed. But not skipping a beat, the man smoothly nocked another arrow, pulled back the taut bowstring, and loosed it straight into the melee.

Someone crashed into Irran who staggered into Joseph, nearly knocking him over and jolting them both back to reality. They were almost to the cart. Joseph's heart pounded as shouldered past a pair of panicked women and grabbed hold of the familiar wooden rails. In a single motion he hauled himself up to see above the crowd.

Joseph's eyes flashed across the plaza to where the battle still raged. The knot of guards from earlier were hard pressed, two of the six men were down. In the center, a bronze sword glinted sunlight as a beleaguered Mamre urged on the defense. Several other guards converged to the rescue from multiple angles around the square, but the attackers surged in, seconds from their prize. One had stepped back from the melee, waving his spear as if to urge the others into the fight…. then froze, as a heavy arrow shaft sprouted from his back.

The man abruptly stumbled a half step forward, wobbling… then sank to the ground, kneeling… where another shaft zipped into his exposed back.

On the opposite side of the cart, a frantic Irran clambered up into the seat. Joseph saw Dad and two of Grandfather's deputies dragging panicked animals by their halters, while Joachim and Ashan had grabbed everything they could and were wading through the crowd towards the wagon. Myrrha and Namluh were already there, having simply bundled up the blankets with all their wares inside and run. More people emerged from the crowd as men and women from camp who'd come to shop now converged on the knot of familiar faces.

The animals were the biggest problem, and Joseph leapt down to help Father. In his peripheral vision, he caught another arrow flash above, and more shouts echoed from the square.

He reached Dad, who strained against eight unruly goats, all trying to bolt in different directions. Grabbing several halters, Joseph helped his dad toward the wagon. They arrived to find people frantically bundling their things into the back, and shoving aside empty barley baskets to make room.

Joseph looped the goats' halters around a small peg on the rear and looked back, his breath catching as he saw the square in absolute chaos. The fire blazed ever higher on the rooftops, orange flames and black smoke spouting out of the house near the square, yet no one seemed to care.

By now, the crowd had thinned enough for Joseph to realize that the battle had largely concluded. He counted seven bodies strewn across the plaza. In the center of the activity, Mamre held his sword high in triumph and stood over a motionless figure, crumpled facedown with two arrows in his back. Mamre's men swarmed into the square from every direction, more than two dozen now, expertly converging on their king. Almost like… Joseph glanced up at the archer still standing on the rooftop overhead… almost like Mamre had planned this.

Two of the attackers had been seized by the guards and another lay on the ground, writhing in pain. Stalking over, Mamre leaned down, and Joseph winced as the king coldly stabbed the wounded man once… then again… no one even looked at the fire.

"Is everyone here?" Jacob's voice interrupted, and Joseph turned to see his father glancing around the cart, tallying everyone. Irran apparently took that as an indication to go, because he flicked the donkeys forward through the milling mass, hauling on the reins to bring the cart around and point them back toward the gate.

Several of the attackers had thrown down their spears and fled, disappearing into the mass of people clogging the road at opposite edge of the square. He dimly caught Mamre's furious shouts, "Find them! Find the traitors!"

Mamre's soldiers did just that, plunging into the crowd where the rebels had vanished. Women shrieked and men shouted as guards from behind corralled a large group into the square, the soldiers separating them out like his family splitting off calves from the cows to be weaned. Women and children were pushed out, along with older men and a few finely dressed fellows. As Irran brought the cart around,

Mamre's soldiers thinned the group down to a couple dozen young men, most in plain work-tunics with a hedge of spearpoints pointing in toward them and...

Oh no...

Joseph caught a familiar shout amid the crowd of suspect men, a voice and a flash of a face he knew well. Myron.

Joseph swore, and almost before thinking, he turned to the square, running towards the guards. By now the majority of market goers had fled, but a number of people still clung around the edges of the square, many crowded down side streets, poised to run if needed. Near the crowd of corralled men in the center, a few terrified wives were shouting to their husbands or frantically pleading with the guards. Joseph hurried up, but before he could explain himself, a stern-faced soldier whipped his weapon around. Joseph ground to a screeching halt, a razor spearpoint tickling at his chest. "Get back," the man snapped harshly. "King's business."

Joseph froze, gulping back a sudden curse as his gaze flashed between the honed bronze and the man's cold scowl. Maybe this wasn't the best place to be. "I..." he stumbled over the words trying to recover. "You... you have one of our men."

He pointed to Myron, who, in the same instant seemed to notice him with desperate shouts, even as the soldiers' spears pressed them in tightly. "Master Joseph! Please sir, tell them I didn't do nothing! Please!"

Joseph gulped at the man's pitiless stare. "So you're one of them too," the guard demanded, scowling like he might just force Joseph in with the other men.

Joseph took a pace back, suddenly reconsidering speaking up. Still, Myron was right there and—

"All of you listen!" A furious Mamre called to anyone who remained. He stalked the square with a mad glint in his eyes, and gestured with his blade. He seemed oblivious to the fact that his city was literally burning behind him. "Watch and see what happens to traitors and those who associate with traitors here in Kiraith Arba! Let this be an example! Finish them all!"

Joseph couldn't believe what he was hearing. Mamre was going to kill everyone, just because some of them *might* be rebels. Yet as he watched, the king gestured to one of his guards and the spearpoints ominously leveled. A woman screamed in forlorn panic at realizing what was about to happen. One man, made a wild rush for freedom, only to stagger to a horrifying stop as he took two spear thrusts to the chest and collapsed, howling in agony.

"Mamre!" Joseph shouted not sure what else to do. "Please, you have one of our people!"

The king glanced towards him, and if there was a flicker of recognition in those flinty eyes, Joseph didn't catch it. Instead Mamre scowled, "Put him with the—"

"Mamre!" Jacob's voice interrupted, bold and commanding, and Joseph glanced back to see Dad crossing the square after him, with only a hint of a limp. "You have one of our people." Father nodded towards a terrified Myron.

Mamre hesitated. He might not precisely remember who Joseph was, but he sure recognized Father. The king's eyes jumped from Father to his new found prisoners, then back. Joseph could swear he almost saw the calculations in the man's head as Mamre weighed Myron's life in the balance.

Father stared the king down, not saying a word, just standing there, until finally the king shrugged, flicking to one of his guards, "Let him go."

The surprised guard did a double take, but raised his spear and a relieved Myron sped out of the trap, even as Mamre called in an obvious foul temper, "Kill the rest! And let this be a lesson!"

Joseph met Myron's gaze, and turned away as the awful screams tore the square.

Chapter 13
Dark Spires

An hour later the beleaguered party had returned to camp. After penning the animals, Joseph stared back across the valley where dark streamers rose like towers above Kiraith Arba. The smoke twisted skyward before reaching an altitude where the west wind caught the foreboding pillar and smeared it across the heavens.

He tried to gauge the scale of the fires blazing in the city, observing how the thick plume of soot above gradually tapered down to just a few thin tendrils near the ground. If what was rising now was just a couple fires, then by comparison, the thicker clouds above must have been a colossal blaze.

Joseph heard a soft rustle in the grass and turned to see his father. Jacob paused beside him, taking a long look at the black column. They'd barely spoken since leaving the city. The cart ride out had been a tableau of stunned silence in the wake of Mamre's cold-hearted massacre, a collective feeling like they'd just witnessed a monster being let loose. For most of the trip back, the only sounds had been the wooden *thunks* of the bouncing cart, a few hushed whispers from the women riding on the back, and occasional exhausted bleats from the rams.

Now though, Joseph swallowed, not sure what to say… "It's a lot of smoke."

"Indeed," Jacob agreed without much emotion. "Mamre let the fire spread for too long. It might have taken a dozen homes from the look of it."

Joseph nodded. The more he thought about it, the more the fire bothered him. In retrospect, he could piece together the rebel's plan — light a fire as a distraction and attack while Mamre's men were busy extinguishing the incipient blaze. Yet... Joseph recalled Mamre stalking the square with a heartless glower, even as the fire spread like locusts behind him. The man hadn't seemed bothered... at all. Joseph had gotten the disturbing sense that he wouldn't have minded the whole city burning to the ground, so long as he was king of the ashes.

And now Mamre was getting exactly that, Joseph realized glumly. He'd slaughtered a score of people for no reason at all and seen a whole block of homes reduced to charred husks.

"I suppose I can see why people wanted to get rid of him," Joseph mused, dourly.

"Careful who you share that sentiment with," Father warned. "I'm sure you can see the importance of treading delicately around such a man."

Joseph nodded, then added a hesitant, "Are... well, I assume there won't be any more grain runs for a couple days?"

"There won't be anyone going to town at all," Father said firmly. "I'll give Mamre the rest of the week to cool off, then I'll have to sit down with him personally, figure out where things stand. Frankly, I'd feel more comfortable if the rest of your brothers were here."

Joseph blinked, picking up the worrying insinuation, "You don't think Mamre is going to make trouble for us?"

Father frowned, still staring at the distant smoke. "Probably not. I'm sure he's quite pleased with himself at the moment. He got what he wanted after all, dead rebels and a display to keep everyone in line. Still, I'd prefer to be safe."

Dad paused, shifting his weight and gazing off at the city to the south for several long breaths. Finally he spoke, this time less dour. "You..." he hesitated, trying to round up the right words like a herd of unruly sheep. "You did very well today, son," he finally said. "I wanted you to know that."

Joseph's surprised focus slid away from the fire, turning to his dad, whose eyes still held their vigil on the black tower in the distance. He sure didn't feel like he'd done well at all, more like he'd almost gotten himself killed. If anything, he'd been low-key expecting Father to tell him not to be so rash. "I… I did?"

"Of course," Father finally turned, his whole posture orienting toward Joseph. Joseph swallowed at the seriousness on Father's face, "You looked after your people, and spoke up for them when necessary. Myron's alive because of you."

Dad laid one hand on Joseph's shoulder, firm, with a genuine sincerity in his eyes, and a smile tracing his face, "You did very well today, Joseph. I'm proud of you."

The words hit like a bolt of lightning. *I'm proud of you.* Joseph wasn't sure the last time he'd heard Father say those words. Perhaps hinted at them a few times, but never just said it aloud. Joseph wasn't sure what to say in answer, but he felt a euphoric warmth radiating out from where Father's hand clasped his shoulder, an unbidden smile slipping onto his face.

"Thanks," he finally mumbled, at a loss for words.

Jacob nodded, squeezing Joseph's shoulder, and in an instant of clarity Joseph realized— this was his chance, wasn't it? This whole time he'd been working to show Dad that he was an adult and he could make adult choices, except now apparently he'd gone and proved it by accident.

During the long hours hauling grain, he'd imagined talking to Father about his marriage dozens of times. But he'd certainly never envisioned a scenario like this. In his head, the conversation typically began with him walking in to speak with Dad, Myrrha at his side, the both of them united.

Joseph swallowed a tight knot of fear in his throat. If this *was* his moment, there might never be another, so he'd better take it. He gulped again, suddenly not sure he could push the words out, until…

"Dad," Joseph drew in a nervous breath, "I… I've had a lot of time to think the last couple weeks and…" he almost couldn't go on, but Dad was looking at him now, expectant.

The last words came in a rush, "I think I know who I want to marry."

Joseph felt his face flush with heat, and for a second his eyes searched for anything to look at except Dad— the grass at his feet, the hills to the east, a hawk circling—

Except… Joseph finally forced his eyes back. Except he was a man, and as such he shouldn't be afraid to look his Father in the eye.

Surprisingly, he saw that Father's grin had broadened. If anything Joseph saw more pride there, almost like Father had been waiting and he'd just passed some critical test.

Before Joseph could wonder too much, Father, gave his shoulder another reassuring squeeze, "Of course, Joseph." Jacob gestured toward the camp, his tone suddenly keen. "If you know who you want, then let's go talk."

***

The front of Father's tent was already open when they arrived. Stooping to duck under the low canvas ceiling, Joseph saw Grandfather Isaac lounging on a pile of cushions amid the sultry heat of the day. Nearby, little Talita busily pulled up flaxen floor mats and stacked them in a pile to have the dust beaten out later. Isaac's eyes were closed and he seemed nearly asleep, although given that he was blind and barely able to walk, that meant very little.

Joseph didn't feel like he'd made much noise, but Grandfather Isaac must have had almost supernatural hearing because he twitched to alertness, sitting up slightly, "Is that you, my boy?"

"It's me, Grandfather," Joseph said.

129

Father stooped into the tent behind him, his focus turning to the young girl working in the corner, "Talita?" The preoccupied girl looked up, as though she'd only just noticed them. "Leave us." Dad flicked a hand for her to go.

She hesitated, her gaze bouncing from Father, to her pile of mats, then to Grandfather, as though she wasn't entirely sure which took precedence. Isaac spoke up though, "Run along, dear."

That finally seemed to settle matters, Talita gave a polite nod to Grandfather and stepped out without so much as a word. Joseph watched her a moment as she left, walking a short distance before breaking into a jog as she made for, what he assumed, was her parent's tent across camp.

When Joseph turned back, Father was busy making Grandfather comfortable, and Joseph found a cushion where he could sit across from the two older men. Isaac asked, "Any more news from Mamre?"

"He seems to have gotten the fires under control," Jacob added a dour, "mostly."

"Ahh, good for him," Isaac nodded, deadpan. "Be a shame if he burnt his city to the ground."

Jacob found a seat of his own. "Joseph and I were just speaking," he explained, "about Joseph's future spouse."

"Were you now?" Grandfather rarely moved in a hurry, but now he sat up, keenly leaning towards Joseph, his eyelids closed but his expression scrawled with curiosity.

The sharp change in Grandfather's demeanor left Joseph unnerved, as though a curtain had abruptly pulled back to reveal the unexpected. Were *his* marriage prospects what Father and Grandfather discussed when no one else was around? Father was clearly making an effort to hide it, but Joseph still felt an anticipation in Dad's gaze that had him nervously rapping on one knee.

Jacob settled back on a cushion with a restrained smile. "So, Joseph, you mentioned that you'd had some thoughts about your future wife."

Joseph gulped, trying to swallow back the unexpected pressure of both men's undivided attention. "Yes," he managed to make the words come out, but only haltingly. "I… I've thought about it a lot and…" he gulped again, "I know who I want to marry."

He drew in a deep, terrified breath, then just let the words he'd practiced dozens of times spill out. "I want to marry Myrrha."

He saw Father's face twist into a confused frown, hardly a good sign. That said, he'd known going in that Myrrha was always going to be a difficult sell, and fortunately Joseph had practiced this conversation *a lot.* Before Dad could raise an objection, he kept right on explaining, "I know she's not who you were thinking, but you said I should marry someone who understood our way of life, and she does. She's smart, and you've seen how great she is with Benji. She's already an incredible seamstress, she already knows how to work with the animals, and…" he swallowed before letting the last bit spill out, "I love her."

He added hastily, "We love each other." His voice faltered as Father's frown deepened. Joseph tried to ignore the sudden cold lump congealing in his stomach. "She's the perfect match," he explained, desperately trying to make Father understand. "And she's not in Seir or Harran, she's already here. If you just give her a chance, I know she'll surprise you."

He paused, his eyes sweeping from Father to Grandfather then back. Father's disapproving frown faded into something arguably worse— disappointment, an expression that stabbed Joseph like a spear.

"Son," Jacob said with a deep sigh, "I know you *think* that you love Myrrha. I remember when I was young, it—"

"I don't *think* I love her," Joseph insisted, trying not to show his frustration, "I *know* I love her."

Father's expression hardened at being cut off mid-sentence. "Joseph," he said bluntly, "you're not marrying Myrrha. I won't allow it."

"Why not?" Joseph demanded, "It's my life, can't I—"

"And I won't watch you ruin your life with foolish decisions," Jacob insisted, his voice rising. "Joseph, one day I'll be gone, and you will be the one leading our people, leading your brothers. It'll be on your shoulders to carry both *my* legacy, and your grandfather's. You're part of a line that runs back to Abraham, and you'll be the one to safeguard everything that our family has built until now. I *will not* let you tarnish that legacy and make yourself a laughingstock by wedding a common slave girl."

"Father, she's not—"

"That is *exactly* what she is," Father snapped, "a *common slave girl*." His tone harshened until the three words felt like a slap in the face. "And no matter what you *think,* your feelings can't change that."

Joseph felt a stinging fury. He couldn't recall the last time he'd been genuinely angry with his father, but if Father's disappointment was a spear thrust to the gut, casually insulting Myrrha just twisted the blade deeper.

Joseph snapped back, not caring if it was disrespectful or not. "How would you know? You barely even know her."

"And you, it seems, know her far too well."

"If you just gave her a chance to—"

"Joseph, I said *No*." Father's voice hardened to flint. "I won't see you marry a slave."

"Then we can free her," Joseph countered. "I don't see the problem. We free her and Althea, then I can marry Myrrha. She's not a slave, and everyone is happy."

Joseph felt he'd made a reasonable point, but instead Father gave a humorless chuckle like he'd only shown his own ignorance. "Joseph, if you were to marry the girl, she would have been freed before the ceremony regardless. Manumitting her a few weeks early changes nothing. She's still spent her entire life as a slave."

"But—"

"Boys," Grandfather Isaac abruptly spoke up, his voice quiet but firm, even despite his age. Instantly Father turned to him, opening his mouth to speak. But for being blind, Grandfather Isaac sure could see pretty well, and he held up a hand. "Jacob, stop," Grandfather said.

For an instant, Father looked like he might speak anyway, but he finally closed his mouth with a sigh.

Joseph almost wished he *had* spoken. In a way that would have proven his point, if Dad could override Grandfather, then why couldn't *he* override Dad?

Grandfather turned towards Joseph with that unnervingly vacant stare of his. "Joseph, it's obvious you care very deeply about this girl, and that's commendable. But you also need to understand that this is a decision that affects all of us, the whole camp. Whoever you marry is someone who we all have to live with. Now, your father, he chose very well and you can hear from anyone what a blessing Leah has been to this camp."

Joseph nearly rolled his eyes as he tried to keep the incredulity off his face. No point letting Father see him scowling. But had Grandpa seriously forgotten that *his mom* was dead? In point of fact, Mom and Grandpa had never even met. And frankly, a few flowery words about how *wonderful* Leah was, wasn't going to change Joseph's mind about her… at all.

Grandpa seemed not to realize though, and kept right on talking. "Your uncle Esau though, I can't say the same thing about his wives. Frankly, they were repulsive, arrogant and haughty. They assumed the world was theirs to be claimed and the rest of us were simply small people to be trodden upon and discarded." Grandfather shook his head with a frown, "I believe part of your father's concern is that this girl you want may not be who you think she is."

Joseph had to bite his tongue not to speak over Grandfather. Showing that sort of disrespect instantly would have settled Father's opinion against him. But he struggled to stifle his frustration as Isaac went into extravagant depth about how *he* didn't trust any of the Canaanite women. Apparently they were all awful, and the only properly raised girls who Isaac knew were the women of their own clan, and that was why *his* wife had been Grandpa Laban's sister...

Joseph *really* wanted to shout and get Grandfather to understand that this wasn't even relevant. Fine, the girls from Canaan might be awful, except that Myrrha wasn't *from* Canaan. She was from Attica *which was in Hellas,* literally, on the other side of the Great Sea.

Joseph glanced over only to see Father eying him with a warning glare as Grandpa rambled on. Joseph stifled a sigh and tried to keep a straight face, but by the time Grandpa concluded his long-winded explanation, Joseph was more frustrated than ever. Yeah, obviously he didn't want to marry a self-absorbed witch either, *nobody* wanted that. Fortunately, Myrrha was nothing like the women Isaac kept on about. If anything, she was the precise opposite. Joseph remembered all the gentleness and love she showed with Benji. He recalled her compassion all the times they'd been alone, and that encouraging smile she always wore that seemed to make every day a bit brighter.

The only benefit of Grandfather's spiraling tangent was that, by the time he finished, the entire discussion had more or less reset. Joseph couldn't understand why Father insisted on being so obstinate, but he gritted his teeth to hold back the deluge of scathing words threatening to come out. "Father, I don't see why—"

"Joseph, the answer is *No,*" Father declared bluntly. "If you were Asher or Gad, I might consider it. But one day you are going to inherit the rights of the firstborn, and I will not watch you disgrace that legacy with Myrrha, of all people."

Joseph snapped, Father's disdain finally setting him off. "Well, it can't be all that bad," his sarcasm sliced sharp as a razor, and even though he knew he was making a mistake, he suddenly didn't care. "After all, I seem to recall you married *common slave girls...* twice."

Father's eyes narrowed, his lips drawing tight, even as he leaned in with a subtle menace. "Well in that case," he said coldly, "I can oblige you. But, just like in my case, I'll expect you to marry a proper girl first. You give her a few children, produce a real heir, and in four or five years, if you're still lusting after Myrrha, you can always take her as a concubine."

The way Father presented the idea, like that was just how things were done, left Joseph feeling physically ill. That genuinely sounded worse. First he'd be forced to marry some girl he'd never even met and didn't love. Then when he was finally *allowed* to marry Myrrha, he'd get to watch his first wife resent her and make her life miserable. It'd be just like Mom and Leah all over again, the endless bickering, fights, grudges… tears. And to top it all off, his son would get caught in the same cycle.

In a flash, Joseph saw the future, and for an instant the horror stole his breath. He saw another boy, just like him, growing up and suffering all the cruelty and nastiness from his brothers… all because he had the *wrong* mother. A little boy always pushed away because of something he hadn't asked for and couldn't control.

He looked up at Dad, suddenly determined. He wouldn't do that to his own sons, bring them up in a world where they hated each other. He met Dad's unyielding glare and said one word, "No."

Father blinked in surprise, and Joseph continued levelly, "I'm going to marry Myrrha, and *not* some girl from Harran."

"Son," Father shook his head, "I told you, if you want to choose a proper wife first then I might consider—"

"Why!" Joseph demanded furiously. "Why would I want *more wives*? Because it's worked out so well for you? Mom and Leah, and Bilhah and Zilpah, it's all been *fantastic*. Hasn't it?" In that instant the dam burst and a lifetime worth of rage and venom all poured out as Joseph's eyes dared Jacob to disagree with him. Pretend that Benji didn't get tormented by his brothers, pretend that Joseph's own life hadn't been constantly punctuated by his older brothers' vicious cruelty.

Joseph threw up his arms as he nearly screamed, "Hasn't it!"

For an instant he saw a flash of pain on Father's face, and another surge of poison boiled out. "Why would I do that?" Joseph demanded. "Why would I do that to my own children?" He blinked back a sudden mist in his own eyes, "What sort of a father does that?"

For an instant Dad didn't answer, his posture tightening. But Joseph could see his words had cut deep. Before Father could recover, Grandfather split the tension with a sharp, "Boys, stop. We can revisit this once you've both had some time to consider the situation."

In truth, Joseph wasn't ready to postpone anything. That would just give Dad time to dream up some flowery words to plaster over this nightmare of an idea, and right now he wanted to fight. "I'm going to marry Myrrha."

Father's expression deepened into a scowl. "Listen to your grandfather, Joseph," he snapped, then shook his head. "We can continue this discussion once you return."

Joseph stiffened, "Return?"

"Yes," Father halted, his expression twisted in a dark scowl. He took a deep breath, and seemingly through force of will, managed to push the worst of the distaste from his face before continuing. "I meant to speak with you once your work was finished in Kiraith Arba, but Mamre side-stepped all of us on that front. I'm sending you out to the field for a few days to oversee affairs. Your brothers are pasturing the sheep at Shechem. Get ready, and I will send you to them."

Joseph frowned. Typically, he might have given a glum nod and gone to fetch his things, but since he was being more blunt than usual with Father, he offered his own dour assessment. "I doubt they'll want me around."

Joseph hadn't been away from camp for an extended time in several months. Partly because taking care of Benji had rapidly transformed into its own, full-time job. There was also the fact that no one seemed to want him along. Probably the more relevant factor.

Last time he'd been out in the fields with his brothers had been early winter, and it had been a disaster. First, one of the animals had developed a limp, and instead of trying to care for the poor thing, Dan, Naphtali, Gad and Asher had just flat out killed it and enjoyed a sumptuous little feast. Then they'd sold a half dozen rams to a passing trader for slaughter. The sale itself was routine enough. But what wasn't, was that on their return they'd flat out lied to Father's face, claimed the rams had been lost to lions. Then they'd cheerfully pocketed the proceeds.

So he'd told Dad the truth, and—

Even the memory of what had happened afterwards still lit Joseph with bristling fury… *sarru* □uzīru, a "lying pig", they'd called him. Which was particularly rich coming from a bunch of thieves.

Father had never explicitly named him as the one to talk, but given that he'd been the only one not punished afterwards… well, even a blind lion probably could have riddled that out. And, mystery of mysteries, ever since no one seemed to want him out in the fields. Which was fine by him.

Father only barely seemed aware of how tense things had been between Joseph and his brothers lately, because he shook his head with a bemused, "Pack some honey-cakes to bring them, and I'm sure they'll be happy enough. And even if not, I still want you to go check on them. I need you to make sure everything is as it should be with the flocks. You should also inform them what happened with Mamre, and have them move to closer pastures until the situation in the city settles down."

Joseph truthfully had no interest in leaving, but there wasn't a real way to say no either. "Yes, Father," he said, frustrated. "I can leave at first light tomorrow."

Jacob frowned, shifting his seat to look outside where the noonday sun beat down. "There's still plenty of light today," Dad declared, more of a command than an observation. "You need to get news to your brothers as quick as you can."

137

"Right," Joseph numbly nodded, reading between the lines. Father wanted him to leave as soon as possible, and any further marriage discussions were suspended until he returned. He debated forcing the conversation back to Myrrha, but sensed he would only be hurting his own case. Reluctantly, he stood, "I'll go pack my things."

Before Father could say more, a frustrated Joseph ducked beneath the sagging tent awning, and stepped out into the sweltering sun.

Chapter 14
The Calm

Regardless of what Dad wanted, Joseph knew he wasn't leaving *right* away. The sun had risen to its zenith and the hottest part of the afternoon lay ahead of him. Hardly the best time to trudge off into the open fields. Besides, after speaking with Father, he felt… jittery, almost shaking, and needed to calm his nerves. After a moment's indecision, Joseph made for his tent. Both the front and back had been drawn open for the air to circulate, and camped beneath the spacious awning, Joseph found his little brother sprawled out on a mat, napping.

There was no point waking Benji just yet, so instead, he set about quietly bundling his gear into a travel pack. Even if Joseph didn't particularly want to leave, there was something cathartically familiar about packing his things. He was casting about for his travel cloak, the one rubbed with beeswax to waterproof it, when he heard a shuffle from across the tent. "Joseph?"

He turned to see his little brother stretching out on his mat and fighting back a yawn.

"Hey, Benji, you get a good nap?"

"Yeah."

Joseph nodded then went right back to his search, rummaging through a wicker basket full of fabrics. Where had he put—

"What are you looking for?" Benjamin's surprisingly energetic tone interrupted from nearby.

"My cloak, the red one."

"Okay," Benji gave an eager nod, awkwardly hovering nearby.

"Uhh… why don't you check *that* basket?" Joseph pointed towards one he'd just dug through. Benji's heart was in the right place, but the boy was still at an age where he struggled to give genuine help. That said, Joseph had learned that if Benji wanted to *help,* it was best to give him something trivial to do before he discovered a more… *chaotic* form of assistance.

For a moment Joseph kept digging, while Benji pulled out the various items of clothing and pronounced an obnoxiously loud *Nope… nope… nope* at each one.

Joseph moved to search another basket, pulling linens aside until—

There it was. He pulled the weatherproofed cloak out from near the bottom of the basket, accidentally dragging something else with it. Joseph stood, draping the cloak around his shoulders… then froze when he noticed the other garment he'd pulled out. It was a dress, long-cut, vibrant yellow… Mom's dress.

For an instant he stared, unmoving. How had that gotten buried all the way down there? Had Myrrha been cleaning and…

"You found it!" Benji's excited voice intruded

"Yeah." Joseph blinked and stooped down, hastily folding the dress and bundling it back into the basket before Benji could pry any more. "Yeah, I did."

His little brother hurried over, finding the cloak where Jospeh had laid it aside and rubbing the waxy fabric between his fingers with a grin. Joseph nodded to him, "Alright, Benji, so I've got a game to play. I need to find a few tunics, a belt, my stick and some spare sandal laces. Then we need to head to the cook tent and get some treats. Sound good?"

Benji's eyes lit up at the prospect, particularly at the mention of the cook tent. The little boy nodded in excitement, "Okay."

And just like that they were off.

There was a lot to pack, but with Benji fetching the simple things, they finished surprisingly soon, and even Joseph was grinning by the end. It wasn't until they were walking back from the cook tent with a sack full of every sort of tasty confection that he noticed Benji suddenly become very quiet.

"You want another honey tart?" Joseph offered with a conspiratorial grin. Surprisingly, not even that lifted Benji's spirits.

"Joseph?" Benji stared up at him, suddenly worried, "Are you leaving?"

Joseph swallowed back a sigh and for a couple of breaths said nothing. He tried to escape the depressing sense that their special moment had just shattered. Finally he answered, "For a few days, yeah."

Benjamin didn't respond, and Joseph reached down, scooping the little boy into his arms as he walked, noticing Benji's small arms clutching him tighter than usual.

When they made it to the tent, Joseph moved to lower his little brother down, but Benji clung on with a surprising tenacity, insisting, "I don't want you to go."

"I know," Joseph gave up trying to put down Benji and instead sat cross-legged in the tent shade. Benji nestled his way into Joseph's lap, and Joseph wrapped both arms around the boy, holding his little brother tight against his chest. For a while both boys sat there. Joseph found himself staring out at nothing in particular, yet feeling strangely content just to be holding Benji. The two watched as the sun slowly drifted above, occasional clouds blanketing the land in traveling patches of shadow, while the breeze playfully tugged at towering oaks in the camp. All the while, Joseph struggled with a strange premonition, like this moment would never come again, and perhaps he ought to hold onto it while he still could.

***

When Joseph finally let go of Benji, he went to find the one other person in camp who would actually care that he was leaving.

"Myrrha?"

The girl jumped at his voice, nearly fumbling the shuttle she was threading through her loom. She turned to see him in surprise. "Joseph?"

Myrrha stood near the left side of her tent, busy weaving in plain view of everyone. And being out in the open he caught an instant edge to her tone, an unspoken *you shouldn't be here.*

Which… yeah, probably. Except at this point he didn't really care if Althea disapproved of *them.* And he couldn't exactly wait for her to sneak off to their usual place to talk. There wasn't time. Besides, he'd already told Father everything, and even if Dad hadn't given his blessing, the talk had left Joseph sick of hiding.

"Myrrha, we need to talk."

She didn't seem interested and instead finished pulling the next thread in her pattern through her loom. Grabbing a simple comb, she began raking the thread into place with a curt, "Can it wait?"

"No, it can't."

If anything, the blunt answer seemed to sharpen the anxious edge to her voice. She gave the thread one last tap into place with her comb before turning to face him with a terse, "What is it?"

Joseph took a breath before the plunge, then, "I have to leave."

"What?" She blinked, stepping closer, then caught herself, seeming to remember that she was in public, and uncomfortably pulled away. "What for?"

"Dad wants me to go check on the sheep. I'll be gone a few days, and you'll need to make sure Benji is okay."

Joseph hesitated before adding, "And I spoke with Dad."

Myrrha's expression turned abruptly more serious at those words, like a part of her guessed what had already happened, "About?"

"About *us*."

Maybe it was something in his voice, or perhaps just that he didn't seem very happy about what ought to have been good news, but Myrrha's face turned ashen pale. "You... but I thought we were going to talk to him together and—"

They had been, but... Joseph shrugged, "It seemed like the right time."

Worry crept onto Myrrha's expression, "Except...?"

"We didn't decide anything," Joseph prefaced. "But—"

"So your father said *No,*" she cut him off bitterly.

"He didn't say... we were at an impasse," Joseph could see she was scared and tried to keep things calm. "But I'll talk with him again when I get back. I'm not going to let..."

Myrrha barely seemed to hear, she turned away her breath coming sharp and blinking as she buried her face in her hands.

"Hey," Joseph laid a hand on her shoulder, pulling her to his chest, "It'll be okay. We'll—"

Myrrha pushed him away though, her eyes brimming with tears, "Why would you do that?" she demanded hotly.

"Myrrha, I didn't mean for this to—"

"But it did," she insisted with a sudden anger that caught Joseph off guard. She glared at him a moment with a fire he didn't recognize, her expression quivering between pain and rage. Then like a wave against the shore, her anger seemed to shatter, leaving only hurt in its wake and Myrrha turned away, sniffling back tears.

For a moment Joseph hesitated, lost. Just like with Dad, he'd imagined a dozen different ways this conversation would go... except not this way. In the moment a part of him desperately wanted to *fix* things, just make everyone happy... except he couldn't do that either.

Instead Joseph stared at the distraught girl. Even crying, Myrrha was so beautiful that he almost couldn't tear his eyes from her. And she was scared wasn't she, he abruptly realized, scared that they were losing each other.

"Myrrha," Joseph stepped close and took her arm, "I love you. And that's not my father's decision, alright." She weakly tried to push him away, but he pulled her against his chest, and looked down at the girl who stood a half-head shorter than him. His eyes locked on hers. "I love you." Joseph repeated, determined. "And when I get back we *will* figure this out."

Her eyes fell with an uncertain, "You promise?"

Joseph smiled, everything else forgotten. "I promise. Always."

She looked up, giving a small nod. And standing there, their lips a mere hands-breadth apart, Joseph did the most natural thing in the world, he leaned down and kissed her. He could feel the jolt of surprise tense her muscles, then her arms laced around his chest as she clutched at him like she was holding on for dear life. For an instant that seemed entirely too short, it was just them.

When their lips broke apart, Myrrha's expression flushed and Joseph couldn't stop the happy grin that stole across his face. He heard a sharp gasp to his left, and his head turned to see Althea, of all people, carrying a small basket and staring at the two of them, frozen in wide-eyed shock. Oh... right, he dimly realized. Everybody had seen that hadn't they. He craned his neck and saw more than a few people nearby hurriedly avert their gaze.

Any other time that might have been a *very* substantial problem, but with Myrrha's arms still clutched tight around him, he couldn't have cared less. Glancing down, Joseph saw Myrrha's cheeks tinged a wild shade of scarlet, even as an embarrassed grin tugged at her mouth.

Oh well, since everyone already knew—

Joseph leaned in again, his lips meeting Myrrha's in an unashamedly passionate kiss. He savored the warm radiance of her body pressed to his chest. And this time, he made sure to take exactly as long as he wanted before pulling away to catch his breath.

They embraced, Myrrha's head resting on his shoulder, and a wondrous contentment soaking into Joseph. It felt like time had paused and if he could just linger in this moment forever, that would be enough. Slowly though, he had a strange sensation that time was finally beginning to flow again and he gave Myrrha one last hug. "I love you, Myrrha," he whispered. "I'll be back in a couple of weeks, and we *will* find a way. I promise."

Her arms squeezed him one last time, and with a terrible reluctance, Joseph let go. Myrrha's blushing cheeks turned an even deeper crimson when she noticed her mom, wide-eyed staring at them like a pair of strangers who'd washed up on the beach.

Before either Myrrha or her mom could speak though, Joseph fixed Althea with a serious look. "It's not Myrrha's fault," he said firmly. "This is something I'll take care of."

Joseph wasn't entirely sure how he intended to do that, but in the moment, it felt like exactly what he needed to say. He met Althea's eyes until the woman finally gave a wordless nod of assent. Then he cast a loving look at the beaming girl before him, and leaned down to give her a parting kiss on the forehead. "I'll be back," he whispered.

Then with a deep breath, he turned and walked away.

Chapter 15
The Storm

Well, that news was about to scuttle its way around camp in an awful hurry, Joseph mused as he strode away from Myrrha's tent. He tried to ignore the sudden chorus of stares prodding him like spearpoints from across the wide circle of tents.

He headed for the outer edge of camp, where he wouldn't have to feel everyone watching. For a while he paced the ring around their encampment, trying to settle his jumbled thoughts. He was going to have to explain what he'd just done, and he didn't imagine Father would be very pleased. But at this point, there wasn't a choice. His secret was definitely out.

He sighed, trying to press back an ominous realization that he'd just sabotaged an awful lot of plans. Even if Father forced him to marry some other girl, everyone would still whisper about what had just happened, that it hadn't been his choice. How badly would that poison things? And what if all this all accomplished was to make Father more determined to have his way? What then?

The possibilities tangled in his mind, his focus drifting from one scenario to the next. Walking with a nervous energy, it was only the sting of sweat in his eyes that made Joseph look up and realize he'd nearly circuited the camp as the afternoon drug inexorably onwards. He would need to go soon, if he wanted to get anywhere before sunset.

Pressing aside the lingering question of what he'd tell Father, Joseph headed back to his tent, where he found the pack he'd prepared earlier. Benji was gone, and given he'd just said his goodbye's, Joseph figured there was no point tracking down his little brother only to repeat the process. Instead, he reluctantly hefted his travel pack, looping the strap across his body. Jospeh added a water pouch over the opposite shoulder, before grabbing his favorite staff and a sling, then turning to leave.

Stooping back outside, Joseph briefly debated strolling straight across the center of camp into Father's tent. As he did though, a puffy white cloud slid across the sun, plunging the whole hillside into a refreshing shade.

Well, he mused, if there was free shade to be had, no point wasting it by taking the quick route. He could still use a few moments to work out what to tell Father. Turning toward the outer ring, Joseph resumed his slow circuit, except this time with a gathering worry as every step brought him inevitably closer to Father.

A few minutes later Joseph had circled around camp to behind Father's tent, and there he hesitated, dreading the final two dozen steps inside. Across the valley, the cloud from before was finally completing its path across the sun. In the distance he could see the thin line dividing bright sunlight and soft shadow sweeping down the western hills and towards them as though signaling that his time to procrastinate was rapidly fading.

Joseph took a deep, preparatory breath, nerving himself as he deliberately strode towards the wall of dark goat hide… then froze as he heard Grandfather's gravelly voice leaking through the leather.

"You're going to have a hard task convincing him he doesn't love that girl, Jacob."

"I'm sure he'll come around," Father said, without much conviction.

"I don't know, I've never heard many stories about young love being particularly rational. I suppose he gets it from you. Didn't you say you worked fourteen years for that bride of yours?"

Father's voice was something close to a growl. "It was for both of them, but it's hardly the same. Rachel was a lot more than just a pretty face."

"And I'm sure your boy feels the same way, even if he's wrong. Maybe you need to give him some space to work that out for himself."

"I would," Father agreed in a sour tone, "except that Althea can't seem to keep that girl of hers away from him."

Joseph froze… what?

Then, like an Aasha game where the dice kept coming up just right, everything snapped into place. Joseph understood perfectly. That was why Althea had been trying to keep them apart and warning Myrrha about getting hurt. It wasn't that she didn't want them together. Now that he saw all the pieces, it felt so blindingly obvious. He was easily the most eligible bachelor in camp, and Myrrha wouldn't have found a better match. There was no sane reason for Althea to want to keep them apart.

Except Father. Father must have noticed the time he was spending with Myrrha and disapproved. So he'd told Althea he wouldn't countenance a marriage and warned her to keep Myrrha away.

Joseph felt a stab of hot fury, his hands unconsciously tightening into fists. How long had Father have been playing him… months now? Not just him— him and Myrrha both. He never had worked out what he'd meant to say to Father, but in the moment none of that seemed to matter as Joseph walked around the front of the tent, and ducked inside with a scowl.

He caught Grandfather mid-sentence, "…take him to meet Esau's girl and see if they…"

The tent went dead quiet, Joseph glaring at his Dad, amid the gut punch of betrayal.

Dad must have noticed, but he put on a forced pleasantness regardless. "Joseph, good. You have your things?"

"I'm ready to go," Joseph replied coldly. Then added, "But you should know, I just kissed Myrrha. I'm sure the news will get around by the end of the day. I figured you deserve to hear it from me.”

Instantly Father’s expression darkened in worry, and he stood in a flash. “You did *what*? Joseph, why would you do that?”

“Seemed like the right thing to do,” Joseph declared with an indifferent shrug.

Father looked down, hand on his forehead and breathing between clenched teeth, “Son, do you even understand how this complicates everything?”

“Well, I’m marrying Myrrha, so it shouldn’t be that awful.”

“Absolutely not,” Father rose to his feet, fairly spitting fire. “I said we’d talk more, but if you’re really dead set on going behind my back and debasing yourself with that slave, then I’ll tell you right now, you’re *not* marrying that girl.”

“Just like you told Althea?” Joseph demanded, so furious that for once he didn’t care how imposing Father was. “Just like you made her do your dirty work to keep us apart?”

Father’s eyes sliced at him like a knife, shockingly unashamed, “I did what I thought was best for all of us.”

“You mean for *you*.”

“Really? You think your mother would have wanted you to marry that—”

“Mom always liked Myrrha!” Joseph nearly shouted. “Don’t pretend you know what she would have—”

“Your mother wanted the best for you! Meanwhile you’re whoring around with—”

“YOU DON’T GET TO SAY THAT!”

“BOYS!” For being as ancient as he was, Grandfather still managed to summon that sharp command in his tone that instantly stilled the tent.

Joseph held Dad’s stony glare, breathing hard and silently daring him to look away, even as Grandfather continued very deliberately. “Both of you, stop this. *Now*.”

For what felt like an eternity the world froze to a tableau, just Joseph and his dad glaring each other down. Finally though, Dad broke off his stare with a scowl and turned toward Grandfather. Joseph looked down, dimly realizing his hands were shaking, then glanced back at the entrance, suddenly eager to get out of here.

Grandfather continued levelly, "Clearly we all need some time for tempers to cool off." Isaac did that trick where he turned toward Joseph despite his blindness and Joseph swallowed under Grandfather's eerily empty eyes. "Joseph, when you return, we'll hear you out, but in the meantime it's not proper to go behind your father's back either."

Joseph's eyes flashed towards Dad with suspicion, but he nodded, "Yes, Grandfather."

Across the tent Father slowly lowered himself down to sitting, drawing in several deep breaths like he was collecting himself. "I've only ever wanted the best for you, son."

Yeah, Joseph thought with a bitter frown, that made two of them. Too bad they couldn't agree on what that actually meant. That said, Father's words were about as close to a detente as Joseph could have expected, and he kept his cynicism to himself.

"Maybe…" Father continued, rapping his fingers against one leg, "when you return, we can take some more time and give consideration to all the options."

Joseph nodded. He had the sneaking suspicion that Father had a very narrow view of what constituted *options* but at least that path ran both ways, Dad would at minimum have to give him a fair hearing. And honestly, if Dad would just talk with Myrrha, give her a chance, he might change his mind.

Regardless, Joseph realized it wasn't the best time to press the issue. Instead, he turned back to the more immediate problem… his brothers.

"I'm ready to leave. Is there any message you want me to convey to everyone?"

"You've packed food for your brothers?" Father asked.

Joseph nodded, "Anything sweet I could find."

"Good," Father nodded. "Go and see how your brothers and the flocks are getting along. Then come back and bring me a report."

"Very well, Father." Joseph felt like he ought to say something more… but he wasn't sure what else there was to say really. "I'll try to be back in…" he did a quick estimate, three days there, plus some time with the flocks, so say, "I suppose a couple weeks."

"Of course," Father agreed, and despite the tension earlier, managed a faint smile like a tentative peace offering, "I'll see you then, Joseph."

Joseph nodded his goodbye, still angry. Then he turned, ducked outside, and left.

Chapter 16
Rachel

Heading north out of camp, Joseph made excellent time, although in truth he wasn't sure if that was good or bad. Moving faster meant he'd find his brothers sooner, and correspondingly get home more quickly… but it also meant he'd have to deal with his brothers *sooner*.

The sun still blazed high above as he headed down the hill from camp and started up the long valley toward Jebus. Occasionally he'd pause, grabbing smooth rounded stones from between the thick tufts of grass, and tucking them into a pouch for later.

Later came five miles down the valley when he spotted a pair of doves hopping about on an exposed tree limb. Slowing his steps and setting aside his cumbersome staff, Joseph crept to within ten paces. Moving almost in slow motion, he carefully unwound the sling he'd looped around his belt. A simple device, just two arm length leather cords with a piece tied between the ends to form a pouch for the stone.

Taking one of his collected rocks, Joseph laid it into the sling pouch, and pulled the leather strips taut, one hand grasping the knotted ends of the cords while the other held the stone in the pouch. In a single smooth movement, he let the pouch drop away, twirling… one, two, three— release.

Whssss—CRACK!

The stone snapped against the branch, bare inches beneath the birds, and both launched skywards in a panic of beating wings and frantic *coo's*.

The release cord swung around, slapping Joseph's chest, and he scowled as he saw the birds flutter off, well out of range. At this distance he definitely should have hit that shot.

Grabbing another stone to practice, he set his eyes on the thick tree limb, aiming to repeat his throw. Loading the sling pouch, he again let it fall into a twirl. One, two, three— Release.

Whssss...

The rock whistled through the tree branches, slapping at leaves as it vanished in the foliage, then continued to impact on a boulder with a far-off *clunk.*

In quick succession Joseph loaded another stone and swung it. One, two three— Release.

Whssss...Thunk.

At least he'd hit the branch, except he'd struck nearly a cubit to the left.

He tried a second time, one two three— Release.

Whssss...CRACK!

Finally.

He stared at the twin scars he'd put on the branch. A couple years ago, when he'd regularly spent time out with the animals, he could have hit the branch dead on, every time, probably from a few feet further back. But it seemed like he'd lost a bit of his magic touch.

That… might be a problem. Years ago when he'd begun slinging, he'd had to endure Issachar and Asher's merciless taunts whenever he missed. So he'd started practicing, and after… oh, about ten thousand rocks… he'd gotten pretty good. At least enough that they left him alone.

Obviously his job was more to check on the animals and supervise than to run around chasing sheep and fighting off wolves. Still, he didn't relish the prospect of having to deal with his brothers *and* them also realizing he wasn't quite the crack shot he'd once been. No, that wouldn't work at all.

Loading another stone, Joseph set to whipping it around with a determined glint in his eyes.

One, two, three— Release.

By early evening Joseph had made it nearly to Ephrath, and his sling arm ached. Turned out, he had been out of practice. Fortunately, he was rapidly making up the difference. He must have shot at least a hundred stones, slowly working the muscles back into form until they started to feel his old rhythm again. Since he had to keep his eyes dead on the target, timing the release and gauging speed came entirely by feel. Unfortunately, there was no shortcut to that beyond practice.

Joseph was skirting around the western flank of the village of Ephrath, when another opportunity arose. Out in the open, three plump doves busily hopped between the low clumps of bluestem grass, pecking at the ground, completely oblivious. Moving very slowly, Joseph laid aside his staff, unwrapped his sling and slotted a stone, all while gently stepping closer. At thirty paces, he couldn't be certain of a hit, but he was certain another step would spook the birds. Focusing on the closest dove, Joseph stood perfectly still, letting it cheerfully hop its way clear of a thick clump of grass to give him a clean shot… then he twirled.

One, two, three— Release.

Whssss… thunk!

The sudden flash of movement caught the bird's attention and several small heads popped up in alarm, but too late. The stone flew true, and Joseph saw his dove limply tumble over as the stone clocked it right in the breast.

The other doves frantically launched skywards even as Joseph jogged forwards to collect his kill. It was a juvenile bird, but still relatively fat. And the fact that Joseph didn't have to share his prize just made it look all the more delicious.

Tying the bird to his belt, Joseph headed back to grab his staff. The sun had already sunk low in the west, and close on the left stood a familiar grove of trees on a low hilltop. They'd moved their animals past Ephrath several times in the past couple years and he knew most of the landmarks along their usual route. This particular grove spread up the eastern flank of the hill, offering decent shelter from the wind as well as deadwood for a fire.

Just transitioning from Mamre to Ephrath the terrain was noticeably more lush, and the forest floor brimmed with greenery. He had no problem finding several broad-trunked oak trees with plenty of medium sized branches scattered beneath.

As the light began to fade, Joseph rapidly gathered enough fuel for a fire, as well as a pile of small tinder sticks. Already the charred remains of a fire pit were visible at the edge of the trees. The small mounds of pebble like sheep poop suggested this was the exact place his brothers had stayed a few weeks prior.

Pushing aside a large chunk of ashy white wood from the fire pit, Joseph expertly piled up his own sticks. Then he dug the fire kit out of his pack, pulling out a clump of flax shavings for kindling as well as a flint, a bit of char cloth and his spark stone.

The spark stone was the true special ingredient. It was dark grey on the outside, but when split open, it contained a dull reddish interior that would strike a spark against the flint. Joseph's stone was a hand-me-down from Levi, the red face rubbed smooth from many uses, but it still worked. After a half-dozen hard *clinks* against the flint, a tiny spark flecked off and caught on the char cloth. Joseph readily transferred it into the bone-dry flax shavings, and a few twigs later he had a small but eager blaze. Once he'd established his fire, he fed in a few larger branches, then set to work plucking and gutting his dove. The process was a mess, but with the help of a small bronze knife, he soon had the bird sliced up and stuck on a crude spit.

The entrails he tossed straight in the fire where they seared and crackled, oozing out a foul, charred smell. He could have thrown them away, but the fresh guts would have just attracted predators... hungry predators... the worst sort. He fed a few more sticks into the fire to incincrate all the nasty bits, then set to the slow work of holding the stick with his dinner over the leaping flames to cook.

Finding a comfortable spot to sit, Joseph idly stared into the fire. After being constantly surrounded by people for weeks on end, he found the quiet solitude refreshing. The last few hours were probably the first time in a long while he hadn't felt urgently stressed about... something. Instead he'd found the adventure of being on his own rather fun for a change. Sure he still faced the looming prospect of having to deal with his brothers... half-brothers, but that was still a few days out, and worrying now wouldn't change their meeting.

For a while, he focused on turning the bird to evenly roast it all the way through. His ears tuned to the *cracks* and *pops* of the burning wood that punctuated the evening symphony of chirping birds. Meanwhile, the sun sagged down below the horizon, dyeing the sky in a fading blush of twilight that melded from orange, to red, to purple as it too scurried away before the coming night.

The next morning Joseph awoke with his back to an oak trunk and his travel cloak pulled up around his chest as a blanket. The sun hadn't yet risen, but already red streaks painted the patchy clouds above to herald its coming.

Trying to stand, he groaned at the stiffness in his legs and the sharp pain that stabbed along his spine after being propped against a tree all night. It took several minutes of gentle stretching to loosen up his arms and neck, then he tried to stand...

"Owww." Given the aching that throbbed in his feet, he might as well have been barefoot on a field of rocks. Apparently, half a day of walking had taken a toll, and he had to spend several minutes massaging the sore spots on his feet before the aching gradually subsided.

All in all, by the time he stood, the sunlight was cresting over the far eastern ridges. He still had half a dove breast left from the prior evening, which, along with a cut of goat cheese from his pack made a passable breakfast. In short order he'd gathered his things, kicked some dirt over the last chilly embers of his fire, and was off with a determination in his step. He had something to do this morning, something important.

Joseph looped back onto the path just north of Ephrath. From there Jebus was visible six miles away, squatting atop its tall hill, like a citadel that kept vigil over the surrounding valleys. In time with the morning light, a steady stream of farmers marched out like ants from the southern gate, swarming down into the fields and orchards that carpeted the valley.

If things went well, he hoped to be well past Jebus by the end of the day. However, after only a short while, Joseph detoured off the path, making for a small rock cairn a few hundred paces from the road. His stomach twisted into nervous knots as he came close.

It wasn't much, a low oblong mound of white stones with a single large rock set at the crest. But as Joseph approached, he hesitantly laid aside his staff before finally sitting down cross-legged at one end. He took a deep breath, then whispered, "Hey… mom."

In truth Joseph wasn't quite sure that Mom could even hear him. He'd asked Father once where people went when they died, and Dad had just thrown out a line about, *they're with God now, son* which… what did that even mean? *With God* as in, up in the sky…? Was that what the stars were then? Or had Dad meant that place, the one they'd seen at Bethel when the sky tore open and they'd seen… God. Was Mom up there?

Joseph dwelt on the possibility for a moment. He liked that idea. He still remembered the song they'd heard from the sky, the rich, flowing notes that thrummed in a harmony of sound. Maybe she got to listen to that all the time. The possibility brought a smile to his face. Mom would have enjoyed that.

He leaned forward, laying a hand on the cairn. He still had no clue what to say, but he couldn't escape the comforting sense that… somewhere, Mom could hear him.

"I… I know it's been a while." Joseph said at last, the words starting to come easier. "There's actually been a lot that's happened though. Benji is doing really well. You'd be proud. He's gotten so big. He's almost up to my waist now."

"He's talking more too. I uhh…" a smile slipped onto Joseph's face, "I was actually his first word, *osef.* For a while he was having a hard time sleeping, but he's gotten a lot better. He's always excited, and somehow he'll just keep going all day long. You would have loved him, Mom, everybody does." He hesitated, remembering his half-brothers harassing Benji a few weeks earlier, then added, "Well, mostly. But Dad and Grandpa Isaac both adore him. Sometimes Dad will even go chase him around and…

Joseph's voice trailed off a moment at the sudden painful memory of Dad and yesterday's argument. "There… there's something else too," Joseph said. "You remember Myrrha, right? She's been helping me take care of Benjamin. Back when you…" Joseph's voice faltered, "…when he was a baby, you were gone and every day it felt like Leah was about to take him away. But Myrrha… she just knew what to do, and who to talk to, and she would watch him when I couldn't. A lot of the time it felt like it was just us…"

His voice trailed off again, his cheeks suddenly warming in embarrassment. It felt absurd, if Mom really was out there and watching, she probably already knew everything, but it still felt strange to force the words out. "I think… I think I love her." He paused letting the statement hang in the air. "I really do, Mom. Maybe that's stupid, I know Dad thinks so, but I want us to be together and be happy, except…" He hesitated as he came to the difficult part. "Except Dad won't listen. I don't know why, but it's like talking to a wall, and I don't know what to do."

Joseph swallowed back a stab of frustration at that last bit. *Dad wouldn't listen*, and not for the first time either. He still remembered the conversation he'd overhead years ago, when they'd been coming south from Bethel, when Mom had pleaded with Dad to just wait. He could have just waited a couple days for her to have Benji... but Dad hadn't listened. And now Mom was dead.

Joseph laid both hands on the pile of stones, bowing his head and blinking back a rush of tears with a whispered, "I miss you, Mom. I wish you were here."

For a moment, Joseph held tight onto that dream. If Mom were here, she'd know how to persuade Father. She'd know what to say, when to talk to him, and how to approach the topic. She would have understood, and she could have told him what to do.

Instead, Joseph felt a bitter frustration at the unfairness of it all. He might as well have been groping in the dark for all the good he'd accomplished trying to convince Dad. If he just had someone who could help.

Joseph's frustrations abruptly ground to a halt as a sudden thought whispered in his ear like a voice on the breeze — a single word.

Bethel.

The thought crystallized in a flash.

God was at Bethel.

Joseph remembered Dad's story, about how he'd traveled and come to Bethel in his moment of greatest need and made a promise with God. God had listened to Father and it had changed everything... so would God listen to him also?

The thought brought an excited energy and a flurry of possibilities whisked through his thoughts. Could God help change Dad's mind?

Joseph gripped the cairn rocks beneath his hands, his mind suddenly seeing the path ahead as clear as midday. He probably could have sat here talking for hours, but suddenly a strange urgency pressed at him. He still had a *very* long walk to Bethel, and for some undefinable reason, he felt that he needed to be there— today, in which case he had better start moving.

Drawing his lips tight, Joseph promised himself that he would definitely stop on the return trip. An excited thought danced to mind, maybe by then he'd have some good news. "I love you, Mom," he whispered. "I'll be back… and thank you."

Joseph pressed his eyes shut, and simply waited a moment in reverential silence. Then, with a deep breath, he stood and set off north with a renewed spring to his step.

Chapter 17
Memories Faded

The valleys around Jebus bustled with farmers. They swarmed the patchwork of farm plots, tending olive groves, fruit orchards and vineyards that were interspersed with golden fields of ripe oats and patches of barley stubble. Even keeping to the path that snaked through the Tyropoeon Valley, Joseph caught stares from farmers that ranged from curious to vaguely hostile.

He was nearing the city proper when the path finally brought him close to a field of oats that was being reaped. Three burly harvestmen in dust-stained work tunics stepped out into the road, barring his way. "What's your business here, boy?"

All three carried curved bronze sickles mounted on short poles, their posture not quite menacing, but straddling the razor edge between polite and unpleasant. He raised a hand to mollify them, "I'm Joseph, son of Jacob, son of Isaac. I'm just passing north."

His brothers would have come through this area a few weeks before and likely sold a number of sheep, so they ought to at least know his family.

Sure enough, the men's hostile demeanor changed like a doused torch. All three relaxed and the leader waved him on past with a nod, "Of course. Fair travels to you."

Joseph breathed a sigh of relief. Good to know his brothers hadn't infuriated everyone. That *had* happened. Sometimes it was a local notable who felt cheated, a farmer whose pasture was eaten down without permission, or just Judah

161

and Gad getting a little too persistent about chasing some farmer's daughter. Somehow his brothers had a knack for finding new and creative ways to leave behind nasty piles of injured feelings. And of course, those hurt feelings typically required money to soothe. Never fun or cheap.

Today though, he made it past the city without further event, only pausing to strip a dozen spade shaped leaves from a cluster of betony stalks. The velvety leaves with a minty spiced flavor were something pleasant to chew on and left him with a relaxed clarity in his head.

He kept a razor eye for game, but the constant swarm of people around Jebus seemed to have scared away the easy prey. Getting north of the city however, Joseph found himself trekking through a wild country of wrinkled valleys and tree-capped ridges that led towards Luz and was bursting with prey. The first few birds he approached took flight quickly enough, but finally he snuck up on an unobservant partridge, walking with slow steps until he was within twenty paces. He calmly slid a rock into his sling pouch, barely daring to breathe, then flicked his wrist to give it a spin.

One, two, three… Release
Whssss— thunk
Joseph grinned in triumph.

He walked nearly the whole day to reach Bethel, following the endless twisting valleys. Even at midday, he ignored the pounding heat and kept moving, hugging the tree line halfway up the valley slopes for shade. That went well, right until he walked beneath a sprawling oak and looked up to find a leopard draped on a low hung limb, observing him with eager eyes.

Joseph froze. One hand clutched his staff as he gently backed away, heart pounding. He forced his steps to stay calm and steady, but eyed the big cat the whole time, making certain not to turn his back. After withdrawing to a safer distance, he moved into the warm sunlight for a while. He made sure to give the tree a wide berth and plenty of wary glances as he headed on.

He kept to the grassy lowlands for another hour until rounding the next curve in the valley and discovering something far worse than a lone leopard. A pride of six lionesses and a fierce maned lion all lounged beneath a sagging jujube tree.

Instantly Joseph cut across to the opposite side of the valley, his staff firmly in hand, even as he fished a rock from his pouch to hold at the ready.

If all his brothers had been here with the animals, they would have grabbed their slings and started bombarding the lions. A few dozen stones from a hundred paces often proved more than enough to shoo away a pride. Unfortunately, being alone, Joseph felt more likely to aggravate the powerful cats than scare them, and just the prospect of being outnumbered seven to one left his mouth dry.

Passing through the valley, he hugged the opposite tree line and tried to skirt past the pride. Typically lions would steer clear of people. There were much easier targets than someone toting around sophisticated long-ranged weaponry… he shot his sling a skeptical glance, then shrugged. Yeah, sophisticated long-ranged weaponry.

Still, even if the lions looked to be lazing away the afternoon, Joseph had no desire to test his theory too aggressively. As he reached the point of nearest approach, he gripped his sling cord tightly, keeping wary eyes on the oversized felines. Even with the lions laying several hundred paces across the valley, Joseph still glanced at nearby trees, quickly picking out one to climb if they swarmed him. They could follow him up of course, but only one at a time. And if he braced himself against a limb to free his hands, his sling would offer a fantastic advantage to hold them off.

In either case, the lions apparently weren't hungry enough to bother with him. And though Joseph kept looking over his shoulder for the next hour, he didn't sight them again once he'd rounded the next turn in the winding valley.

By the time he sighted the squat town of Luz, the sun had long since begun its western descent, and after quite a bit of sling practice, Joseph was several birds richer. Alongside the limp partridge tied to his belt, he'd added two meaty doves and a tiny sparrow. Granted, the sparrow was more a happy accident of target practice than an intentional kill, but he still beamed at having sniped the minuscule bird at forty paces.

Their family's altar hadn't moved from its hilltop, but he still had difficulty finding it. The last time he'd been here, the immediate few cubits around the altar had been blasted to a char by the light from heaven. Now though, the loose pile of stones had completely grown up with tall thistles, their stalks flecked with dagger-like needles and their bulbous seed heads closed up like green candle flames. A few mallow shoots with their hand-sized leaves sprouted around the base, while tall stalks of grass completed the disguise. Amazing how much the place had utterly changed. Joseph remembered the altar from when they'd left Bethel as neat, well-fitted stones, but now it exuded a worn, battered age.

He'd had a great deal of time to think about what he wanted to do, and the first step was to restore the altar to a semblance of its prior dignity. Trying to pull out the thick thistles with their needle spikes would have torn his palms, but he still spent a few moments striking off the thistle tops with his staff, clearing away the tall grass and pulling mallow stems. Then, he set off towards a nearby copse of trees to gather deadwood.

Collecting enough wood took several trips, all while the sky transformed to a deep ochre above. However, he soon had a sizable assortment ranging from small twigs to thick wooden hunks stacked at his feet. Piling some of the larger pieces on the altar he then set about the business of arranging his sacrifices, starting with the tiny sparrow which he positioned towards the back. He grabbed for the partridge from earlier as his centerpiece then froze with an abrupt realization… what about the blood?

That was one specific that Father was very particular about, *the life of the animal was in the blood.* Father would typically drain the blood from the sacrifice into a bowl and pour it out before the altar. Obviously, some of those details weren't feasible given that Joseph didn't even have a bowl with him.

For a moment he considered just not bothering. The sun would soon set, and he would waste a great deal of time draining the blood from his birds. It probably didn't matter… except… Joseph's mind flashed back to the last time he'd been here, the sobering memory of a pillar of light so bright he'd been nearly blinded even with his face pressed to the ground.

What if it did matter?

He knew Father certainly wouldn't have gone to all that trouble for no reason. Years back, Joseph had asked why they drained the blood and Dad had simply said that was the way it should be done, the same as his father and Abraham had sacrificed. At the time Joseph had been ten, and he'd idly decided that just meant *all his ancestors* were crazy. But now he wondered if perhaps they understood something he didn't. Sure Grandfather Isaac could be a bit eccentric, but he hadn't become as wealthy as he was now by being crazy.

Joseph stared a moment at the altar. He'd come all this way, caught all these birds, and he needed to talk to the God of Creation because he had one essential problem that was about to push his entire life down a path he didn't want…

Maybe this wasn't the moment to be careless.

With a resigned sigh, Joseph pulled the sparrow off the altar and headed over to the nearest tree, an oak with several low branches. Lashing up all four birds by their feet, he took a small bronze dagger and sliced open the back of each of their necks, allowing the blood to begin draining. He made sure they were suspended high enough that a passing fox couldn't just leap up and snatch a free meal, then headed out to begin gathering more wood.

This might take a while.

It must have been an hour later when Joseph cracked his spark stone against flint over a batch of kindling, watching as a few precious sparks sprinkled down until…

Yes.

His char cloth caught a flicker of slow burning flame and he quickly sprinkled in a few powdery leaf bits for kindling. Slowly, he added more fuel until he had a low fire going in a depression twenty feet in front of the altar. Overhead the scattered clouds shone a rich purple in the dying twilight, and to the west, the last sparks of day had scurried away. The evening star had already risen like a golden ember in the sky, and now the orange glow of Joseph's fledgling fire illuminated the four birds he'd laid out on the altar.

He had drained the blood as best he could, and now with a fire to hold back the night, Joseph turned to his sacrifice. He'd debated whether he should fully sacrifice all four animals or keep some of a bird for dinner. After some consideration though, he had concluded that if marrying Myrrha was important enough to come here, then she was important enough to offer the best he had. If he went a little hungry tonight… so be it.

Now that he had piled kindling around the altar, there wasn't much left to do. He spread the pair of doves to either side, set the little sparrow in the back, and laid out the partridge in the center, its breast toward the sky and its wings spread wide.

Stepping back, he surveyed his handiwork in the gathering darkness. It looked good. It wasn't much against the rams and bulls Father offered, but it was what he had, and he knew that God was certainly here, so…

Taking a long hunk of deadwood, Joseph hovered one end over his diminutive starter fire. Soon orange flames began to tentatively cling to the wood. Pulling it back, Joseph carefully walked the impromptu torch over to the altar, where he pressed it against a small pile of sticks at the base.

He held his breath as the fragile flames licked at the altar wood. For an instant, the fire almost died…

Then Joseph saw a small tendril of flame spiraling up from one of the twigs. Grabbing another handful of dried grass stems, he sprinkled it in among the tinder, the parched grass erupting in bright flickers as the fire established itself.

Then, in a hungry rush, the fire began to spread. Joseph had always been amazed at the dichotomy— how fire could be so fragile and weak when small, yet transform into a ravenous monster when it grew. In just a few heartbeats, the fire licked across the altar, a brilliant inferno erupting with heat that forced him two steps back.

For a moment Joseph stared with a boyish awe at the leaping flames. Then, remembering why he was here, he stepped back onto a bare patch of ground and knelt amid the firelight. He wasn't entirely sure what to say. Usually when Father made sacrifices, it was with an invocation of thanksgiving, but right now he really needed something from God, and he didn't know the formal words for that.

When Father had first come here all those years ago, he'd offered a deal with God. But truthfully, Joseph wasn't certain that was the correct solution. He didn't get the sense that Father's bargain had necessarily made anyone's life better. If anything, it had complicated things and left Dad wary of returning to Bethel at all. Joseph didn't want that.

Glancing up, Joseph saw the flames starting to take the birds, soft feathers scorching and blackening in the blaze. And in that moment, the answer settled in his mind like a stone finally drifting to the bottom of a riverbed. He should just explain things and ask for what he wanted. God had already sent him dreams, hadn't He? Joseph hadn't asked for those, but if God cared enough to do that, then surely he'd understand now. Besides, except for the birds, he didn't have anything to offer God anyway, so…

"Lord," Joseph began tentatively, not shouting, but speaking loud enough that God ought to be able to hear him. "I know you're up there, and I need some help."

Strangely, once he started talking, the rest of his words flowed easily enough, how he didn't want to marry Uncle Esau's daughter or a girl from Harran who he barely remembered from ten years before. How he wanted Father to listen and understand, and at least consider that there were other options. How he cared about Myrrha, how she'd proven herself a dozen times over. And how the absolute last thing he wanted to deal with was more women fighting over him and wounding everyone around them in the process.

The words seemed to go on and on, and somewhere in the middle it began to dawn on Joseph that this was about more than just him and Myrrha. Father had merrily gone about planning Joseph's whole life for him. Not only had he already picked out a bride, but Father had also chosen him to lead their camp one day and Joseph had an ornate tunic in his pack to prove it. In a way, Jacob had already decided that they would stay at Mamre too. After all, they were building stone granaries, and they couldn't tote those along if they left. To top it off, Joseph thought bitterly, Dad was now down to choosing who he could be friends with because he might make a mistake and that certainly couldn't be allowed. It might ruin the plan.

Joseph gritted his teeth. *Dad's plans,* he mused bitterly, that was why Mom was dead too. His father made all these wonderful plans and once he'd set his mind to it, he didn't let anything stand in his way. Yet when things went wrong, Father also wasn't the one who had to live with the consequences. No, Joseph swallowed back angry bile, that was *his* job.

He thought of his brothers, knowing all too well the miserable, lonely days he was in for when he did finally catch up with them. A full week, stuck stewing in the frigid nastiness of people who despised the very sight of him. And all because Father had *planned* for him to be over all the rest of them.

Joseph hadn't asked for that. He didn't *enjoy* being a pariah. Yet it had happened, and without any say on his part. Most irksome of all, Father clearly had no clue how icy things truly were between Joseph and his half-brothers. If Dad *had* realized, Father wouldn't have sent him at all. Literally *anyone* at camp would have been a better choice.

Yet here he was.

Opening his eyes, Joseph looked up, surprised to see the last light had completely vanished. Before him the altar fire blazed, but not with same bright intensity as earlier. Instead the flames had wilted back as easy fuel had turned to ash and the larger branches burned more slowly.

With his confused, rambling prayer still hanging in his mind, Joseph stared into the heavens. His eyes slowly adjusted to the field of needle-prick stars poking through the black veiled night. A part of him had secretly been hoping that God would appear like He had last time, in a storm of brilliant shining power that sliced open the sky.

Another part was glad that God hadn't though. Last time had been incredible, yet utterly terrifying. Joseph's gaze drifted back to the crackling altar, trying to summon up the words to distill down his frustration. "God," he said, his voice quieter than before, "I want my own life. I don't want to have to marry someone that Dad chooses, I want to make my own choices, pick my own path, and I don't understand why that's so hard for him to see."

For a dozen heartbeats Joseph waited, silent, letting the sounds of the night press in around him. All around came the popping crackle of the fire, the pulsing chirps of a thousand crickets and the quiet whispers of the breeze across the grass.

Finally, when he didn't hear an answer, he settled back, not sure if he was disappointed or relieved. In a way he did feel better… maybe… maybe just from admitting what was happening. He turned back to his own little fire, and discovered it had burned down nearly to the coals while he'd been busy.

In the far distance, the long mournful howl of a wolf drifted through the night, soon followed by several others. Nothing close enough to be concerning, but Joseph still used the sound as motivation to bring him out of his quiet trance and get to the simple work of stoking the fire. In a few moments he had it burning bright enough to scare away predators.

The summer night was still warm, and putting his back to the altar fire, Joseph found himself idly staring at Luz in the distance. For a time, he watched as the last sparks of orange firelight gradually winked out across the town. Meanwhile the moon rose, full and bright, casting a fine silver rain across the rolling hills.

Eventually Joseph yawned. The altar fire had mostly burned itself out, but he stoked the smaller fire one last time. Then, laying down, he pulled his cloak around him for a blanket and with a hundred worries still circling in his mind, he slowly tried to get to sleep.

Chapter 18
Brothers of Strife: Part 1

Four Days Later

Reuben stooped down beside Asher, his hand touching the paw print in the sandy streambed, a deep pressed oval pad with five razor tipped-toes. The sand of the dried-up stream bed easily crumbled inwards beneath his fingers, marring the otherwise perfect specimen. The loose soil, combined with the excellent condition of the track, meant it couldn't have been here long, a day at most.

His eyes darted a cubit to the side, easily spotting several familiar imprints, the long double ovals of sheep hooves. A half dozen pairs dotted the sand, and numerous other hoof prints were faintly visible on the firm packed soil of the stream bank. They'd brought the sheep across here yesterday afternoon. From the track's condition, he doubted it had been here then, which meant…

"Well, it's certainly a bear." Reuben dourly agreed with Asher's original assessment. "Probably came through last night."

Following the direction pointed by the claws, Reuben stepped up onto the bank, then knelt down on the plain, his eyes scanning the hard packed earth until…

There… his hand shot out, touching a second track, this one nearly invisible, just a crescent of five claw points etched in the dirt. He found one track, then a second further on and scowled. "Hmm, decently sized from the stride."

Reuben turned back to Asher, who nodded and pointed across the valley. "I think he came from those trees."

Reuben followed his brother's gesture to a stand of trees a half mile across the flat Dothan plain where the valley ascended into rugged hills. "That's reasonable," Reuben agreed. He stood to his full height, an irritating half-head shorter than the much younger Asher. "So, did he come back, or keep heading south?"

Asher shrugged, with an unconcerned, "I haven't seen any more tracks."

"That doesn't mean much," Reuben said absently. Turning, he looked toward the steep, tree-capped hill where he and his brothers had set up camp. They'd settled on the lower east slope with a good vantage across the Dothan valley, nearly to the city. But if the bear had continued this direction, the animal could easily have climbed up the opposite side of the hill without them ever knowing. It might still be lurking up in the trees right now, eying an early lunch of lamb. Alternatively, the creature could have simply cut back across the stream at another point and headed home. If it had, then they were worrying about nothing… but if not, they might very well have a fight on their hands this afternoon.

Asher was typically allergic to anything that even whiffed of extra work, but before he could make himself scarce, Reuben continued, "Follow the stream bed back around the hill." He pointed off to the southwest, his finger carving a line to the where the Hadera stream cut a steep ravine between their hill and a longer ridge. "Check for a return trail. I'll follow it back east, and keep an eye out along the way."

"Reuben," Asher grumbled, "I'm sure the bear already—"

"Just check," Reuben snapped. "And if you don't see anything, circle around the back and keep a weather eye on the hilltop. I'd like to know if there's a bear up in the trees waiting to chew our butts."

Asher clearly wasn't enthused at the prospect, but Reuben glared down his younger brother until Asher finally assented with a grumbled, "Alright."

Reuben waited until Asher had actually turned and started following the parched stream bed east before taking off in the opposite direction. A sullen scowl slipped onto his face. Reuben honestly didn't understand why everything had to be so difficult. Father had put *him* in charge, yet no one seemed to listen... at all.

Reuben followed the stream half a mile west across the flat plain. He found mainly thick patches of sheep prints, a few scattered antelope tracks and several pad prints that marked a passing wolf pack, but those were at least a week old. He also came across several spots where clumps of tall grass had been unnaturally smushed flat. However those were surrounded by faint sheep tracks and marked out by green stalks that had been distinctively nibbled down to blunt ends. Finally, coming parallel to their campsite, he turned south and made a beeline for where a thin tendril of smoke trailed skyward, a beacon to mark their presence.

Walking into camp, a sharp gust wafted the smoky scent of crisped meat to his nose. And Reuben scowled as his eyes canvased the grassy terrace to discover their encampment even *more* of a chaotic mess than earlier.

In the center, a sheep carcass sat spitted across the firepit, charred and barely recognizable after the left flank and ribs had been picked clean last night. Nearby, Gad busily picked blackened bits of meat from the roasted animal, alternately popping one into his mouth before tossing another to *Quppû,* the smallest of their three sheepdogs. In keeping with the theme of *No One Doing Their Respective Jobs,* the powerful white sheep dog had her haunches firmly planted on the ground, her head excitedly bobbing to catch the tasty morsels out of mid-air. Nearby, Simeon lazily lounged beneath a broad oak, doing absolutely nothing, and Naphtali sat near his bedroll absently carving a piece of wood. Meanwhile

Dan, Levi, and Judah squatted across the firepit from him in a tight cluster, their heads leaned over something.

"So, is anyone actually watching the flock?" Reuben loudly demanded as he stalked into camp.

There was a time when his strolling up in a foul mood would have had everyone scrambling. However, quite to Reuben's simmering fury, today his brothers barely budged. Naphtali at least looked up… for a moment, then his gaze went straight back to his carving.

"Don't worry about it," Simeon didn't even bother to stand. "I sent Issachar and Zebulun out to keep an eye on the sheep."

Reuben repressed the abrupt urge to pound Simeon's smug face. Perfect. *Stupid* and *Useless* were now in charge of the animals. "Well, in that case, you might be interested to know that Asher just found bear tracks north of here." Reuben pointed up the slope toward the tree-capped crest, "It may be up in the woods right now."

He'd expected that to, at minimum, elicit some concern, but instead Judah finally turned away from his huddle, exasperated. "Yeah, Reuben, we know, there's always something. But I'm sure they can manage the sheep for an hour." He added eagerly, "Check this out."

His lips drawn tight in frustration, Reuben paced over to find his other three brothers huddled around a small pair of scales. Several drawstring pouches of silver bits sat between them— their haul from yesterday afternoon.

Yesterday, Judah and Dan had taken a number of sheep up the valley into Dothan, to sell at market. They'd returned, their pouches brimming with silver, and one of their pack donkeys loaded down with fresh wine to boot. Reuben hadn't seen the final tally, but apparently the people of Dothan had bought them clean out. They'd even contracted for another dozen animals to be delivered this afternoon. That was, incidentally, how they'd justified slaughtering a ram last night for their own, slightly drunken, celebration feast.

They weren't supposed to be slaughtering animals from the herd like that, but realistically, Reuben had long since ceased to care. A few years ago, it might have bothered his conscience, but… that was before Dad had basically disowned him and…

Reuben caught his mind following down a familiar trail and consciously forced the infuriating thoughts away. Sometimes it could be a curse to have the time to dwell on things.

Instead he focused back on the silver at his feet. "How did we do yesterday?"

"Dan's still tallying it up," Levi said, watching as Dan carefully added silver bits to one side of the scales to balance out their *five sheep* weight on the other side.

"I'm sure we did well though," Judah added. "Dan and I both cut some excellent deals."

"Yeah," Dan agreed dryly, as the scales finally tipped into balance. "I almost felt bad about a few of those trades."

The four waited a moment as the scales bounced up then slightly down before leveling in balance. Dan then expertly scooped off the silver bits, pouring them into a large drawstring pouch that they'd been adding to for the last several weeks. Father's *cut* of the sales.

The weighted side of the scales plopped back to the dirt. "How many are still unaccounted for?"

"Just three," Dan said, taking off the *five sheep* weight, then putting on the *one sheep* weight and beginning the process anew.

Reuben blinked in disbelief, his eyes flashing to the ample bag of silver that still remained. "Only three?"

Judah grinned, "Told you we made some good deals."

They still had to split the remainder ten ways, but even so, Reuben found his mood suddenly much improved. He might actually come away from these last few weeks with something substantial to show for his efforts. It would certainly be better than the miserly pittance Father might distribute out to them when they made it back to camp.

Reuben nodded to last night's meal, still spitted over the warm coals a few paces away. "Are you accounting for that one too?" he asked.

"Nah," Dan shook his head dismissively, "we'll just say the bear got it. Easier to keep the stories segregated."

"And you're sure you've gotten your tally, right?"

Dan finished balancing the weight once again. "Don't worry about it," he said confidently. "I've been keeping totals on everything. Even if Father has dreamer boy look through the ledger, he won't find anything suspicious."

Reuben nodded, standing with the sudden feeling that this might turn out to be a good day after all. "Alright, you all finish up then head out to help graze the sheep."

Reuben turned to the others still sprawled around camp, "Gad, Naphtali, you two are with me. Let's go. And Simeon… try not to be completely useless." He knew from long experience that trying to *make* Simeon do anything would end in a fight. But mocking was nearly as effective.

Sure enough, Simeon stirred with a scowl. "Oh please, I do more than any two of you combined."

"Huh," Reuben shook his head, "could have fooled me."

He turned to go, then glanced back to the three, busy counting money. "Levi, when Asher shows back up, don't let him spend half the morning laying around either. He can work like everyone else. Gad, Naphtali, let's go."

The whole rest of the morning dissolved into a haze of bleating animals and rocky hillsides. Issachar and Zebulun had the animals grazing on a low rise just south of their camp and Reuben spread everyone out to keep a cordon around them. The sheep had started grazing early enough that some dew still lay on the grass, but by midmorning that was gone, the bronzed sky above burned with an unrelenting heat, and it was clear the animals were tiring.

Around noon, with the sun scorching everyone, Reuben finally decided to bring the sheep in. Calling to Levi and Issachar, the three of them slowly pushed the sheep off the hilltop and down into a wide, bowl-shaped depression beneath their campsite. There a grove of towering cedars rose skyward and the sheep clustered in the shade of the sprawling branches.

A half dozen, rough-hewn, cisterns sat at the low point of the depression funneling in water from the slope to store during the long dry spells of summer. Leaving the rest of his brothers to the arduous task of hauling up buckets of water for the thirsty sheep, Reuben trudged his way the short distance up the slope and back to camp.

Asher hadn't found any returning bear tracks earlier, which meant the animal was potentially still hiding in the trees above their camp. But after eyeing the forested hilltop all morning, Reuben had yet to see any signs of the bear. He was beginning to hope the creature had simply wandered by on its way to somewhere else. On his right, the Dothan Valley spread out below, a serene, dagger shaped plain flanked by the hilly wilderness to either side. Several miles up the broadening valley, the town of Dothan was barely visible, squatting on a low hilltop. A patchwork of fields below it were dotted with neat patches of wheat stubble, rows of vineyards and green clumpy orchards.

Reuben's eyes idly lingered on the city until... wait... was that?

He shaded his eyes with one hand, staring into the distance at a lone figure in a robe that flashed with bright blue and silver. The figure barely constituted a speck in the distance but, he watched for a moment... yeah, a speck that was bee-lining straight towards them. Reuben only knew one person with a robe those colors who'd be out here looking for them.

He stared another minute, his sharp eyes struggling to resolve the figure, then the frown crept back onto his face and turning away, Reuben swore.

Within a few short minutes the remainder of his brothers began trickling back into camp... and there were more curses.

Chapter 19
Brothers of Strife: Part 2

"Maybe we can haul off what's left of the carcass and bury it?" Naphtali pragmatically suggested, as one by one, the rest of them gathered and the speck slowly resolved itself into the clear image of Joseph.

Reuben glanced down at the rock-strewn hillside. Good idea, but not enough time, particularly in this soil. "You volunteering, Naph?" he asked dryly.

Before Naphtali could answer, Judah interrupted with a dismissive, "Just say the thing broke its leg and we had to put it down."

"Been there, said that… doesn't work," Dan answered with barely a pause. "It's the first thing the little spy will spill to Father. Then we're either lying, or we're letting the animals die. Either way *we're* the problem."

That dour synopsis elicited a pause from everyone. Reuben recalled last year when Joseph had told Father about Dan, Naphtali, Gad and Asher doing… basically what they were doing now, eating the flock and pocketing a share of the sales. They'd been dressed down by Father in front of everyone, and as the oldest of the four, Dan had taken the brunt of Father's sharply worded disappointment.

Reuben paced to the fire pit and back, uncertain, even as their time ran abruptly short. Joseph would be here in half an hour, and truthfully, the remains of last night's meal might just be the least of their issues. What if Joseph started snooping and discovered their *surplus* silver? The sum they'd amassed now made what Dan had skimmed last time look rather trifling. That could earn them a lot more than just a stern talking to from Father. And what happened when they went on to the next town and the brat started questioning why sheep prices were suddenly double what they'd been in Dothan?

Reuben froze with a mounting horror. What about the sheep they'd negotiated to sell today? Already he could see Joseph prying into every little detail and asking a dozen inconvenient questions. Forget the next city, what if he asked why prices in Dothan had doubled *overnight*? Sure they could lie, but Reuben had already witnessed how Father trusted his conceited little brother with anything involving numbers. He let loose a frustrated obscenity.

"Really, Reuben?" Simeon's thick baritone interrupted as he trudged up the hillside. "You gripe about my work, then leave Levi and I to finish watering the sheep?"

"Joseph's coming." Reuben just thumbed towards the gradually approaching figure on the horizon.

"Huh?"

If Simeon *did* have the wit to recognize the implications, he sure didn't show it. Instead, he calmly shaded his eyes, idly peering off into the distance a moment before frowning and mumbling a bemused, "Huh… what a surprise." Then added a dispassionate, "You know, we ought to end that little rat. Show him what all his dreams are worth."

Reuben rubbed his forehead, irate. No, they weren't stupid enough to start slaughtering their own family. "Can you just *try* to be serious for once, Simeon."

His eyes rested on Joseph a moment, lingering on the boy's robe… the beautiful one Father had gifted him. The one that should have — Reuben tried to halt the stinging thought that weaseled into his mind — the robe that should have been his.

And now Father's favorite intended to strut into camp like a peacock and spy over everyone's shoulder. It burned at Reuben like—

"What's wrong with you idiots?" Levi's cheerfully oblivious voice interrupted as he followed behind Simeon. "Somebody die and forget to tell me?"

Reuben was hardly in the mood to explain things… *again.* Simeon got the words in ahead of him with a deadpan, "No, worse actually." He pointed toward Joseph on the plain below, "Here comes the dreamer."

Levi stared a moment, one hand shading his eyes, then swore loudly, "*Aplu karkittu.*"

Son of a whore… Reuben mused glumly. That about summed it up. He enjoyed a flash of sick amusement as Levi's head turned first to the fire pit with its incriminating evidence… then to Dan, with their ill-gotten silver… then to the sheep beneath the cedars below that they'd be selling later today.

"*Šahātu, šahātu— ŠAHĀTU!*" Levi swore furiously. "I swear that rat has some magic to just show up when he does." He kicked a nearby stone, sending it skittering across the slope. That at least seemed to vent some of Levi's boiling anger, his next words were more businesslike, "Any ideas, Reuben?"

Simeon interrupted, his tone deadpan calculating. "Like I said, we should just end him. Problem solved."

There was a disturbingly icy dispassion to Simeon's casual suggestion that gave Reuben a heartbeat's pause… like… Simeon wasn't just kidding.

A surprised silence swept across the group at the suggestion, seriously made. A sharp breeze gusted up the hillside, briefly plastering Reuben's tunic to his chest, before dying into an abrupt, knife-edged stillness. Then, Zebulun spoke up, one hand unconsciously going to his recently broken nose with a dawning, "Yeah… why not?"

The group erupted into chaos. Reuben tried to restore reason, "Simeon, we're not going to kill—"

Issachar interrupted with an angry, "You know he deserves it!"

"You heard all his talk about being king over us!" Asher scowled.

"Probably make things better for everyone," Gad agreed.

Reuben couldn't believe this. Did they not hear what they were saying? Did no one remember the last time someone had agreed with one of Simeon's crazy ideas? They'd killed half a city and nearly gotten their entire family wiped out.

"We can't kill anyone!" Reuben had to shout to even be heard.

"Of course we can," Simeon insisted, boldly stepping right past Reuben into the middle of the group. "You think anyone's ever going to know?"

Simeon's eyes roved across them, sparkling with that effortless, captivating command that Reuben had always envied. "Come on, let's kill him and throw him into one of the pits." Simeon gestured to the cisterns at the base of the hill. "We can say that a vicious animal ate him. Then we'll see what becomes of his dreams!"

Reuben tried to speak up and take control of the spiraling situation, but the rest of them had already dissolved into frenetic arguments at the proposal. Reuben glowered at his next youngest brother who wore a smug, satisfied grin at having just stirred the pot to perfection. "Really, Simeon?" he demanded, furious. "How is this supposed to help anything?"

But no one seemed to hear him amid the bristling shouts. In the chaos, he saw Simeon gesture towards the cisterns at the base of the hill and head off to examine them, the others excitedly trailing in his wake.

Levi moved to follow last of all, then hesitated, seeing Reuben's stunned disbelief. "What's your problem, Reuben? You of all people know he deserves it."

The words stung Reuben like a wasp. Levi turned to go, but Reuben was still tempted to punch him. *And...* what was Levi's point? Did Reuben like Joseph? No. He despised the uppity little brat. Did it grate how Father had chosen Joseph over him? Obviously. Did he want to see the boy brought down a peg… or three? No question. But would murdering him be the answer?

Reuben didn't see how, even as he hurried to catch up with everyone else.

Father wasn't going to suddenly care about *him* just because Joseph was dead. It wouldn't even earn Reuben back his position as heir, the honor father had ripped away to give to his own favorite. He'd already seen Father's fury when Dad had discovered that he'd slept with… really, *been seduced by*, Bilhah last year. Reuben knew with bitter certainty that Father wasn't about to just forgive him for that.

So what was the point? Drench his hands in innocent blood and bring a curse down on himself? Even if Joseph was dead, Father would probably choose…

Reuben's thoughts crashed to a halt, his eyes focused on Simeon a dozen steps ahead, busily egging on the rest of them. A possibility smashed in Reuben's mind like a drumbeat.

Would Father choose Simeon as heir after Joseph?

Technically, Simeon was the next oldest, although admittedly, with his own share of problems, most notably that he was completely insane. But staring at his eager younger brother, Reuben couldn't escape an unnerving prickle that Father's favor was exactly what Simeon expected.

In a flash Reuben's resolve hardened. There was *no way.* Not for all the silver in Canaan would he let Simeon be in charge of anything. Joseph was arrogant, but Simeon would get them all killed, probably over something stupid to boot.

And in that instant, Reuben had an epiphany.

A dozen steps ahead, Simeon reached the cisterns at the base of the hill. He stooped down to peer inside as everyone gathered around. Reuben's gaze swept across his brothers. It was obvious Simeon had cinched his argument with several of them, Issachar nodded eagerly while Gad and Asher shared wolfish grins. But not everyone seemed happy with the arrangement, even if they didn't object. Dan and Judah still wore deeply uncomfortable expressions, while Naphtali hung back several steps, saying little.

Reuben shouldered his way into the group, taking advantage of Simeon being distracted… then he just asked the obvious question. "Simeon do you even hear what you're saying? You're talking about cold-blooded murder of our own brother. Do we really want that curse hanging around all our necks?"

Glancing around the circle, Reuben saw from the flutter of nervous expressions that he had finally struck a chord. They all knew that murdering family, especially unprovoked… was bad news, the sort that would haunt you for the rest of your life. That was just inviting God to punish you. It didn't even matter what god you worshiped — Father's God, Ba'al, Asherah, any of the Canaanite gods — everyone knew not to kill family.

Standing from where he'd stooped to look into the cistern, Simeon rolled his eyes… and utterly mis-stepped. "Seriously, Reuben, are you scared of a little curse?"

"No, I'm just not stupid," Reuben snarked. In a flash he could see even Levi's expression turn hesitant at Simeon's brashness. Maybe they *were* afraid, he mused… as they should be. "What if there was a better way?"

Judah frowned, "Such as?"

"Let's not kill him," Reuben said. "We can let nature take care the job for us." Catching their confusion, he strode over to the cistern, peering down into the dank chasm beneath. A long crack in the plaster lining ran down one side of the cistern, allowing the collected rainwater to quickly drain away. Stooping down, he reached a hand inside, and he felt none of the typical cool humidity to indicate there was anything more than parched dirt at the bottom. Standing, Reuben continued, "Why should we shed any blood? Let's just throw him into this empty cistern here in the wilderness. Then he'll die without our laying a hand on him."

Even Issachar and Zebulun nodded at that idea. It was a fine distinction, leaving someone to die versus killing them.

But an important one. Physically killing someone? There was no going back from that, no denying what had happened. Leaving them to die though… well they might survive, there was always a chance. If God wanted them to live then He could figure that out. And besides, if Joseph ended up in a hole and couldn't escape… that wasn't exactly their problem now was it?

Clearly there was enough of a difference to assuage everyone's conscience. Judah and Dan both seemed to like the idea. Simeon was the only one wearing a scowl, probably sad he didn't get to smash something today. "Are we agreed?" he asked.

A chorus of nods came back.

"Good," Reuben said, nodding back towards camp.

As everyone began to trickle away, Reuben paused a moment, once more kneeling to peer into the cistern and mentally gauge the depth. Throwing Joseph into the cistern wasn't the same as killing him… not at all really. Who knew, once they left, *anyone* might happen along and pull him out if they found him here.

Such as himself.

Depth was difficult to gauge, but he guessed the cistern was about ten cubits to the bottom, so he'd maybe want the long rope to be certain. That should be doable. He'd come back, pull Joseph out, make sure he got home safely, and permanently put paid to any of Simeon's ambitions. Perhaps, Reuben mused, it might help mend some fences between him and Father too. A ray of hope stabbed his chest at the prospect. Maybe, for a change, Father might just be proud of *him*.

Chapter 20
Tombs of the Living

Joseph wasn't certain if he was glad, disappointed, or just flat out irate at finding his brothers here. He'd wasted half a day scouring the familiar fields around Shechem before bumping into a farmer who'd informed him that they'd decamped and moved the flock to Dothan.

Despite that news meaning he had another long day's walk ahead of him, a part of him had been relieved to learn they had left. It meant one more day free from the misery that was their company. But, as Grandfather liked to say, all good things had to come to their end, and judging from the distant camp in the *usual place*, it seemed his time alone was concluding as well.

Traipsing through one of the innumerable olive orchards that quilted the flatlands of the Dothan valley, he diverted past the gnarled trunk of an obviously well pruned olive tree. Joseph could tell from a glance that it would be a good year for olives. The tree was loaded down with immature fruits like hundreds of small, green peas. And he'd seen dozens more just like it this morning. The figs and grapes around Shechem would struggle during particularly dry summers, but olives, especially older trees like this, could shrug off even the worst drought. He knew that all too well. About five years back, they'd seen no rain for months... and that autumn they'd eaten a *lot* of olives.

As he strode by, Joseph idly picked off one of the leaves, a stretched oval about the length of his little finger. He proceeded to stare at it a moment as he walked then tossed it aside before snatching a similar leaf off the next tree he passed and repeating the process. Anything to take his mind off having to deal with family.

Reaching the edge of the orchard, Joseph found a narrow footpath heading west up the valley. The wheat fields were ripe, a sea of chest high gold. Drawing near, he saw dozens of men working to bundle up sheafs of grain, even in the heat of the day. Ahead a single donkey cart pulled out of one field, laden down with wheat bundles and bound for the threshing floor. The farmer behind the reins slowed as he neared. His eyes lingered cautiously on Joseph's robe, a rich ornate blue with silver banding, the vibrant colors not yet bleached by the sun. "And who might you be, young sir?"

"One of the sons of Jacob," Joseph raised a hand in greeting. "Looking for my brothers."

"Ah," the man nodded, warming noticeably at the news, "they'll be up on that hill, there." He turned to point to the spot Joseph had already been angling for.

Before Joseph could even offer a polite thanks, the busy man flicked the reins, and the donkey lurched forward, leaving just a polite, "Safe travels."

Joseph watched him depart, then sighed and continued his trek, aiming towards a hill at southern edge of the valley.

He spent the next half hour watching the hill slowly swell up until it towered above him, all the while mentally rehearsing what he would say. Typically, whenever he showed up to help, Reuben or Simeon would brusquely point him towards the animals with a curt *Go try and be useful.* Really it just meant, *leave us alone.*

He'd been stranded out there for hours once, everyone else trickling back to camp until it was just him and the sheep with the sun pouring down on his head. Eventually he'd gone back to camp also, only to find everyone else enjoying a multi-hour break.

Well, until he'd showed up that was.

Then Levi had proceeded to light into him about *responsibility,* and how he should never have left the sheep all alone. There'd been much shouting as Levi roused the camp and the usual scowls from his brothers at having their day ruined. Somehow, by the time everyone stomped back to check on the animals, Joseph found himself heading straight back out with them and resentfully simmering over the insinuation that *he* was somehow to blame.

Today wouldn't end like that though. Joseph had made sure to wear his best robe, the one Father had given him. Usually that would have been a mistake, traipsing around out in the tall grass and chasing after sheep was never gentle on nice clothes. In fact, he'd actually spent most of the journey walking in just a work tunic, the original white linen long since faded to a dull grey from years of dirt and grim that never quite washed out. But when he'd entered the Dothan Valley, he'd stopped, changed into a nicer under tunic and put on his ornate robe.

Already, he'd resolved that if Reuben and Simeon tried to push him around, he'd give them a hard *No*. He wasn't just another herdsman that they could shove into the most menial role possible. He was here, first and foremost, on business from Father, and this robe was the proof, both to them and himself.

If nothing else, he intended to do an accounting of what had happened since they'd left Mamre, along with assessing the condition of the herd. Then, *maybe*, if they needed help, he could switch into work clothes and assist. But that was *not* why he was here. He repeated the mantra over and over to himself as he reached the base of the hill and looked up to see his brothers' camp on the eastern slope.

It was obvious that the sheep had grazed here. The hillside was littered with clumps of grass trimmed unnaturally short, and the thin, spindly stalks of weeds with all the leaves stripped away. Hiking his way up, Joseph wiped the sweat from his forehead, and made sure not to snag his tunic on the few scattered thistles, one of the things the sheep *wouldn't* eat.

He found his brothers camped in the shade of a tall oak. A pair of pack donkeys had been tied to a low branch, while the camp itself consisted of little more than a blackened firepit set in the center of several tents. Joseph counted all ten of them, either seated or sprawled out in a loose ring, hugging the patchy shade to avoid the midday heat. They must have sighted him from well off, but as he strode into camp, only Levi even bothered to glance up, raising a hand with an uninspired, "Joseph," in greeting. No one else even turned to face him.

That said, Joseph could guess why. The fire burned slowly now, just a single ashy log smoldering to keep the heat alive. But above it sat the blackened carcass of a roasted ram.

He knew what that meant.

By some strange fortune, his brothers had left an open spot for him in their loose circle. Usually, they would have shut him out and forced him to almost fight for a place. But today he found a seat in an empty patch of shade.

It might have been a sign of respect... except he was certain most of them would have died before showing him even the slightest courtesy, so...

Glancing around the circle, a nervous twinge prodded Joseph's gut at the almost tactile frost radiating off everyone. Enough to send a shiver down his spine despite the hot day.

"How's it been?"

There came a strained pause, until Levi finally spoke, his response an awkward beat late and strangely flat, "It's been fine."

Joseph nodded, one hand fidgeting with the fringe of his sleeve, while his eyes strayed to the roasted ram. He still had the pastries from four days earlier bundled in his pack, although he wasn't sure how to broach the topic amid the icy reception. "So uhhh... you've been eating well, I see?"

"Yeah," Issachar snapped harshly, "we have been."

Issachar abruptly pushed to his feet, and Joseph met his gaze, stiffening at the almost feral glint in his half-brother's eyes.

He expected Issachar to stalk off, but instead his brother came right toward him, fists balled in a hot fury. A jolt of panic surged in Joseph's arms, and he scrambled to his feet. His eyes swept across the rest of them, and in a surreal flash, saw a hungry pack of hyenas staring back.

Issachar came straight at him, and Joseph stepped back, bewildered, "Issachar what are you—"

Issachar swung.

Joseph stumbled back. His foot caught on a rock and he fell, sitting down hard. He looked up to see Issachar dive at him, and Joseph gasped as the older boy's full weight crushed down on his chest.

Nothing made any sense, but in the vacuum of reason, a part of Joseph's mind that had fought a hundred frantic scrambles instinctively took over.

Issachar straddled his chest and Joseph's elbows rose to protect his face, meeting a sharp pain as Issachar's fists wailed on him, once… again. Joseph grappled back, smacking the next wave of flailing punches away, then grabbing one of Issachar's arms by the elbow and pinning it against his brother's chest.

Joseph's other arm looped around his brother's torso, and more by instinct then thought, Joseph did the one thing that might save him, something they'd practiced hundreds of times in years past. With his crazed brother slightly off balance, he jerked Issachar close, and threw all his strength into a desperate roll.

The world flipped sideways, then back… suddenly Joseph sat on the chest of a surprised Issachar, and without an ounce of hesitation he smashed an elbow straight at his half-brother's face.

Once, and—

Crack!

Joseph felt more than heard as something inflexible struck his back, leaving a stripe of burning agony on his skin. "Get off him!" Zebulun roared.

Gasping, Joseph limply tumbled off Issachar. He dimly felt his cloak catch with a sharp *Riiiiip*. He couldn't get away though. He ended up on the ground, staring upwards in horror as Zebulun viscously whipped a staff right at his head.

Joseph caught the first blow on his elbows. Then Zebulun pulled back for another strike, and Joseph made a desperate lunge at his half-brother, grabbing his knees to unbalance him.

Something blunt smashed at Joseph's cheek, and his vision swam as Zebulun roared, "Let go!"

The staff smacked at him again, although without the murderous power of before. This close, Zebulun tried to kick at his chest, but with Joseph's arms death-gripped around his legs, all he did was lose his balance. Zebulun swore and helplessly toppled backwards, crashing to the grassy turf with an enraged, "Owww…!"

His mind a haze from the pains seared across his body, Joseph staggered as he tried to crawl on top of Zebulun to finish things—

Then a force like an angry bull slammed into his side, and Joseph's world twisted as he was nearly punted off Zebulun. Rolling over on the grass, he frantically gasped for breath. Everything strobed in agony — his head, back, arms — hurting so much tears of pain welled unbidden in his eyes.

Staring skyward, he dimly registered Simeon's figure towering above him, a cruel, murderous glint in his eyes. Joseph's mind blanked, another foot stabbed at his side, and he instinctively curled into a ball. More blows struck, and Joseph's world faded into a haze of pain.

Chapter 21
Falling

Joseph fell, the world plunging away beneath him until—*Smack.*

His body flooded with a new anguish as he crashed into something hard. He didn't move... couldn't move. All he felt was an awful throbbing in his head that came in slow, miserable pulses. The pain ebbed and surged like the sea in a storm, rising swells that crashed over him so he could barely think, before slowly dimming, offering a tantalizing relief, only to rush back with a splitting fury.

For a long time, he could barely breathe, his ribs stinging at each inhalation. He struggled to find the strength to even open his eyes, and one question bobbed in his mind like a leaf in a stream— *why?*

The thought came and went, sometimes rising to his awareness before being sucked back down beneath a river of jabbing stings and pounding aches that stubbornly refused to dim. It didn't make sense.... he hadn't done anything.

The surreal memory of the fight dominated his thoughts. Everyone had just... turned on him, in a heartbeat, and the burning hatred he'd glimpsed in Issachar's furious eyes was seared into his mind.

The unnerving image cut through his physical pain. He hadn't even recognized his brothers. He'd known them his whole life, for better or worse. Yet meeting them today, it was like the brothers he'd known had been stolen away, possessed by strange monsters with death in their eyes. His family was... gone.

And he hadn't a clue as to why?

His mind slipped back across everything. He had a blurred remembrance of being on the ground, then strong hands crushing his arms, hauling him upright, gasping. He could barely stand and Simeon loomed up before him with that terrifying mad grin. Asher shouted somewhere nearby, *Take the stupid coat!*

More voices crowded in, Issachar flashed into view, rubbing his jaw with the furious demand *Make him pay!*

A foot lashed at Joseph, searing his knee, then more hands grabbed at his robe. "No," he pleaded weakly, "don't…"

His arms were jerked back as his ornate robe was nearly torn off him with another painful *riiiiiip.*

He winced at the sound, all of Myrrha's intricate art ruined in an instant. Then more voices drowned out his thoughts, Gad calling out, "Come on, let's get rid of him!"

Zebulun's sneering agreement, "Yeah, what about all your dreams now?"

He was certain they were about to kill him, "Please," he pleaded, "I didn't—"

Something struck him in his kidneys and Joseph gasped at the new spike of pain. "Shut up." Asher's harsh voice intruded, physically shoving him ahead.

He'd stumbling forward, he didn't know how far, dazed, confused and bewildered. His legs more dragged than walked, each step a symphony of collective hurts, even as he desperately tried to reason with them, "Please don't. You don't have to—"

A dark hole loomed on the ground before him.

"Bye bye, little brother," Simeon's mocking tone spat behind him.

Then a push. And… falling.

Joseph lay there as his world slowly faded to blackness.

***

Joseph stirred awake. His face pressed against a soft patch of coolness. The chill pressed in around him, nipping at his extremities, and when he attempted to roll over, pain shot up his elbow, enough to jolt him back to awareness. His eyes popped open to find a sideways world of gloomy shadow.

Where was he?

His hand touched the cool floor, his fingers coming back dry and chalky. It might have been night, except for a ring of white brilliance that shone on the floor. He felt he ought to know what the ring meant, but his head throbbed and he couldn't seem to organize his thoughts through the drowsy haze.

It meant something though, he was certain.

He was…

His brothers!

The remembrance struck him like a bolt of lightning, memories rushing back. They'd thrown him and…

With a panicked urgency Joseph tried to sit up but gasped as sharp pains slashed at his ribs and arms. He made it halfway before his muscles nearly locked up and he slumped back to the dirt with an agonized, "Owwww."

For several moments he lay there, the only motion he could manage being to breathe deep and try to ignore the aches. Finally, after a few more abortive tries, he managed to find an angle where his arms didn't scream when they moved. With a tremendous effort, he slowly pushed himself up to sitting.

For a disoriented moment his eyes wandered the gloomy chamber, the dark shadows only barely held back by the blazing circle of white on the floor. Was it nighttime already or…

His gaze rose to a domed ceiling with a circular hole in the center, and Joseph winced at the stark brightness pouring through from above. It took a moment for his eyes to adjust, but finally he resolved a blue sky through the hole in the roof. A lone, puffy white cloud breezed its way past far above, and in an abrupt flash, Joseph understood… it wasn't nighttime at all. His brothers had… Joseph swallowed hard, they'd thrown him into one of the cisterns.

Ironically, the cisterns were how he'd known specifically where to search for them. They always camped here because of them. The holes shaped like giant clay jugs stored days' worth of water for the animals, even well into summer after the Hadera brook typically ran dry.

Blinking against the brilliance from above, Joseph focused back on his gloomy prison. The walls were a shadowed white plaster, marred only by a single long crack that stretched from the floor halfway to the curved roof. This was the cistern that leaked, wasn't it? The one that only ever filled after a big rain, then quickly ran dry. Father had spoken about fixing it on several occasions, but they'd never had the time, except in the rainy cold of winter when the cistern was perennially damp and too miserably chilly to bother with.

Swallowing back a parched dryness in his throat, Joseph suddenly wished someone had. He'd barely drunk anything on his morning walk here, and already his aching body craved water. Cistern water was foul, but with nothing at all… Joseph gulped back a sharp fear. Years ago, he'd witnessed a herdsman who'd gone too long without water. The man had stumbled into camp in a raving delirium. Would that happen to him too, trapped down here to inexorably lose his mind to a maddening thirst?

Surely it wouldn't come to that, Joseph tried to reassure himself. They wouldn't leave him here… would they?

Would they?

A part of him whispered an answer he was terrified to hear, and Joseph tensed as a spike of dread hammered straight to his heart.

They might.

Ignoring the slow pounding in his head, Joseph stumbled to his feet and gasped at the pain of moving. He limped his way to the nearest wall where his hand met the smooth, cool surface, no handholds. He gulped. No way out. Stumbling to the center he vainly tried to reach up, the bright light above contrasted with the darkness all around, giving the impression that his hand might be just at the edge. But nothing. He had to try, but deep down he knew he couldn't reach. These cisterns were two or three times as deep as he was tall. Even with a rope he'd need someone to pull him…

Up above he suddenly heard noises — shouts and whoops — the familiar voices of his brothers. They were close, driving the animals by the sound. With a mounting desperation and no idea what to do, Joseph gasped, "Help."

The first word came out little more than a faint croak. But wetting his lips, he managed a real shout, "HELP!"

The voices above stilled, only for an instant, but long enough to know they'd heard.

"SOMEBODY! PLEASE!"

Above the shouts resumed, he caught a muffle of Reuben's voice, "…keep those back…Levi split them off…"

Then Dan's "…need a dozen. That's fourteen… stop…"

Joseph shivered at the realization; they were going to leave him down here. This might be his last chance. "DAN!" He shouted as loud as he could. "NAPHTALI! PLEASE, I DIDN'T DO ANYTHING!"

…nothing.

"JUDAH! LEVI!" He tried to think of anyone else who might not completely hate him… at least, not enough to kill him.

Again the voices above hesitated, and Joseph frantically pleaded, "HELP! ANYBODY!"

The voices resumed, but then, miraculously, a head cut a shadow in the light above, and Reuben's harsh voice reverberated in the cistern, "Shut up, Joseph. You'll just make things worse."

"Reuben," Joseph had never been more relieved to see his brother's face, "Please just get me out. Whatever I did, we can—"

"I said shove it," Reuben snapped loudly. Then, abruptly lowered his volume to little above a whisper. "Look, just try not to make a fuss," Reuben insisted. "I'll figure out something. But try not to rile everyone up in the meantime."

Joseph gulped but nodded, "Alright… but I need water. It's completely dry down here."

Reuben hesitated a second, then another black shadow appeared in the opening next to his face, "Catch," Reuben called.

He tossed something down, but despite Joseph's best efforts he fumbled the bouncy leather pouch and it slumped to the floor… a waterskin, he realized. He could hear Reuben's frustrated sigh overhead, but grabbing the pouch, Joseph found the impact had left only had a small hole in the leather that he could easily pinch shut. "It's fine," Joseph called back, before adding, "Thank you."

Reuben's only answer was another sigh, as his head vanished from the cistern opening. Joseph stared after him a moment… *figure out something*… what did that mean?

Up above the shouts resumed, and Joseph's gaze turned to the slightly broken, squishy leather of the water pouch in his hands. It was only a quarter full, but some water was certainly better than the all-consuming thirst he'd been staring down. Holding the hole tight closed, he tilted it back and gulped down a deep draught, sputtering as some of the fluid went down his windpipe. Just the wetness on his tongue felt like a miracle unto itself, and no sooner had he swallowed his first gulp then he raised the pouch for another.

***

Standing near Levi, Judah watched as Reuben tossed a waterskin into the well then rose from his crouch at the cistern's mouth and turned to jog back towards them.

"You're giving him water now?" Levi asked, suspiciously

If the question did bother Reuben, he didn't show it. Instead, he shrugged. "Just trying to shut him up," Reuben said. "Unless you want to listen to his wailing all afternoon."

Judah caught an accusatory edge to the words, one that left them all uncomfortably silent. He swallowed back a sudden lump of shame that seemed stuck in his throat, his gaze falling to the dirt. Levi's expression remained a mask of stony indifference, but Judah noticed his brother stubbornly digging the end of his staff against a tuft of grass, like he was trying to uproot it. An old fidget, from when they'd been kids…

Judah finally spoke to dispel the awkwardness, "It was probably a good idea, Reuben."

The three focused back on the sheep, where the rest of their siblings had just finished splitting off twelve rams, corralled in by Simeon, Dan and Asher. Reuben spoke rapidly as they headed toward the small flock, "Levi, I'm going to go with you and Dan into town. I want to meet this buyer of yours."

Levi cocked his head quizzically, joking, "What, you don't think he's real?"

"Just want to know who we're doing business with. Who knows, you two might not be with us the next time we're here." He nodded as they approached the others, "Best take Simeon also."

Levi chuckled in dour amusement, then shouted, "You hear that, Simeon?"

The large man looked up in absent surprise, wearing an expression that said he'd just now been deeply engrossed in the act of standing around doing absolutely nothing. "Hear what?"

"You're coming with us."

Sure as the sun, Simeon's natural indignation traced his features in a frown, his voice a challenge, "Who said that?"

Judah saw Reuben roll his eyes, "Would you prefer to remain ignorant then?" Reuben swiped a weed with his staff, irate. "I mean, that's fine. Doesn't bother me if you have to come crawling to one of us to figure out who we do business with in Dothan."

Judah always found it deeply amusing how deftly Reuben played Simeon. As if on command, Simeon bristled, defensive, "Oh *that*. Well, of course I'm coming. Just waiting on you all to get going."

With that Simeon wheeled, his eyes searching the rest of them and picking out whoever was nearest. "Asher," he called, imperious, "you're with us too. Somebody has to watch the sheep while we're doing business."

Judah held back a snicker at Simeon's sudden change of heart, even as Reuben turned to him, "You're in charge while we're gone. Keep an eye on things and…" Reuben's voice trailed off, and he glanced back toward the cistern, with an empty-eyed stare. Finally he sighed and shook his head, "Try to get the camp in order. I want to leave first thing tomorrow."

It seemed like Reuben hovered on the cusp of saying more, but finally turned away, waving his staff for his own party. "Come on! Let's get to town."

Judah watched as they set off, herding the sheep before them. It was probably for the best that Simeon and Levi were all going, give them both a chance to cool off…

He paused, had that been Reuben's plan all along? Get the oldest most influential firebrands out of camp? Judah considered the possibility a moment before nodding to himself. Interesting.

He was just left with Zebulun, Issachar, Gad and Naphtali. Before the four could dream up any more crazy ideas, Judah strolled over, interrupting them. "Come on, let's get some food."

Throughout the whole saga, the roasted ram from last night had remained spitted over their fire pit, an unspoken witness. The fire had long since died back to the coals, leaving the meat cold, and now flies eagerly buzzed around the half-eaten carcass. Judah noticed several vultures silently soaring above also, their wings outstretched as they circled like a ring of black omens.

Digging into the ash to find the hot coals beneath, he added a lump of parched deadwood, coaxing the flame to life to help shoo away the bugs. He couldn't do anything to stop the vultures though. Obviously, they were eyeing the remains of last night's dinner, but his apprehensive gaze kept darting back to the cisterns at the base of the hill. If they left tomorrow, then the vultures would be down here in short order to feast on the remains of the ram, and then... he felt queasy considering what... *who* they might be eying next.

In short order, the low flame had warmed the meat and Judah found himself picking off choice bits from the ribs. But instead of bursting with tender, juicy flavor, the meat tasted like ash in his throat. He forced himself to eat, more out of habit than desire, but even food couldn't distract him. Soon Judah found himself glancing back down the hill, his eyes lingering on the cisterns for long heartbeats.

Chapter 22
Evil Deeds

Sitting with his back to the cistern wall, Joseph thirstily quaffed down a final gulp of Reubens' water, then held up the skin, trying to squeeze out every last drop. When nothing came out, he lowered the empty pouch, regarding it with frustration. Finally, his eyes unconsciously drifted back to the only thing of interest in his… his tomb. He found himself staring at the hole in the roof, the light so tantalizingly close, yet impossibly far. Things were not looking up.

Already he'd explored a hundred possibilities for escape in his head. The methods ranged from the mundane, *someone coming along to help,* to the genuinely fantastic, *a giant bird swooping down to rescue him.*

At its core though, short of a miracle, his problem boiled down to a very simple reality. He needed a rope… a rope and someone up top to hold it.

Neither of those things seemed terribly forthcoming.

At least the pain had dimmed to manageable aches. His ribs were a mass of bruises that stung to the touch, and a sharp burn simmered where he'd taken a staff across his back. The front of his elbows had been hammered raw and he could definitely feel a pigeon egg lump forming above his cheek. But so long as he didn't move it was… bearable.

But then what?

The thought circled like a vulture above, ever present. What was he supposed to do… wait around and pray someone took pity on him?

Yeah, Joseph thought with a bitter despondency. That strategy didn't instill him with much confidence, especially now that his brothers had made their feelings pretty obvious.

How was he supposed to get out of here? For a while he stared at the hole in the roof, the question hammering a drumbeat in his head. He doubted any of the locals from Dothan would happen along. Down in the fertile valley he might have clung to the hope that some farmer would reliably stumble upon him, but not here in the hilly wilderness. Nobody came up here except to graze animals.

So what to do? He had to get back to Benji and Myrrha and… and Dad. Joseph swallowed hard as he briefly glimpsed the awful alternative, just sitting here staring impotently up at the same hole in the ceiling until his eyes closed for the last time.

No. He shoved the thought from his mind, the dread bringing with it a crystal clarity. He had a whole life ahead of him that he had to get back to— and it couldn't end here.

He grabbed hold of the terrible urgency, finding the strength to finally push himself to his feet. *It could not… end… here…*

"Ahhhhh!"

Joseph took a step and gasped at a new pain, a sharp pinch between his ribs. Sliding back to the floor, the stabbing sensation remained until he leaned to the left, opening up his chest and finally bringing some relief. It vanished as abruptly as it had come, but the stinging memory lingered, and for a time, he didn't move…. was afraid to move.

Meanwhile, the tide of resolve seemed to crest then beat itself out in impotent waves until only a frigid, miserable despondency remained. He stared at the smooth, inescapable walls. What was he going to do?

Maybe Reuben did have a plan, he mused grimly. His last real hope. The depressing irony wasn't wasted on him. His brothers had tossed him in here, and now his only realistic option was to hope they decided to pull him out.

Still trying not to move, Joseph found his aimless gaze drawn to the oval patch of sunlight on the floor. He blinked, abruptly realizing it had moved from earlier.

When he'd first seen it, the sunbeam had been shining down near the center of the cistern, and now it nearly touched the wall to his right. For a while Joseph watched, falling into a distracted trance as he tried to spot the slow, incremental motion.

The oval patch of light had just reached the wall, the first tendrils crawling up the grey plaster that lined the cistern when a noise snapped Joseph back to reality. Voices. Overhead.

At first the voices were distant, familiar but indistinct, maybe Zebulun and Gad although he couldn't make out the words... then they abruptly fell silent. Joseph strained to hear, and caught the faint swish of feet in grass until...

"Joseph?" Gad's voice called, "You down there?"

No, he'd up and flown away, Joseph mused sourly. What sort of a question was that?

Given that he'd also caught Zebulun's voice earlier, he assumed they'd just come to mock him. His eyes couldn't help but drift toward the circular hole above, but he didn't answer.

"Joseph?" Gad's voice was insistent. Joseph might even have mistaken the tone for kindness. But after the awful looks in his brothers' eyes earlier, he knew better than to expect any empathy there.

He hoped they'd go away, but a moment later a face appeared overhead, silhouetted in the streaming sunlight. Gad's tone sharpened, "Hey, you still alive?"

"What do you think?" Joseph snapped venomously. Maybe they'd get bored and find something better to do than taunt him.

He assumed he'd succeeded. Gad's silhouette hung there an awkward second, then disappeared—

Until Joseph's eyes caught a flash of motion from the hole and something soft slapped at the dirt floor.

Joseph stared, wide-eyed, certain the light was tricking him… it was… a rope?

Gad's head reappeared, "Well, come on. You want out or what?"

Joseph blinked, stunned. What?

There must be some trick, right? Like Gad wanted to drop him when he was halfway up. Probably some sort of sick joke to it all. He'd been fooled that way enough times before to be wary.

Gad just cocked his head though, his voice urgent, "We don't have all day, Joseph."

"What's the catch?" Joseph demanded, disbelieving.

Gad let out a frustrated sigh, "Think of it as a favor, alright?"

That made, *absolutely* no sense. Joseph couldn't recall the last time Gad had done him anything that might *accidentally* have been construed as a favor, let alone intentionally. His gut insisted that something was wrong, but… the rope was right there, and Joseph desperately needed a way out.

What were the odds? He figured maybe one in ten that Gad *wasn't* messing with him. But that was still a chance, he realized with an icy urgency, a chance that might not come again.

Standing slowly, Joseph didn't feel the sharp pain from earlier come rushing back. He didn't know how he was supposed to climb ten cubits with his body a mass of aches, but, grabbing the rope tight, he found a loop tied at the bottom and threaded his foot through.

"Hang on," Gad said, his face disappearing overhead.

Joseph mentally braced himself for another cruel disappointment, waiting for the other end of the rope to slap him on the head as they tossed it in and chuckled at getting his hopes up.

But instead he nearly rocketed into the air, strong arms above hauling the rope upward. In a few heartbeats he was at eye level with the rocky cistern top, where he grabbed the lip with one hand. The rope tugged upwards again and

Joseph scrambled out of the nightmarish hole in the ground. His sore ribs stung where they rubbed against the rough stone, but even gasping at the sharp pain, he couldn't stop a wonderful surge of relief at just seeing the wide expanse of the sky overhead. "Thanks, Gad." Joseph pushed himself to standing and gratefully turned toward his half-brother, "I don't know—"

His voice abruptly trailed off and Joseph froze. Why was Issachar here?

Issachar sported a purpling lump above his cheek from earlier. Between his cruel grin and dagger honed glower, Joseph instantly realized something was very *very* wrong.

The worrying thought flashed through his mind, maybe he'd been safer down in the cistern.

***

Half an Hour Earlier

From Judah's perch on the hillside, he could watch Reuben's group escort the sheep towards Dothan. The journey to the city and back would take several hours, not to mention the business aspect of the trip. Down below, the valley fairly crawled with farmers and workers, many still enjoying long naps beneath olive trees to escape the blistering midafternoon heat.

That time might be nearly over though. Wispy clouds had crawled across the sky in the last hour, casting behemoth shadows across the valley. As Judah watched, he spotted several farmers slowly lumbering back to their labor in the fields.

Looking beyond his brothers, Judah's sharp eyes paused at a group winding their way through the valley, who clearly *weren't* farmers. They weren't from anywhere around here either, at least judging by the fact that they were leading trains of... *camels*?

Unusual.

His own family owned a few camels, Father had brought them from Harran, but few people here cared for them. In the ten years since they'd arrived in Canaan, their herd had dwindled to a shadow of its former size. For most tasks, they'd found it easier to simply use donkeys, everyone had them and understood how to work with them. They could be saddled with just a few blankets and some straps while camels required the most absurd scaffolding to even be rideable, not to mention the *quality* of said ride. Judah knew from firsthand experience that camels could be... awful creatures... at the best of times.

The only people who put up with the animals were the ones who had to, people from the desert, where water was scarce, the heat was miserable and only camels could endure.

Barely touching his food, Judah stared at the unusual procession for several moments. Now who exactly could that be?

Probably Ishmaelites, he guessed. Their caravans occasionally came through here. Judah had never dealt much with them though, and they possessed a mercilessly cutthroat reputation when it came to the art of trade. Most people avoided them entirely... if they could, which given the rarities the merchants carried, wasn't always possible.

As Judah watched the caravan slither its way westward, another thought popped, unbidden to his mind... a tiny spark that promised a fascinating possibility. He glanced down at the cistern once again, then back to the long strings of camels...

Where was their final destination?

He knew it must lie somewhere to the west. They would have come from across the Jordan, where the verdant fields gradually decayed into an endless scrubland. Once they reached the coast, Judah knew they would turn either north or south. If north, they'd go at least as far as Byblos. Some caravan masters journeyed all the way to Hattusha in the highlands. And if south, there was only really one possible destination... Egypt.

In either case, those were all a *long* ways away. Hattusha was further from Canaan than even Harran. And Egypt... well, it was safely walled off behind its own vast desert. Judah's eyes flicked back to his four remaining brothers around the fire. He caught Naphtali covertly peering down the hill, ostensibly looking at the flock below... except he was chewing his lip with a profoundly guilty expression. As Judah watched, his half-brother looked up, jumped slightly at realizing he was being observed, then turned back to his own meal, subdued.

Judah sighed then gazed back out at the approaching caravan. They all wanted quit of Joseph, certainly... but maybe that didn't require him to die and bring a curse on them all. Technically, he just needed to go away, far away. Maybe that could be arranged.

Judah allowed himself a calculating nod, perhaps it was good Reuben had thought to get Simeon and Levi out of camp for a few hours.

"Naph," Judah said abruptly, "who would you say that is?"

Naphtali looked up in surprise, following Judah's pointed gesture. He stared a moment. "Might be Ben-Tov's people," Naphtali finally assessed. "Hard to tell from here, but it looks like them. Five camel trains... that's about right." Naphtali looked back to Judah, "You looking to buy something? You know you'd get a better deal in Dothan or Luz."

"Looking to sell, actually." Judah said, for once grateful for all the odd trading lore that Naphtali seemed to soak up like parched ground.

"I hate to break it to you, Naphtali continued, rather matter-of-fact, "but I doubt they'll be interested in *more* animals, even for slaughter. If it is Ben-Tov, he'll have packed enough dried meat to keep them stocked for weeks."

"What about a slave?" Judah asked, thoughtfully.

Naphtali blinked, while Issachar, Zebulun and Gad all looked up, confused. After a bewildered moment, Issachar blankly asked, "What slave?"

"Joseph, you idiot." Judah nearly reached over to smack him, except his brother already had a nasty bruise from earlier.

"But I thought—"

"Yeah," Judah cut his little brother off. "Don't do that, it never ends well."

Judah's eyes fell to the rest of them, meeting a chorus of skeptical expressions. He pointed towards the snaking train of camels out on the plain, winding its way ever closer. "What if this is our chance to be rid of Joseph for good, except, nobody has to die."

Zebulun, shrugged with a defensive, "I thought that's what we were already doing."

Even as Zebulun spoke, Judah could glimpse on his face what a stinking lie they both knew that was. Yeah, sure, they weren't killing him, they were just leaving him in a cistern to die in three days... completely different. When Reuben had proposed the idea, it had seemed almost clever, but now that he considered actually carrying it out... well...

"Hear me out," Judah said. "What do we gain if we kill our brother and cover up his blood?"

His glance roved across them, and Judah could see the truth written on Gad and Naphtali's faces. They understood. They might not like Joseph but killing him left all of the feeling queasy. "Come, let's sell him to the Ishmaelites and not lay a hand on him," Judah proposed, "for he is our brother, our own flesh."

Judah could swear their eyes lit up like a row of torches at the idea. Naphtali gave an eager nod, while Gad thoughtfully rubbed his lip. Zebulun put his hands together and leaned in, fingers peaking in interest. Only Issachar frowned, his hand going to the recently acquired welt above his cheek. "But what if he comes back? What then?"

Gad chimed in, "He'd be a slave, it's not like he could just leave."

"Exactly," Naphtali said, "and besides, if that is Ben Tov, then they're going to Egypt, he won't be coming back. Just to get there, you're talking days of travel through the desert with bandits, heat, no real landmarks. Even if he escaped, he'd have to join one of the caravans to even get a guide back to Canaan."

"So we're agreed?" Judah said, before Issachar could interject any more of his stupid into the conversation. He looked around and saw nods from all corners.

"And we split whatever we get for him?" Zebulun asked.

"Well," Judah mused, joking, "as the person who came up with the idea, I think I'm entitled to—"

"Yes, we will," Naphtali interjected, with a sharp glower.

"Fine, even shares" Judah chuckled. "Naph, you're with me, let's go see if it really is Ben-Tov, and if we can strike a deal."

Chapter 23
Cruel Favors

"Oh, sure," Judah nodded. "He knows all about camels."

Turned out it had been Ben-Tov's caravan. It had taken some time, but Judah and Naphtali had finally tracked down the caravan master amid the lengthy camel trains. Now Judah busily reassured the older, heavyset man as he waited for the rest of his brothers to arrive. Bizarrely enough, Judah was actually boasting about his little brother for a rare turn.

Ben-Tov nodded with skeptical, penetrating eyes. "You *say* he knows about tending camels, but has he ever worked with them? I have not seen many here in Canaan."

"We're not actually from here," Naphtali interjected, with a chatty, almost conversational air. "Both of us," Naphtali gestured to himself and Judah, "grew up in Harran."

"Harran?" Ben-Tov frowned, stroking at his long, pointed beard. "But I thought you said your honored grandfather was Lord Isaac. I know he's lived here for many years."

"Grandfather has," Naphtali nodded. "But *our* father, Jacob lived in Harran for several decades. That's where our mother's side of the family is from. We left there…" Naphtali shrugged, trying to tally up the seasons, "I suppose about ten years back. Father acquired our camels there, and we haven't been able to get rid of them since. Like you said, no one here seems to understand how to work with them. We've taken to cutting our bulls and hoping the herd dies out eventually. Horrible creatures, honestly."

That finally elicited a chuckle from Ben-Tov, who might just have smiled beneath his thick, full-faced beard. "Indeed, they come with some unique challenges."

While Naphtali kept Ben-Tov occupied, Judah's eyes were drawn back towards their camp, wondering what was taking his brothers so long. He let out a sigh of relief when he saw that Gad had just emerged from around the side of the hill, with Issachar and Zebulun close behind, shoving Joseph ahead of them.

Judah turned back, only to see that Ben-Tov had followed his gaze, the older man's eyes gleaming with a canny, calculating spark.

Before Judah could say anything, Ben-Tov probed, "This brother of yours, what has you so eager to get rid of him?"

Naphtali began to speak but Judah interrupted, "Think of it as doing him a favor."

Ben-Tov's eyebrows arched, sarcastic, "Some favor, I'd say."

"Well, given that the alternative is him dead..." Judah trailed off with a shrug. He caught Naphtali squirming uncomfortably at the blunt admission. That said, he assumed a merchant like Ben-Tov would have an acutely tuned sense for lies. Trying to brush over the truth might just land them in a worse negotiating position.

"If you'd prefer," Judah added, "you can say that you're saving his life."

Ben-Tov chuckled at that, a deep-chested throaty laugh that left Judah uncertain if he'd said too much. After a moment, Ben-Tov shook his head, an amused gleam in his yes, like a joke only he could hear, "You boys are the same ones that killed Hamor? Am I right?"

Judah nodded, then added, "Look, you said you're heading to Egypt. You sell him to someone there and everyone's happy."

"Of course," Ben-Tov nodded, still obviously entertained, "*everyone*."

Turning, Judah saw the rest of his brothers were close. Zebulun had his arm looped through Joseph's, locking the boy's elbows behind him so he couldn't run. That didn't stop Joseph's furious eyes from lancing Judah, "What is this, Judah?"

Next to Zebulun, Issachar's expression twisted in a cold scowl, "You'd better shut up, Joseph," he snapped, balling a fist and angrily slugging Joseph straight in the gut.

Joseph doubled over, gasping and Judah winced, mentally cursing his little brother. That had probably just cost them a shekel… if not more. They'd brought Joseph wearing nothing but a wrapped loin cloth and already his ribs were darkening into a splotchy tapestry of bruises on clear display for Ben-Tov.

Next to him, as if on cue, Ben-Tov observed dryly, "I hope you haven't been mistreating him too harshly."

Naphtali interjected hurriedly, "Just a little roughed up, that's all. Nothing a few days won't fix."

"No broken bones?"

"He wouldn't be walking if there were."

Gad strolled up with a respectful bow to Ben-Tov, "Hello, sir. Here he is."

Ben-Tov returned a perfunctory nod, then strode over to examine the boy. Joseph coughed, wincing, his head hung low and hunched over as much as he could be with his arms pinned behind him.

Regarding him, Ben-Tov abruptly switched languages, speaking several throaty words that Judah couldn't follow at all. Whatever the man had been expecting, no one answered. Not wasting time, Ben-Tov then grabbed Joseph by the jaw jerking his head up. Judah caught confusion and a flicker of fear on his half-brother's face. Joseph tried to turn away but Ben-Tov held him in an unyielding grip. The trader pinched open his mouth, and examined him with an emotionless, calculating ease.

Judah couldn't escape a forlorn chill that scurried down his back as Ben-Tov suddenly jabbed a finger into one of the bruises on Joseph's chest. The boy groaned, writhing in pain but Zebulun held him firm. Ben-Tov finally withdrew his finger, only to immediately prod at the other side of Joseph's chest for another painful moment. Abruptly, Ben-Tov wheeled back toward Judah, leaving Joseph gasping.

The caravan master's eyes dulled with a cold detachment as he flatly declared, "I'll give you five shekels for him."

Judah nearly choked, at the scandalously low offer, but retained his composure. "I think thirty-five is a fair price."

In truth, thirty-five was a bit high. Thirty was reasonable. However, as Ben-Tov apparently had no shame, Judah didn't feel compelled to open with a fair offer either.

Naphtali added, "He's young, strong, healthy."

"Healthy might be an exaggeration," Ben-Tov noted dryly, nodding to the welts on Joseph's chest.

Judah scowled, his frustration building and starting to understand *exactly* why Ben-Tov's people had such a foul reputation. "Those will be gone in a week." Judah snapped, "nothing's broken."

"True," Ben-Tov nodded, half to himself. "I suppose ten might be reasonable."

"Thirty."

"Twelve."

Judah's scowl deepened, "He's a young man in his prime, most markets they'd start the bidding at twice that."

"And yet this is not *most markets,*" Ben-Tov observed, utterly dispassionate. "For all I know he might die next week after the way you lot have been treating him."

It pained Judah to go lower. A part of him cringed at being so obviously taken to the wash bucket, but… "Twenty-five," he more growled than said.

"Fifteen."

Judah pursed his lips, realizing what a snake he was truly dealing with. Unfortunately, Ben-Tov was right: this wasn't a typical market, they didn't have any other buyers and Ben-Tov seemed acutely determined to squeeze every last shekel out of them. "Twenty," Judah nearly spat, "Final offer."

"Eighteen." Ben-Tov calmly countered, one hand absently twisting the tip of his pointed beard.

Judah's eyes nearly popped out of his head. Twenty was a steal, and they all knew it. He glanced at Naphtali who shrugged, equally disgusted.

"You know what," Judah resolved not to get cheated and decided to take the risk of walking away, "Gad, throw him back in that hole, this isn't worth—"

"Twenty, then," Ben-Tov smoothly interrupted, his fingers abruptly ceasing to twist his beard tip. "You have a deal."

***

Joseph's chest stung like a dozen dagger wounds, and past the aching pain he only dimly registered Judah talking to the strange man with the pointed beard. The man had jabbed so hard that Joseph had thought he was trying to break a rib. And behind that sharp pain crouched an ominous unease at the cruel, inhuman way the stranger had looked him over… examined him.

He caught the strange man's words, "You have a deal." And looking up, he saw Judah and the man shaking on…?

The stranger spun away, shouting to his people, "Aamil! Gabir! Take him!"

What?

All Joseph's unease coalesced into boiling panic. Two lithe men with daggers strapped to their belts and razor tipped spears in their hands, abruptly broke off from the caravan and started towards him. In a flash the whole scene snapped into focus, they were trying to get rid of him. They were—

"JUDAH!" he shouted, writhing to escape Zebulun's vise grip until his arm sockets screamed. "You can't do this! You hear me! You can't—"

"Oh, shut up." Issachar pointedly turned, holding up a threatening fist.

Hands grabbed Joseph's arms, shoving him towards the plodding train of camels. One of the strange men welled up in front of him, grabbing his wrists and forcibly pressing them together. Joseph weakly tried to fight as the iron-gripped man wrapped a cord around them. It felt useless though, and before he could really grasp what was happening, his wrists were tightly bound, the man jerking him ahead.

Joseph's eyes flashed back to Judah… to all his brothers who were just standing there… watching. In the back of his mind the awful reality sank in like a long acacia thorn, they were selling him. They couldn't do that, it wasn't right, they…

The cord around his wrists jerked again, and Joseph stumbled forward a pace.

"Judah, please," Joseph looked at his brother, suddenly terrified.

Judah just stared back, unmoved.

"Judah… Naphtali… please, you don't have to—"

The guard's brusque voice sliced in, "Move it, kid. We're leaving."

The rope jerked again, and Joseph felt himself irresistibly pulled further from his brothers, his home, his life, his…

"JUDAH!" he shouted, frantic, angry, scared, "JUDAH, YOU CAN'T DO THIS!"

Joseph tried to dig in his heels, fight, anything to halt this nightmare, and ahead the caravan guard's expression narrowed to a scowl. "Come on."

"NO!" For a desperate instant Joseph didn't care, "You can't do this," he snarled, "I am Joseph ben Jacob, and you cannot just—"

The guard roughly jerked the rope, Joseph's feet slid on the soil and he pitched forward, tasting dirt.

Joseph's scattered aches lit up like a wildfire. For a moment he lay there groaning, tears brimming unbidden in his eyes.

"Get up," the guard's voice sounded above, more impatient than angry.

Joseph felt himself forcibly hauled upright by his wrists, and stumbled to catch his footing. While he'd been down, the guard had tied the end of the cord onto the nearest camel saddle. He rapped the creature on the rump with his spear haft, and with a renewed vigor, the animal thudded along, tugging Joseph behind.

A horrible terror gripped Joseph, this couldn't be happening, this couldn't be happening, this…

He looked back to see his brothers. Issachar and Zebulun had both turned to leave, walking back towards camp. Gad glanced away guiltily and Naphtali seemed to be pointedly looking anywhere *but* him. Only Judah met his eyes. A part of Joseph despaired, knowing there was no hope, but, "Judah," he pleaded, his eyes wet, "please, stop this. PLEASE!"

Nothing.

The camel relentlessly jerked him forward another stumbling step. Another pace further from home. The cold reality sank its teeth into him. People needed him at home. What about Myrrha, what about Father, what about — the thought struck Joseph like a sling stone to the gut —what about Benji?

At the thought of his little brother, Joseph suddenly dug in his heels, willing himself to pull the entire camel train to a stop. His eyes bored into Judah, who was still close enough to hear. "Don't hurt Benji," he begged, "please, whatever you do, don't hurt Benji…"

"I said, move!" the guard's harsh command intruded. The man's spear haft prodded Joseph forward. He nearly tripped, staggering a few paces to keep up with the camel train. And when he finally caught his balance and looked back… Judah had turned away… they all had.

It was just him now, Joseph realized with a mounting dread… just him… alone.

Chapter 24
Trekkers of the Wastes

Joseph stumbled along behind the camel for what seemed an eternity. Wearing just a loin wrap and a pair of thin sandals, he felt the sun mercilessly burn down on him while only the faintest puffs of a breeze provided any relief. As they reached the western edge of the Dothan Valley, sweat trickled down his face and into his eyes. With his hands tied, he was forced to lean down and wipe his forehead on his upper arm.

Already, every step brought a dull ache to his ribs and a sting in his left knee. And from his spot in the middle of the caravan, he could see the narrow, winding pass through the wilderness rising up before him.

With each breath, the dry air rasped in his throat until it was parched and cracked. Already, any memory of Reuben's waterskin had long vanished, leaving just a persistent, worsening thirst.

A dozen paces ahead, the caravan guard who'd tied him up walked next to one of the camels. Joseph hadn't wanted to speak to the man at all after his humiliating treatment earlier. But now his misery steadily trounced his pride, and wetting his lips Joseph finally called, "Water."

The man reacted like he hadn't heard, and after an awkward hesitance, Joseph called again, louder, "I need water."

The guard glanced back, wearing an indifferent frown, "You'll get water later."

Joseph stared, dumbfounded. In this brutal heat, water was the one thing that *no one* negotiated about. It was essential, it might taste of old leather or be pulled out of a murky well, but everyone understood that no water was a sure way to die. Finally, he insisted, "Please, I'm thirsty."

No answer. This time the guard didn't even look back.

A sudden wave of frustration swept Joseph, his tone turning bitter, "Are you trying to kill me?"

No response.

They walked on another dozen paces, the guard still in front, the words hanging between them. Finally the guard strolled up several animals ahead, and casually grabbed a water pouch strapped to the saddle of one camel. Joseph's mouth moistened at the tantalizing sight. Right there, in full view, the man tilted back the skin and took a long, deep draught. Then, he casually tied it back onto the camel and let the train tromp ahead. Falling back into his place, the man turned and flashed Joseph a smug, infuriating smile.

Joseph unconsciously flexed his wrists, vainly fighting against his binds as he glared venom at the snide man. He jerked at the rope holding him to the camel, his whole body tensing in fury. Oh yeah, it'd be really funny when he passed out from heat exhaustion. Unfortunately, he wouldn't be around to appreciate the joke.

For a moment, his eyes flashed to the heavily loaded beast, wondering if maybe he could spook the creature in his own quiet revenge. He didn't want to get dragged, but perhaps he could just disorder the caravan and get some rest from their relentless pace. Looking to ensure no one was watching, he delivered a swift kick to the camel's hind leg.

Instead of lurching forward though, the docile beast half turned its head toward him, resentful, and emitted a deep, belching grunt as it plodded on. An instant too late, Joseph realized he might have made a mistake. Up ahead, the guard turned, eyeing him suspiciously.

The guilty part inside him urged Joseph to look away, but instead he met the man's gaze, shrugging as though it was a mystery to him also. Thankfully, that seemed to do the trick, and after a moment the guard faced back ahead, allowing Joseph to breathe a sigh of relief. Slowly the tension drained from his body, leaving behind an elegant symphony of aches for him to stew in.

As they continued the long trek up into the hills, the sun began its slow march downward into the west. After another hour, Joseph struggled to walk in the oppressive heat, his mouth completely dry and his vision becoming hazy. To either side, fertile tree-capped hills rose up as they traipsed through the canyons of greenery. The ground was hard though, stones tearing at the soles of his sandals. Stepping on a loose rock, Joseph felt it shift and he stumbled, nearly turning his ankle.

The trees here were tall, groves of soaring oaks and cedars. They passed into a string of shadows and the pulsing heat of the sun vanished, replaced by a stiff breeze that finally provided him a chance to cool off. He wasn't sure he could go much further when, up ahead, he heard someone shout. The call repeated back down the camel trains as his mind struggled to decipher the words.

Abruptly, the camels ground to a halt with a chorus of throaty grunts, and Joseph staggered to a stop, nearly ready to collapse. For a moment, he dimly wondered if they were under attack, but the guard didn't break into a run, and soon Joseph slumped down on the turf, miserable beyond caring.

He absently stared at a knee-high tuft of emerald grass sprouting up two feet in front of him, his eyes defocused as he tried to ignore the painful rasp each breath brought to his throat. He only looked up at the sound of footsteps to find the guard approaching, a pouch hanging from one hand.

"Please," Joseph croaked, his eyes fixated on the waterskin, "I need…"

The guard glowered down on him, before dropping the skin into his lap. "Try not to guzzle it all at once," he snapped. "We move again soon."

Joseph barely heard the second part as he eagerly unstopped the waterskin. Lifting it to his lips, he feverishly gulped down the cool liquid—

That was a mistake. With his mouth turned to sand, he swallowed wrong, and immediately coughed half the water onto the dirt as he tried to clear his windpipe.

"Told you," the guard declared, shaking his head and pacing off.

Joseph didn't care. Coughing one last time, he took another smaller draught to wet his throat, and over the next few minutes, he managed to slosh down as much water as he could.

By the time the guard returned, Joseph felt… at least able to go on. He'd also had a few desperate moments to consider his situation. He caught one more mouthful before the man fairly tore the waterskin away with a gruff, "Get up."

"Listen," Joseph whispered, urgently, "I'm not supposed to be here. My father, Jacob ben Isaac, he's a very wealthy man. If you free me, I'm sure he'll reward you with—"

The man cut him off with a derisive chuckle, "Please, boy, you expect me to believe that?" His face split in a cruel grin. "Those were your brothers who sold you, right?" Joseph gulped, not answering.

The man just chuckled again, mocking his silence. "You think I'm that dumb? I'd wager your father hates you just as much as the rest of your family. I'm sure he'd be *real pleased* if I brought you back."

The words lit a fire in Joseph, "No, that's not— AHHHH."

His words died in gasps as the man struck his bruised ribs with the spear haft, then turned away with a smug, "Best keep that talk to yourself. Not everyone here is quite as *merciful* and *understanding* as me."

Joseph glared after the man as the caravan gradually lurched into motion, his teeth gritted in undiluted rage… yet utterly powerless.

Over the next few hours, they came down out of the rocky hills and into the verdant greenery of the coastlands. The sun rode ahead of them, a brilliant orb sinking toward the horizon. Finally, they left behind the towering oaks and dense thickets of the hill country and came to a place where scattered fields and pruned orchards dotted the land around a small village, Labaya.

With the light dying, Joseph guessed exactly where they would stop. Labaya wasn't walled, but the cluster of homes sat atop a gentle swell in the landscape. Down at the base stood a familiar well, one where Joseph and his brothers had halted to water their own animals on several occasions.

Slowly, the strung-out trains of animals circled up, and the men of the caravan launched into a bustle of activity. Joseph counted five different trains, each ten animals long, and all of them loaded down with sagging pouches, wooden chests and heavy sacks.

There must have been twenty men among the different trains, most toting spears and sporting stiff leather armor. Joseph could spot the stark difference between the guards and the camel drivers who wore much looser tunics and mostly tended the animals.

As everyone gathered, Joseph caught more than a few questioning eyes directed towards him, several men staring and pointing as they spoke among themselves. Amid the hail of looks, Joseph felt the painful lack of even a tunic for basic modesty. Standing in front of two dozen strange men with just a loincloth and his hands bound, he swallowed back the creeping desire to curl up somewhere and disappear.

After the day he'd had, Joseph genuinely could have slumped over next to the camel and passed out. Before he could though, he spotted the man from earlier, the unnerving one who'd just... the word left him feeling sick... *purchased* him. The man made a beeline for Joseph's particularly cruel guard. After a quick exchange of words, Joseph involuntarily tensed as the man stalked over, spear in hand.

"Get up, lazy," the guard snapped, and cracked him across the back with the blunt end of his spear before Joseph even had a chance.

The blow wasn't very hard, but Joseph hissed in pain as it inflamed a half dozen bruises from earlier. Wincing, he scrambling to his feet, only to find the guard still glowering at him. "If you travel with us, then you have to earn your keep," the man declared with his characteristic bluntness.

Right, Joseph thought bitterly, as though he'd *chosen* this. Maybe if he was particularly lazy, they'd drop him off somewhere. He was smart enough to keep that idea to himself though, and directed his resentful glare to the packed dirt at his feet.

"And speak when you're spoken too," the guard snapped, irate. He slapped him across the chest with the spear haft once again, leaving Joseph cringing.

"Understand?"

"Yes," Joseph gasped, fighting back his outrage at the man's casual cruelty.

"Good." The guard stepped close and leaned down to deftly untie his hands. "Ben-Tov wants you to check all the camels and refill the waterskins." The guard hesitated a second before adding a sharp, "Well, get to it."

Joseph massaged his sore wrists, nodding, and turning to go. But before he could take two steps, the man's spear haft swept down in front of him, blocking his way. "And what do you say when spoken too?" the guard demanded like an irate teacher.

Joseph very much wanted to pound the man's face in, but he forced out a mumbled, "Yes."

"Yes… who?"

Joseph blanked… he didn't know this guy's name; they'd met four hours ago and exchanged about twenty words. What did he…? Oh, Joseph's face flashed hot at the furious humiliation, and for a half second, he actually considered flat out running to get away from this nightmare. Unfortunately though, he knew he wouldn't get far in open daylight... probably not even out of camp.

Staring down the prospect of being beaten up for... the fourth time today, Joseph swallowed back his pride and spat out the words, "Yes... sir."

The guard flashed that infuriating smirk, then slowly, he raised his spear out of the way and gestured Joseph on.

At least refilling the waterskins was a task that Joseph could do well enough. The rest of the caravan had set about either unloading the camels for the night, cracking flint to spark a fire, or gathering deadwood. Weaving past them, Joseph limped his way down the lines of camels, collecting any empty skins.

The ache in his knee had worsened during the last part of their walk, and he really just wanted to sit down. However, a quick glance confirmed the guard's eyes were still honed on him, probably looking for any excuse to use his spear a bit more. Joseph sneered to himself, probably didn't get to use it much except on people who couldn't fight back.

Collecting four skins from the first camel train, he limped over to the well, and set to the mundane task of refilling them. With two people he could have bucketed up water and poured it in, but on his own, it was easier to just tie the existing skin cords onto the bucket frame and drop them both down.

Dunking the waterskins into the well one by one and waiting for them to fill, Joseph cast a quick glance back at the impromptu camp. The guard was still there... still watching. Joseph turned back to the well, but in his mind a single insistent thought hammered like a drum— he had to get away.

That seemed obvious enough. He couldn't leave Benji and Myrrha and Dad. Not like this.

But how was he supposed to get away?

Deciding that the first skin had filled for long enough, Joseph steadily hauled it up until the pouch peeked over the upper lip of the well. The flexible leather bag was about half full, which was the best he could reasonably expect with this method.

Tying on another skin, he let the bucket plunge back down and found himself absently staring off across the green plains of the coastlands amid a whirlwind of thoughts. He could run away tonight, the idea sparked in his mind… maybe…?

Joseph shook his head, pushing the possibility away. That would only work if they *didn't* watch him, and the chance of that was just about nil. He remembered back when father had bought Fannah and Remmi from a slave trader in Shechem. They were supposed to be maid servants for mother and Leah. The first thing Father had cautioned when they'd returned to camp, was to keep a weather eye on the two for the next few days.

Joseph even dimly remembered treating it a bit like a game to spy on them. Well, at least until he'd realized the two were just helping with chores. At the time he hadn't understood why they they'd seemed so upset. What was wrong? The girls got to be part of the camp just like everyone else.

Pulling up the bucket once again, Joseph sighed, pushing away the memories… well, now he understood. He could grasp in exquisitely painful detail why the girls had looked so miserable. And he could also assume that Ben-Tov's people would likewise be keeping a sharp eye on him… at least for tonight and tomorrow. Besides, even if he could have slipped off right now, he didn't even have a tunic, let alone food, or a weapon… how long would he last, traipsing half naked through the wilderness?

No, Joseph resolved, if he wanted to get back to Father, he couldn't just wait for a chance to run. He would need to be smart about his escape, which meant he had some planning to do.

It took about a half hour, constantly walking back and forth from the camels to the well, to refill all the waterskins.

By then the rest of the caravanners had bedded down the camels, started a small fire, and broken out food. Their meal looked to be a combination of dried meat and some barley they were busy boiling over the fire to make porridge. One of the locals had come out from the village earlier to barter with the leader, who Joseph had now heard multiple people call Ben-Tov. They'd haggled several minutes before the man turned away in evident disgust.

Joseph had stared after him, wondering at his chances of getting to the man and explaining who he was. His brothers had been to Labaya many times before. Back when they'd camped near Shechem they'd grazed near the village often enough. That said, they'd never been particularly welcomed by the villagers, and Joseph himself hadn't been here in years. Still, perhaps if the villager saw him…

But the man had turned to leave without even a glance Joseph's direction. The more he considered it, the less Joseph was certain they'd even remember him, let alone be willing to purchase him from Ben-Tov on just his own word.

Maybe it didn't matter. While he'd been filling waterskins he'd worked out a better plan anyway. The reality was that he'd likely only get one chance to escape, probably in a few days when everyone got tired of watching him like a hawk.

Perhaps there would come some moment when either everyone was asleep, or some unexpected happening threw the caravan into chaos. In either case, if he tried to run now, he'd just make them all the more alert going forward. Besides, at this exact moment, he wasn't entirely sure he could run, even if given the chance. He was hungry, tired, everything hurt and he'd just walked most of the day.

Unfortunately, despite how deeply the decision stung, that meant that tonight and tomorrow he had to do exactly what Ben-Tov and his people said. If he ever wanted them to let their guard down, he didn't really have a choice but to play the part.

While Joseph had worked, the sun had faded to orange embers on the horizon. Turning to the campfire, he hesitated, uncertain about being near any of these people… except that he was really hungry.

Before Joseph could make up his mind though, he saw Ben-Tov of all people beelining straight towards him. "You, boy," the caravan master snapped, stalking up with a scowl, that left Joseph wanting to shy away, "get some clothes on."

Joseph blinked as the man unceremoniously tossed a wad of clothing at him. He caught it to his chest, staring a moment in shocked bewilderment, even as Ben-Tov added, "Get some food." He thumbed toward the fire. "As long as you work you can eat. When you're done, find Gabir." Ben-Tov pointed across the fire to the guard that Joseph had already learned to loathe. "He'll get you something to keep warm tonight. You do what he says, and this doesn't have to be hard."

Joseph cringed internally at the prospect of being under Gabir's thumb for even another hour, but Ben-Tov seemed earnest enough, and Joseph nodded a hesitant, "Okay."

Partly out of habit, he looked up when he spoke, looking Ben-Tov straight in the eye. Maybe it was a trick of the gathering dusk, but he could swear the man with the pointed beard regarded him with an indulgent, almost amused air… like Ben-Tov already guessed everything Joseph was plotting.

Joseph quickly looked away, unnerved.

He couldn't know, right?

For maybe a second too long, Ben-Tov didn't seem to move at all. Finally, he snapped in his gruff voice, "I'll want that tunic back, so try not to ruin it."

Joseph could swear the man was about to say more, but an ill-timed burst of raucous laughter from the fire behind drew the caravan master's attention. He made to leave, then glanced back at Joseph, "Get some food, boy."

Then Ben-Tov was gone, stalking off amid the bustle of people.

Joseph stared after him though… did he know? Was it that obvious that he intended to run? For a moment he'd gotten the strangest sense that, not only did Ben-Tov know exactly what he was planning, but the man also *knew* that Joseph *knew* that he *knew*. In which case they were all just players in some elaborate game where the prize was… Joseph swallowed hard… his life? At least his future.

Joseph bit his lip as the grim possibility sank in. He was playing for all the pebbles now, wasn't he.

The thought harried at him a second, until his stomach jolted him back to reality with an insistent gurgle. Right, he mused, if he intended to win, he'd probably better start with a good meal… and go from there.

Chapter 25
The Coastlands

The next morning the first tendrils of dawn had barely brushed the eastern horizon when a foot nudged Joseph's back, poking through his hazy sleep.

It nudged again… harder.

"Go away," he mumbled, trying to roll over beneath the blanket.

The act of moving jolted him awake as seemingly every muscle in his body lit up in pain, and he gave a low groan, "Owww…"

"Oh, stop your complaining," a gruff, unfamiliar voice spoke overhead.

Joseph tried to move his arms… except he was in some sort of nightmare where he couldn't and…

His eyes snapped open, his confused mind taking a moment to register that his wrists were bound. He looked up, only to see a hulking man with a thick beard and a spear in hand towering above. Joseph blinked, trying to piece together where he was, until the memories cycloned back in a rush — the cistern, his brothers selling him, and the murderous trek yesterday.

The awful realization settled like a rock in the pit of his stomach. But looming overhead him, the caravan guard — Gabir, he remembered — seemed completely disinterested.

"Get up," the man said. "We're leaving soon. Trust me, you'd rather walk than be dragged."

The man turned and strode away. Joseph wasn't entirely sure if he *would* prefer walking. Just trying to push himself up to sitting, every muscle in his body stung with a razor-edged stiffness.

It took him several moments just to wobble to his feet, even as all around him the caravan bustled with frenetic activity in the early light. Men hastily loaded up the camels with sacks and boxes. They then coaxed the beasts up to their feet, checking harnesses and bundling up their belongings from the night before. Gabir had tied his wrists and roped him to one of the camel trains the prior evening, so Joseph finally found himself *forced* to move as one by one the workmen checked their way down the train of animals.

With little else he could do, Joseph watched numbly as the men packed up their spartan encampment, and within minutes they were walking once more. The worst pains from yesterday had faded, but only to be replaced by persistent, throbbing aches as his muscles cried out for relief.

The surges of dull pain as he stumbled along lent Joseph's thought a sharp clarity. A clarity that left him stewing in mounting frustration as the sun rose to a burning orb on the horizon behind them. He shouldn't be here, the thought stung him nearly to the point of rage. How could his brothers have done this? They… did Judah even realize what they'd done? How they'd—

"Boy?"

Joseph jolted out of his darkening mood at the interruption. Gabir was watching him, he realized with a gulp. The guard had fallen back almost alongside, the bearded man regarding him from beneath thick, unkept eyebrows.

Joseph assumed the cruel man meant to torment him again this morning. But after a moment of nerve-wracking silence, the guard finally spoke, with a far more mundane question, "What's your name?"

Joseph blinked, caught off guard, "Uhhh… Joseph, son of Jacob."

Gabir nodded, "You speak any Egyptian?"

"Egyptian?" Joseph asked, suddenly wary, "Why would I—"

"I asked you a question." Gabir cut him off with a threatening edge.

Joseph hesitated. Had Judah told them about Scribe Tefibi teaching him? Did they expect him to know Egyptian? He knew a little, mainly numerals… and of course all the obscenities… Tefibi had never been the most restrained man. But did that have implications for what happened to him?

The whirl of questions whipped around him for an instant before Joseph came to a snap judgement— better they didn't know anything yet.

"I uhh, don't really speak Egyptian."

"Hmm," Gabir remarked slowly, eying Joseph as though he suspected a lie. "Well, in that case, I suppose there's no time like the present to begin learning. I guess we can start with the basics—"

"But why would I need…" Joseph's voice trailed off as he realized he'd interrupted the guard. He cringed, anticipating the spear blow he expect to follow.

This time though, Gabir walked alongside him a moment, letting the painful silence hang in the air. And glancing up, Joseph caught a smirk curling at his lips. "Where do you think we're heading, boy?" Gabir spoke, mocking, and almost wistful at the same instant. "Egypt. Wonderful place. You might like it." Gabir paused, thoughtfully, then added, "Well, I like it— excellent food, lots of fish, date bread and enough beer to drink ten men under the table. Granted, everyone's a bit obsessed with death, and I suppose the people can be a bit snobbish, but they get over it if you have money. And the women…" Gabir let the words trail off, his grin widening.

Finally he gave a nostalgic sigh, adding, "Don't worry, though, I'm sure a lad like you will get a chance to find out *aaaaall* about Egypt. But before that, you need to learn how to talk like the locals, Ben-Tov's orders. They look down on speaking Akkadian there. And I'm sure you'd much prefer to end up in a respectable house in Avaris."

"Now, the first thing you…"

Joseph didn't hear the rest. His mind ground to a horrified halt. No, they couldn't… that was so far away. Basically the end of the world. In a flash he understood how Myrrha must have felt all these years, so impossibly far from home that there was no chance of ever returning.

A slow wave of anger boiled up inside as well. Had Judah known? Of course he'd known, Joseph thought bitterly, probably planned this. Fury surged in his chest as the reality sank in, they'd made sure he would never get home and—

"Owww!"

Joseph's head snapped up, his ribs stinging, only to see Gabir staring at him, suddenly much less jovial than a moment earlier, "You hear anything I just said?"

"I…"

"You'd better start paying attention," the guard warned. "Or else this is going to be a *very* long trip — for one of us. Now, we call it Egypt, but the locals call it Kemet, means The Black Land, it's named after the soil. Not like this dirt," he scuffed one foot at a patch of bare, tan soil. "It's dark and rich… you'll see when we get there."

"Now say it, *Kemet*."

Joseph gave a tentative attempt, "Ka-met."

The man shook his head. "No, smoother, all one word and drop the *ahh* sound." He enunciated again, slow and precise, "K-ehhh-met."

***

The next three days blurred into a haze of walking and work with every spare second crammed to the seams with Egyptian lessons. Gabir seemed to warm slightly after the first day… or at least Joseph thought so. Regardless, they fell into a familiar pattern, and so long as he behaved, Gabir consented to untie his hands while they traveled. It was only so that Joseph could take turns with one of the workmen leading the camel train, but to Joseph, just being able to swing his arms was a tremendous blessing. That, and it was a relief not having to stumble along at a camels pace to avoid being dragged behind.

As far as teachers went, Gabir was… not awful. Joseph gathered he was illiterate, but he had clearly spent plenty of time in Egypt and seemed to enjoy having someone who was forced to listen to his lessons. They were hardly groundbreaking, just basics such as…

"Say it with me" Gabir tried again "*rn-ee*."

"*Rn-ee,*" Joseph mimicked. "*Rn-ee, Joseph.*" He added, "My name is Joseph."

He'd apparently done a decent enough job and the guard nodded. "Good, just remember that *my* and *name* are reversed and combined into a single word."

"Right," Joseph nodded, "So it's literally *name, my, Joseph.*"

"Correct, a lot of the language is like that, very…" he paused, searching for the correct term.

"Systematic," Joseph suggested, mostly out habit.

"Yeah…" Gabir nodded, seeming almost pleased at the word, "Systematic."

The first day they traveled all the way to the Great Sea, that endless expanse of cerulean blue that stretched beyond the western horizon. The land transformed from a rugged mix of tree-capped hills and vales covered with patches of tall grass, into a verdant paradise of greenery. They went by several small villages surrounded by orchards of proud date palms and wide vineyards. As they passed close, Joseph could see the grapes, thick clusters of hard little green balls, just beginning to redden into a dark crimson.

From the coast they followed the road south, pausing for the night almost within sight of the shore. Unfortunately though, even if Gabir trusted him during the day, come nightfall, Joseph was deeply discouraged to find that the man still bound his wrists and roped him to one of the camel saddles.

That was… a problem. That night Joseph intended to pretend to doze off, but actually stay awake and experiment with unbinding the knot. Instead his tired body betrayed him and he fell straight asleep, plunging into a deep slumber.

The next day they passed Jaffa, a small, walled port town, with several tubby ships docked in its harbor. They reminded Joseph of giant round barrels, cut in half and set afloat with sails. His family didn't often come this far west. They kept to the hill country with all its scattered cities and villages. He'd only been to the Great Sea a handful of times. Walking along the coast for a whole day, he saw the landscape transform from orchards, to sandy beeches, to wild palm groves, then to vineyards and so on… yet the sea remained, unchanged.

A part of him was astonished at just how vast it was, like he could walk the shore forever and still not find an end. Several times he caught himself gazing out across the blue when it came into view, sometimes staring at ships, but often just imagining what was out there. Kaphtor and Attica, he knew were somewhere across the sea, but he'd rarely considered what that actually meant, how genuinely far away they were.

He intended to work out an escape plan that day. But between Gabir's endless lessons, leading the camels, plus helping unload and tend to them that evening, *and* refilling all the waterskins, Joseph found the day somehow vanished before him. It wasn't until he sat down to eat dinner that he realized he hadn't done much planning at all.

That evening he considered perhaps trying to cut his bonds in the night and run off. But he'd need a knife… didn't know who he'd steal that off… or how. Maybe a sharp rock instead, he mused, but glancing around, he didn't see any of those either.

They were common enough in the hills, where most of the stones were the familiar white, jagged limestone. When he started carefully eying the ground though, he was surprised to realize there weren't many rocks here at all. The ones he did see were worn and rounded. There was probably a metaphor in all that about the difficulty of life in the hills versus along the shore. But mainly Joseph found himself silently cursing his ill fate as the darkness gathered and Gabir tied him to a camel for the night.

He might stumble over a rock while walking. But with Gabir hovering near him like a hawk, he didn't see how he could inconspicuously pick up a stone… or hide it for that matter, since he only had a tunic and his hands.

He tried not to worry too much, right now they were still coming closer to home. He'd spent days walking north to meet his brothers, and now they were moving back south down the coast. As the camp slowly drifted to sleep that evening, he fumbled for a while, trying to untie the rope that knotted him to the camel harness. However, in the chilled darkness with his hands tied tight, he couldn't get much purchase. The need for silence killed any dreams of working quickly. His fingers fumbled for several minutes, feeling out the tightly bound strands, but without making any noticeable progress. Joseph quietly kept at it, with an urgency born of panic. But eventually, after a tense eternity, his fingers came away from the saddle, sore, exhausted, and unsuccessful.

Sourly admitting defeat, Joseph settled back on the hard dirt. Probably wouldn't have mattered anyway, he thought glumly, pulling his blanket tightly around him his as best he could. He'd still be running through the night, his hands tied, with no food and no water. Probably not a recipe for success.

He lay there a moment, the discouraging failure beginning to sink in, then, staring at the stars he whispered a quiet prayer.

He wasn't certain that God would hear him if he didn't have anything to sacrifice, but his desperation had been building for three days now, and he felt he had to try. "God," he whispered, not sure what to say, "Please… save me. I just want to go home."

A part of him still clung to the hope that a miracle might happen. That God would tear asunder the sky, burn down among them, and save him. Put his life back on the path he was meant for. Anything but… this.

But as he stared upward at the ocean of stars above…nothing happened, and eventually, Joseph drifted off into the world of dreams.

Chapter 26
Ashkelon

The next day continued much the same— more lessons in Egyptian, more camels, more walking. But as the sun began its daily plunge into the Great Sea, the landscape gradually changed. Wild trees and brush gave way to acres of precisely ordered fields, orchards, and vineyards marked out by squat stone walls.

The barley fields were carpeted with fresh stubble and in other fields workers scythed and bundled tall sheaves of wheat and oats. Vineyards spread up hillsides in neat rows, their trellises mounded with leaves, while orchards of olives, pomegranates, and date palms filled in between. The shoreline transformed from a long band of golden sand into one pockmarked by wide, ankle-deep salt pools, where barefoot men raked the brine water and condensed out valuable, white salt flakes.

Slowly a sprawling city came into view to the south, and cresting a small rise, Joseph missed a step at his first real look. Tall white walls ringed a hill by the sea, and from within, tall apartments and towers jutted skywards. Delicate trails of smoke danced above the hill, while villages and farms sprawled at the base. Further out to sea, Joseph saw several ships clearly making for the city, and at the mouth of the harbor, a single fat ship had just edged its way into view.

"Is that…"

"Ashkelon," Gabir nodded, momentarily forgetting his lessons at the marvelous sight. "You ever been?"

Joseph shook his head. He knew Grandfather Isaac had lived near here back when Father had been young. But from Father's stories they hadn't gotten along well with the locals and eventually had been pushed back into the hills.

"Well, don't worry," Gabir said, "you'll get to see it up close tomorrow. Maybe closer than you'd like too."

That night they camped in the shadow of the massive city walls, and the next morning Joseph awoke to a mad bustle as Ben-Tov strolled like a whirlwind through the camp.

"Get the animals up! Barak, Caleb, stop lazing around! Gates open at sunrise, and I'll not be late to market!"

Groaning at the early hour, Joseph nonetheless rose. Gabir was nearby to free his hands, and stumbling around with a lingering grogginess, Joseph fell to the familiar routine of his morning chores. In short order he'd helped pack their gear and begun to saddle the camels to move.

Apparently they weren't taking all the animals though. Stalking past Joseph, Ben-Tov pointed to the first camel in the train, "We'll just need that one for today."

Joseph untied the sluggish camel from the rest of the train, and set to work loading it down with the bags and chests. Soon enough the creature was ready, but didn't seem in any hurry to leave. "Come on," he growled, digging in his heels to try and drag the stubborn beast a step forward. For its part, the camel just stared at him with a lazy indifference.

Meanwhile, a scuffle developed among the guards. Joseph looked over to see something of a shouting match, apparently over who would get to head into the city and who would be stuck watching the animals. Eventually Gabir's group must have won out, because the man strolled over with a curt, "Follow me, boy, we're going."

Trudging up a steep hill, they reached the main gate just as the sun finally crested above the eastern hills. The towering walls illuminated in a blaze of white, and up close, Joseph finally got a feel for their astonishing scale. He'd thought Kiraith Arba impressive, with its low ramparts and vaulted gate, but the walls of Ashkelon utterly dwarfed it. They must have risen twenty… thirty cubits into the air, and as he crowded in with so many others through the city gate, Joseph craned his neck back to glimpse the parapet.

The gate itself was another marvel, vaulted like at Kiraith Arba, yet tremendously long. It could almost have been an extended cave they walked through. He marveled, were the walls really that thick? Ten, twenty, thirty paces. He'd seen the city from the outside as they approached and the walls ran a vast circuit at least a mile long, perhaps more. He couldn't fathom the amount of work required to cut and dress that much stone.

Everything about the city made home feel small. Breaking into the daylight on the other side, Joseph was confronted by an endless ocean of faces. People and animals crowded the streets, bustling past with barely a second glance, while shopkeepers shouted over one another at their storefronts.

"Jugs, pots, urns, amphoras! Best prices in town!"

"Fresh bread, straight out of—"

"Copper, silver and bronze work! Whatever you need! Anklets, necklaces, bracelets and torques!"

Amid the hurricane of noise, Joseph distantly caught the sharp clangs of smiths hammering metal, while to his left a potter molded out a jug at his wheel, and a pushy woman shoved linen tunics at passers-by. The town seethed with utter chaos and…

This was his chance, Joseph realized with a jolt.

If he could escape here, no one would find him, no one would even know who he was. If he hadn't been leading one train of camels, he might have ducked off into the crowd right then. Now that he considered it, that might be part of why Gabir had insisted on him taking the camel's halter in the first place. But when they got to the market, there would be a pause, and so long as he was quick about it…

Their group made it down the first street into Ashkelon, and as they moved further from the gate, Joseph found that the most aggressively pushy of the merchants were left behind. The buildings crowded in around him though. They soared two or three stories tall, clad in white plastered adobe and lending the city a claustrophobic air. All he could do was follow the camels in front of him, and after several seemingly nonsensical twists and turns, Joseph was completely lost.

Burrowing deeper into the labyrinthine city, the constant noise of the town pressed in on him. Hundreds of people crowded around in a mind-numbing blaze of colorful clothes, clogging the streets and only grudgingly making way for their troop. Meanwhile, a breath of wind swirled the stale city air and he caught a pungent whiff of fish. It lay half buried beneath a dozen other scents that left his nose reeling, the concentrated odors of animals, urine, incense, roasting meat, fresh bread, oil, oven smoke and… a whiff of what smelled like rose perfume?

They took another abrupt turn, and Joseph nearly bumped into a girl. She was only a couple of years older than him, short with brown hair and a lightly tanned complexion that said she'd spent plenty of years indoors. But while the other women he'd seen in Ashkelon were clothed in vibrant reds, and yellows, she wore only a threadbare tunic, the linen dirtied to a puke brown. She looked up at him, fear in her eyes as she mumbled a hasty, "I'm sorry," in what he numbly recognized as Mycenaean and shuffled aside

It was only then that Joseph noticed her wrists were bound. A rope around her waist tied her to another frightened girl in similarly tattered garb a few paced ahead, and another…. and another. Five women, bound in a line with a finely dressed merchant standing a few steps ahead, engaged in animated conversation with another man.

And they weren't the only ones. Joseph's eyes flashed around, his heart turning to ice when he saw several men on his left crammed into tight wooden cages. Most had their heads hung low in dejection, while one leaned on the thick wooden poles that barred them in, gazing out blankly. The street they'd turned down swarmed with slaves everywhere Joseph looked.

Nearby he saw a downcast young boy, no more than ten, being poked and pinched by a pudgy, silver-haired slave trader, who was bartering animatedly with the boy's owner. Up ahead, the street widened out into a small square where dozens of men gathered around a raised rock dais. A forlorn man stood on the dais, his hands bound. Meanwhile an auctioneer rapidly called out bids as hands went up among the crowd. "Twenty-one shekels! Anyone for twenty-one? He's strong, healthy, speaks Hittite and Akkadian— twenty-one to you! Do I see twenty-two?"

They passed down the wide street. Joseph's stomach twisting as the press of people crushed in on every side, traders with greedy, calculating smiles, and a host of hollow-eyed men and women.

So this was what a true slave market was.

Back in Shechem there had been *maybe* three slave traders who each wandered through once a year... if that. Kiraith Arba had Ashur and Namtar, traveling brothers who would bring back slaves from various cities. Usually they took orders though. A merchant showing up with more than ten slaves to auction would have set the city abuzz. Here, there must have been at least a hundred different faces — terrified, confused, smoldering with rage — all caught amid of sea of hopeless resignation that almost physically pressed on him.

Joseph's gaze was inexorably drawn to the forlorn man on the auction platform —brown hair, olive skin and garbed in a filthy tunic, as the auctioneer loudly cried, "Sold! For twenty-eight!"

He couldn't look away from the surreal scene, the bound man being roughly tugged off the platform, while a sobbing woman was prodded up. Was that what would happen to him, Joseph thought, a horrible, leaden lump gathering in his stomach.

The auctioneer called again, "Next up, we have what you've all been waiting for, a whole shipload of fresh stock from Libya. We'll start with this girl, strong Amazigh blood, docile and not a day over twenty-two. Good hands for weaving, strong enough for a laundress, and I've been assured she can cook. We'll start the bidding at fifteen shekels. Do I see fifteen?"

They passed by and amid the rumble of the crowd the last Joseph caught was "Fifteen to you sir! Do I see seventeen? Seventeen for the young…"

Joseph plodded numbly ahead, horrified. He couldn't end up in a place like this. He was freeborn. He didn't belong here. As their troop navigated out of the slave market into a less sickening part of town, Joseph resolved he had to get away… and soon… very soon.

They turned onto a narrow north-south street, the buildings casting gloomy shadows. He jostled his way past a party of muscular young men headed the opposite direction. One shot him a skeptical eye, but the others seemed intimidated by the bizarre sight of the camel. As if on cue, the beast looked up, gave a deep, almost mournful grunt, and the pair hurried past. From there they turned onto an east-west road, where the rising sun cut a golden stream through the buildings, lighting the road to where the real market began.

On either side of the narrow street, shop owners stood near the doors, shouting to draw customers. This appeared to be the weavers' street, as Joseph saw a dazzling array of fabrics on sale. Nearby three different shop owners engaged in a shouting match to sell linen bolts, all of them apparently having the 'lowest price in Ashkelon'.

Down at the end of the street, the true market square came into view, and Joseph blinked in amazement. The square was a blur of vibrant colors— men and women in a rainbow of exotic clothes bustled past vendors peddling food beneath red, yellow and tan awnings. Already the fresh scent of bread reached his nose, mingled with whiffs of perfume and simmering incense, along with the tantalizing aroma of slow roasting meat.

The square buzzed with excitement and anticipation. Voices surged at him from every direction, layered one atop the other, and drowning his senses. He caught the clatter of bumping carts, the *heehaws* of donkeys towing them, gruff shouts and like a metronome, the far-off *clang... clang... clang* of forge hammers in the city. Left to his own devices, he might have been lost in the bazaar forever, but following the tail of the camel in front of him, they finally came to a small clearing in the square.

It soon became apparent why there had been a scuffle for the privilege of coming inside. Almost before they'd tied off the camels, Joseph noticed several of the herdsmen and at least a few guards slipping away into the crowd. He was still staring when a hand smacked at the back of his head, and Ben-Tov's impatient voice snapped, "I didn't buy you so you could stand around gawking, boy. Unload the camels. And do a proper job. Lay everything out so people can see."

Joseph bristled at the abrasive man, but forced it aside, offering an apologetic, "Sorry, sir."

During their long days of walking, he hadn't actually gotten the opportunity to see what was packed onto the camels. But coaxing each camel down to sit on its belly, Joseph set about untying a heavy burlap sack from the wood framed saddle. He pulled it open, only to be hit with the sweet, slightly smoky scent of incense that he recognized instantly— myrrh. The burlap had been double bagged, but peering inside, his jaw dropped open as he saw tan, aromatic pebbles— a thousand fabulously expensive bits of resin.

And this was just *one* bag. Under the spell of his own amazement, Joseph quickly pulled down several more bags, each as rich as the last. Mounted on top of the camel's saddle frame sat a large chest. As he began to untie it, Gabir called a sharp, "Careful with that!"

It was heavy, so much so that Gabir had to come grab the other handle. The two of them lugged it over to where Ben-Tov was already busy negotiating with a tall, richly dressed man who carried a self-important whine in his voice.

Joseph flipped open the chest lid to reveal small pottery urns racked inside and packed with straw. They were only about a cubit long, too small to carry wine or common pressed oil. "What is it?" Joseph asked.

In response, Gabir removed the wax cap of one with a sharp twist, and a calming, woody scent with hints of sweet pine wafted out. Joseph stared into the urn, drinking in the intense but pleasant aroma given off by a thick amber liquid within.

"Balsam," Joseph murmured in amazement. His eyes darted to the chest, as it truly registered what a fortune he'd been leading around on camel back for the last few days. No wonder Ben-Tov had so many guards.

He was familiar with balsam. It was mainly harvested across the Jordan, not that far from where they'd lived in Shechem actually. But it was expensive, and used sparingly.

Samas kept a small supply. If Joseph remembered correctly, Myrrha had said it was good for relieving swelling and reducing pain. They had a jar maybe half this size for the entire camp, and Father had complained egregiously when they'd run out and been required to buy more.

Just this chest represented a stunning quantity, and this was only one camel out of… fifty.

Joseph blinked, jolted back to the loud and busy market by Gabir's voice, "Well, get too it. Unload the rest of the sacks."

Joseph didn't object to the work. At this point his intense curiosity might have had him pulling open sacks anyway. Along with the myrrh and balsam, he found a bag with more resin bits tied to the next camel. These were a woody brown though, and exuded a fruity, amber scent that he recognized like an old friend. Labdanum.

He didn't know much about balsam or myrrh, just that they came from trees, but labdanum he'd actually harvested before. It came from rockrose leaves. Short scrubby bushes that grew in patches. When the goats would graze them, the sap would stick in their fur and beards and Joseph and his brothers had spent many, *many* hours combing the dried bits out to be sold at market. It too was expensive, although after all the middle-men had taken their respective cuts, Joseph had never felt terribly well compensated for the extravagant effort required. Still, just this one sack held a *lot* of labdanum, and there were six sacks per camel plus another chest of balsam. It represented an absurd amount of wealth.

By the time Joseph finished off-loading all the bags, a crowd of eager buyers had gathered around Ben-Tov and the two men acting as his assistants. They'd clearly made a stir, showing up unannounced with such rarities. Now Gabir and several of the guards who had remained, stood around looking particularly threatening to deter would-be thieves.

Amid the chaos, Joseph abruptly realized that no one was looking at him. For the first time in days there was nothing to do, and Joseph's eyes darted among the distracted guards as he stood near the camels. Was this his chance?

For a few moments, he hesitated. Someone must be watching him, right? Glancing around the bustling market, he saw people everywhere. A few local boys stood nearby, gaping at the exotic camels, while men in fine colored robes hurried past, trailed by slaves and servants in simple tunics. Finally, his eyes paused, lingering on a trio of muscular men with a confident, distinctly independent air about themselves. They strolled down the avenue not far away, clearly heading about some business.

Joseph glanced back to his own group, half expecting someone to stalk over and scold him for lazily standing around. But no one seemed to have even noticed. Gabir briefly glanced his general direction, but the guard's eyes didn't seem focused on Joseph at all. The guard turned away, and in a flash, a single dominate realization crystallized in Joseph's mind. This was it, his moment. Right now.

Joseph took once last look around. Still no one watching. Gabir stood ten paces away, conversing with its another guard and nodding at something across the square, but not looking at him. He glanced down at the camel who had been his constant fellow for the last three days, and who now stared at him with probing eyes. Apparently, it was the only one aware of his existence at all.

Did the camel have a name, he idly wondered? He'd never asked. Oh well, too late now. "Well, I'd say it's been fun, but it really hasn't." Joseph nodded and met the creature's absent stare. "Anyway, let's hope we *don't* meet again."

If the camel had thoughts on his odd goodbye, it didn't share them, and with a sudden anticipation, Joseph turned and hurried off into the swarming crowd.

Chapter 27
Threads Unbroken

Joseph didn't run. He wanted to. Every muscle in his legs screamed at him to run, to get as far as he could before someone noticed his absence. But running was perhaps the one thing that would *definitely* give him away. Instead Joseph walked, quickly but deliberately, down the cobbled road that ran alongside the market square.

He specifically chose a direction opposite of the way they'd entered the city. Trying to backtrack probably would have ended with him taking a wrong turn in the tight, chaotic streets and finding himself completely lost. Besides, backtracking would mean going back through the slave market, and right now just the thought of that place made him sick to his stomach.

So he headed the opposite way. He knew that there were three gates into Kiraith Arba, so certainly the much larger Ashkelon had to have more than just one.

Almost without realizing, Joseph followed the three heavily built men from earlier. Even from fifty paces back, they stood out in the crowd and seemed like they knew where they were heading. The townspeople flowed by like a river around him, but Joseph kept his eyes on the three, weaving past the servants and workmen choking the streets.

A loud shout spilled out from a side street, a crier calling, "Make Way! Make Way!"

Joseph's heart froze in his chest as five armed men with spears turned onto the main avenue, shoving people aside.

For an irrational instant he was terrified that they must be coming for him, somehow they knew he'd run away and—

He was caught up as the press of people hurriedly swept him toward a white plastered wall on the side of the road, clearing an open path through the middle of the street. One man didn't seem to realize he needed to move, and the lead guard cracked him upside the head with a spear haft, "Stand aside!"

Caught in the swirling crowd, Joseph was shoved against the wall next to a short, poorly dressed man who pressed so close that Joseph could catch his very distinctive stink. He was tall enough to see past the man, to where a trio of curtained palanquins born by bulky man-slaves swept after the guards. Joseph stared, his eyes following the rich fabrics that veiled away the occupants. Who were they?

The palanquins passed by quickly, and like an exhaled breath, the pressure of the crowd eased. The street resumed its typical tumultuous activity, and a nearby shopkeeper shouted, "Get your oil here! Pressed and strained olive oil, pay by the mina!"

Joseph stared after the palanquins for an instant though, still marveling at who they could be to let them shunt aside everyone so casually.

Further down, the group took another turn and disappeared from view. It was only then that Joseph realized something else. The trio he'd been following had vanished… and he had no clue where he was.

Had Gabir noticed he was gone yet?

Probably.

Joseph pushed aside an anxious twinge. It didn't matter, lost amid all these people he might as well have been a tree hiding in the forest. Besides, he doubted Gabir and Ben-Tov would search in the direction *away* from the gate, and short of scouring the whole city, there was no way Gabir could hope to track him down.

Which meant he was free… the realization left him almost ecstatic. Nearby the woman still ranted about her oil, but for a moment Joseph didn't care. He slumped against the white plastered wall beneath the shade of the shop awning, an awful weight lifting from his chest, and the strength momentarily draining from his limbs. For a long moment he just breathed. It was over, he'd escaped.

Joseph was still trapped in his own head, trying to work out what to do, when a shrill voice jolted him back to reality, "Looking for some oil, young sir?"

"Huh?" Joseph blinked as the shopkeeper woman held up a jug of oil.

"Olive oil," the lady insisted. She stood a half head shorter than him but still managed to look imposing. "We have the best quality in town. Bottled straight from the oil press. One jug and I promise you'll taste the difference."

"I…" Joseph stammered, "I'm fine."

The woman's expression soured, "Well move along then. Can't have you getting in the way of *real* customers."

Joseph nodded, trying to avoid a scene, as he stumbled back into the road.

He joined a stream of people heading… vaguely west. Not the direction of home, but it took him away from the market square. Occasionally, he glanced back, his eyes scanning the crowd for Gabir or one of Ben-Tov's men.

He didn't see anyone though. Obviously, they were likely searching for him by now, but every moment that passed lent him a budding confidence. They wouldn't find him… not here. They were probably still scouring the road that led back towards the slave market.

Unlike the narrow streets that seemed to be the norm in Ashkelon, the road he was on sprawled out wide enough for large traffic, and was paved to boot. He hadn't gone far when more shouts went up, "Stand aside!"

Again Joseph found himself pressed against a storefront as a heavy wagon trundled past, towed by a pair of donkeys. The rancid smell of the city seemed to worsen the further west he went. He had scented whiffs of dead fish in the main market, but here the reek lingered like a noxious cloud. He wrinkled his nose as a puff of wind only seemed to strengthen the odor.

Ahead the street slanted sharply southwest, and turning the bend, Joseph saw exactly where the awful smell was emanating from. Laid out before him was a long avenue with a plaza at the far end, and everywhere Joseph saw fish, fish, and more fish.

The smell was enough to make him gag, dead and rotting meat and guts all nicely putrefying beneath the blazing sun. He passed a strangely cheerful man wielding a bronze cleaver at one table, with a mound of fish guts a cubit high haphazardly shoved off to one side.

Everywhere in the aquatic charnel house, lifeless fish hung limply on hooks, their vacant eyes eerily following Joseph as he walked. And among them he caught glimpses of abominations that looked nothing like fish at all. Several grotesque creatures had been laid out on a table. One had a proportionally giant mouth brimming with needle-like teeth and two little ridges for eyes, while the rest of its body seemed almost comically small. The huge head tapered down to small fins and a bare stub of a tail, like some bizarrely stunted monstrosity. Another table was laid out with horrifying sea snakes, the bodies colored deathly black with a single white streak. The thick-bodied creatures must have been two or three cubits long and Joseph skirted past them with a shudder.

The awful pall of the market only worsened, but down at the end of the street, he saw something that beckoned like a siren. A wide gate was cut into the wall, and trying not to breathe through his nose, Joseph instantly beelined for the exit. And freedom.

The gate was flanked by a single pair of bored, spear toting guards in leather armor. Stepping through the broad portico, Joseph breathed deep as a breeze from beyond finally whisked away the foul smell of putrid fish. It was replaced by the crisp scent of salt as he emerged through the gate to find himself staring out at… the harbor?

Joseph had never seen a real harbor. Nashu had occasionally spoken about the grand harbors at Knossos and Phaisos where dozens of ships found their berths, and based on what he saw now, the harbor in Ashkelon must have been comparable. From the gate a steep slope led down to where broad docks jutted out into the sea like giant fingers.

Fat, tubby merchant ships sat like jeweled rings among an armada of small fishing skiffs. Most of the fishermen had already returned for the morning, and he saw only a few final boats still straggling into the harbor. Meanwhile, down on the narrow shoreline, dozens of fishermen busied themselves cleaning their nets and tossing aside unwanted fish for flights of white pelicans that danced slow circles above.

Down on the docks, one of the merchant ships must have just arrived, because men swarmed like ants around the vessel. A steady stream disappeared below only to re-emerge, hauling off a seemingly endless bevy of barrels, sacks and crates that they then loaded onto waiting wagons. Even as he watched, Joseph was forced to step aside as another cart clambered up the hillside and rattled on past, heading into the city.

As he did, his eyes finally left the grand harbor vista and noticed something else — the walls. The wall he'd just come through had seemed oddly slim compared to the monstrous edifice they'd entered beneath this morning, and now he understood why.

To either side, the city walls towered like giant sentinels, fencing in the harbor and running straight into the deep waters. That meant the only way he could escape Ashkelon from here was by diving straight into the Great Sea itself, which...

Joseph shook his head, suppressing a shudder at the thought. Absolutely not. Chest deep in the Jordan was about as close to deep water as he *ever* wanted to get.

He reluctantly glanced back at the gate he'd just come through, forcibly ignoring a twinge of worry. Well, it wasn't like he had any other options. And... he mused optimistically, at least now he could be certain Ben-Tov wouldn't think to look for him in this direction.

He let his eyes rove around the magnificent harbor for a final moment, then turned and headed back into the smoggy reek of the fish market. His first order of business was to backtrack down the main road until he wasn't gagging at every breath. From there though, he hesitated.

He couldn't stay on this road, that much was certain. It would take him straight back to Ben-Tov in the market. But then where to next? He knew had to get out of Ashkelon, preferably before nightfall. In both Kiraith Arba and Shechem, townsfolk had never been kind to unknown strangers who wanted to loiter after the gates closed for the evening. He doubted Ashkelon would be any more tolerant.

But if he had to get to a gate… where even was the nearest gate? Joseph chewed at his lip, his eyes glancing around. Behind him a now familiar call rose about the rumble of the city, "Make way! Out of the road!"

Turning he saw yet another wagon coming, and this time he managed to move aside in step with the crowd instead of just being thrust out of the street. He backed into a narrow side street, and as the cart clattered by, found himself staring down a shadow shrouded alley. The path was cramped, barely wide enough for two men to walk abreast, with double story homes stacked high on either side. The only person he saw was a shambling old man thirty paces down where the street turned out of sight.

Unlike the main road, the side alley wasn't properly cobbled either, more like a dirt path strewn with half buried stones, their tops smoothed by the collective wear of many feet. But…. Joseph mused to himself, it wasn't like *he* cared about fancy cobbled streets. Plus, he sincerely doubted that Ben-Tov and Gabir would have a raindrop's chance in summer of finding him if he kept to back roads. They'd be scouring the main streets all while he'd slip right past and out of the city. The prospect of keeping one step ahead of the caravanners warmed Joseph's chest. In a snap he made his decision and plunged into the back streets of Ashkelon. He was smart, he could find his way, and he'd back home in no time.

***

An hour later Joseph was seriously questioning his assumptions as he faced down yet another bewildering dead end. Nothing about this city made any sense. Take here, where someone had apparently decided to build their house right into the middle of what should be a path. He could hear the siren sounds of a road right across from him, shouting shopkeepers, the drone of voices, and the slaps of a hundred footfalls. Yet, for some infuriating reason, the city seemed to be conspiring to keep him trapped back in this maze.

Joseph turned back in disgust, ignoring the lingering malodor oozing through the street. He made certain to skirt well clear of a spot where someone had disgustingly dumped an entire chamber pot worth of… waste into the alley from a window overhead. How did anyone even live in this hole of a city?

He'd always thought of Kiraith Arba as a beautiful gem on a hill, but treading through the guts of Ashkelon, all he'd seen so far was excrement, trash, poverty and misery. He'd stepped over beggars laid out drunk on the street, and wandered past packs of children in threadbare rags, playing amidst piles of festering garbage that no one seemingly could be bothered to move. He'd passed empty-eyed people shambling around in tattered clothes and grubbing through trash piles, who almost seemed worse off than the slaves from earlier. At least the slaves were fed.

Hurrying back to the last intersection, Joseph couldn't escape a mounting worry. He looked up, sliding several steps to one side to peer past a rooftop and gauge the position of the sun. He'd been attempting to head north, but kept getting turned around, and in the narrow twisting streets it was nigh impossible to go in anything resembling a straight line. Even

251

worse, of the two branches this lane took, both had dead-ended, which meant he had little choice but to back-track to the previous intersection and navigate a new path from there.

He was certain he'd find his way out… eventually, except he didn't have that long. Every moment he lingered was another moment for Ben Tov's people to scour the city, and the dread of them finding him had been slowly pooling like poison in his gut. Stepping past a molding mound of kitchen scraps, he paused at yet another intersection. A tall, featureless wall plastered in the ubiquitous beige white of Ashkelon stood before him. The path he'd originally come down led back south, while the street he'd just backtracked angled off northeast. The only other option headed west, toward the sea and in about ten paces appeared to turn back south… the exact wrong direction. Increasingly desperate in the strange city, Joseph stared blankly at the wall, his intuition deserting him.

Finally he laid one hand against the rough plaster, "God," he whispered, "please get me out of here."

He waited a second, a small part of him hoping beyond hope for a miracle.

Nothing happened…

Typical.

Joseph shook his head and pulled back his hand, suddenly gripped by a terribly loneliness. He was about to turn away when a soft *Meeeeow* drew his gaze to the top of the nearby wall. A plump yellow tabby sat on its haunches, head cocked slightly askew, gazing down on him with slitted amber eyes and a characteristically feline disdain.

Joseph watched the cat a moment. That was one *very* well fed kitty, he mused. A rotund belly bulged beneath a flawless, shining coat that screamed to everyone the cat hadn't come across all those meals by being a scrapper.

Probably a pampered pet to some rich merchant's daughter that had never had to catch a mouse in its life.

As if knowing his thoughts and wanting to flaunt its posh existence, the cat rose, imperiously strolling along the wall down the one street Joseph had yet to check. The cat probably lived in a large house right on the other side of this wall, Joseph realized. A place where everything was just… normal, he thought with a sudden pang of jealousy. No running from slavers, no frantically trying to get home, no wondering what would happen to Myrrha and Benji if he didn't…

Joseph shook his head, his hand once more touching the rough plaster, like he might steal away a glimmer of that serenity for himself. No, none of that insanity on the other side of the wall, just people going about their lives.

Feeling more lost than ever, Joseph walked after the cat. Maybe it would take him around to the front of the house. Maybe not. Maybe it didn't matter.

The path proceeded to turn back the wrong direction, but only for a few steps. Following the haphazard footprint of the building, it then turned toward the ocean, and within ten more paces it abruptly turned again. Suddenly, despite the odds, Joseph found himself heading back the way he'd been trying to go this whole time, north.

With a budding excitement he hurried ahead, weaving past a trio of grubby children excitedly kicking a leather ball. A few more steps took him to the entrance of a fairly wealthy home. Passing the hinged double gates that marked the entrance, Joseph followed the road further and soon heard the distinctive din of a major thoroughfare ahead.

In short order, and to his tremendous relief, he stumbled out onto a paved avenue, the shouts of vendors ringing in his ears. "Get your salt by the sack!" an eager man called to anyone nearby.

The enthusiastic vendor turned to Joseph, nearly thrusting a bag of salt in his face, "See that, young man? Best salt in town, any quantity you want."

"Sorry, not right now." Joseph pushed the bag away and hurried past, rather hoping that no one noticed him much at all. Now that he'd finally found himself back on a main thoroughfare, the urgency of escaping Ashkelon had latched onto him like the talons of an angry falcon. He could see the city wall towering above the houses ahead, and sure enough, two short turns later, Joseph saw a gate, sitting at the end of the road like a long-lost friend.

Hurrying forward, he breathed a wonderful sigh of relief as he slipped past the guards and strode into the vaulted entryway, his head held high.

He done it.

Joseph found himself laughing in pent up emotion. Seemed Ben-Tov's people weren't so clever after all. The realization lit his footsteps with a surge of euphoria. He'd actually done it. He was free.

Exiting the long tunnel of the gateway with a spring in his step, Joseph's gaze immediately went to the east. From here he couldn't quite see the crumpled ridgeline in the distance that marked the ascent into the valley where Mamre lay. The far horizon was veiled behind tall palms, disappearing into a haze of orchards and vineyards, but Joseph knew he'd see it soon enough. Just one last hill to climb and he would—

Gabir's cold voice abruptly intruded from behind, "Going somewhere, boy?"

Joseph jumped in shock, a jolt like lightning freezing his limbs. He half spun right as a sharp crack lit up the back of his head in pain. Joseph's vision swam and he tumbled to the dirt, seeing stars.

Chapter 28

The Edge of Nowhere

Sitting with his hands bound and roped to a heavy camel saddle, Joseph glared at Gabir. Ten feet away, illuminated by the failing red light of evening, the guard busily scarfed down his meal with a perverse gusto. The man had very deliberately *not* given Joseph anything, and after not tasting a bite since entering Ashkelon that morning, his stomach protested with a demanding gurgle.

Joseph tried not to show weakness… but it was hard when inside he felt an utter fool. In retrospect it seemed so obvious, of course Gabir and Ben-Tov's men would have staked out the gates. Why bother scouring the city when they could just wait for him to come straight to them? And so he had.

Joseph wanted to vomit, and not just from the throbbing, goose-egg lump on the back of his head. This had been his one chance, his single opportunity to get back home… to see Benji again, and…

Joseph shook his head, his eyes falling to the well-trod clumps of grass as he desperately tried to summon up a new plan, some solution to fix this… yet found nothing. Escaping tonight was flatly out of the question. After today's misadventure he would have a leaf's chance in a storm of sneaking away. And tomorrow came the desert, the endless expanse that Joseph had always dimly thought of as marking the end of the world itself. Once they were out in the wastelands, there was no return. If he ran he'd just condemn himself to an awful end, raw hands scraping in the parched dirt for water, while jackals and vultures circled, eager to pick at his bones.

For a time, the despair kept building inside Joseph, roiling like a pot about to boil over. Finally he looked up to see Gabir finishing his meal with a delicious smelling round of bread covered in honey.

"My Father will pay you," he said at last, "if you set me free and take me back to Kiraith Arba, he'll give you whatever you want."

Deep down Joseph knew with a crushing certainty that the offer wouldn't sway Gabir in the slightest. Yet, standing on the cusp of a journey from which there was no return, he at least had to try.

Gabir looked up from his bread, regarding Joseph with penetrating eyes, then finally shrugged, "I doubt he pays better than Ben-Tov."

Joseph hesitated, his eyes going to the now familiar string of camels bedded down for the night with all their baggage piled alongside, a staggering fortune in incense and resin. Could Father match a share of that?

Maybe…

Joseph swallowed back the sour despair, and admitted the truth. "I don't know, he might."

Gabir gave a chuckle at that statement and Joseph looked up, bewildered, to see the guard shaking his head with a hearty laugh. The man's dismissive tone stung at Joseph, each chuckle sinking like a barb into his chest. Finally, Gabir settled down shaking his head with a bizarre mirth in his eyes. "Well, at least you're honest, boy," Gabir said. "I'll give you that."

When Gabir had caught him earlier there'd been a cold, terrifying fury on the man's face. But after hauling him back into camp, Gabir had simply gone back inside Ashkelon without so much as a word.

Joseph had spent the whole day dreading his return. But now, the long day at the market seemed to have drained much of the man's anger. Instead there remained a dry humor that had Joseph confused, wondering if perhaps the Gabir *was* warming to him in some small way.

Gabir continued, "Your Father is Jacob son of Isaac son of Abraham? Am I correct?"

"Yes."

"Is that the same Jacob who murdered Hamor a few years back? Sacked Shechem if I recall correctly?"

Joseph swallowed, wondering if for once he might actually be getting somewhere. "Technically it was Hamor who started the fight."

Gabir leaned forward a handsbreadth, "But your father finished it?"

"My brothers, mainly," Joseph explained, the old bitterness welling to mind. "Father would have chosen peace if he could have."

Gabir leaned back, nodding to himself. "Interesting," he mused. "And your brothers, the ones who did in Hamor, what do they have against you?"

"You mean specifically, or in general?"

Gabir chuckled at the answer, "How about in general."

"Father wanted to make me his firstborn heir." Joseph slid around so his back was to the camel saddle. As he spoke, he idly staring at the rope around his wrists, snaking back to a tie-off on the saddle itself. "My brothers are all older, so obviously they weren't very satisfied with the arrangement."

He hesitated, then added a hopeful, "I wasn't lying, my father would pay a great deal to someone who brought me back safely."

"I don't know," Gabir mused thoughtfully, "I would insist on quite a lot."

Joseph nearly froze at Gabir's calculating utterance. In an instant he saw the sudden crack in the man's bronze facade and determined not to waste his opportunity. "My father possesses great wealth in sheep, and goats, and cattle," Joseph assured Gabir, trying to be tempting without slathering on the promise of riches too heavily. "He could make you a very wealthy man. It's barely two days easy travel to our camp."

"Ahh, but would he really honor a deal such as that?" Gabir said pointedly.

"My father is an honest man."

In answer, Gabir regarded Joseph with a penetrating stare. A sudden derisive grin curled at the guards' lips, and Joseph was gripped by a terrible sensation like the ground plunging away beneath his feet. "Your father's reputation speaks for itself, boy," Gabir said, shaking his head. "And not as commendably as you might believe. I wonder, if we walked up to his tent, just the two of us, and I demanded a vast sum for your safe return, would he beggar himself to pay it? Or would he simply take you, have a good chuckle, and send me on my way?"

Joseph swallowed back a stab of wounded anger at the scornful amusement now apparent on Gabir's face. The man was toying with him, wasn't he? Just a cruel little game to pass the time.

Even so, almost out of instinct Joseph found himself defending his family anyway, "My father remembers his friends," Joseph snapped, adding a more ominous, "As well as his enemies."

Infuriatingly, Gabir seemed to find that statement even more amusing. "I'm sure he does."

The man chuckled and stood. Strolling over to the camel saddle Joseph was leaned up against, he untied a neatly packed bedroll.

Joseph fumed at the man's mocking voice, wishing he had just some way, *any* way to strike out against him. "I take it you don't care about wealth then?" he muttered sarcastically.

Surprisingly, Gabir's hands halted untying the various saddle knots for an instant. "Quite the contrary," he said, his fingers resuming their work. "I certainly wouldn't have come all this way if not for a great deal of silver promised at the end."

"But it's not as simple as you might think, boy." Gabir walked back around the front of the camel saddle to tower over Joseph. He held a flaxen mat bedroll tucked beneath one arm and folded blankets in each hand.

Without warning, he dropped a blanket in Joseph's lap then turned and strolled over to begin laying out his own bedding. "Have you met Buarch?" Gabir briefly paused his work, pointing across their camp to a trio of men enthusiastically playing what looked like a game of Mia. Joseph saw the three busily passing around a covered cup, each giving it a shake. Finally, someone called the bluff, and the first man set the cup in front of the third with a triumphant grin.

The third man gave a low groan that drifted across camp, and Joseph turned back to Gabir. He didn't know which man was Buarch, but he'd met none of the three, so in a way it didn't change his answer. "No," he shook his head.

"He's a cousin of mine," Gabir said, unrolling his bed mat with a flick that spread it smoothly across an open patch of dirt. "Married to my oldest sister. She and I have always been close. Now, imagine the shame I'd bring down on her head if I ran off and abandoned everyone, just to chase a few silver bits from your father."

Gabir shook his head, "Imagine my own wife, having to live with the humiliation."

The man made a sweeping gesture around the camp, both to everyone in general and no one in particular. "Ben-Tov and a few of his people are Ishmaelites, but most of us are from the tribe of Midian. Sons of the same Abraham as you, in point of fact."

"If the gods are willing, when we return home, my wife will have given birth to our third child. I'll get to hold her, see both my boys and tell them stories about Egypt."

As he spoke, Gabir had been laying out his blanket, a genuine fondness gracing his face. But suddenly he paused, looking straight at Joseph, serious again. "You should get some sleep, boy. You'll need your strength tomorrow. The desert can be a cruel place."

Joseph already knew that well enough. For a moment he stared at the dirt, trying not to let his terrible despair show. Just his luck to be stuck with a captor for whom all the silver in the world might not be enough. He needed a new plan, some way to escape before they were too far gone, yet as desperately as he tried to marshal one, Joseph found instead a cold, inexorable fear seeping into his soul. He fidgeted, his bound hands finding a clump of freshly sprouted grass, the usual deep green color washed to a purplish black in the twilight. He began plucking the smooth-edged blades, his fingers absently shredding them into pieces, even as his despair deepened.

It was Gabir's voice that finally jolted him out of his reverie. "And, boy, don't try to run again."

Joseph looked up blinking in surprise. That was the first Gabir had spoken about what had happened in Ashkelon.

The guard didn't seem so much angry as simply stating a matter of fact when he continued. "Everyone tries to run once, but if you try it again, I assure you it won't go well the second time. And once we're out in the sands, there's nowhere to run anyway. Is that understood?"

Joseph nodded, swallowing back his own despair, but Gabir stared him down, reiterating, *"Is that understood?"*

Joseph sighed, muttering, "Yes."

"Yes, *who?*"

The words tasted bitter in his mouth, but Joseph forced them out. He was wise enough not to look the man in the eye, but still glared at Gabir's legs with a sullen, powerless defiance, "Yes, *sir.*"

***

The desert found them slowly.

After a sleepless night that filled Joseph with gnawing despair, the caravan continued south along the coast road.

The sun blazed like an oven above, and all day the foul stink of camel breath seemed to chase him, only ever a few steps behind if the sea breezes should falter.

Slowly the world transformed around him. The barley stubble and ripe vineyards of Ashkelon gave way to endless ranks of ripening olive trees interspersed with ever more desert palms. The soil beneath his feet turned from a rich loam and clay mix to a softer, almost sandy dirt from which scrub bushes cautiously poked out.

That first day they passed the city of Gaza on the coast, a stout, walled settlement, yet strangely small in comparison to the behemoth Ashkelon that they'd left behind. A few miles later they stopped for the night, making camp above a dry wadi, and near a solitary well that sat beneath the watchful gaze of some ancient crumbling fortress.

The guards seemed doubly alert now. Spears almost always close to hand, and slings laced around their belts. Joseph imagined that was intended to keep him from running away again, but the more he watched Gabir the more that explanation felt inadequate. Even when quizzing him on Egyptian grammar, Gabir rarely looked at Joseph. Instead his eyes roved the plains around them, searching… always searching. And Joseph couldn't for the life of him puzzle out what for.

The next morning, they set out with freshly filled waterskins before the sun had even crested the eastern horizon. The camels Ben-Tov had taken into Ashkelon had seen most of their merchandise sold off and replaced with even *more* waterskins. Joseph wondered at them having so many and inwardly groaned at the extra work of filling them. But as the scrublands slowly melted into an endless plain of flat bronze, he began to understand why.

Chapter 29
The Golden Sea: Part 1

"*Dau*," Gabir declared in an absent voice, even as he stared off toward the south, "It means bread."

"*Dau*," Joseph dutifully repeated, plodding behind as the caravan crawled down the reverse slope of *another* sand dune.

Almost out of habit, he tried it out in a simple sentence, "*Erdee dau. Ee hakar.*"

Roughly, *Give me bread, I'm hungry.*

Almost without thinking Gabir bantered back in Egyptian, "*Natka bahee eewaf stya re.*"

Joseph's Egyptian had improved dramatically in just the last week, but Gabir's snappy delivery still managed to jumble the words in his head. He was forced to slowly translate the sentence in bits, before finally fitting everything back together."

You — can have — meat for — stare at?

No.

Smell?

No, smell was *st-ish-ya* instead of *stya*

What was…

Right, *meal,* he belatedly realized. *Day meal* specifically. Or more commonly, *lunch.*

Then he registered what Gabir's full sentence actually meant and groaned.

You can have meat for lunch.

He was talking about that disgusting goat jerky they'd been chewing on for the last two days. Joseph still hadn't

262

gotten the salty ick out of his mouth from this morning. A part of him wondered at how Ben-Tov kept the caravan together given how miserly the man was with his supplies.

Although… Joseph bemoaned inwardly, perhaps there was some twisted logic to having terrible food, it certainly made everyone eat less and thus lasted longer.

Trudging on and now dreading his next meal, Joseph tried to ignore the relentless heat. The hot rays beat down from above, while the sand reflected back a miserable fire onto his face.

He wished they could have stayed close to the sea. The first day after leaving Gaza, they'd followed the coast road for a while, usually staying within sight of the vast cerulean blue sea. Joseph had no great love for deep water, but as the day's heat poured down on him like hot embers, the cool waters had beckoned.

It was right there, the chill waves sloshing on the beach a few hundred paces away. Meanwhile they wandered right on by, apparently suffering amid the sweltering heat for the sake of… suffering.

Gabir had seemed distant, distracted, sometimes forgetting to insist Joseph practice his Egyptian for minutes at a time. His eyes always focused south and west, almost like he expected someone.

Which was absurd, Joseph quickly decided. The only people dumb enough to be all the way out here were *them*.

He'd been nearly ready to push past Gabir's outward focused watchfulness and straight up insist on going over for a quick dunk in the sea. It was right there, and he didn't see why they couldn't at least wet their clothes to stay cool.

Joseph had been gazing longingly out to sea when he saw it, a ship crawling its way up above the horizon. He'd only seen ships a few times and found it endlessly fascinating how the white squared sail peeked above the horizon first, then the fat tubby bottom followed, as the large boat edged into view. He couldn't figure out why the ship did that, unless it was rising up out of the waves—

Joseph turned at the sound of a new pair of footfalls. He'd been monotonously listening to his and Gabir's steps so long that a third pair of feet sounded like an unexpected new instrument joining a familiar song. Ben-Tov strode his way down the caravan line, his footsteps sounding more urgent than usual, a quarter beat faster perhaps.

"We're heading south," he declared in passing.

"South?" Gabir questioned.

"Just out of sight of the coast."

Joseph didn't see how there was any particular logic in that. But Gabir nodded as though it made perfect sense, and Ben Tov hurriedly strode past to the fifth and final camel train tailing behind them.

Gabir said, "You heard him, boy. We'll jog south a bit." He gestured ahead to where Joseph could now see the first camel train in the long line veering sharply to the left.

Joseph cast a longing look back at the waters. "Why not stay near the sea?"

In response Gabir pointed towards the ship slowly inching its way up to parallel with them, "Because of that."

What?

Usually Joseph wouldn't have questioned orders. It wasn't as though Gabir wanted his input anyway. That said, he *really* wanted to take a dip, and like a simmering fire spreads into an inferno, his curiosity rapidly got the better of him. "It's just a ship."

"Yes." Gabir agreed, offering an indulgent, almost mocking nod, "a ship with people onboard." The man paused his steps, breaking the steady rhythm of footfalls, as he fell back to walk alongside Joseph's camels.

Gabir spoke like he was hinting at something, but mull on it as he might, Joseph couldn't see what. Ahead, the third train of camels turned to snake south after the others, and Joseph followed suit. Behind him, Gabir took a waterskin from the camel and tilted it back, quaffing down long gulps. Finally, he walked up next to Joseph. "Get a drink," he pushed the waterskin into Joseph's arms. "It's easy to forget out here. If you're not careful you'll start getting dizzy and be no good to anyone."

That Joseph knew well enough. *Water is life.* Father had drilled the mantra into him and his brothers like a tent peg.

Accepting the smooth leather pouch, Joseph took several slow gulps before lowering it to catch his breath. The water was warm, with a tangy aftertaste from the leather, but compared to the blistering heat of the sand, the pouch felt cool to his hands.

Passing the water back to Gabir, Joseph frowned, his mind still stuck on the ship. "I don't get it, are you worried they're going to see you going to Egypt to trade as well?"

Gabir didn't answer for a moment, and Joseph had almost given up on solving the riddle when the man said, disdainfully, "That's assuming they're going to Egypt to trade at all. They might have a… *different* cargo in mind."

A different cargo such as… Oh, Joseph realized in a flash. His mind leapt back to Ashkelon, to the slave market. All those people from across the world being shoved onto the auction platform. Of course, they'd come in by boat.

Suddenly he saw the ship in an entirely more sinister light. Slavers prowling the coast, waiting to descend like hornets on anyone they passed. That was what had happened to Myrrha and her mom, he thought queasily, at least from the snippets he'd gathered over the years. A bunch of men in boats landed near their village, slaughtered anyone who fought back, dragged everyone else screaming aboard the ship, then vanished into the endless blue.

Still though…

"They wouldn't attack Egypt though?" Joseph asked, "the Egyptians have a mighty army. It'd be suicide."

"That they do. But they can't be everywhere at once," Gabir shook his head. "And the slavers aren't there to fight the army, they just cruise along until they find an unprepared village then swing into shore. Only takes a couple hours. By the time someone goes for help and the soldiers arrive… they're far gone.

Only thing the army is good for is keeping places like Ashkelon in line. Supposedly the king there bans anyone from selling Egyptian slaves in town. Doesn't want to rile up his neighbors. I doubt the Egyptians could take the city, but they could certainly burn the fields and trash everything beyond the walls if they had a mind to. But that just means the slavers sail off to Kaphtor or Tarsus to sell their cargo instead."

"But the Egyptians have their own ships too," Joseph insisted. "They could just chase the slavers down." That he was certain of. Abraham had spent several years in Egypt and Grandfather Isaac had relayed marvelous stories of the boats there, the great armadas that cruised the river during the floods. Surely, they could dispatch a few to overwhelm a lone ship.

"Those boats aren't for the sea," Gabir shook his head, "they're for the river. Don't ask me the difference, but I spoke to a sailor in Byblos once who claimed to know all about it. According to him, most of the Egyptian boats wouldn't even last a day on the seas. They'd get pounded into driftwood at the first swell."

As Gabir spoke, they came to an abrupt rise in the terrain, a spot where the dirt had abruptly crumbled away and left a cubit high step. For Joseph it was no problem, but the camel immediately balked, grinding to a halt with a low grunt.

"Oh, come on." Joseph pulled hard on the rough rope of the halter. Unfortunately, a couple hundred pounds of him, versus a thousand pounds of camel was a losing battle.

He tried pulling again, digging in his heels as he grunted, "Move… you… stupid…"

A sharp *thwack* came from behind the camel, and with a mournful groan, the beast finally took a tepid step up the miniature cliff.

Gabir stood near the creature's rump with a short crop in hand, "Keep moving."

Joseph certainly felt there was still no love lost between him and Gabir, but he nodded, with a mumbled, "Thanks."

The guard didn't answer, and as they traipsed southwest, Joseph cast one last look back to the sea, sweating in the roaring heat. He really would have liked to take a dip in the water.

Back in the moment, Joseph tried to ignore the prospect of the nasty goat jerky he'd be forcing down later and pushed his thoughts anywhere else. Unfortunately, the endless dunes offered little to distract him.

He stared blankly at the camel train a dozen steps ahead. It was same camel whose rear he'd been following for days now, marked out by a bare patch on his rump, right below the saddle. Oh, well, Joseph kept up his steady trudging, good thing the camel knew where they were going.

Struggling up the next steep dune, his feet sank ankle deep into the loose sand of the slope, his leather sandals filling with yet more abrasive grit. He was getting tired this. Yesterday at least had been flatlands as far as the eye could see, but this morning they'd reached the rippling sandhills, the *ka sha'ee.*

From afar they towered up— beautifully molded golden mounds that glittered in the rising sun. The dunes ran in belts, striping the land from northeast to southwest. Joseph guessed they'd come two or three miles inland, and from the top of the first he'd been able to glimpse the far-off blue of the Great Sea. They'd gotten a welcome taste of morning shade on the reverse slope as well. At first the dunes hadn't seemed so terrible at all.

And then they had gone on… and on… and on. Now it was past noon, the sun had soared back to its scorching zenith and Joseph was sick of the exhaustingly eternal up—down—up—down—up—down.

Trying to shake some grit out of his shoes, he looked to his feet as they crested the dune and—

"Oww…" Joseph's head snapped back up as he walked straight into a motionless Gabir.

"Sorry," he mumbled, stepping around the man and hoping to avoid an angry swat, "I didn't..."

Gabir didn't even seem to notice. Instead the man's eyes stared south once again, looking at—

"Raiders!" The loud call went up from ahead.

Raiders? The enormity of the word took an instant to register. Joseph tensed, his gaze instinctively darting left to follow Gabir's. He caught a flicker of white among the golden waves and his chest knotted... who would be all the way out here?

More frantic shouts went up, "Look to the south!" "They've got slings!" "Hold the camels!" Then Ben-Tov's deep baritone voice from ahead, "Circle up!"

Gabir abruptly wheeled on Joseph, who stared in frozen shock, "Move it, boy!" he snapped.

"But where..."

"Ben-Tov's at the front, get to him!"

Right, okay. Joseph managed a nod, and pulled hard on the halter to haul the camels out of their languid pace. The rough rope bit at his palms, and the lazy beasts barely seemed to budge. "*Arāru gammalu.*" he swore at the beasts, lapsing back into Akkadian. "Move!"

He hauled again, his heels digging trenches in the loose sand. Maybe it was the panicked shouts from all quarters, but this time the camels finally seemed to gather some sense of urgency and grudgingly cantered into a quick walk.

As the camels plodded past Gabir, the man turned, giving them several hard swats on the rump, which did seem to energize the creatures... slightly. Joseph pulled until his arms burned.

Finally Gabir turned away, and jabbing his spear deep into the sand, his fingers went to the sling tied around his belt. Unrolling it, Gabir dipped into a pouch of stones at his hip and deftly loaded one. Joseph saw him pause, still as a tree, his eyes scanning the dunes until...

One, two, three... Release.

Gabir didn't speak, but the form was identical and the habitual words drummed in Joseph's head. His eyes instinctively followed the shot and Joseph gulped when he saw three men shrouded in white robes. They swarmed out from behind the corner of the dune barely fifty paces away. Two toted spears while the third carried a sling.

Gabir's shot went low, the stone impacting in a fleeting puff of sand in the dune. Still backpedaling and desperately pulling the camels for everything he was worth, Joseph stared at the trio. His heart froze as the raider with the sling stared *directly* back at him, twirled his sling and…

One, two—

"*Ezû!*"

Joseph swore and dove for the ground in front of the camels.

Sand gritted on his elbows, and something *thumped* into the dune nearby. Overhead the camel gave a confused, deep throated bellow.

Joseph rolled over, sand everywhere and his heart racing as he scrambled to his feet. Two paces away, a fresh indentation in the ground marked the impact, a speck of grey stone peeking out. Reaching down, without really giving it much thought, Joseph snatched the rock, fitting it into the palm of one hand, then looked back to the lead camel, which gave him a quizzical stare.

They'd politely halted at seeing him go down, and now seemed uninterested in resuming their plodding forward gait. Joseph only dimly registered the camels though, instead his eyes went straight back to the slinger.

The white robed man's eyes bored into Joseph with an intense concentration. Joseph's mind blanked as the raider quickly loaded a second stone, anchored one foot back and twirled once, twice—

CRACK!

The bone jarring snap struck like a bell across the sands. The slinger's head jerked back at an unnatural angle, and the man collapsed, motionless.

Joseph blinked in disbelief. His head swiveled back to Gabir barely ten paces away, as the man tossed aside his sling. The other two raiders rushed at him, their feet kicking up sand as they converged.

Two on one, horrible odds, Joseph dimly thought. Yet an undaunted Gabir tugged his spear from the sand and went at them with a sneering roar of "*Sumaktar!*"

Joseph blinked, rooted to the spot as a dozen questions swirled about him. Should he run if they killed Gabir? Could he get away? Was this another chance to escape? Could he hide? Should he help? What if he didn't?

Then a single overriding thought sliced through the rest like a falcon through starlings— they'd just tried to kill him. And just like that, Joseph realized exactly which side he was on.

He pulled back his hand holding the sling stone and hurled it as hard as he could. And at ten paces he probably couldn't have missed if he'd wanted to.

The two white-clad men had slowed. One circled around to pin Gabir in the back, and Joseph's stone cracked him right in the back of the head.

The reaction was instantaneous. The man's spearpoint drooped, one hand clutching the back of his head with a sharp gasp. Almost too fast for Joseph to follow, Gabir took the opportunity and lunged forward, his seeking spearpoint impaling the man straight through the gut.

He must not have been armored beneath those white robes, because the raider crumpled with a pained scream. Gabir jerked the spear loose then spun towards the second man who'd tried to rush him while his back was turned.

The man hesitated at his partner's wail, and in that flash of indecision, Gabir batted his spearpoint aside, and slammed up the butt end.

SNAP!

The third raider tumbled backward, red streaming from his temple where Gabir's spear haft had slammed home.

Standing over the unconscious man, the guard quickly reversed his grip, and ran the final man through as well.

Only then did Gabir turn back to the camels. Joseph could swear he caught the faintest nod of appreciation from the man before, "KEEP GOING, BOY! HURRY!"

Right. Joseph hauled the halter with a renewed strength, even as Gabir was in among them thrashing camel rumps with his spear haft.

The camels sped ahead, this time at nearly a run, and cresting the next dune, Joseph found a sight to make his heart sing in relief. The others.

Chapter 30
The Golden Sea: Part 2

The rest of the caravan had grouped up in the gentle depression below. The first two camel trains had already combined into a loose semi-circle of animals and the third was just joining them.

Eight of the caravan guards formed a loose line in front of the camels, spears leveled as they squared off against as many raiders. Already there were signs of a stiff fight. One of the guards and four of the white robed men were splayed out on the sand in dark patches of crimson. Two more white robed men were limping, while a third bore scarlet streaks on the ivory fabric swathing his arm.

Meanwhile Ben-Tov stalked two paces behind the rank of guards, sling in hand and barking out orders as the third camel train joined them. "Hold the line! Kedan, get the camels here! Circle up!"

Somehow, amid the whirlwind of activity he saw Joseph and waved him on. "Hurry! We don't have all day!"

Joseph hauled the animals pell-mell down the slope, his feet sinking deep into the loose sand, and the scared animals bellowing right behind.

He saw Ben-Tov scan the field, and freeze, seeming to notice something. Without hesitation, he twirled his sling.

One, two, three… Release.

Joseph followed the stone as it zipped straight to a slinger who'd popped up atop the next dune. The man took the hit dead in the chest and tumbled backwards with a strangled cry.

Gasping, Joseph reached the rest of the caravan, with Ben-Tov's shouts ringing in his ears, "Circle the camels! Keep them calm!"

A sling stone sang overhead, and another lanced right into one of the packed camels, punching a hole in a bag of resin that cascaded onto the sand like a waterfall. The camel jerked wildly, pulling the others in front and behind, and Joseph fought just to hold the lead camel in place, "Steady!"

Behind them, he saw the last train cresting the hill at a dead run, leader, guards and beasts all tearing down the slope. Joseph gulped when he saw the state they were in. Unlike the middle trains, the tail of the caravan had five guards attached. They should have been able to hold their own nicely, but now only four guards remained, one clutching a limp arm as he ran. Right behind them, more raiders appeared on the crest, spearpoints glinting in the noon sun.

Slings met the raiders though, several shots whizzed past and one raider tumbled out of view with a yelp.

As the last camel train nearly skidded to a halt amid their little knot, Ben-Tov called out, "Spears, pull back behind the camels."

Huh, Joseph jolted up from soothing the lead camel, certain he'd misheard. Weren't *they* supposed to be defending the camels, not the other way around?

Despite his confusion, the guards did in fact pull back. The camels had been circled up into a loose cordon, and as the men slipped back inside, there seemed at least a momentary sigh of relieved safety.

But looking out at the raiders, Joseph's heart sank. There were at least twelve facing the caravan across the narrow depression, and as he watched, ten more men crested the rise behind them, several bearing slings.

So far things clearly hadn't gone the raiders way though. Joseph mentally tallied up the bandits' losses and was shocked to realize they'd lost almost ten men with twenty still alive. By his reckoning, if they'd gotten off a proper surprise, thirty men together could have swarmed the lead of the caravan then mopped up the survivors. They must have been forming up for the assault when they'd been spotted, he realized. That one fact had saved them… so far at least.

Staring around at the overwhelming numbers however, and comparing it to their own guards, several of whom were already injured, Joseph questioned how long they could hold out. A full attack might just overrun them.

Joseph tried to swallow back his fear and found himself unconsciously casting about for a weapon. If this really was the end, at least he could give himself a chance. His eyes fell on what might have been Ben-Tov's spear staked forgotten in the golden sand, that might—

"Hold your stones!" Ben-Tov abruptly shouted, "We want to talk!"

Huh? Joseph turned, absolutely lost and trying to catch a glimpse of Ben-Tov through the tight crowd. Talk? Because they had so much to talk about?

Peering over a camel's head at the men up above however, Joseph was surprised to see several slingers hesitate. Their slings loaded and held at the ready, but otherwise motionless.

Ben-Tov called again, "Which of you is in charge?"

Another instant of tense silence until, "You can surrender now merchant if you want to live. Otherwise, we've got no words for you!"

Joseph figured that pretty much settled things, and began mentally planning to make a break for the spear in the sand nearby when—

"So you prefer to watch more of your men die for no reason?" Ben-Tov shouted. "If you're willing to leave, I'll give you a pair of fully loaded camels to take back. You walk, we walk, everyone's happy, nobody else dies."

Joseph finally pinpointed the speaker for the raiders. He was with the group up on the hill, a short man toting a spear, his face and hair buried beneath the flowing white garments. The bandit shook his head at Ben-Tov's offer, his voice harsh and his posture contemptuous, "I think we'd rather take them all! Slings, let them have it!"

Joseph tensed, ready to duck behind the massive camel at the first stone, but up on the rise the slingers hesitated… maybe because they had no one really to shoot at. Ben-Tov's irate shout answered, "If you kill the camels, you won't be taking anything back to Ashkelon! And good luck finding this fool place again once you're gone! I haven't seen a landmark in ages!"

"Doesn't change a thing!" The leader of the raiders stepped forward, his foot sinking into the sand on the side of the dune even as he jabbed the sky with his spear. "We can come down there and root you out like the rats you are. Then it'll be my spear in your gut, old man!"

"You'll bring home a lot more dead of your own if you try!"

With the pause in the fighting, Joseph at least had the lead camel starting to calm down. Out of nowhere the creature spit, landing a stain of bile on his already dirty tunic. A nervous reaction on the camel's part. Joseph did his best to sooth her, stroking her muzzle and murmuring quiet words. The last thing they needed was a panicked stampede.

Ben-Tov and the bandit were still trading barbs. "Every one of my men will fight to the bitter end!" Ben-Tov called.

The bandit scoffed, before shouting to the rest of the guards, "You men there, if you want to stay and die for this old fool be my guest. But I swear, if you come out right now, I'll grant you water, supplies and safe passage! You have my word, on the gods themselves!"

Clearly he expected that to have some effect… but no one budged. Joseph didn't even hear a whisper of discontent. Glancing back, he only saw hard-eyed men clutching their spears. Even the camel leaders held loaded slings now. He dimly realized that he was the only one of them who *wasn't* armed and spoiling for a fight.

Ben-Tov clearly saw that too. The old caravan master waited a resounding moment before calling, "Not going to work, son! Everyone down here has a share in the profits! A lot of them borrowed to buy in! If this caravan is gone, there's nothing for most of them to go home too! So what do you say, my offer's still on the table!"

"I'd say we're done talking!" the bandit leader snarled. Taking another pace ahead, he jabbed his spear sunward, "KILL 'EM ALL!"

Joseph's breath caught, certain they were about to die. Then the bandit to the immediate left of the leader lowered his own spear— and skewered his boss right in the back.

Despite the blazing heat, the world froze. The leader of the raiders screamed in pain and tried to turn, right until the bandit tore his reddened spear free and clocked him with the butt end. The leader tumbled senseless to the sand and slow motion rolled halfway down the dune, leaving a streak of dark scarlet on the golden slope.

The surreal instant seem to drag into forever, and the motionless bandits stared as their leader's body dragged to an ignominious halt. The scene might have descended into pure chaos, except in that heartbeat before everyone could recover, the still living bandit pointed his spear down at the clumped caravan and called, "Let's talk about this deal of yours!"

Joseph breathed a sigh of stunned relief. He might just survive after all.

But the new leader followed up with, "But we'll need more. We want a whole camel train!"

"Not going to happen!" Ben-Tov shouted. "But how about as thanks for ending that last fellow, I'll toss in an extra camel."

The guards remained tensed taut as bowstrings. But Joseph could swear he caught a hint of calculating excitement in Ben-Tov's voice now that the trader was negotiating.

"Eight then!"

"You're breaking me, but four!"

"Seven!"

"Five's the absolute best I can give!"

"We want six!"

Joseph looked over and saw Ben-Tov through the press, grinning, even as he let the offer hang for a heartbeat, until, "Five! But I'll throw in one of our water camels for free! I'm sure you boys are getting a little thirsty all the way out here! Do we have a deal?"

The bandit leader hesitated, his spear lowering in indecision until—

"Deal! Send out the camels!"

Ben-Tov's voice lowered, "Uri, cut the camels loose!"

"But, sir, that's—"

"Cut—them—loose."

Uri hesitated until, "…yes, sir."

Ben-Tov spun, eyes searching, "Where's the boy?"

Before he could duck away, several strong arms pushed Joseph forward. The camel harness slipped from his hand as Gabir called, "He's here."

In a moment Joseph stood in front of Ben-Tov. A guard who must have been Uri stepped forward, holding the reins to another camel. "Alright boy," Ben-Tov nodded toward the bandits. "Take the camels over, nice and slow."

Joseph's mouth dropped open, "M… me?"

"You hard of hearing?" Ben-Tov glowered. "Yes, *you*."

The halter rope was thrust into Joseph's hands, and before he could object, he was shoved past the barrier of camels. Standing out where all the bandits could see him, Joseph gulped. Gabir's voice hissed close behind, "If you want to stay alive, boy, try not to look quite so terrified. Now move."

A spear butt shoved Joseph from behind, and he stumbled forward. Rubbing at the sore spot on his shoulder, Joseph looked back to see the camel's blinking eyes blankly regarding him… and absolutely no way to return to the comparative safety of the group.

Well, he thought dourly, good to know he was the one person who they didn't mind getting killed. His eyes went to the bandit leader glaring from the dune above... nothing else to do.

Swallowing his fear and hoping it wouldn't show in his eyes, Joseph forced himself to take a step forward.

Behind him, Ben-Tov called again, "Last thing! One of my men is still back there. We want the body to give him a proper funeral. Then we'll be on our way!"

In response the bandit leader nodded to two white clad men who disappeared behind the dune crest.

Step by step, Joseph closed the distance until he was right in front of the bandit leader. But when he offered the camels the leader didn't take the halter. Instead he gestured to his people, "Check the bags."

That meant Joseph had to awkwardly wait there as the bandits fumbled to open several bags and verify the contents. Watching the leader, he couldn't identify much past the robes, but the face was young, maybe Judah or Levi's age.

The leader's glare abruptly swept from the animals to Joseph, with a calculating intensity that made Joseph look away, a disturbing thought springing to mind. The man *would* take the halter eventually, right? Or would they want *him* as part of the deal too?

A shiver like a beetle scuttled down Joseph's spine, and he looked back toward the caravan, hoping for some sign. He might not like Ben-Tov, but every muscle in his body screamed that he didn't want to end up under the thumb of these crazies.

The bandit kept staring, and Joseph's nerves boiled inside like thunderheads, until a flurry of curses abruptly drew his focus. One of the men had cleverly thought to check the contents of a sack with his spearpoint and been rewarded with a flood of resin bits spilling onto the ground. Now the bandits scrambled in the sand, frantically scooping up the precious resin. A moment later two men crested the dune, dragging a limp, bloody figure, and unceremoniously dumping him at Joseph's feet. "He's all yours."

Joseph wasn't sure he could drag the body all by himself, but right now he'd do just about anything to get away from these people. So, taking both wrists, he pulled hard, his feet sinking deep into the sand, and the corpse carving a shallow depression along the dune.

Somehow he actually *did* reach the bottom while the bandits were still vainly trying to refill their leaking sack. As he did, several guards broke from the circle in a rush of activity.

Gabir helped him grab the man, and together they threw the body onto one of the water camels. Meanwhile, more guards collected the rest of their deceased comrades. Joseph panted hard from the exertion, but before he could catch his breath, Ben-Tov strolled by, commanding with a quiet urgency, "Quick, over the next hill. Keep the camels side by side. Move while they're still busy."

Chapter 31

The Edge of the World and Beyond

Once they were away from the bandits, Ben-Tov set a grueling pace. Water breaks were short, and by Joseph's reckoning, they headed further south into the dune-streaked wastes. Instead of being strung out in a single long column, the camel trains now walked side by side in a block five ranks wide. Ben-Tov always stalked ahead though, relentlessly leading onward. They turned more than once to throw off pursuit, although Joseph wasn't sure what that accomplished when they left a trail of indentations in the sand as obvious as a stream.

Still, he mused, feeling the warm, but persistent north wind gusting in from the sea, the breeze might obscure and eventually obliterate their tracks if they got a lead. Maybe. Joseph had all the time in the world to consider the question, since Gabir seemed to have abandoned even a pretense of Egyptian lessons. As afternoon stretched into evening, he still couldn't decide if they were finally safe, or just preparing for a restless, knife-edge night's sleep.

Still Ben-Tov didn't stop.

The sun before them turned red, and Joseph fought a yawn, blinking back his own weariness. Soon the bronze dunes cast murky shadows until every downslope seemed a descent into a gloomy vale, only to find a dying light at the peak of the next rise.

Only when the orb had fully descended into the west, the amber sky glowing with purple and scarlet, did Ben-Tov

280

pause, abruptly grinding to a stop in a small dip between the dunes. "We camp here," he declared. "No fires."

After the grueling day, Joseph was ready to simply lay down and pass out. But the camels still needed care. As the daylight fled into the west, he hurriedly went down his camel train, untying sacks of resin and hauling down wooden chests of balsam in a familiar pattern.

Nearby he was dimly aware of the guards bickering, some voices sounding pleased and others disappointed. Under normal circumstances he might have been curious, but with his arms tired and his feet aching, he pulled his blanket from a pack and flopped down next to the camels when he finished.

The sand still retained a pleasant warmth, and wrapping the blanket tight, Joseph discovered at least one pleasantness of the dunes… it was remarkably easy to sleep on a comfortable cushion of sand.

Above him the myriad stars peeked out to resume their nightly vigil. And closing his eyes, Joseph let himself fall into the abyss of dreams.

Voices called to Joseph in the darkness. A girl's plaintive wail, "Joseph!"

Myrrha, the realization struck him like lightning through the haze. He had to find—

"Joseph, where are you?"

He tried to shout, tell her that he was here, yet his voice came as a hoarse whisper, unable to find the breath he needed.

More voices rose, Father, Benji… Mom.

Stumbling in the blackness, Joseph tried to find them. He tried to run, but his feet sank deep into the sand. Every strenuous step might have been scaling a mountain as he slogged his way to the top of the dune. And there a horrible creature reared up to halt Joseph— a man in white robes, the face young, furious and dimly familiar. He lowered a spear at Joseph's chest, blood shining like scarlet fire on the blade, and death glinting in his eyes. Beyond him Myrrha screamed, "JOSEPH!"

But he couldn't pass. Joseph tried to run but his feet were sucked into the sand. His muscles fought in vain terror to pull his legs free as the man thrust his spear at Joseph's chest and…

Joseph bolted upright, panting, his blanket a tightly tangled mess around his legs. Fear pumped in his veins and his eyes darted wildly until…

It was a dream, he dimly realized. The panic drained from his arms as he leaned back on his palms.

Just a dream.

His breaths slowed as the bizarre images slipped away like water through his fingers.

"Get back to sleep, kid." A low voice in the night jolted Joseph, his head jerking towards a shadowed figure sitting a dozen feet away. He recognized Gabir's voice instantly, but in the cold light of a half-moon, the man's tan face was dyed a deep azure. His figure sat as a dark, motionless monolith against the pale sand. "It's late."

Joseph blinked, hesitating at the prospect of facing his nightmares again, of plunging back into that chaotic realm. After a moment's indecision, he chose in favor of avoiding it for a time. He pulled his blanket close against the chill of the desert night then sat up, propping his back against the flank of a nearby camel. "Are you not sleeping?"

"Someone has to stand watch," Gabir declared simply.

There was no invitation to talk in the words, and for a time, Joseph said nothing. The cool of the desert night nipped at his face while everywhere the dunes were bathed in a silver mist of moonlight. Normally the night was awash with sound— crickets, owls, jackals, wolves, all alive in the darkness. Yet here in the desert, it was strangely quiet. Only the whispers of the wind prowled the dunes, a wild, restless murmur that rose and died and rose again in a ceaseless dance.

Joseph found the night strangely serene. Here was a place with no distractions and only the low howl of the wind to cocoon him away from the rest of the world. A place where he could think.

The bandit's face from earlier was still vividly etched into Joseph's memory, and he couldn't help but wonder if the dream carried some hidden meaning. Should he have tried to go with them?

He could have. Ben-Tov had hardly been in a position to stop him. At the time he still recalled the strange foreboding he'd sensed at the prospect. Yet he'd realized afterwards that Ben-Tov had somehow seemed to know they were from Ashkelon... perhaps they would have taken him back there?

The question circled round and round, the uncertainty taunting Joseph, until finally he broke the dark silence with a question, "Gabir, the bandits today. Who were they?"

"Just bandits I suppose. Sometimes they hide out in the wastes, preying on travelers."

"But Ben-Tov spoke like he knew they were from Ashkelon?" Joseph pressed.

"Oh... that," Gabir mused, half to himself. "If you'd been paying attention, instead of trying to sneak away, you'd have noticed them at the market. They spent ages poking through bags of resin, asking questions, tried to chat me up about where we were headed... then just walked off. Didn't even make an offer."

"Ben-Tov assumed they might follow, maybe try something in the night. None of us realized how many there were."

Joseph frowned at the realization, "They followed us for three days?"

"They couldn't attack too near the city," Gabir said bluntly. "The King of Ashkelon would have hunted them down if word had gotten out. If he doesn't keep the desert road clear, the Egyptians might get the idea to come and do it themselves."

"Out in the flatlands there was no way to sneak in close. Even if they overran us, someone might have escaped to ride back to Ashkelon. The dunes are a good place to surround someone though, and bodies are easy to lose in the sands."

Gabir let the words hang, and Joseph swallowed hard. Well at least that answered his question— what would have happened if he'd tried to flee with the raiders. He would have just been one more loose end to snip. Probably wouldn't have seen the sun set tonight, he though soberly.

"You did well today," Gabir added. "Kept your wits, didn't panic. That's important in a tight spot."

Joseph didn't feel like he had, but nodded in an absent agreement. A least he'd hidden his terror well enough… that was something.

The night fell quiet again, and a sudden gust of wind whipped up the sand around them. Joseph closed his eyes, tasting the slight crunch of dry grit between his teeth. For several moments the gust rose to a howl, bits of fine sand pelting his cheek, until suddenly the wind faded, the air cleared and the desert sank back into its serene tableau.

Joseph brushed his hair, bits of dust sprinkling down, and finally opened his eyes to see Gabir's dark lump of a figure still unmoved.

Behind Joseph, the camel's breathing struck a steady cadence, unbothered by the wind and sand. The belly rhythmically puffed out then fell back at each exhalation. The monotonous beat might have lured Joseph back to sleep, until Gabir finally asked, "Who's Myrrha?"

Joseph stiffened, suddenly wary, "Who told you that name?"

"You did. You kept mumbling it over and over before you woke."

Joseph's lips drew tight, not sure if he should answer, "She… she's a girl… someone I knew back home."

"Ahh," Gabir nodded, as though he'd understood the whole story in only a few words. Then added, "I'm sorry."

"Yeah," Joseph agreed, not really in the mood to say more. He leaned back, staring at the blue-silver dune, wishing that home wasn't so terribly far. For an instant he imagined that their camp sat just beyond the crest of the dune. A short walk to his own tent, and he'd find Benji and Myrrha waiting, happy to see him. They'd wonder where he'd been, and he could tell them of the strange surreal dream he'd lived through the last few days.

Amid the empty silence of the sands, Joseph held his eyes open for a while. But slowly his alertness from earlier drained away. His eyes drooped shut, and barely realizing, Joseph slid back into the exotic and enigmatic realm of sleep.

***

Four days later, Joseph was tired, sunburnt and thoroughly ready to be quit of this miserable desert. It was barely midmorning, the camels stank, and already the sun blazed like a furnace in the sky. Meanwhile the sand just went on… and on… and on…

He'd never imagined so much sand in the whole world. The adventurous part of him dimly wondered if they might, at some juncture, actually stumble over the edge of the world. It must be out here somewhere.

After a second day moving in a tight column, Ben-Tov had apparently decided they weren't being tailed any longer. The caravan had once more spread out, with Joseph's camel train finding its customary spot, fourth in line. Now it was just him, Gabir and endless Egyptian practice to keep him busy.

Piecing the words together for a moment, Joseph asked in Egyptian, *"Are you sure we haven't walked right past Kemet?"*

Gabir shrugged, *"We're following the road."*

Were they though? They were supposed to be following *The Way of Horus,* a road named after the Egyptian falcon god… or something. Joseph didn't really see how being a bird qualified this Horus to have his own road, which… maybe that was the point, because this wasn't a road. Joseph wasn't even sure that the term footpath qualified. It was just the desert, with the slight caveat that they'd looped back toward the sea and now caught occasional glimpses of sparkling blue waters.

As far as Joseph could tell, the only thing that might have marked this out as a path was a single deep well they'd passed yesterday. Where of course, he'd had to spend hours — *literally* hours — drawing water to replenish their skins and allow the camels their deep, endless drinks.

Otherwise, Joseph still saw no signs of civilization… nothing. He knew Egypt was big but…

"*What if we missed it?*" He asked in Kemeti.

Gabir chuckled, answering, "*Boy, out here so long as you're heading west, you couldn't miss Kemet if you tried.*"

Gabir point skyward, and Joseph followed his gesture to see a solitary falcon idly circling overhead, soaring high on thermals as he peered down at them.

Oh great, Joseph mused sarcastically, the falcon god. Maybe he was out taking complaints about his road. Joseph sure had a few to register.

Joseph watched a moment, his neck craned back as they walked. Finally, the bird tired of its display and majestically wheeled away, cruising off northwest towards the sea. The sight of the falcon did prove that perhaps, *something* was close, but Joseph's impatience kept nipping at him. Where was this place?

Then he smelled it… a whiff on the breeze of water. He caught a refreshing humidity in the air, mingled with a riot of undertones, the fresh cleanliness of the Jordan swirled with the musk of decaying vegetation. Beneath that lay more scents, a hint of fish, and something sweet but not quite floral, all underlined by a crisp dash of salt breezing in from the sea.

Joseph sniffed... lost the smell... and sniffed again, catching it. He glanced at Gabir, who's eyes twinkled in an amused grin.

"Told you."

The smell came again, now stronger. After the arid emptiness of the desert, the new scents lit him with sudden excitement. Traipsing over the next few dunes, the aroma strengthened and Joseph began to catch more familiar smells, the crisp, earthy notes of barley stubble, and something that might just be lemons. The damp humidity in the wind grew noticeable too, soothing a throat sore after a week of parched breaths.

They kept on. Cresting another sandy rise, Joseph's heart dropped as he caught his first sight of what could only be Egypt.

Before him the world abruptly transformed. The barren sand simply fell away, sloping down thirty feet into a vast verdant plain. Spread out to the horizon lay a patchwork of palm orchards bursting with greenery, and golden fields of fresh cut barley stubble. Clusters of small homes dotted seemingly every rise in the landscape. A mile off, a squat, tan-walled fortress crouched upon a hilltop, a moat trenched on all sides. Its towers fluttered with blue banners marked by a stylized golden eye.

In the distance Joseph's sharp gaze saw what looked like a city, and at its foot lay a colossal ribbon of deep blue that stretched back to the southern horizon.

The Nile.

Joseph stared at the stark incongruity, his jaw hung open and his mind refusing to believe the paradise they'd stumbled into. Gabir's voice intruded, "Beautiful, isn't she?"

Joseph nodded numbly, his eyes peering toward the river where a fleet of boats cruised like toys in the distance.

Gabir continued, "She can be a deceptive place, but she does have her moments." He drew in a long breath through his nose and exhaled, oddly pleased. "Smells like Kemet." He nodded to where the rest of the caravan was already descending the slope. "Come on, we still have a lot of ground to cover."

With that Gabir strode forward following a steep path down the slope. Joseph hesitated, lingering at the cusp of this exotic world. For a moment, his head turned back the way they'd come… back home. Toward the place where people waited for him.

He felt so impossibly far away, but prayed that in some small way Myrrha could hear him across the gulf. "I'll find a way back, Myrrha" he murmured, "To you and Benji. I promise."

He let the words slip away, fluttering on the breeze for a single heartbeat… then they were gone, and Joseph had to hope that at least his promise knew the way home.

Then, swallowing hard, he turned and pulled the camels along. Stepping across the strange line between barren sand and soft grass, he shook his head in amazement and strode down into Egypt.

Epilogue

Myrrha hummed a quiet tune as she stitched. Gradually she'd covered half her cushion with yellow and white daisy blossoms. The pattern had proved simple enough once she'd finished the first bloom, and now she stitched with only half her attention on her work. Instead she watched where Benji and Nathanial had cleared a circle on the ground and now busily flicked pebbles back and forth, occasionally bursting into excited exclamations.

She struggled to grasp the allure of playing with rocks in the dirt... she honestly would have considered it a punishment. But the two boys seemed happy enough. Maybe boys never really graduated from playing with rocks, she thought with an amused grin. Joseph certainly hadn't, he'd just gotten to an age where he slung them instead of flicking them. Myrrha wasn't sure that was much of an improvement.

Still, she thought cheerfully, Joseph had offered to teach her how to sling. She could always take him up on the offer when he returned, might help her grasp what exactly made rocks so much fun.

Myrrha giggled at the thought and kept at her stitching. The sun rose toward midmorning, but sitting in the entrance to Abby's tent, Myrrha found it pleasantly cool. She finished three more daisies before looking up to see her mother and Abby strolling back across camp, returned from their morning excursion. Both carried reed baskets fairly brimming with sprigs of fresh cut greenery and herbs.

Finishing with another daisy, Myrrha gave a deferential nod as Abby walked up, "Everything alright?"

"As best as I can tell," Myrrha gestured to the two boys still engrossed in their game. "No one got hurt, although I'm not sure who's winning."

Abby smiled fondly at her son, then shook her head, "I'm sure they'll let us know later. Come on Althea."

The two women ducked inside with their baskets, and leaving her cushion incomplete, Myrrha followed. "Did you find it?"

"We did," Mother declared, pulling several leafy sprigs out of her basket and segregating them into small piles for each different plant. "We got a whole plant worth of verbena for you. And some hyssop leaves and myrtle for Tirtzah. Should be just what she needs for her stomach."

She looked at Myrrha, "You told Fannah to make her a garlic loaf? Right?"

"Fannah said she'd bake it this afternoon."

"Good," Mother actually seemed pleased for once as she piled up a half dozen sprigs of verbena in front of Myrrha, velvety, pale green leaves studded with clusters of miniature white and purple flowers. "You know how to prepare the tea?"

Myrrha nodded, "Yeah."

She reached down to take the sprigs just as Mom absently added, "And don't use it all at once. I picked enough for a few doses."

Yeah, Myrrha could tell. She kept that to herself though and just nodded, as she gathered them up. "Okay, Mom."

"And don't drown it in honey, or you'll upset your stomach."

Myrrha rolled her eyes, finally failing to keep all the sarcasm out of her voice, "Got it."

Mom clearly caught the exasperation which earned Myrrha a sharp look, but after a moment her mother's expression softened, her voice offering an olive branch. "Right, I'm sure you know what to do."

Holding the sprigs in one hand, Myrrha turned to leave right as a little bundle of excitement crashed through the

entrance and nearly barreled into her. "Benji, what are you—
"

The little boy spat out a single breathless word, "Joseph."

"Huh?" Myrrha blinked, the word taking a moment to register, then hit like a charging bull, "He's… he's coming back?"

Benji nodded, beaming, But Myrrha froze. In the crowded tent, her eyes flashed to Althea, whose olive branch smile had abruptly withered and died.

Her mother had *not* approved of Joseph kissing her. And she fully expected him returning to rub that particular wound. She'd tried to explain that *he'd* kissed *her*, not the other way around, yet Mom still acted like it was solely her doing. She felt that Mom hadn't even wanted to listen, she'd just swept in with an overbearing lecture about protecting her reputation and *not giving everyone the wrong idea.* Which…

Myrrha shook her head, frustrated. Sometimes she wondered why her mother couldn't just let her be happy. Yeah, fine, Mom didn't want her to get hurt, but what if it hurt more to keep being wedged apart?

She'd noticed it more and more the last week and a half since he'd left. First had come several days of frostiness between herself and Mother, followed by a growing loneliness inside that had gradually crystallized into a stark realization— she missed Joseph… a lot. He was the only person here who saw her — *really* saw her. With him she was so much more than just little old nobody Myrrha and… she missed him.

Just looking at Mom, Myrrha could already hear the lecture coming. However, little Nathanial picked that moment to wander into the tent with a loud, "I'm hungry."

At just the mention of Joseph, Abby was obviously keen to be anywhere but here. She took the opportunity to scoop both her son and Benji into her arms and slide outside, "Come on, you two," she said. "I think I saw Dhra making soup for lunch."

In a moment they were gone, just leaving Myrrha to cast an apprehensive side glance at her mother. Unexpectedly though, Althea's expression softened, still not pleased but not angry either. She sighed, and Myrrha blinked in shock when instead of haranguing her, Mom nodded towards the tent exit and forced a tentative smile, "You'd better go."

She… she should?

Her mother seemed to sense her confusion and added a reassuring, "Just… be careful."

"I will," Myrrha nodded, stunned but in a good way for once. Gathering the last of the verbena, she hurried outside.

Benji hadn't quite spoken truthfully when he said *Joseph* was coming back. From the entrance of Abby's tent, Myrrha could see some distance down the valley, and sure enough, she marked several figures making their way toward camp. At first glance her heart fell at noting that none of them wore Joseph's distinctive blue tunic with silver bands. But the reasonable part of her knew that meant little. That coat was hardly the sort of thing he would choose to wear for a long journey where it could snag on tree branches and nettles. Frankly, she thought with a flash of satisfaction, if he *had* been wearing it, she would have some sharp words for him about properly caring for his garments.

The figures were still too far off to distinguish. Joseph took offense at the fact, but he, Zebulun, and Issachar all looked similar enough that she couldn't have picked them out at a distance if she'd tried.

Instead, she watched a moment and decided she had awhile before they arrived. Enough time to make that tea.

There was always a fire kept burning in camp, and usually plenty of spare kindling for general use. Currently Dhra was slow boiling a pot of stew over the low flames in the central pit which steamed with the rich, delicious aroma of broth. Several smaller fire pits stood nearby, burned low and covered with white ashes. Poking around in one, Myrrha found a few warm coals still buried beneath. In short order she had coaxed it back to life and set a copper teapot to boiling water.

She watched as Benji, Nathaniel and Abby busily pestered the camp cook for an early helping of stew. Both boys pleaded piteously with the stern-faced cook, and Nathanial capped it off with a sorrowful, "Pleeeeease... we're starving." Meanwhile Abby stood behind him, nodding with a mock seriousness.

Myrrha giggled as Dhra finally relented, telling them, "Fine you two can have some, but only if you tell me how it tastes."

That seemed a wonderful bargain to the two boys and in short order they were showering a smug Dhra with praises. Myrrha set about steeping her tea, and in a few minutes, it had cooled enough to not burn her mouth.

The verbena had a sharp lemon tang, a little sour but hardly unpleasant, especially compared to some of the wilder remedies she'd seen Samas put together. She sipped her cup a while, making a conscious effort *not* to peer after Joseph.

As the travelers in the valley neared, they were obscured behind the ring of tents and Myrrha struggled against the urge to hurry to the edge of camp and watch from there. She forced herself not to though. She *wasn't* about to be the lovesick little girl caught staring at Joseph from the edge of camp. Certainly not after promising her mother she wouldn't make a fool of herself.

Instead, Myrrha fought back the butterflies in her stomach, and tried to be patient. By the time she got down to the dregs of her tea, several other people had gathered around for food. Apparently, they'd decided that Benjamin's and Nathanial eating must mean it was well and truly time for a meal. Who cared if the sun still had an hour until noon?

As more hungry stomachs gathered nearby, Myrrha caught several people nodding to something behind her and a low mumble, "Look who's back."

Feeling that propriety had reached its reasonable limit, Myrrha turned, a smile brimming on her cheeks as she saw…

Not Joseph?

Issachar, Gad and Levi had all walked into camp and were making for Jacob's tent. She felt a flicker of disappointment, then froze as her eyes caught a flash of blue cloth in Levi's hand. Her heart skipped a beat.

Was that?

Suddenly all sense of propriety vanished, and Myrrha stood. Hurrying over, her eyes fixed on the familiar shade of deep blue fabric wadded in Levi's fist but stained with something dark. The dread gathered like a cloud around her. It couldn't be… right?

Except as she got close, the cloth looked more and more familiar. She caught traces of silver stitching and… was that blood?

She met Levi a dozen steps before Jacob's tent, and ground to a dead halt, her eyes fixed on the cloth. No… it…

Levi paused at seeing her, his grip loosening on the cloth so it could splay out… and confirm Myrrha's worst nightmare. Joseph's coat.

For a desperate instant her feet rooted to the ground and her eyes flashed to Levi. It was a mistake right? It must have been torn or… please let it be a mistake.

She saw the grim expression on Levi's face… on all their faces… as if understanding her question perfectly. Levi shook his head, and the truth struck her like lightning.

No.

Myrrha couldn't breathe. She swayed, barely able to stay upright.

No… no… no…

Levi kept walking and Myrrha turned away, her world crashing around her as a storm of tears clouded her eyes.

No.

Stumbling through the awful haze, she found herself at Mom's tent, the tears pouring down her cheeks as she sank to the ground.

No.

Her breath came sharp and rapid, her mind a blur. It was a mistake, it had to be a mistake… Joseph couldn't be gone, he… he couldn't—

"Myrrha?" A little boy's confused voice chimed behind her.

Myrrha froze, suddenly wishing the ground would swallow her up as the awful reality sank in.

No.

How did she tell him? How was she supposed to explain that Joseph wasn't coming back…

Myrrha sobbed low and miserable, even as Benji stepped around in front of her, his voice worried. "Myrrha?"

Not sure what else to do, she scooped him up, squeezing him tight. Terrified. Heaven above, what was she supposed to tell him?

Benji tiny hands clutched her back, but his voice sounded scared, "Myrrha, what's happening? Where's Joseph?"

Myrrha didn't know how to explain. She sobbed, even as her mother's confused voice interrupted, "Myrrha, what is it? What's wrong?"

And as the tears streamed down Myrrha's face, another voice rent the midmorning, a man this time. Emanating from Jacob's tent came a terrible, bereaved wail.

TO BE CONTINUED

Afterword

Well that's it, you made it to the end of the Days of Joseph: Part 2. If you appreciated this dramatization of Joseph's story and want to share it with others, I encourage you to leave a review. Reviews help others discover the story and contribute to the continuing success of the book. If you're reading online that can be as easy as flipping on through to the end and leaving a rating.

If you're eager for more of Joseph's story, fear not, he will return and he has plenty of story still ahead. In the meantime, I've written a short story covering Joseph's adventures years before this book, when his family first returned to the land of Caanan. You can check it out here: *The Days of Joseph – Mahanaim* on Amazon.

If you want more full length Biblical Historical Fiction, then I'd encourage you to explore my other book, *The Days of Elijah*. And if science fiction is your thing, you can check out my space adventure series, starting with *Medea*.

If you'd like to receive email notifications when I release new books, you can head over to my website

Jnoblewrites.com, click on New Releases and sign up for email notifications.

Finally, if you'd like to reach out to me personally, you can email me at johntheauthor1@gmail.com.

With all the housekeeping stuff out of the way, I wanted to talk about the world Joseph dwelt in, and hopefully answer some common questions about the way it's portrayed. Obviously, this book is a dramatization, and the truth is that we actually have frustratingly few details about Joseph's personal life to work with. As a general rule, I've tried to keep as close as possible to known historical evidence and fill in the gaps as best I know how.

Delving into the historical details behind this book I'll briefly mention that, if you want to play Aasha yourself, it's a real game. We don't know the original name, but if you search for "The Royal Game of Ur" you can find a modern version and even try it out online. The modern game is a re-creation based on gameboards found in digs throughout the Middle East. Speaking from experience, it's surprisingly simple, fun, and a lot faster than monopoly.

Getting into more serious territory, I'd like to discuss the discrepancy that most people probably noticed straight away. Joseph's "Coat of Many Colors" isn't quite the same technicolor dream-coat that it's often depicted as in cartoons and plays. So what gives?

Well, this is likely a case of a word's meaning being lost in translation. The phrase *pas·sîm* kə·□ō·ne, commonly translated as a 'multicolored coat', occurs twice in the Bible. Once in the story of Joseph and again in 2 Samuel 13: 18-19. There it is simply translated as a long-sleeved tunic, specifically the sort worn by virgin daughters of the king. Now, are these two instances separated by close to a thousand years referring to the exact same thing? Unlikely, but they do both seem to refer to an ornate tunic of some variety although not necessarily a striped robe. The origin of the 'coat of many colors' interpretation actually comes from the Greek translation of the Old Testament, the Septuagint, where Joseph's robe is translated as a "various colored coat." That translation has stuck around in one form or another ever since, and is the source of all those pictures of Joseph wearing a striped rainbow coat that they pull out in Sunday School.

I'll leave it to the reader if they want to keep with the traditional view of Joseph's coat and simply say that I've taken the view that the coloration is open to substantial interpretation. Because of that I chose a blue and silver color scheme for his coat that I imagine would have looked very sharp.

With that said though, there are plenty of clothes described in this book, and I do want to pause and emphasis just how important clothes were in the ancient world. In the modern world, we often view clothes as something to throw on before work, or nice things to wear for an evening out. Our main concerns are: how many layers should I put on for the cold, do these colors match, and does this dress make me look fat.

That sort of utilitarian view of clothing is only possible, however, because of automatic spinning and weaving machines that have transformed the textile industry in the last four hundred years. Prior to the industrial revolution, clothes were made much as Myrrha does throughout the last two books, very tediously and with great care. Because of this, in the ancient world, clothes were a very conspicuous form of wealth and vastly more expensive.

To make something as simple as a wool tunic, wool first had to be carefully combed to remove impurities, then tufts were *carded* or laid out in a cross-hatched pattern on a board to help interweave the fibers into a fluffy mat. That mat was then wrapped around the top of a staff called a distaff and a thread was carefully teased out or *spun out* by hand and wound around a spindle. This spinning was an extremely tedious process where working too fast might break the thread.

And that's just to get the thread that you buy at the store for a couple dollars. From there, that thread had to be woven into fabric on a loom, a process that involved hanging the vertical threads and using a hand shuttle to laboriously guide through each strand of horizontal thread.

In the modern world this is all automated, and we can go purchase our 300 thread count sheets for a reasonable price. But to manage this in the ancient world would be beyond prohibitive. Those 300 thread count sheets have 150 horizontal threads *per inch* that had to be hand woven. A ten foot or three meter bolt of cloth would have 18,000 (yes *eighteen thousand*) horizontal threads that had to be drawn through one at a time.

Needless to say, a common workman's clothes in the ancient world were not a terribly high thread count. Even then, clothes could still be absurdly expensive. A Roman price list issued by the Emperor Diocletian in 301 AD to combat rampant inflation includes the expected daily wages of a laborer *with maintenance* (which means the effective cost of hiring the person was likely much higher since you were likely paying for room and board) at about 1/3 the price of a winter tunic. It's always a little finicky translating ancient prices into modern terms. Simply converting silver denarii or gold ducats into modern precious metals prices tends to understate the real value. But making $15 per hour, imagine paying between $360 and $500 for a basic shirt and jeans, and you perhaps begin to feel some of the ancient world's pain. Farmer's sandals, think *work boots*, ran a similar price. And of course prices only went up from there. For a tunic from Laodicea in particular (because I guess those were particularly nice), you'd be out about $10,000. And three quarters of a pound of undyed silk fabric, which might perhaps be sewn to make a woman's dress, was fixed at a mind boggling $57,000 plus or minus a few thousand.

So yeah, in ancient terms, Joseph receiving his fancy robe with cool embroidery was very much the modern equivalent of a rich kid whose Dad just bought him brand new Porsche with racing stripes, while all his other brothers had to drive old Honda Civics and go digging in the couch cushions for gas money. Put in that light, you can start to understand why Joseph's brothers resented the special treatment he was receiving. You can also begin to see why their revenge was the equivalent of deliberately wrecking his Porsche and getting it towed back to the house.

People in the ancient world were, of course, very much aware of how to flaunt their wealth with extravagant clothes. It often became such an issue that many medieval cities had what are called sumptuary laws, or laws that regulated who could wear what and in what quantity. These laws imposed penalties on people of the lower classes who tried to *dress up* too much, but they also partly stopped the rich from engaging in a ruinous arms race to display ever more ostentatious garb.

In short, clothes in the ancient world were very much a status symbol. To an ancient observer, Joseph wearing his ornate robe, verses his work tunic, verses a worn slave's tunic sent very different status signals that would have been instantly picked out by everyone around him.

With that aside, I'll briefly mention a few other things. First off, if you're an actual ancient Egyptian scholar, I apologize for my butchering of the language, please know I tried. For everyone else who is unaware, ancient Egyptian, much like ancient Hebrew, has no written vowels which means that, to take an English example, *Halo, helo, holo, holy, hula, hole, hale, hail, heel, and hulu...* are all just written HL and the meaning is derived from context. Thus, we sadly have no idea how words were often pronounced and even the names of major Egyptians gods such Amon are sometimes translated as Amun or Amen.

Second, I'll briefly touch on the geopolitical situation, as there are several exciting moments in this book. To the best of my knowledge we have no specific evidence of Mamre's underlings trying to depose a tyrannical king, or of bandits attacking Joseph's caravan on the way to Egypt. However, those are things that would have happened *very* routinely in the ancient world. Many ancient *kings* were really little more than local strongmen who commanded the loyalty of a group of followers and ostensibly ruled a small patch of the local surroundings.

When you read about so-and-so having thirty kings in his army, that's talking about people like Mamre or Hamor from the previous book. Someone like Hamor would be an excellent example of a small-scale ancient king, and Mamre at Kiraith Arba would exist toward the larger end of that spectrum. A position such as Mamre's could be very tenuous as it relied on the support of his warriors beneath him. If enough of his lieutenants got together, it would not be uncommon to dispose of a tyrannical leader and choose a new one.

Similarly, banditry, piracy and slave raiding were sadly ubiquitous in the ancient world. Often bandits weren't full time brigands as we think of them, but rather locals who might get together and decide to make some quick money at the expense of travelers. A caravan like Joseph's could easily be hauling around life-changing quantities of valuables and prove a tempting target. Joseph may, very well, have had a boring, uneventful trip to Egypt… but maybe not. Frankly, we don't know.

I'll wrap up with a little bit about Joseph. I've always personally disagreed with the common interpretation of Joseph in this story as some *arrogant, whiney, entitled son.* Admittedly, he might have been. But I feel this is an extreme view that gets reinforced when people pick out this passage to teach lessons about humility and consequently trump up Joseph's perceived negative qualities.

Was he lonely and perhaps a bit of know-it-all? Did he fantasize about the day when he didn't have to live in fear of his brothers bullying him? Yeah, probably. I imagine I would have felt much the same. In a similar vein though, I also find it difficult to imagine him just strolling up and excitedly taunting his brothers with his second dream, especially after his first dream had received such a poor reception. That's why, in this account, the revelation spills out in rather more tense circumstances. Again you're free to disagree, but I've tried to approach Joseph's character from a sympathetic perspective and give him the benefit of the doubt.

That said, whatever your thoughts about Joseph's character, I don't think he was stupid. If anything, Joseph was likely educated, at least by local standards. I can't prove that he necessarily knew math or was literate, but given his later positions of note in Egypt it's likely that he had some basic scribal knowledge. As we'll discuss in a later afterword, the Egyptians loved to appoint people with a flair for administrative ability to all sorts of unusual positions. In that context, Joseph knowing basic math and having a rudimentary grasp of writing would have been a substantial leg up later on.

Another thing that I can't prove relates to Joseph's love life. Obviously, we don't know if Myrrha or someone like her ever existed in Joseph's life. However, as a seventeen-year-old favored son of a petty chieftain, Joseph's eventual marriage would have been a topic of hot interest to plenty of people. In a world where marriages were at least partly political, Jacob likely would have conducted an extensive search for a bride. The options he pushes for in the book, mainly one of Joseph's female cousins either from Esau's or Laban's side of the family would have likely been the leading candidates in real life too, with perhaps one of Mamre's daughters or a similar highborn girl from Kiraith Arba coming in as a possible third choice.

A slave like Myrrha would have been an absolutely terrible partner in Jacob's eyes. But with that said, ancient people weren't stupid either. Love and compatibility were also important considerations when arranging a marriage, just not the *only* considerations. Certainly, if Joseph had wanted to marry Myrrha, it might not be completely beyond the realm of possibility, although he also would have been in for a stiff fight from his father.

On the topic of Joseph and Jacob fighting, while I can't prove that Joseph's last conversation with his father was them fighting about a girl, I will point to the text where Joseph's parting statements do seem oddly curt. Maybe it's just me, but phrases like, "*I'm ready*" (Genesis 37:13 HCSB) aren't quite brimming with the fond goodbyes we would expect between Joseph and his father. Granted, this just opens up a myriad of possibilities ranging from my own dramatic interpretation, to the more mundane consideration that perhaps no one recorded the full exchange because it took up too much space and paper was expensive. It could just be that the abbreviated version seems curt today in a world with very different social norms.

As one final note, we don't know if Joseph stopped by his mother's grave, or paused at Bethel to make an offering and ask for God's help. However, both sites were very much on the route he would have traveled. And his prayer, that God would let him have his own life and stop his Father's meddling, is very much drawn from my own experiences. I have on several occasion asked God for oddly specific things, only to receive exactly what I'd asked for, except in a package that was radically different than I'd imagined. It's happened enough that I suspect it is a pattern, not just in my life, but in other's lives as well. I can also say, that much like Joseph's case, the experience of getting exactly what you ask for is sometimes deeply painful. But, I can also say that, just like in Joseph's case, it does usually lead somewhere, so long as you keep walking forward and don't give up along the way.

And while there's much more to say, I'll cut things here and simply thank you again for reading this story. It's one possible interpretation of history and hopefully you enjoyed it. There will of course be another exciting installment following Joseph's adventures in Egypt. And perhaps not the story you're expecting either… at least not yet.

And to end, I really ought to thank the Lord God for helping me to finish this story. I can't claim any divine or special insight into Joseph's tale, as I mainly just read a bunch of dry history books and spent several hundred hours dreaming stuff up. But I can say this was a technically challenging book to write, and that I mainly penning it during a difficult and stressful period of my own life (one of those, getting exactly what I asked for sorts of situations). I certainly needed some divine help at more than a few points to keep going and I'm glad it's finished.

And with that said, hopefully you're as excited as I am about Joseph's future adventures. I'll leave the usual citations below, then I'll see you in the next book.

Citations

Ancient Hebrew doesn't have quotation marks, and dialogue was routinely paraphrased. That said, I used exact dialogue from the Book of Genesis where translators provided it. I mixed and matched Bible versions to find the translation I felt flowed best within the rest of the narrative. Below are the biblical references for the book. The Chapter in *this book* where the citation is used is listed first and the biblical chapter and verse numbers are listed second. The appropriate version citations are shown last. If you have ten minutes, I'd encourage you to check out the source material as it's only a quick search away. Note: full verses are often cited but only the dialogue is actually quoted.

1. Chapter 6: Genesis 37:9 (NIV)
2. Chapter 7: Genesis 37:10 (NLT)
3. Chapter 13: Genesis 37:13 (NLT)
4. Chapter 15: Genesis 37:13 (NLT)
5. Chapter 15: Genesis 37:14 (NLT)
6. Chapter 19: Genesis 37:19 (NLT)
7. Chapter 19: Genesis 37:20 (HCSB)
8. Chapter 19: Genesis 37:21-22 (NLT)
9. Chapter 22: Genesis 37:26 (NIV)
10. Chapter 22: Genesis 35:27 (BSB)